PRAISE FOR
The Royal Governess

"A beautifully woven and exquisitely detailed story of strong upstairs-downstairs women whose lives entwine during some of the most significant periods of modern British history. . . . A novel that will stand the test of time. I loved it."

—Heather Morris,
New York Times bestselling author of *The Tattooist of Auschwitz*

"An intimate view of the royal family at a time of great uncertainty and change, *The Royal Governess* is a beautifully written and richly detailed piece of historical fiction. Marion Crawford's dedication to her charges, as well as her passion for education and reform, shines through the pages. Through her eyes, the reader is transported back in time and thoroughly immersed in the lives of the British royal family. A delightful read!"

—Chanel Cleeton,
New York Times bestselling author of *The Last Train to Key West*

"Wendy Holden absolutely delivers in this perfect blend of story and history. *The Royal Governess* is a fabulous read for not only devotees of period fiction and the British royals, but anyone with a hunger for a well-crafted tale. Lovers of *The Crown* will adore this!"

—Susan Meissner,
bestselling author of *The Last Year of the War*

"A moving, gorgeously written page-turner. We peek behind the Windsors' swagged silk curtains—the insider details are a total delight—but the story's beating heart belongs to the devoted royal governess, Crawfie. Holden takes the reader on a glittering, unforgettable journey."

—Eve Chase,
author of *The Daughters of Foxcote Manor*

THE DUCHESS

WENDY HOLDEN

BERKLEY

New York

BERKLEY
An imprint of Penguin Random House LLC
penguinrandomhouse.com

Library of Congress Cataloging-in-Publication Data

Names: Holden, Wendy, 1965- author.
Title: The duchess / Wendy Holden.
Description: First edition. | New York: Berkley, 2021.
Identifiers: LCCN 2021022748 (print) | LCCN 2021022749 (ebook) |
ISBN 9780593200353 (trade paperback) | ISBN 9780593200377 (ebook)
Subjects: LCSH: Windsor, Wallis Warfield, Duchess of, 1896-1986—Fiction. |
Windsor, Edward, Duke of, 1894-1972—Fiction. | Great Britain—Politics
and government—1936-1945—Fiction. | GSAFD: Biographical fiction.
Classification: LCC PR6058.O436 D88 2021 (print) |
LCC PR6058.O436 (ebook) | DDC 823/.914—dc23
LC record available at https://lccn.loc.gov/2021022748
LC ebook record available at https://lccn.loc.gov/2021022749

Welbeck Fiction Limited UK hardcover edition: August 2021
Berkley trade paperback edition: September 2021

Printed in the United States of America
1st Printing

Book design by Katy Riegel

To Noj, Andrew and Isabella

THE
DUCHESS

PROLOGUE

The Duke of Windsor's Funeral
London
June 1972

In his coffin of English oak, on the Royal Air Force plane, he had gone before her. Wallis had not wanted him to be alone on that last journey. But grief had weakened her, and her physician insisted she stay in Paris. A few days later a plane of the Queen's Flight arrived to bring her to England for the funeral. Now they were almost here. Below, London spread flat and gray. There was the squiggle of the Thames, there the Tower, Tower Bridge, St. Paul's.

Wallis stared at her reflection in the cabin window. She had never felt old before. He had made her feel youthful and beautiful always. But with him gone she was suddenly a woman in her late seventies.

Her once-smooth, pale skin was furrowed and powdered. Behind her brave red lipstick her mouth was wrinkled. Hair that had been naturally black and glossy was now dyed and lacquered. Only her navy-blue eyes were the same. Framed thickly with mascara, they registered shock and bewilderment.

She still could not believe it. It was a dream from which she would soon wake, in her bedroom at home in the Bois de Boulogne. *Bwah de Bolone*, as he always drawlingly pronounced it.

Opposite, her companion shifted in her armchair. "The Queen's

Flight might be the most prestigious in the world," she remarked. "But no one could claim its aircraft are the most luxurious."

Wallis gave Grace a weary smile. She knew her old friend was only acting the spoiled part, trying to distract her from the trials that lay ahead. How would she bear a single moment of any of it? And yet borne it must be.

"I suppose her Purple Passage has proved useful," Grace conceded, referring to the invisible red carpet in the sky that only the Queen's Flight could use.

"It's called Purple Airspace," Wallis corrected. "As well you know!"

Grace had been Princess Radziwill in a former marriage—Jacqueline Kennedy's sister, Lee, was the current one. Grace had moved on to become the reigning Countess of Dudley. She and Wallis went back years; besides a dry sense of humor, they shared a similar taste in clothes and an outsider's perspective on the British upper class. Both were foreigners—Grace from Dubrovnik—and neither had been born aristocrats.

"I'm grateful to Lilibet anyway," Wallis went on. "She's been very kind. She came to see us, which was good of her."

After decades of cold war with the Windsors, the call had come out of the blue. The Foreign Office relayed that the queen wished to visit her uncle at his Paris home. She would come during her five-day state visit to France.

Lilibet had clearly heard about the ex-king's cancer. Someone had said that after the failed radiation treatment his life hung by a thread. She wanted to say goodbye but only afterward had the high-stakes game that was the run-up to the visit been revealed. Britain's ambassador in Paris had been adamantly against the idea. It would, he had warned, spell disaster for Anglo-French relations if the ex-monarch died before the present one left England. The state visit would have to be canceled and President Pompidou would be greatly offended.

The farcical aspect this lent the situation would, in other circumstances, have amused the former Edward VIII. But he rose to the occasion. His country needed him. He was important in a way he hadn't been these past thirty-six years. Through sheer strength of will he hung on and waited during the whole of the royal visit. Lilibet did not hurry, dazzling banquets at Versailles and the British embassy in one tiara after another before touring Provence and attending the races. Finally, accompanied by Princes Philip and Charles, she arrived at route du Champ d'Entraînement on a sunny May afternoon.

Grateful as she was to her niece-in-law, Wallis could not help being struck by the hideousness of the royal-blue hat and the horrible matching box-pleated suit. Amid the riot of pattern, Lilibet's bow-shaped diamond brooch and three strings of perfect pearls were completely lost. How could such a naturally pretty woman with such wonderful skin contrive to seem so plain?

In his overcoat Philip had looked like a testy bank manager, while Charles, his striped shirt clashing with his floral tie, had just looked uncomfortable. Beneath his checked tweed jacket, his shoulders sloped. His eyebrows too; his face wore a permanent expression of weary disappointment.

Wallis had felt sorry for him. She knew what it was to be steamrollered by the Windsors. And Charles was obviously terrified of his father, whose mannerisms he seemed condemned to imitate: pulling at his cuffs, clasping his hands, even walking with one arm behind his back.

As she entered the airy marble-floored hall, Lilibet had glanced without comment on the great silk Garter banner fixed to the ornate balcony. If she was surprised, in the drawing room of an abdicated monarch, to take tea under his full-length portrait in kingly robes and another of Queen Mary in all her splendor, she did not show it.

Philip had been another matter, lounging against the Louis

XV sofa and gazing satirically around at the collection of Meissen pug dogs and Black Diamond and Gin-Seng, their panting real-life counterparts. "Is it true you've got one called Peter Townsend?" He had smirked.

"We used to," Wallis had answered levelly. "But we gave the group captain away."

"Ha. As did Margaret, of course."

Tea over, she took Elizabeth II upstairs to the orange sitting room on the first floor. Uncle David, as she called him, using the name the family always had, was fixed and threaded with tubes and clamps to the drip that sustained his life. He had, however, insisted his doctor hid the latter behind the curtains and the former beneath his clothes. His wizened face, still handsome beneath his combed silver hair, blazed with delight when Lilibet came in. He did his courtly best, rising from his wheelchair with great difficulty to bow and kiss his royal visitor on both cheeks. Still the fashion plate, he had sported a perfectly cut blue blazer and a silk cravat round his withered throat. They talked for exactly fifteen minutes.

But afterward, once the queen had left, David seemed annoyed.

"Oh, David. You didn't ask her about my HRH again?" Exasperation and love twisted within Wallis. Surely he hadn't wasted a precious—and final—personal interview with the sovereign on something so utterly pointless. The Windsors would never let her be a Royal Highness, and she didn't care anyway. But David did, passionately, and had spent a lifetime trying to bring it about.

Wordless, spent from the recent effort, he shook his head. But he was growling, trying to speak, and she gathered he was irked by his doctor not being presented to Her Majesty. "Monsieur Thin would have remembered it all his life."

She shook her head. Oh, the irony. No one was ever more

aware of the power of the Crown than David, who had been so eager to give it up.

He had lasted just nine days after that. On the night he died, black ravens, harbingers of death, sat in the bright leaves outside his window. They had come for him. When, much later, she was called by the nurse, it was to see that Black Diamond, who always slept on his bed, now lay on the rug on the floor. The pug too knew what was about to happen. At 2:20 in the morning, the onetime King Edward VIII of Great Britain, Ireland and the British Dominions Beyond the Seas, Emperor of India, breathed his last. It was May 28, 1972.

CHAPTER ONE

Honeymoon in Paris

1928

The hotel room was dingy and had an odd smell. There was a brass double bed whose counterpane sagged in the middle. The floral wallpaper was faded, with rust-edged stains.

Two long windows looked out into the street. Wallis went across to them. The window opposite had dried-up plants and dirty curtains.

She had not expected Paris to look like this. All the way over on the boat from Dover she had imagined views of the Eiffel Tower. But Wallis was an optimist, and never more so than now. This was her wedding day. A fresh start. A new life.

There was a mirror on the wall by the window, positioned to throw light on the face. Critically, she examined hers. She was no longer young—thirty-four at her last birthday—but she looked pretty good, she thought. Poised, sleek, fashionable. And hopeful, most of all.

Her wedding outfit—primrose-yellow dress, sky-blue coat—made a colorful contrast to the glossy black hair center-parted and curled in two "earphones." In her pale face her lips were a bold slash of red. If, in her dark-blue eyes, there was still something sad behind the sparkle, that would not stay long. Everything would be fine from now on.

They had married that morning in London. At the Chelsea Register Office, as both had been divorced. But Wallis did not regret being unable to wed in a church. She had done that the first time around, and to a cad. Ernest could not be more different. He was a fine, kind, honorable man, and she was a lucky woman.

A movement in the mirror caught her eye. She saw that the bellhop who had brought their bags up was still standing in the doorway, scratching himself.

"Ernest," she prompted, smiling. "I think he expects a tip."

Her new husband rummaged in his overcoat pocket and handed over a small coin. The boy looked at it, raised his eyebrows and disappeared.

Wallis heaved her suitcase onto her bed and snapped the locks open. In the dingy surroundings, her dresses, new for the honeymoon, bolstered her feelings of optimism. She had bought them all for a song and altered them herself. She was clever with her needle and had once thought of a career in fashion. After the divorce, the idea of supporting herself, of becoming an independent woman, had strongly appealed.

But her shattered self-confidence and her lack of practical skills had made this more difficult than she expected. And once she met Ernest, she had abandoned the effort altogether. He had been a port in a storm, quite literally, as his family owned a shipping firm. When he announced he was leaving America for the London office, and asked her to marry him and come too, she had seized the chance to begin again.

She shook out a dress and thought about the great Paris fashion houses. She was keen to see them even if there was no chance of buying anything. Money was tight, hence the shabby hotel room. Hence the tiny stone in the ring on her finger, so small it struggled to catch the limited light.

The family firm was in trouble, although Ernest was determined to turn it round. There were also the alimony payments to his first wife and young daughter. He had thought that would annoy her, but it didn't. On the contrary, she was pleased that he already had a child. She was in her early thirties and the prospect was fading, but after her own miserable childhood, she had no wish for one anyway. She felt sorry for her little stepdaughter, whose life had been upended by her parents' divorce. When Audrey came to stay with them in London, Wallis would give her a good time. They would be friends.

She felt Ernest's solid, reassuring presence behind her. He came close and put his large hands over hers. She leaned her head back, into his chest, and relished, for a few moments, his tall broadness, the feeling of utter safety, of being cherished and protected.

"Don't do that now," he murmured into her shoulder. He meant the open case before her.

"But I have to unpack. My things will be so creased." The cheap material needed to be hung to look good.

He pulled her closer. His mustache was tickling her neck. "Who cares if your things are creased? I'd like to crease them some more!"

Her reaction was as instant as it was unexpected. Panic swept through her like a tidal wave. An alarm bell shrilled loudly in her head, and her heart rose in her throat, banging violently. The urge to wrench herself away was overwhelming, and only by inhaling slowly, shudderingly, could she gain any control.

Ernest had not noticed. He was sliding his arms round, pressing his body into her back. Through his coat and jacket she could feel how aroused he was.

"Wallis," he murmured into her ear. "I've wanted you for so long."

As his hand explored her breast, her whole body screamed silently. Her teeth began to chatter. She clamped them hard together so he would not hear. He pushed her gently forward, onto the bed. She fell like a stone, hands by her sides, and lay rigid, face pressed in the cover. Its sour smell filled her nostrils.

She braced herself, as if against some expected blow or other act of violence. Great waves of heat followed by sickening swirls of cold were chasing each other round her stomach. She could not breathe. She turned her head, gasped.

He seemed to take this as encouragement, perhaps as a pant of desire. His hand was on her thigh now. It was pulling up her dress; she could feel his fingers on her stocking top. She was going to be sick; she pressed her mouth and body hard into the bed. If those fingers got through, if they touched her . . .

Oh God, no. Please, no.

She must have spoken aloud. The fingers stopped. The hand pulled away. Beneath her ear, there was a grate and groan of bedsprings as he sat down. "Wallis, whatever's the matter?"

She raised her head. He sat at the other side of her case, his overcoat still on. His basset hound face with its round brown eyes registered absolute bewilderment.

She could not blame him. Throughout their short courtship, kissing was as far as he had gone. He was the very pattern of chivalry and had treated her with the utmost respect. But on their wedding night he was naturally hoping for more. She was a divorcée, after all, a woman of experience. That he had absolutely no idea what her experience had been was not his fault.

Perhaps she should have told him, but what could she have said? That she had, for nine years, been married to someone who had beaten and abused her, who drank himself senseless, who had not only forced himself upon her but made her watch him with other women?

How could she have told him? Ernest would have been appalled; it would have lessened her in his eyes. It lessened her in her own. She had pushed her first husband into the depths of the farthest cupboard at the back of her mind, the one marked "The Past," and done her level best to forget.

It had worked, or appeared to. After the divorce, as she recovered and looked to the future, her time as Mrs. Earl Winfield Spencer Jr. seemed increasingly like a bad dream. She had thought she could move on, but that Win—as he was known—had destroyed her ability to enjoy physical intimacy, even to take part in it, was something she had not suspected. Until now. Now—on her wedding night.

She hung her head. What could she say? That she was damaged goods, in every sense? Would he even believe her? He might think she had known, that she had trapped him. Her panic had drained away to leave a sense of utter hopelessness. She had no idea what to do.

She could feel his eyes on her and tried to guess their expression. Accusing? Angry? She could not blame him. But when, eventually, she screwed up the courage to look at him, the basset hound eyes were gentle.

"We're married now," Ernest said softly. "I love you. Talk to me."

Wallis stared at him for a moment. Then she looked down at her hands, at the ring, took a breath, and talked to him.

CHAPTER TWO

Win had burst into her life in 1916. Her grandmother had recently died, and after the required period of mourning, her mother decided that Wallis needed a little fun. She sent her to stay in Florida with her cousin Corinne, who was married to an air base commandant.

Fun it certainly was. Wallis had never seen an airplane before, let alone a pilot as dashing as young Lieutenant Spencer with his close-clipped mustache and worldly air. They met on her first morning and saw each other every day. When, with bewildering speed, Win proposed, she accepted. She was nineteen years old.

"Mother adored him," Wallis said ruefully now to Ernest. "Which should have been a sign. She has terrible taste in men. She married twice more after my father died and chose someone worse every time."

"Alice didn't like me, for sure." Ernest shrugged his wide shoulders.

It was true that Alice had admired Win's charm and derring-do. Her new son-in-law, she considered, fell far short of this dashing ideal. "That bowler hat and mustache! He's like an American actor playing an Englishman!"

"But he *is* English, Mother. Well, half."

The connection was on his father's side. Ernest felt it strongly. Though he had grown up in America and been educated at Harvard, he had spent the war in the Coldstream Guards, an elite British regiment. He was passionate about British history and during their courtship had taken Wallis around the New York art galleries, showing her portraits of English rulers and describing their reigns.

"Stop!" Wallis would laughingly implore. "I'm from the States. We're a republic, remember. If we'd wanted all this royal stuff we'd have hung on to it."

But by far the worst of Ernest's crimes in Alice's eyes was his failure to understand her sense of humor. She regarded herself as a wit and on their first meeting had told him the most cherished of her amusing stories: how she fell down the stairs in the five-and-dime. An assistant rushed over and asked if he could help her.

"And whaddya think I told him?" Alice demanded as Ernest stood awkwardly twisting his hat.

"I don't know, Mrs. Warfield. What did you tell him?"

Alice's gaze switched gleefully to her daughter, who was standing apprehensively by. "Tell him, Wallis! Tell him what I said when I fell down in the five-and-dime!"

Wallis turned to her fiancé. She said flatly, "Mother told him to take her to the five-and-dime coffin counter." As Alice dissolved into hysterical laughter, Ernest looked blank. Their relationship had never recovered.

Wallis was aware that her husband thought her mother delusional. She didn't disagree. Her difficult relationship with Alice was something else she had been glad to escape from. She returned to the subject of her first marriage.

She and Win had married in Baltimore; she had worn white velvet over a petticoat of heirloom lace. Her bridesmaids wore wide picture hats. She was madly in love, or so she thought.

Then, on their wedding night, Win pulled a bottle of gin from his suitcase. It was an introduction to what would become the third person in their marriage.

"And the drinking got worse when the war came," Wallis went on.

"Win was desperate to fly in combat, but somehow it never happened."

She paused again.

"Go on," prompted Ernest.

"One day, after he'd been drinking, he dragged me into the bathroom. He . . . assaulted me. Then he left, and as he went, he locked the door. I lay there all day. . . ."

She stopped. Evening was coming. Oblongs of coral light, cast by the setting sun, shone on the faded wallpaper. She remembered lying on the cold tiled bathroom floor, her mouth full of the brassy taste of blood and her mind churning with anguish. The shaft of sunlight through the small, high window had moved across the wall as the hours dragged by. It was next to the street and she could hear people passing. But calling for help was out of the question.

"Why?" asked Ernest.

She sat on the bed edge, bending over, both arms wrapped round her middle as if to protect herself. She raised a hand to cover her eyes. "I don't know," she muttered. "I should have. But it was a small community. Everyone knew everyone's business. And Win was popular. People would have been surprised. Perhaps I was worried that they wouldn't believe me. Or maybe . . ."

"Maybe what?"

"Maybe I thought it was my fault. Maybe I was ashamed."

Ernest groaned. "Oh, Wallis."

She lowered her hand and glanced at him. His basset hound eyes were glistening but had a furious glow to them too. She went on.

"Then, much later, Win came back. I heard him unlock the bathroom door . . ."

She shut her eyes, but the image of herself cringing in terror against the bath, anticipating another beating, was seared on her memory and could not be erased. "He didn't come in though. He left the door open and went to bed. I lay there for a few more hours. Then I spent the rest of the night on the sofa, and the next day I left."

"You filed for divorce?" Ernest's brow was furrowed. She guessed he was trying to work out the timings.

"We separated. I went back to live with Mother. She didn't want me to divorce. Warfields and Montagues didn't do that sort of thing." Throughout Wallis's poverty-stricken childhood she had been reminded of her descent from the foremost families in Baltimore. It was like being a modern American version of *Tess of the d'Urbervilles*.

"Of course they didn't." A wintry smile crossed Ernest's features. He had often been told about the illustrious family background. Along with the famous sense of humor, it was Alice's favorite subject.

"And then Win went to join the US fleet in the Far East. He'd kept writing to me, and gradually he persuaded me that the Shanghai posting would be a new start." Another one. Just how many new starts had she had?

Shadows were gathering in the room. Across the street, in the window opposite, a red bulb had come on. Its glow evoked another room, dark and sour-smelling, a room with a red paper lantern. A woman in a dirty wrap with cynical eyes. A mat-strewn floor. A rumpled bed.

"So that's why you were in China," said Ernest. "I remember it came up on one of our first dates. You never really said what you were doing there."

She had met him in New York the winter before last. He was a friend of Mary Raffray, an old schoolmate. An inveterate matchmaker, Mary was keen to throw them together. But Wallis hadn't been interested. After the horror of Win, marriage to anyone was out of the question. Besides, Ernest Simpson was not her type. He was pleasant but rather plodding. And he wrote terrible poems. She received the first one after a card party.

I'm afraid I'm just a joker
When it comes to playing poker
It would give me greater solace
To have the skill of Wallis

"His poems are *terrible*," she complained to Mary.

"I think they're meant to be bad. He's trying to amuse you."

"I don't want him to amuse me."

Ernest persisted, even so. As did Mary, constantly feeding him lines. "Wallis was once on a train that was halted by bandits!"

"Bandits!" Ernest's thick eyebrows soared into his low hairline.

Wallis spoke through gritted teeth. "It was when I lived in China. It was fine."

Next morning another poem appeared.

If I ever met a bandit
I feel that I would hand it
To Wallis to dispose of
Because banditry she knows of

"Well," she said now, "that's what I was doing there. Trying to rescue the marriage. At first it was fine, but it soon all began again, the drinking and violence, and worse . . ."

She stopped and looked at the floorboards, unable to carry on.

"Worse?" prompted Ernest.

She looked at him pleadingly, but on the other hand, he needed to know. This, after all, was the very heart of the matter, that their time in Shanghai, a city notorious for its sex trade, had provided Win with endless opportunities to indulge his existing vices and acquire new ones. Sometimes he had forced her to come with him. She would cower in the corner, face to the wall, listening to his degradation.

"*Banditry she knows of*," Ernest said when she had finished. He added slowly, "I had no idea how true that was."

Neither of them spoke after that. The shadows deepened. The room was almost entirely dark now apart from the red light in the room opposite. She stared at it, wondering if it really was a brothel, wondering if there was a Win in there at the moment, and a Wallis waiting for him at home. She wondered what Ernest was thinking.

That he seemed sympathetic was a relief. But the greater relief was that he knew.

"I'm sorry," she said eventually. "You deserve better."

"As do you," he returned, with heat.

"I think," she said hesitantly, "I just need . . . a little time."

His answer to this was to stand up. He was still wearing his overcoat and she hers. The wedding night hadn't even got that far, she thought.

Ernest smiled at her. "Let's go and have dinner."

CHAPTER THREE

As their hotel was central, near the Tuileries, it was the walk of a few moments to pass from the gloomy street to the splendid rue de Rivoli.

They went along the grand arcades, under the great lanterns. Across the road was the Louvre, and beyond the park, the Eiffel Tower rose up in the west. The sight of them made her heavy spirits soar. This was more the Paris she had been expecting.

"I've found a place round the corner that's famous for its pot-au-feu," said Ernest. He was a great consulter of guidebooks.

"What's pot-au-feu?"

"It's a kind of simple French peasant dish."

Wallis smiled as if this were the most delightful possible prospect, as it clearly was to Ernest, and not at all as if her own thoughts had gone down the oysters-and-chilled-Chablis route. Funds were low, after all. They should eat within their means.

A splendid hotel entrance approached, with braided flunkeys in top hats and a glass revolving door. Wallis slowed down to look at the interior. Through the polished plate glass it appeared glittering and palatial. She could see pillars, gilding, mirrors, chandeliers. Longing pulled at her.

A shining car glided up, headlamps blazing, and the flunkeys shot

forward to open the doors. A woman in a silver dress emerged, tossing a fur wrap carelessly over a pearly shoulder. A tall man in white
tie and tails joined her, and together they sailed into the hotel, leaving
behind them a trail of delicious scent.

Wallis sighed and made as if to walk on, but Ernest pulled her back.
"Shall we go in? Have a drink?"

Her heart leaped. "Can we afford it?"

"No, but it won't hurt just this once. We *are* on our honeymoon.
Come on."

And she came on, grinning in delight, before he could change his
mind.

The click of her heels on the marble floors sounded thrillingly in
her ears. She glimpsed a stunningly opulent dining room. The hotel
bar had classical murals and a pianist playing jazz in a corner. The
people at the other tables looked happy and rich. There was a murmur
of conversation, a tinkle of glass and china, the occasional low laugh.
Just sitting there made her feel special and beautiful. And made a
handsome blade out of homely Ernest. The table candle gave his eyes
a mysterious depth. Under the pleated silk lamp, his curly dark hair
shone.

A waiter glided over with a silver tray from which two tall glasses
rose. As her champagne cocktail was set before her, Wallis thought
what a work of art it was, the bubbles swirling from the sugar cube,
the deep-red cherry and the yellow curl of lemon peel nestling in the
glinting amber depths. She inhaled the rich scent of wine and spirits.
She would sip it slowly, make it last.

The waiter carefully placed small shining silver bowls of olives and
nuts and a silver holder with tiny linen napkins pressed into triangles.
A pair of small silver-rimmed plates followed. Wallis's eyes sparkled.
She loved the ceremony of it, the beauty of the objects, the sheer life-
enhancing glamour of it all. It was making everything better. After
the evening's miserable beginning, this was a new start.

"You're enjoying yourself," Ernest said, sounding amused.

She took a sip, savored the powerful hit, and nodded. "I adore places like this."

He raised his thick eyebrows. "You'd like to be rich, I daresay."

"Oh, no, Ernest!" She stretched out a pale hand over the table and covered his. The little diamond winked in the light. "I couldn't ask for anything more than you."

She meant it, sincerely, but there was also some truth in what he said. She would have liked to be rich. She had observed wealthy people throughout her life and formed the view that while money made some people miserable, in general it made things fun. But there were some things that it could not buy, and a kind, supportive and understanding husband was one of them.

"I've married the best man in the world," Wallis said sincerely.

"And I the best woman." Ernest leaned forward to pick up his glass. "Here's to us!"

They talked of the future, of what their life together in London would be like when they got back. Ernest's sister had found a house for them, which neither of them had yet seen.

"It's a good address, Maud tells me," Ernest said. "And it comes with staff. A cook and a maid."

Wallis wrinkled her brow. "I could do the cooking," she suggested. She enjoyed it and was good at it. Her trusty Fannie Farmer recipe book was the one thing from her first marriage she had kept. "It would save us money."

"Good idea," said Ernest. "You could cook for all my business dinners. I'll be having plenty of those to strengthen my contacts and get the old firm going again."

Wallis loved the sound of this. She would be more than just a wife, she would be helping Ernest in his work. As there would be no children to look after—until Audrey came to visit, of course—she would need something to do. "And it would be a good way to meet people," she said. "Make friends."

Ernest speared an olive. "Yes, and Maud will help you with that too. She's very well connected."

"Is she?" Wallis knew little about Ernest's sister apart from the fact she was older than he was.

"There's a baronet in her husband's family. In the ancient hereditary titles of Great Britain, that's—"

The little diamond glittered as Wallis laughingly held up her hand. "Stop! I'm not interested in ancient titles! I'm interested in modern people!"

Ernest took it in good part. "Well, Maud knows plenty of those too. She moves in all the best circles. Her husband is very rich."

Wallis was interested. "Really? Why?"

Ernest crunched a nut. "Irish linen."

Wallis glanced at the napkins. This was exciting news. She imagined Maud to be a slender brunette version of her brother: tall, sophisticated and dressed like the woman in silver they had seen getting out of the car. She would introduce Wallis to her many glamorous, interesting friends. She would have a ready-made social circle. There would be parties, and they would go to the theater together. London was famous for its theaters. There were nightclubs too, with celebrated bands. Everyone seemed to flock to the British capital.

The cocktail was expanding within her, filling her with joy and excitement. "I'm looking forward to making friends with the British," she said, draining the last of her cocktail. "Living in London is going to be wonderful!"

"I'll drink to that," said Ernest, finishing his too.

"Shall we have another?" she asked, wryly pleading.

Ernest looked surprised. "It's time for dinner. The pot-au-feu."

The waiter came over and expressionlessly exchanged their empty bowl of nuts for one freshly filled. It gave Wallis an idea. The cost of another cocktail each would not be greater than dinner out, even the most reasonable peasant dish in Paris. They could dine on free nuts and olives.

"Please?" she begged Ernest. Who knew, after all, when they would come somewhere like this again.

He shook his head in mock exasperation. "Wallis, when you look at me with those eyes, how can I ever refuse you?"

He could not refuse her a third one either. It had a more practical purpose than its predecessors. She may be sitting now in the glowing cocktail bar. But not far away was the shabby, shadowy room where painful confessions had been made. Where, for the first time, they would share a bed. For both these reasons, when eventually they went back, Wallis wanted her feelings numbed by alcohol.

And so it proved. They made a merry, unsteady couple returning through the rue de Rivoli's lanterned passages. At the dark and deserted hotel, they shushed each other amid snorting laughter up the four floors of battered stairs. The dreaded entry into the room was something, in the end, Wallis hardly noticed. She was so tired that the sight of the sagging bed was actually welcome.

Until she saw that the case was still on it, its lid open, one dress abandoned across it.

"What are you doing?" Ernest asked tiredly.

From the cheap little wardrobe, where she was rummaging for coat hangers, Wallis flashed him a bright, exhausted smile. "I forgot to hang my dresses up."

His face fell. "Wallis. There's no need to worry. I won't . . ." He sighed. "You can trust me. I won't hurt you."

She realized that he thought she was playing for time; that she thought, after all she had said, he was going to force himself on her as Win had. She saw that he understood how little she trusted men, how little reason she had had to. She was deeply touched. Her eyes glistened as she looked at him.

"Ernest, I do trust you. And you can trust me. I won't hurt you either." She paused, and smiled. "But I really must hang my clothes up. Otherwise they'll look awful tomorrow."

He was in bed by the time she had finished. As there was no bathroom in their room, he had undressed in the shared one down the corridor. She used the wardrobe door as a screen. As she changed into her nightdress, he lay on his back with his pajamas buttoned to the neck, eyes closed. Slipping in beside him, Wallis heard something crackle under her pillow. It was a small piece of paper, folded. She held it up to the only available source of light: the red glow from the window opposite.

> *To my little Wallis wife*
> *On the start of married life!*

The sound of paper alerted Ernest, who obviously hadn't been asleep at all. His face in the darkness looked abashed. "I forgot I put that there. It was when we first arrived. . . ."

"It's sweet," she said. "Thank you." She leaned over to kiss him softly on the cheek. Avoiding his eye and what question might be in it, she lay with her back to him. After a while, regular breathing told her he really was asleep this time. She stared at the red-lit floral wallpaper until she too drifted off.

It was dark when she awoke. Her head felt tight from the alcohol. But it was something else that had disturbed her. She listened. She thought she could hear running feet. There were distant bangs that gradually came nearer. Then a crash on their door. The sound made her jump violently. Then a cry. "*Feu!*"

Feu? Wasn't that French for "fire"?

Ernest still lay on his back, snoring. It didn't look as if he had moved.

She nudged him. "Ernest!"

He grunted, then turned over.

She seized him. "*Ernest!*"

The banging and shouting outside had increased. The running

feet now sounded like a stampede. Wallis realized she had not seen a fire escape. They didn't seem to go in for them in Paris, even in a tall building like this. They were on the fourth floor.

Sheer panic drove her out of bed and toward the light switch. "Ow!" objected Ernest, screwing up his face as the bulb's pitiless glare flooded the room. He clamped both hands to his head. "Uhh . . ."

She was pulling her coat on over her nightdress. "Ernest, there's a fire! We've got to get out!"

Ernest was out from under the covers like a shot. He opened the door, took her arm and pushed her into the passing crowd. It happened so quickly there was no time to speak. Before she knew it she was being carried along. She turned, looked back, yelled, "Ernest!" But the door to their room had closed.

She turned and tried to walk back against the tide. But the people behind her pushed her forward. They were coughing and holding handkerchiefs to their faces. There was an overpowering smell of smoke.

"*Ernest!*" Where was he? Why had he not come out of the room? A terrible thought struck her. Was it because she could not be a proper wife to him? Had she angered him? Or had he decided to let events take their course, as life with her would not be worth living?

"*Continuez, madame!*" shouted the large man behind her, a vision in long johns and a vest.

Her eyes smarted with the smoke, but also streamed with tears. It was all her fault. She should never have married him. She had ruined him, destroyed a noble and generous man.

The crowd swept her, stumbling, down the spiral staircase and into the tiny hallway at the bottom. When last she had seen it, the hall was dark and empty, but now light blazed on old ladies in bloomers and young men with bare chests. It was like being in a surreal dream; strangers in their nightclothes, the world out of joint, the air full of smoke, everyone shouting and shoving. She fixed her attention on the one thing that mattered, the bottom of the staircase, willing with all her might for Ernest to appear.

She heard someone say the fire was on the top floors of the hotel. At that, the last of her reason vanished. With the strength of madness she shoved her way back toward the stairs. This time, even large men in long johns would not stop her.

"Let me through!" screamed Wallis.

She had gained the bottom of the stairs when an arm clutched her. She dragged it away and pushed forward. It grabbed again.

"Wallis!"

The voice was Ernest's. She opened her eyes and found herself staring into his creased and friendly face. It seemed to her the most wonderful and most beloved face in the world. Then she saw that he was fully clothed.

"You stayed to get dressed?" she gasped, disbelieving. He had put her through all that anguish and fear so he could put on his suit and overcoat?

He held up her suitcase. "No, Wallis. I stayed to get your dresses. I know how much they mean to you."

The Duke of Windsor's Funeral
Heathrow Airport
June 1972

There was a bump as the airplane's landing gear made contact with the tarmac. The flight attendants appeared from the cabin next door. Their smiles were bland, professional, but Wallis sensed their curiosity as the plane slowed to a standstill.

"Who will they send to meet you?" Grace was wondering.

Wallis didn't care. Life had become vague and floating, like an untethered balloon. Nothing felt real anymore. But she knew that David would care, and care very much, who made up the official reception for his widow.

"Mrs. Temple Senior?" Grace was asking.

"Her Majesty Queen Elizabeth the Queen Mother, you mean," Wallis corrected, smiling at this use of David's old nickname for his brother's wife. If Lilibet when little had resembled child star Shirley Temple, there had been far more of the ruthless stage mother about Elizabeth.

"Do you think she'll be the welcoming committee?"

"Shouldn't think so." Wallis hoped not. That bitterest of old enemies would have to be faced sooner or later, even so.

"She been in touch?"

"No."

"Not at all?" Grace was amazed.

Wallis shrugged her narrow shoulders. "Still blames me for the abdication and her husband's death, I expect."

Across the tarmac were shining cars and a row of dark-coated, waiting figures. Prominent among the latter was someone tall and erect with silver hair.

"They've sent Mountbatten!" Grace exclaimed. "That's outrageous. He's not a member of the royal family!"

"Thinks he is though," Wallis said. "Always has. And I'm not a Royal Highness, anyway. Just Your Grace."

"Nothing wrong with being a Grace!"

The air hostesses approached; time to get out. For a second Wallis clung to the seat. Her limbs had turned to water. She could not face it. She wanted to fly straight back to France.

Grace slid her arm through her friend's. "Come on," she urged Wallis. "We Graces must stick together."

They emerged into the daylight, which, despite it being June, was chilly. The cold penetrated her bones; gray sky pressed down like a lid. It wasn't raining. But this being London, it wouldn't be long.

As she descended the steps, she clung to a railing to steady herself. Mountbatten marched over, tanned beneath the silver hair.

She watched him roll an appreciative eye over Grace before turning to clamp a solicitous arm about Wallis. She proudly pulled away. "I'm a widow, Louis. Not a cripple."

They were to travel alone together while Grace and Dr. Antenucci, Wallis's physician, rode in the car behind.

Sensing her alarm, Grace enveloped her in a swift hug. "See you at Buckingham." It was what the French called the palace. They were all guests of the queen for three nights, until the funeral was over.

A smell of leather rose richly from the car seats. "Her Majesty has blocked off all the cross-traffic," Mountbatten remarked as they glided off.

Wallis had a sudden image of Lilibet in a policeman's uniform, directing the cars with bossy white gloves. It seemed oddly appropriate. "Why?"

"So you don't get held up and stared at. It will be a straight route through."

Wallis had never even thought about intersections. But staring crowds would not be a problem. She was here to represent her husband, who had briefly been their king.

"I wouldn't mind," she said. "I'm sure people would be respectful."

He was settling himself in his seat; there was a brief, skeptical lift of his eyebrow. Irritation shot through her.

"David was very popular," she reminded him. "The most popular Prince of Wales in history."

"Oh yes." Mountbatten's tone was sardonic. "No one who knew him when he was *Prince of Wales* will ever forget him."

She forced down her indignation and tried to change the subject. "How are they all? The family?"

"Very well. Looking forward to seeing you."

"There's a first for everything, I guess."

His long mouth stretched in a faint smile. "Oh, you'll be surprised. Your sister-in-law especially will welcome you with open arms. She wanted me to tell you so."

This was sufficiently amazing as to make Wallis drop the pretense. She stared at Mountbatten. "Are you kidding?" Had the years finally softened that hard old Bowes-Lyon heart?

Mountbatten inclined his neat silver head. "Her Majesty Queen Elizabeth the Queen Mother is deeply sorry for you in your present grief."

"Really?" She felt a weight roll from her shoulders.

"Yes. She remembers what it was like when her own husband died."

Ouch. "That's very . . . um . . . comforting to hear."

"Good. She hoped it would be."

Wallis turned away to the window. Dull beneath its granite sky, London slid past.

"You know, Louis," she said after a while, "it wasn't me who killed George the Sixth."

"No, it was stress. He hadn't been trained to be king, like his brother had."

She sighed, exasperated. Another myth that had gained traction. "David was never trained to be anything. His father never let him attend a single meeting or showed him a single red box."

A skeptical silence greeted this. She ignored it. "George the Sixth died of lung cancer. He was a human chimney. It was cigarettes that did it, not the stress of suddenly becoming king. And, while we're on that subject, no one ever enjoyed being queen more than Elizabeth."

Mountbatten was looking out his own window too. "But that's the thing about history, Wallis. It's not what you did that counts. It's what people think you did."

CHAPTER FOUR

The New Mrs. Simpson

Upper Berkeley Street
London
1928

The rain hurled itself against the sitting-room windows. Outside, on the narrow iron balcony, the water pooled. It had rained every day since they got back from Paris, or so it seemed to Wallis.

She was trying hard not to feel disappointed in London. But nothing had yet measured up to expectations.

"Maud's been marvelous to find the house for us, hasn't she?" prompted Ernest the day they arrived back from honeymoon. It had been hot and sunny when they left Paris, but rain now dripped from his hat.

Beneath her own sodden, ruined pillbox, Wallis had forced an appreciative smile. "Maud certainly has."

It was obvious the moment Wallis laid eyes on Maud that her hopes of a friend were doomed. Ernest's sister was, for a start, a good twenty years older and dressed even older than that. Her baggy tweed suits were light-years from the soignée sophistication of the woman seen in Paris. But none of that would have mattered if she was friendly, which she was not. With her beady dark eyes and compact build, she was like a bossy and cross little bird. Her surname—Smiley—seemed ironic to say the least.

And while she had undoubtedly helped them with the house, Wallis regretted not persuading Ernest to let her look for one herself. She would not have chosen 12 Upper Berkeley Street. It was part of a narrow terrace north of Oxford Street whose neighbors pushed in on it, seeming to squeeze so it had no air. By night the ancient pipes rattled and banged, and by day the ill-fitting doors and windows let seep in the filthy London fog. It was coal dust from millions of smoking chimneys mixed with a sulfurous miasma from the river, and was especially thick and smelly now that winter had come. Londoners called it smog or pea-soupers and seemed almost proud of it, but Wallis loathed the way it billowed in the street so she could not see a hand in front of her face. It roamed around the house like a dirty cat, leaving a layer of black grime on every surface.

The Upper Berkeley Street house belonged to someone Maud knew, a Lady Chesham, so Wallis wondered whether the person being helped was her, rather than them.

Especially as the cook who came with it seemed nonnegotiable. When Wallis, hesitantly, had mentioned doing her own cooking, Maud was aghast.

"A lady doesn't cook for herself!" she exclaimed. "A lady doesn't work at all!"

Wallis had resigned herself. Arguing with Maud would only upset Ernest, who seemed rather cowed by his older sister. And there may be things to learn from Mrs. Codshead, the cook who came with the house. Wallis was keen to acquaint herself with English cuisine.

Unfortunately, Mrs. Codshead turned out to be the least suited for her profession of anyone Wallis had ever met. "She's almost brilliantly bad at it," she observed to Ernest during their first weeks in London, when Mrs. Codshead had served up yet another mush of cabbage and yet more hard and black-veined rabbit legs. "It's actually easier to cook cabbage so it's crisp and green. You have to be a real genius to reduce it to wallpaper paste, like this."

Ernest raised an eyebrow. "Well, you're always saying this place needs redecorating. So wallpaper paste might have its uses."

They had turned the terrible cooking into a private joke. There was a particularly repulsive meat dish that Ernest christened "Dead Man's Leg" while Wallis dubbed a gritty, grayish pudding "Nun's Toenails." A watery and colorless casserole that seemed mainly bones was "Skeleton Stew."

These days the awful food seemed less amusing. The fact that they were paying for it especially. Their arrival in Britain, the much-heralded new start, had coincided with an economic crisis that worsened by the week.

The economic picture was dire, as Wallis knew more than most; Simpson Spence and Young, Ernest's family firm, was proving far more difficult than expected to turn round. Wallis and Ernest had less money now than when they had married, and the prospects were grim.

London remained unexplored; its theaters, its nightclubs with famous bands, its concert halls with celebrated orchestras, its grand hotels with ballrooms. Thanks to lack of money, these delights were now completely out of reach. Ernest, too, seemed to be receding. Anxiety and exhaustion were having strange effects on him. He had started declaiming Latin aloud; he had won a prize for it at school, apparently, and revisiting this success seemed to bring him comfort. Stress was also bringing him out in boils, particularly on his neck. She would apply poultices while he read Virgil in the original. Never had the night in the Paris bar seemed so long ago.

She tried, all the same, to revive some of his old Paris spirit. One night out, she reasoned, wouldn't break the bank. "How about a club? The Café de Paris?" She'd seen it in magazines; it was popular with cabaret stars and had a great curved staircase designed for spectacular entrances.

"I don't think so."

"Or the Embassy Club?" She'd seen pictures of that too, lined with mirrors and red velvet banquettes. "The best bands play there." She had not danced for so long.

"Those places are very expensive," Ernest warned.

"We'd just have one drink and watch people?" She was pleading like a child. "Like we did in Paris?"

"Wallis, we didn't have one drink in Paris, we had three!"

And thank God they had, she thought now. It didn't look as if she would ever see a champagne cocktail again. She felt like a bottle of champagne herself, one that had been forgotten in the icebox and had all the bubbles chilled out.

She had been in London six months now and still had not made one single friend. Once Ernest had gone to work, time slowed to a crawl. But once he got back and sat with his books, it seemed slower still.

Isolation gnawed at her spirit. Never in her entire life had she felt quite so lonely. She hated the feeling he was drifting from her. They had felt, albeit briefly, like a team, united in hope and ambitions for the future. Now they seemed far apart. By unspoken but mutual consent, they slept in separate rooms these days.

Sensing he was terrified by the extent of his financial difficulties, she tried to talk to him about it at dinner, encourage him to share the burden. But Ernest only told her not to worry. Male pride, she guessed. He felt obliged to provide and cope. He seemed to have forgotten that the model of masculinity she knew did neither of these things—it did the opposite.

"I have an idea," announced Ernest one night as they tackled a plate of Skeleton Stew. "You're always saying you haven't explored London."

She brightened immediately. Was he about to relent and say they could go to the theater after all? But his next words sent her soaring heart sinking again.

"London's full of historical attractions," Ernest went on.

She took a deep breath. "You mean galleries, museums and such?"

"Exactly!" His eyes shone. "Fascinating places. And do you know what the best thing of all is?"

"Tell me."

"They're all free!"

And so it was that—armed with Ernest's guidebooks—Wallis's small lone figure, umbrella raised against the ever-present downpour, explored the precincts of Parliament and walked beneath St. Paul's great dome. At the Inns of Court she huddled on garden benches as black-gowned barristers flapped importantly past. In Westminster Abbey she dutifully sought out the rather plain wooden chair where royal careers commenced and the magnificent tombs where they ended. Having been informed by Ernest that London railway architecture was the best of its kind, she visited the soot-blackened spires of St. Pancras station. The platform was crowded with beer barrels and burly men with strange accents. The roof was a vast arched iron vault and the redbrick walls suggested a medieval cathedral or fort. It wasn't just that an Englishman's home was his castle; his station was too. There was a beauty to it, Wallis conceded, although mainly due to its suggestion of escape.

CHAPTER FIVE

The weather got worse with the winter dragging on, and Wallis more hopeless. Would she ever find a kindred soul in this cold old town? The only people she had met so far were business contacts of Ernest's. They occasionally came to dinner with their strange English table manners. Such as eating with both knife and fork, not just fork as Americans did, and getting straight on with it rather than waiting for everyone to be served. She thought this bold of them given how bad the food was. But Dead Man's Leg and the rest of it seemed more than acceptable, amazingly. Bad dinners, like bad weather, seemed expected in this strange new city.

Conversation had rules too. Wallis had been regarded as witty in the past, but here her jokes fell flat. She found that English words, especially place names, were spelled differently from how they were said. Clipped British speech was hard for her American ear to catch. She practiced her English pronunciation diligently, working hard to flatten her rolling Southern drawl. "Barth, not bayath," she would repeat, like a stateside Eliza Doolittle, as she soaped herself in the tub at night. She read all the newspapers to be up on British topics and pestered Ernest for details about every guest, so she could draw them out with questions.

But no one wanted to be drawn out. The men spoke exclusively about the stock exchange while the women discussed the royal family. In the last few months Wallis had heard more about the infant Princess Elizabeth and her mother, the Duchess of York, than she had ever thought possible. The Prince of Wales was another obsession. His good looks, his radiant charm, his popularity were endlessly recited. The man was a living god, apparently.

"It's crazy," she said to Ernest. "You'd never think Britain was the mother of Parliaments."

She had visited Westminster too, on her round of historical sights. It had been unexpectedly beautiful, all spires, statues and blazing color. A reflection, she had assumed, of British respect for democracy. So why all this veneration for a family whose position depended on birth alone?

Ernest sighed. "Just don't argue with them, Wallis. I'm trying to drum up business. Try to look interested."

"But I don't know anything about them!"

"Read the Court Circular," advised Ernest.

She found it in *The Times*, a daily account of royal doings. To her republican, skeptical ear, its sycophantic language struck a bizarre, eighteenth-century note. *His Majesty was pleased. . . . Her Majesty graciously replied.* Neither King George nor Queen Mary ever looked either pleased or gracious in their photographs as they cut a ribbon or laid a foundation stone. But compared to their subjects elsewhere in the newspaper, the ones on hunger marches or strikes or standing in the ever-lengthening dole queues, they had plenty to be pleased and gracious about, Wallis thought.

Meanwhile, filling the day remained her greatest challenge. She made herself go for walks, pulling the collar of her tweed coat tightly around her chin, wincing as the freezing wind sent leaves rattling round her ankles.

She visited the great art galleries and did her best to find them interesting. Her favorite was the Wallace Collection. Quite apart from its amusing resemblance to her name, the paintings there were delightful. The *Laughing Cavalier* lifted her spirits and she enjoyed imagining what the haughty Velázquez ladies would say to Maud. But it was the larky, frilly Fragonards she loved best. His sunny pastoral world was such a contrast to the dreary city outside. Wallis longed to be on that flower-strewn swing, in the midst of that jolly party.

Or any jolly party, frankly. There were parties going on, she knew. Her perusal of the newspapers, the gossip columns, the social pages, had shown that some people in this cold wet town were having a high old time. They were called Bright Young Things. Their faces were fashionably blank, their chests fashionably flat. They seemed always to be at balls and dances, and almost all of them had a title.

The doings of society beauties such as Lady Bridget Poulett, Lady Edwina Mountbatten, and Lady Anne Armstrong-Jones were breathlessly followed in the press. Young titled people in Britain commanded the sort of attention that film stars did in America.

These well-connected women were often referred to as debutantes. A little research revealed that this meant they had been presented to the king and queen at court, which meant Buckingham Palace. This happened every summer, and those hoping to be presented at the next season needed a well-connected lady to sponsor them. Shot through with a sudden hope, Wallis asked Ernest to ask Maud on her behalf.

No, was her uncompromising answer. "Apparently you can only present someone once every three years," Ernest explained wearily.

"And next summer she's presenting My Elizabeth," Wallis guessed crossly. "My Elizabeth" was how Maud always referred to her daughter, a younger version of her mother. "Maybe there's someone else who can do it." She looked hopefully at Ernest, as if he could produce someone with contacts from among his shipping connections. Perhaps one of the royalty-obsessed wives.

But Ernest's basset hound face was gloomier even than usual. "It wouldn't be any good, Wallis. Apparently you can't be presented if you're divorced."

She gasped at the unfairness of it, churned with indignation. "That's so ridiculously old-fashioned! And I bet it doesn't apply to men."

"On the contrary," said Ernest. "If you're a divorced man you not only can't appear at court, you have to resign your army commission, leave your club and chuck yourself in the Thames."

"You're not serious!"

"Perfectly serious," he returned, poker-faced. Then his face split in a smile. "Well, I'm serious about the first two. The last one I might just have made up."

She was relieved. There were traces of the old Ernest yet.

She continued doggedly on her cultural visits. One afternoon, as darkness was gathering, she was near Piccadilly in search of St. James's Palace. An icy rain had started, and she hurried along trying to avoid drips from buildings and filthy water from splashing tires.

In the low winter light, jewels winked in the windows of Cartier and Van Cleef and Arpels. She felt she could hold up her hands and be warmed by the blaze from behind the glass—the fire-like rubies, flashing emeralds, burning sapphires, the white-hot diamonds most of all. She passed the glass front of a dress shop. The sign above the door read CHANEL in thick black capitals. Her thoughts flew back to the Paris honeymoon, where she had gazed hungrily in the window of the very same designer.

Simple, sophisticated, yet beautifully designed clothes, with attention to what a woman's actual shape was. But far too expensive for her. She stared at the display: a sleeveless evening dress, a gray silk jacket edged with fur, wool jerseys with broad pockets. A brooch on a dress flashed invitingly. One day, she thought to herself. One day.

She went on to the palace, but her mind was still on clothes. The redbrick, white-trimmed gatehouse emerged from the mist with its castellated towers and gold-edged clock; she tried in vain to remember who had built it and who now lived there.

There was a big arched gate with sentry boxes on either side. A couple of scarlet-clad soldiers stared straight ahead, the weak autumn sunset glinting on their bayonet tips.

As Wallis watched, they stood stiffly to attention and clamped gloved hands on their rifles. The great gates now swung open, and a magnificent black limousine appeared. It glided toward her, engine humming, silver grille shining, plate-glass windows agleam. In the murky afternoon its headlamps glowed like yellow eyes.

Barely visible inside at the back was a solitary male figure. The pale, boyish profile and flash of bright hair seemed familiar. She remembered now that St. James's Palace was the home of the Prince of Wales. Excitement flooded her; even Chanel's clothes were swept away—it was something to have seen the idol of the empire. Finally she could impress Ernest's shipping contacts.

"But you know," she said to him over dinner that night, "what was really odd about it?"

Ernest was frowning over the financial pages. "Mmm?"

"He looked so unhappy." She paused, recalling her powerful impression of a private side of the prince, one hidden from public view. "It was so strange," she went on, as Ernest did not reply. "In his pictures in the papers he's always smiling. But he looked the absolute picture of misery."

Ernest turned a page of his newspaper. "Well, I don't see why you're worrying about it. You're a republican. You laugh at the Court Circular, and you once told me that if America had wanted all that royal stuff you'd have kept it."

She chuckled. He was right. She had said that. But the prince she had seen in the car didn't look like all that royal stuff. He had looked like a deeply unhappy man. Republican or not, her heart had gone out to him.

CHAPTER SIX

Winter finally turned to spring, but this did not really improve things. Budding trees and rising shoots never failed to remind Wallis of how, as a schoolgirl, she had remained alone in Baltimore while all her wealthy peers went off to their country homes on spring break. None of them ever invited her along.

It had been hurtful but also confusing. According to her mother, they were grand people themselves. "Never forget, Wallis! You belong to the first and finest families of Baltimore."

So why then, Wallis would wonder, were they so poor? Why was home a succession of shabby apartments with a frequently changing cast of stepfathers?

As she grew older she learned that things could have been different. After her father's early death, his relatives had tried to help his widow and baby daughter. Grandmother Warfield had given them a home, and Uncle Sol, her father's brother, an allowance.

But Alice had rejected all this, presumably finding it restrictive. And so had begun the uncertain, impoverished, peripatetic life. Ostracism was the result and Wallis the principal sufferer. She was left out of parties, talked about, shunned. Alice's famous sense of humor and refusal to take any of it seriously only made things worse. "Who cares what they think?" she would say despite the obvious fact that her daughter did, desperately. That she could have grown up in the

Warfield mansion, not a succession of dingy boardinghouses, was particularly hard to forgive.

When she was grown up, Wallis had resolved, she would never have children. She would never impose her own selfishness on a small and helpless person. Nor would she act recklessly or marry badly. She would not repeat her mother's mistakes.

But it seemed that she had repeated quite a lot of them. She still felt vulnerable and powerless. She was still left out of parties. She still had no money. The sight of spring blossoms brought it back, made it worse.

Even so, she knew she was lucky compared to many. The unemployment rate was still rocketing, and many millions were now on the dole. Whether the newly elected Labour government under Ramsay MacDonald would, as they promised, "end misery, hunger and starvation within three weeks of coming into office" seemed unlikely to Wallis.

She wished she could help Ernest somehow. He was still battling to save the firm, but with no result that she could see. Money was tighter than ever, and the obvious economy was food shopping. If she bought it herself she would save them money; she was sure she could get things better and cheaper. But Ernest insisted it remain the domain of Mrs. Codshead. Wallis suspected it was because of Maud. Small as she was, and tall as Ernest was, she had the power to terrify him, like a mouse menacing an elephant.

The whole English system of food procuration seemed strange to Wallis. Mrs. Codshead never seemed to go near a shop; instead, the butcher, greengrocer and dairyman delivered directly to her. These supplies and their cost were listed in a series of small books that were fiercely guarded. Wallis saw them, grubby and grease-stained, on the same night every week when Ernest brought them up from the kitchen and went over the household expenses with her.

She understood that pondering for hours over what had been spent on liver or potatoes was Ernest's outlet for his worries. But the system of pounds, shillings and pence was a mystery at first, as were many of the bills, which didn't seem to relate to the meals.

In recent weeks, he had particularly queried the meat bill, which did seem high given the poor quality of what they were eating. Did Dead Man's Leg contain meat, or offal?

"But then again," Wallis observed, "if anyone could make fine steak taste like scrag end, Mrs. Codshead could."

Now her grasp of English currency was surer, Wallis had definite suspicions. Mrs. Codshead seemed to be buying the best of everything but serving up the worst. One morning, as the smell of boiled cabbage rose from the basement to the sitting room yet again, Wallis decided she had had enough.

She had rarely ventured belowstairs during her time in Upper Berkley Street. It had been clear from the start that her presence was not welcome. But now she felt that had probably been for a reason.

In the scullery off the kitchen the housemaid was scrubbing potatoes. Her hair hung lankly over her face. Wallis saw how raw her hands looked. She was supposed to be dusting, sweeping and cleaning, not being made to do the cook's donkey work. But that was an argument for another day.

Wallis entered the stone-floored kitchen. Predictably, a large pan of boiling cabbage raged on the stove beneath a rattling lid. The stinking steam covered the windows. On the solid wooden table, a large knife lay in a red mess of mince.

The door was open into the entry, the dank yard reached by a flight of iron stairs from pavement level. It was this route that the tradesmen used for their deliveries. In the doorway stood Mrs. Codshead, broad back turned. She was talking to someone, meaty hands clamped on solid, aproned hips.

The parts of the window not entirely steamed up revealed her interlocutor to be the butcher's boy, a squint-eyed, unprepossessing youth. Seeing one meaty hand leave a hip to receive some coinage,

Wallis instantly guessed the solution to the mystery. Mrs. Codshead was ordering expensive meat, receiving cheap meat, and splitting the difference with the butcher's boy.

She felt a surge of indignant rage. "Mrs. Codshead!"

The cook whirled round, a startled expression on her broad red features. "Gave me quite a start there, ma'am." She slapped her thick sausage fingers over one of her vast bosoms. "Got a dicky 'eart," she added.

Wallis doubted Mrs. Codshead had a heart at all, let alone a dicky one. "I'd like to talk to you about the food."

"Ma'am?" A warning glint had appeared in the cook's small eye.

"Let's start with the cabbage." Wallis waved a hand at the seething pan on the stove. "I prefer to have mine steamed in the French way."

The cook crossed her fat forearms belligerently. "Lady Chesham likes hers the English way. That's how we do it here."

Wallis stood her ground. "Well, it's not how they do it where I come from. And I give the orders now."

Mrs. Codshead glanced sideways at the knife, its blade smeared with bloody mince.

"I think we've probably exhausted your repertoire," Wallis went on. "Some of your, um, specialties have come round quite a few times after all. Your sago pudding, for instance." She winced, recalling the gluey, frogspawn-like mess, then turned the grimace into a bright smile. "Time for a fresh approach, Mrs. Codshead."

"Fresh approach!"

"Yes. I'll be doing the food shopping from now on."

The butcher's boy, who had been gleefully following the drama through the steamed-up windows, now looked considerably less amused. Mrs. Codshead's puce face drained to the color of gray dishwater.

"Ladies don't do their own shopping!" she exploded.

"Possibly not," Wallis replied calmly. "But *I* do."

+ + +

"I see Mrs. Codshead's resigned," Ernest observed later. The cook, on her way out, had slapped a grease-stained envelope marked "Mr. Simpson" on the hall table. He waved it at Wallis now. "She says she's never been so insulted."

"She's been lucky in that case. Given how bad her cooking is."

Ernest was fretful. "But what about the accounts? I've no idea where she's put those books."

Ernest clearly hadn't looked in the kitchen grate, where the smoldering remains were probably just about still visible. "Maybe she's taken them with her," Wallis suggested. "I'd better do the marketing, anyway. For now. The cooking too. Just until we get someone else."

Wallis had already identified the someone else. The scullery maid, originally housemaid, had something quick and intelligent about her. Something that, with careful attention, could be trained up. Her name was Lily, she had discovered.

"Maud's not going to be very happy," Ernest warned.

"No," agreed Wallis, looking down to hide a smile.

CHAPTER SEVEN

Summer had arrived, and with it the London season. The social pages abounded with parties and balls. As she still had none of her own to go to, Wallis now went to watch other people's. Why not? It was a free show that took place every day of the week. She just had to look in the morning papers to get the details from the social pages.

"Forget-me-not blue will form the very lovely frock of tonight's blue-bred debutante Miss Margaret Whigham," ran one breathless account, "for whom her mother, Mrs. George Hay Whigham, is giving a ball this evening at No. 6 Audley Sq. It promises to be a very smart affair."

Wallis made a note of the address. Miss Margaret Whigham's ball would do very nicely, she thought. Quite apart from being curious about the blue-bred debutante herself, she had read that the family's Mayfair mansion had a bathroom that took over an entire floor. It was the work of fashionable designer Syrie Maugham, whose signature color palette was white.

It was a warm summer evening and a large crowd had gathered outside the Whighams' vast house. An imposing front door, opening to admit the arriving elect, revealed a marble-floored hallway filled with flowers and lit by a glittering chandelier. Glimpsing Miss Whigham in her sparkling turquoise tulle standing at the foot of a sweeping staircase, the onlookers sighed with admiration.

Wallis had noticed that society's have-nots seemed uncritical of society's haves. It was the same at society weddings. Again, thanks to the newspapers, it was common knowledge which churches had well-born brides in Hartnell dresses emerging beneath the crossed swords of regimental guards of honor most Wednesdays, Fridays and Saturdays. If it was a particularly grand union, the pavements were jammed with onlookers and the traffic backed up for several miles. People in rags with holes in their shoes would even gate-crash the ceremony itself, scrambling over the pews and clinging to pillars. Yet they did not come to jeer but to admire.

Wallis realized that she was taking part in the national sport, which was not actually cricket or football but watching the cream of high society dressed to the nines. The unspoken agreement seemed to be that the gulf between rich and poor was tolerated if the former entertained the latter. This was especially evident in the Mall, where, as the season got going, huge numbers gathered to watch the debutantes going to the court presentations.

Having failed to gain the entrée herself did not stop Wallis being interested in the ceremony. The scale of it was astonishing. The day Maud presented her daughter, Wallis watched in amazement as, from Trafalgar Square to the very gates of the palace, the wide processional route completely filled up with beetle-like black cars. Each contained a white-clad, feather-topped daughter of a noble house and her guardian mother.

The crowd watching from the pavements, from in the trees in some places, seemed less deferential than those at the weddings and parties. Some people went right up to the windows of the stationary cars, stared in and made remarks about the girls inside, which ranged from the flattering to the disobliging but were always frank.

But for all the gauntlet of popular opinion they had to run, it was hard not to envy those who passed, quite literally, through gates that were closed to her. She would, she thought, rather be in the cars than in the crowd, national sport or not. She remembered Ernest's words in Paris.

You'd like to be rich, I daresay.

And her reply.

Oh, no, Ernest! I couldn't ask for anything more than you.

Did she still feel that way? she wondered. Ernest barely spoke to her these days; at dinner, he rarely put down his newspaper. She wondered if he had even noticed he wasn't eating mushy cabbage anymore.

Doing her own shopping was trickier than she had expected.

The fishmonger was rude when she asked for filets all the same size. "Fish aren't stamped out like cars on a Ford production line, you know."

The truculent butcher was little better. She usually had to show him the diagram in her cookbook before he gave her the cut she wanted.

Lily, at least, was proving a success. Under Wallis's tutelage, the former skivvy was blossoming into a capable chef. Wallis and Ernest now sat down nightly in a well-dusted dining room at a table covered in a pretty cloth. The vegetables these days were crisp and steamed and the food of immeasurably better quality. The cook's backhanders, it turned out, had extended to the fishmonger, greengrocer and dairy, all now altered to different and better suppliers. The bills, even so, were much lower.

But did Ernest appreciate any of it? See it, even?

One evening, as Lily finished carving the chicken and left the room, Wallis leaned over and tapped the back of Ernest's newspaper. "You don't talk to me anymore," she said when his surprised, slightly indignant face appeared. "I feel that I hardly see you."

"I've been working late a lot," he objected. "Things at the office . . ."

An angry retort hovered on the end of her tongue, but she held back. Bitter experience had given her a horror of rows.

A few days later though, Ernest had a dinnertime surprise. "I thought I would take you somewhere. For a treat."

Her heart beat faster. Her eyes sparkled. She lay down her fork in excitement. Perhaps this time he really would suggest the Embassy Club? Or the theater to see Noël Coward's latest, *Bitter Sweet*?

"I thought we could visit Warwick this weekend," Ernest said.

She wrinkled her brow. "Who's Worrick?"

"*Where*, you mean," he corrected genially. "It's actually spelled *War-wick*. It's got a castle, a church with some splendid medieval tombs and a famous almshouse."

She felt her soul sink through the soles of her shoes. She stared at him desperately while he told her that he had booked the hotel and everything was settled. They would leave the following day.

As the city receded, Wallis felt her disappointment ease. The English countryside was beautiful. The landscape was rolling and gently swelling. Fields were gold with corn or a gentle green. Rivers flashed and shone. Splendid trees shaded cattle and sheep just as in a Gainsborough painting. The roadsides were colorful with wildflowers, and the sky above was bright blue.

She had noticed something else too. Every now and then, the hedges at the roadside gave way to smart stone walls. They would run along for a mile or so until they reached a magnificent entrance whose gateposts were topped with heraldic beasts. If Wallis looked back as they drove by, she would see an impressive pile of stone topped with towers and turrets, or a pillared classical frontage.

"Who lived there?" she asked Ernest.

"*Lives* there, you mean," he corrected. "They're the stately homes of England."

She could not believe that the vast and beautiful houses, of which there seemed so many, were actually still occupied. But according to Ernest they were the ancestral homes of England's ancient noble families. Some of the names he rattled off were the same as the glamorous young women she followed in the social pages. She imagined them in these places, slouching about the long galleries and great halls in the way that debutantes did, tummy forward, back arched, hand on hip.

She felt rather stunned. She had observed, in London, the poor watching the rich at play. But no one watched in the country. These were completely closed aristocratic worlds and a level of privilege she had never suspected existed.

Warwick, when finally they reached it, looked quite pleasant. The main street was attractive, with large-windowed Georgian hotels over whose doors heraldic emblems shone colorfully in the sun. Ernest drove past them all and into a shadowy backstreet where waited a cramped and poky establishment evidently closer to their budget. Wallis smiled gamely as she carried her bag in.

There was barely time to unpack; Ernest had a schedule. He marched her around, pointing out what he imagined were objects of interest but she secretly thought were objects of boredom. Chancels and corbels, misericords and mounting blocks, milestones and finger-posts, linenfold and wattle and daub. To please him she assumed an expression of patient attention as he described the function of flying buttresses, how stained glass was made and that Crusaders always had crossed legs on tombs. As if they needed the lavatory, she thought to herself.

They returned to the hotel to dress for a dinner they made only by the skin of their teeth, the dining room shutting promptly at eight. The other guests were peppery retired majors with handlebar mustaches and purse-lipped wives, all so old that she and Ernest, though hardly youthful themselves, brought the average age down by several decades. Afterward they sat in a dank guest sitting room with a weak fire, the fug of pipes and a silence so thick she could hear the majors' wives' knitting needles drop. Wallis tried to talk to Ernest in whispers, but the disapproving glances and angry sighs were hard to ignore.

"Magnificent, eh?" Ernest said the next day as they stood before Warwick Castle. Its great stone walls connected massive towers. A bridge over a grassy moat led to an arched entrance with a sharp-edged portcullis. Inside there were no rooms to see that people actually still lived in. Only dark stone chambers with huge, empty fireplaces. She walked through as quickly as possible and waited for Ernest on a bench outside.

He came out sometime later, looking cross. "I don't see what's the use unless you stop to look at things. You can't do a castle like that."

"I did look at things," Wallis said composedly.

"Oh yes? Give me an example, then."

"That death mask of Oliver Cromwell in the entrance hall."

Ernest looked doubtful. Despite having been inside far longer, he clearly had not noticed it. "Really?"

"Really. He had the most enormous mole. It looked like a pea stuck to his face."

From the castle Ernest marched them back into town, pointing out various objects of boredom along the way. "And there's the bear and ragged staff." He gestured at an inn sign. "It's the symbol of Warwickshire."

"That's a *bear*? Why is it chained to the post?"

As her husband explained bearbaiting she felt revulsion. How *barbaric*.

At the Church of St. Mary, Ernest insisted on climbing the 160 steps to the top. The dark, winding narrow stair seemed to get narrower as they went up. She pressed her elbows tight to her sides, but the shoulders of her precious best coat still scraped against the stone and she kept missing her step and bumping the toes of her one good pair of shoes.

Halfway up it struck twelve, and when the tower bells rang out, the shattering noise caused Wallis to cling to Ernest in terror. She had barely recovered when they reached the top and she staggered out after him onto the platform. For all it was a summer day, a powerful wind was blowing, which beat at her face and tore at her hair and made the gold weather vane above wobble violently back and forth. She held on to the parapet and looked down at the steep roofs, the gardens, the lanes.

Quite suddenly, the urge to jump possessed her. To end it all. It seemed quite rational. Why not? What was there to live for? She wanted to escape; here was her chance. She leaned over the edge. It would be so easy to tip forward. A rush of air, then all her problems would be over.

Back down in the church, she collapsed in a pew, drained and shocked. Meanwhile Ernest paced around, oblivious to how close he had come to being a widower. Guidebook in hand, he was raving about the painted figures round the windows. "They portray the nine orders of angels!"

Wallis glanced up from her clenched fingers. "*Orders* of angels?"

"Seraphim, cherubim, thrones, dominations, virtues, powers, principalities, angels and archangels," Ernest happily confirmed.

"So there's a class system even in heaven?" Heaven had obviously been designed by the British. Just as well she hadn't thrown herself off the tower. Her hopes of getting in would have been zero.

Ernest was examining more tombs. She dragged herself up and followed. He was crouched over some carving, painstakingly deciphering the medieval Latin. "Just think, Wallis!" His brown eyes were bright with enthusiasm. "The chap in this tomb knew Henries IV, V and VI and presided over the trial of Joan of Arc! Imagine!"

Wallis was actually imagining lunch. She yawned and stretched, hoping Ernest would take the hint.

"Let's visit the crypt," he suggested instead, and disappeared down a dark staircase.

When she found him in the darkness he was staring at something in the corner, an ancient wooden chassis with two wheels at the back and one at the front. It looked vaguely like a large wheelbarrow.

"It says here it's part of a medieval ducking stool," Ernest reported from below. He had squatted down before a small framed notice and began to read out the description. "Women were tied to it and lowered underwater for whatever number of times the court decided."

Disgust surged through her. "*What?*"

"Only women of immoral character," Ernest said cheerfully. "And it was hundreds of years ago."

Wallis thought about the bearbaiting, the dreary inn. She thought of the beautiful, private palaces of the elite. The sheer hopelessness and unfairness of everything pressed on her. She took a deep breath. "Ernest. I've had enough."

He scrambled to his feet. "Absolutely. We'll go back to the hotel for lunch."

She held up a hand. Her face was set. "I didn't just mean I'd had enough of Warwick. I've had enough of *everything*."

+ + +

Ernest feels a churl
To have upset his little girl
He vows he will be better
And so has penned this letter

Wallis smoothed out the note that Ernest had hidden in her napkin. It was lunchtime in the hotel's silent dining room. The majors and their wives glared at the sound of the paper being unfolded. Ernest's eyes were anxious. Pushing aside the urge to say she was leaving and never coming back, she gave him a wan smile. "Fine, but can we go back to London?"

They set off straightaway and reached Upper Berkeley Street just before dinner. Lily, neat in her dress and apron, opened the door and handed a brown telegram envelope to Wallis.

She tore it open, scanning the message. "It's from Washington. From Aunt Bessie."

"Your mother's sister?"

Wallis nodded. "Mother's ill."

"Oh, Wallis, I'm so sorry."

Wallis wasn't. Not entirely. Alice had never had a day's illness in her life. Whatever it was, she would recover from it. In the meantime, here was the escape Wallis was looking for.

The Duke of Windsor's Funeral
London
June 1972

By now Wallis had thought to recognize somewhere, but nothing was familiar. From the distant height of the plane, it had seemed so. But peering out of the car, she could see this was a new London. These great concrete and glass buildings had all been put up since her day. The city had moved on.

Mountbatten was going through the funeral program. She listened but could hardly take it. The lying-in-state with David on a bier, his coffin draped with the royal standard and with soldiers at all four corners. The funeral, then the burial at Frogmore. She must face the royal family alone at all of it.

"And tomorrow is the Trooping the Colour."

In a flash she was back there: 1936. David's first Trooping the Colour as sovereign. His first assassination attempt too. She could still hear the pistol clatter on the cobbles under his horse. A quick policeman had saved him, but David had not batted an eyelid; his self-possession had been superb. Afterward, he had joked about it. "The Dastardly Attempt," he had called it, and refused to take it seriously. A couple of hours later, he had been playing golf.

"They are Trooping the Colour?" she said to Mountbatten in surprise. "That's happening?" Didn't ceremonials get canceled after royal deaths? And this wasn't just any royal death. David had been king of Great Britain and Ireland, Emperor of India and the Dominions Beyond the Seas. Not that those darn Dominions had been much darn use. They had ganged up on him along with everyone else.

Mountbatten looked shifty. "Everything was in place, so it was decided to continue. David died quite suddenly."

But hardly unexpectedly, she wanted to point out. The monarch herself had been to visit him, had seen how close the end was. But now the queen would ride out in full uniform and review her troops as if the passing of their former commander in chief was of no consequence.

Her indignation gathered force. "And tomorrow's June third. The thirty-fifth anniversary of our wedding."

"There will be a tribute to the late king at the Trooping the Colour," Mountbatten assured her.

"What sort of tribute?"

"The band of the Scots Guards will play 'The Flowers of the Forest.'"

She closed her eyes.

"You might find it hard to bear," her companion suggested.

No kidding, she thought. One measly bagpipe tune to commemorate the passing of a king? She clenched her fists inside her gloves.

"It might be better to watch it on TV, in private." He looked at her. "I would avoid the lying-in-state too."

"What?" She met his eyes incredulously. "Of course I'm going to that."

"You don't think it would be difficult?"

She forced away the irony. "Louis, come on. I've got to show up somewhere. David would expect me to."

"Really, I wouldn't advise it."

She took a deep breath. "I know I'm not very popular in Britain."

He did not contradict her.

"I'm notorious. I get that. People blame me for everything that happened. And for things that didn't happen too." She paused, took a deep breath. "But David was my husband, and he was king. Not for long, but king nonetheless. As his widow, it's my duty to go to see him at Windsor. See the chapel. The crowds."

"Crowds?" He seized on the word incredulously.

"Well, the people filing past his coffin."

As Mountbatten raised his eyebrows and sighed, she leaned over and grabbed his arm.

"Louis . . . they are filing past, aren't they?"

When he did not answer, she felt nausea. She had expected the visit to be difficult but not in this way. She had imagined every scenario except indifference.

Finally, they reached the Mall. At the far end, like a threat, lurked the palace. She watched the heavy gray front approach. Her last visit here had been in 1935, at a Jubilee ball for George V. She could see, even now, those ice-blue Hanoverian eyes, feel them skewering her across the ballroom as she fox-trotted round.

She had forgotten how hideous the Victoria Memorial was. The gold figure atop the bulging marble gleamed dully. The barracks-like building reared, blocking out everything else. How David had hated it; "Buckhouse Prison," he had called it. Even when king he had hardly lived here. He'd moved into two dark little rooms but barely bothered to unpack his boxes.

Damn you, David, she said silently as they slid in through the gates. *It was me who was supposed to go first.*

CHAPTER EIGHT

Embarking for America

London
1929

Ernest drove her to Southampton. At the dockside reared a black cliff topped with four red funnels. He reeled off various facts about the *Mauretania*: that it was the fastest in the world when built, the noteworthy aspects of its engines. She listened politely. It was the last time she would have to, after all.

She would not be coming back. Her mother's illness, she had decided, was the perfect excuse to leave her marriage. She would tell Ernest when she was safely back in America. But perhaps he had sensed something. As the *Mauretania* pulled away and the stretch of water between ship and shore widened, he was still waving to her from the dockside. He continued with his farewells as the liner retreated through the port, out to sea. As Southampton, and the rest of England, disappeared into the mist, Ernest's figure was the last thing she saw.

She turned from the rail, dug her hands in the pockets of her coat and walked back to her stateroom—second class, but with almost the same facilities as first, Ernest said. Her fingers felt something sharp and papery. A note; he must have slipped it in as they were saying goodbye. She stared at the familiar careful handwriting:

Oh my little Wallis!
I'm quite without solace
Your being at sea
Is such sadness to me

Exasperation and affection swept through her, along with a heavy-treading guilt. She knew she had been unfair to Ernest. To leave without telling him, without giving him a chance to put things right. On the other hand, it was obvious what was wrong and had been ever since they had arrived in London. But the causes were beyond his control; they related to the class system, to finances. If there was something he could do about her lack of friends, let alone their financial position, he would have done it by now. Similarly, if there was anything she could have done about shrinking from his touch and refusing him her bed, she would have. Could they have made it work, if circumstances had been different? Perhaps, perhaps not. Perhaps it had been written in the stars all along.

There were no stars yet. A sunset like a huge red penny was sinking into the sea. The sky was streaked with pink; coral and crimson spread across the moving water. It felt like the end of something; another marriage, possibly. In the depths of her memory, something suddenly gleamed.

It was some years ago, after her divorce from Win. To help her in her search for a new direction, her friend Mary had suggested an astrologer.

"I had a wonderful experience with one. She did my horoscope and you wouldn't believe the number of things she got right."

Wallis had been dismissive. "I don't believe in that rot. I'm too much of a realist."

Mary laughed. "Rubbish. You're a hopeless romantic and always have been."

Too true, Wallis thought glumly. Why else had she married Win?

"Anyway, you don't have to believe it. The real satisfaction comes in just sitting there while someone talks seriously about you and your future for half an hour. It's extremely flattering and much cheaper than going to a psychiatrist."

This argument was much more appealing. Not long afterward, following an unsuccessful job interview at a department store, Wallis looked up Mary's astrologer in the telephone book. Despite what seemed to her an exorbitant fee of ten dollars, she made an appointment.

On the day arranged, Wallis half expected a tent with a crystal ball. But the astrologer worked from a midtown office not unlike a dentist's. A neat receptionist ushered her briskly into a tidy room with nothing otherworldly about it. The woman who sat there was ordinarily middle-aged and wore a plain dark suit. Even her gaze didn't seem especially penetrating.

Wallis sat down, scoffing inside and cursing herself for the waste of much-needed dollars. She answered the woman's questions—her birthday and the exact hour of her birth—quickly. She wanted to be finished as soon as possible so this undignified experience could be put behind her.

The astrologer spent a long time silently consulting books and charts on her desk. The flick of the pages and the slither of the maps were all that could be heard for a while. Eventually the woman looked up. "I have cast the horoscope. You will have two more marriages in your life."

Wallis started awake immediately. "Two *more*? But I'm only just getting out of the first one."

The astrologer met her eye steadily. "Two more," she repeated. "And in middle life you will exercise considerable power."

"What sort of power?" demanded the staggered Wallis. Middle life couldn't be too far away; she was in her early thirties as it was.

"The aura is not clear," said the astrologer. "But you will become a famous woman."

She had emerged from the astrologer's more convinced than ever that the whole thing was hocus-pocus. Two more marriages? One divorce was disastrous enough, two unimaginable. Her mother had married three times, the worst of all examples to follow. But now, holding Ernest's poem and staring over the sea, Wallis realized that the first part of the prediction had come true.

The *Mauretania* was decorated in the heavy palatial style popular with the Edwardians. The second-class lounge featured a glass roof, potted palms and button-back armchairs. There were newspapers arranged neatly on the polished mahogany tables. Wallis picked one up. The front page featured a smiling Prince of Wales in full matinee-idol mode. She remembered the sad-faced figure she had seen in the back of the car and her impression of seeing something hidden and private.

Later, having unpacked, she went out on deck. The sky was dark now and the stars coming out one by one. She stared up at them, thinking of the sailors through the centuries who had charted courses by the constellations. Those great adventurers. She wanted to be an adventurer too. When she got to New York she would try again to start a career. And this time she would succeed. Maybe that was what the astrologer had meant. She would become rich and famous through her work, be head of some big store or something.

She sipped on a martini she had got from the bar. Its strength increased her sense of invincibility. Yes, she would get a job. Once Alice had recovered.

Her mood dipped. It was hard not to blame at least some of what had happened on her mother. Had they stayed with Grandmother Warfield, life would have been different. She remembered the big shady rooms, the grand old lady in her rocking chair. Growing up in the family mansion, she would have known none of the stigma and poverty Alice's caprice had condemned them to. And which she had made so many mistakes trying to escape. Staring over the dark ocean, she felt resentment swirl within her as the water swirled round the ship.

A few days later, she stood again on deck and watched the *Mauretania* sail into New York Harbor. Liberty proudly raised her lamp against a fresh blue sky and the towers of Manhattan sparkled in the early sun. After cramped and dingy London it all looked so big, so bright, so modern and hopeful. The shadows of the night before had gone and a happy relief rose within her. This was where she belonged. This was home. The future.

In the dingy brown Washington bedroom, she took Alice's wrinkled, near weightless hand.

Across the bed, Aunt Bessie, her mother's sister, was battling to control her emotion. "It's happened so quickly." She shook her silver head, tears filling her faded blue eyes. "She got sick, then sicker."

The change was shocking. Alice's body, once curvy and robust, was barely visible beneath the faded counterpane. The once-blooming cheek was wrinkled, the formerly thick glossy hair a dry gray plait. She was fifty-nine but looked twenty years older.

Wallis was still in her coat and gloves. It was all so unexpected, so completely bewildering. After all the other hurts she had inflicted, her mother was now going to die with typically dramatic suddenness. She would leave Wallis alone in the world with their differences unresolved.

It had started with a vision problem, Aunt Bessie whispered over the sagging bed. Having consulted an optician, Alice had been sent to a doctor, who diagnosed a blood clot behind an eye.

"But she was lucky. Apparently she would have been paralyzed if the blood clot had got to her brain."

Alice's eyes flew open, one clouded and dead-looking. "Guess the clot went up to my brain anyway," she wisecracked, her voice a whispery croak. "But it couldn't find the poor thing."

Wallis felt impatient. Even now, at this latest of all late stages, was her famous wit all her mother could think about?

Her mother was peering at her through the eye that worked. It rolled about, trying to focus. "Bessiewallis? That you?"

Wallis hadn't heard her full name for many years. It was the Baltimore habit to give children two names and run them together.

"Yes, Mother. It's me."

Alice was croaking something. Her wasted face held an urgent expression. Her papery hand folded round Wallis's with surprising strength. She bent forward, trying to catch the words. Then she glanced up at Aunt Bessie. "She wants to talk to me alone."

Bessie nodded her silver head. Watching her tiptoe out, Wallis steeled herself. Was this about Ernest? Alice had never liked him. She winced at the thought of her mother's satisfaction on hearing the marriage was over. Or maybe this was about the finest families of Baltimore. For all the good they had ever done her, Wallis thought.

The wasted hand gripped hers. The faded voice croaked. Wallis bent again to listen. She frowned, blinked in surprise. She must have misheard. It was surely impossible that Alice could have uttered the two words she had never said before in her life, and which at certain points might have made a considerable difference: "I'm sorry."

"Sorry for what, Mother?" Wallis asked when it was repeated and there was no doubt.

"For what I put you through," Alice muttered.

"Put me through?"

"When you were small." Alice took a rattling breath. "Why we lived the way we did. It must have seemed strange to you. But I had no choice."

Wallis's surprise gave way to suspicion. What had sounded like an apology was only a piece of self-defense. "You had no choice to leave Grandmother Warfield's?"

"I did not."

"But why, Mother? They'd taken us in. Grandmother and Uncle Sol. He'd given you money, for goodness' sake."

Her mother's hand spasmed at the mention of her uncle's name. Alice was staring at her, her clouded gaze agitated.

Quite suddenly, a memory came back to Wallis. A room in the dark Warfield mansion. She was outside in the passage. Her uncle and her mother were in the room, standing close together. Very close. Then a rustle, a cry, a gasp, and her uncle suddenly staggering backward, as if pushed, before rounding on Alice and snarling at her.

"You are completely dependent on me!"

"I'll make my own way," Alice retaliated.

"Without me you would starve!"

"And I would rather starve than do what you want!"

Wallis took a deep breath. "He tried to take advantage of you? Uncle Sol?"

The hand squeezed hers in confirmation. "He used to come in my room," Alice croaked. "At nights. If I locked the door he'd rattle the handle, threaten me."

Wallis winced. She knew about the rattling doorknob too. And like Win her uncle had been thickset, forceful. A bully. Her mother had been young and vulnerable. A defenseless widow with a child.

There was a stir from the bed. "He wanted to buy me, so he gave me money. But it was never the same amount. Sometimes hundreds of dollars. Sometimes a dime. He showed his power every which way."

Wallis felt sick with guilt. "I didn't understand."

"How could you?"

"And all those years, you just let me think the worst. That you'd done it for your own selfish reasons."

"I'd rather that than the truth. But it was hard." Alice swallowed and closed her eyes. "It hurt me to see you left out of things. People cutting us in the street. I used to try to cheer you up, laugh about it, try to convince you it didn't matter. But maybe that was the wrong thing to do."

Remorse blurred Wallis's vision. She had believed all this time that her mother had first caused her sufferings and then trivialized them and failed to understand them. But now she saw the bravery and humor with which Alice had borne her difficulties. She leaned her head on the wasted hand and let her tears run over it. "Oh, Mother."

Truly, to understand all was to forgive all. She had had no idea. And now at this moment of conciliation Alice was dying, worn out as much by ill luck as ill health. Life was so unfair. Rage blazed through Wallis, followed by a feeling of bleak devastation.

Alice opened her eyes again. "Bessiewallis," she whispered sleepily. Wallis bent her head near her mother.

"Ernest," Alice croaked.

Her heart sank. The son-in-law Alice had never approved of. Never forgiven for his bowler hats and for not getting her jokes. Her mother did not need to know he would not be around for much longer.

"I'm glad you've got Ernest," Alice whispered, to her surprise.

She was looking at Wallis as if she were the only person in the world. The gaze felt like sunshine, warming her skin. But she knew it was love.

"I love you too," she said, but she was not sure her mother could hear her anymore.

But after a while she stirred and spoke again. "When you were a little girl," Alice breathed, "and you had trouble sleeping, I would get into bed with you and stay awake until you dropped off. I wanted you to feel that if you were afraid, in the darkness, someone who loved you was with you. Did you know that?"

Wallis could not answer. A thick lump had filled her throat. She stood up, walked round to the other side of the bed and lay down next to Alice. She took the hand that was nearest to her, put her head on her mother's shoulder and kept vigil while the daylight faded in the windows and shadows gathered in the corner of the room.

The funeral, as befitted a daughter of a famous Southern family, was in Baltimore's leading church. Many of the city's great and good attended, accepting Alice in death as they had snubbed her in life.

The eulogy emphasized her sense of humor and revisited some celebrated jokes, such as the Fourth of July party Alice attended with her third husband. "Here on the Fourth with my third," she had written in the visitors' book. Under a snapshot of herself sitting on this same husband's knee she had put "On My Last Lap." The people in the church shook their heads and chuckled as if a well-loved member of the community was gone and not a troublesome woman who constantly strayed over the line of propriety. Watching them contemptuously, Wallis thought of how the unwanted attentions of a powerful man had caused Alice's social ostracism, and how she had bravely used jokes to lighten the darkness cast over both their lives. The famous sense of humor had not been vanity; it had been concealing despair.

The burial was at the main cemetery, in the Montague plot. Watching Alice's coffin being lowered into the ground, Wallis bid her a silent goodbye. It was also an apology. She saw it all so differently now. Finally she understood how, far from being a bad example, Alice had been the very best. Wallis felt glad to be her daughter in a way that had nothing to do with fine families. What Alice had really stood for was not pride in her background but courage in adversity.

At the wake following Alice's burial, in a medium-smart Baltimore hotel, Wallis told Aunt Bessie she intended to stay in America.

"You can't be serious!" The old lady's teacup crashed into her saucer. "You can't divorce Ernest!"

On her own saucer, Wallis's cup nervously rattled. She had not expected opposition from this reliably genial relative. After explaining the misery of her life in London, she had anticipated Aunt Bessie's wholehearted support.

"Ernest is a good man!" Aunt Bessie placed both cup and saucer down on a nearby table in order to give the matter her undivided attention. "Even your mother came around to him in the end."

But Wallis was determined not to give any ground, not even that. "But I'm so lonely, Aunt Bessie."

"Well, join the club." Her aunt's tone was brisk. "I've been lonely too. Many times. Loneliness has its purposes. It teaches us to think. And what would you live on anyway? Your mother left you hardly enough for a new dress."

Wallis didn't need reminding. She had sat in a local lawyer's wood-paneled office to be told that, as the final indignity after a lifetime of setbacks, Alice's savings had been almost wiped out by the stock market crash.

"You can't leave Ernest," Aunt Bessie went on. "He adores you. It's cruel to abandon him."

Wallis wanted to reply that it was cruel not to.

If she left Ernest now he might find someone with whom he could have a full physical relationship. But this was hardly something she could say to her octogenarian aunt at a funeral. Instead she said, "I'm going to get a job."

Bessie looked skeptical. "What sort of job?"

"I'm still looking," Wallis said evasively. But inside she was crumbling. She wondered if anyone in the entire history of the world had ever made quite such a mess of things. The year she had married Ernest, 1928, had seemed like the worst year of her life, but 1929 was beating it hands down.

"You'll be a double divorcée with no money and nowhere to live," Aunt Bessie summarized.

Wallis knew it was childish, but the power to destroy suddenly seemed the only power she had. She stuck out her chin and folded her arms. "I don't care. I'm leaving London."

Aunt Bessie eyed her sternly. "Have you even spoken to Ernest about any of this?"

"What would be the point?"

"If he knew why you were unhappy, he might do something about it."

"Well, he couldn't. No one could."

"You haven't even given him a chance. Doesn't he deserve one?"

Wallis did not reply.

Her aunt's gaze was considering. "You said you had no social life. What if you got one?"

"That's not going to happen. I don't know anyone."

"You know that baroness woman."

"Maud? She's not a baroness, she's—"

Bessie batted this away. "Who cares? She knows people, doesn't she?"

"Well, yes, but . . ."

"So make Ernest make her introduce you to some. And make him move."

"You make it sound so easy!" Wallis cried in frustration.

Bessie's old eyes sparked in her wrinkled face. "Of *course* it's not easy! But, Wallis, you're a Montague on your mother's side and a Warfield on your father's."

"Not that again!" Wallis put her hands to her ears. Even her mother had resisted saying that at the end. "What good has it ever done me? What good did it ever do her?"

The old lady's blue eyes flashed. "My point is that you don't just give up! Where's your pride? Your backbone? Your mother made many mistakes, but giving up was never one of them."

Shame crashed over Wallis like a heavy wave. She thought of the courage that Alice had always shown, even on her deathbed. Bessie was right. She owed it to her brave mother to try again.

When she called him, the relief in Ernest's voice surprised her. It was almost as if he had suspected she might never return.

"Of course I'll talk to Maud," he exclaimed. "And I'll start looking for a new house right away. Now just come back, Wallis. *Please.*"

CHAPTER NINE

Upper Berkeley Street
London
1930

Ernest had just returned from work and she had news. But first, she must settle him in the sitting room with a drink. When the whisky had started about its work, she would tell him.

After a while, when his shoulders relaxed and he had stretched his legs out before him, she put aside her interiors magazine. "I think I've found a flat," she announced.

Ernest rubbed his tired face. "A flat? I thought we were looking for a house."

He had been, at first. But the office, as ever, had got in the way, so she had taken it over. She had enjoyed investigating the property market, and after an extensive search for something modern and new, had found it in a just-built mansion block, Bryanston Court, only slightly northwest of where they sat.

"It's got amazing potential," she told him excitedly. "I'm thinking a white color scheme. White walls, white sheepskin rugs, white leather chairs, ivory silk cushions, mirrored screens." She had not forgotten Syrie Maugham's all-white bathroom for the Whighams.

"Are you sure?" Ernest looked doubtful.

"Oh, absolutely. It's very fashionable at the moment." She picked up the interiors magazine and waved it at him.

"Not about the white. About the flat."

His gaze lingered on her. He had realized, she saw. A small apartment would be an admission that children were no longer a prospect. Her heart started to thump. Quite suddenly and unexpectedly, a critical moment had been reached.

It was warm in the room, but her teeth were chattering. Ernest swirled the whisky in his glass and spoke gently. "I don't need any more children, Wallis. I have a daughter already, although I never see her and she never answers my letters."

Audrey had never, after all, come to London. The stepmotherly relationship Wallis had hoped for failed to materialize.

New York was a long distance and an expensive voyage away. A bitter ex-wife had something to do with it too.

His round brown eyes were pleading. "So I don't need children, Wallis, but I hope, even so . . ." He stopped, obviously searching for the words.

She was perfectly still. Panic churned inside. She waited, as for an ax falling.

"When we got married you said you needed time . . ."

She closed her eyes and saw the Paris hotel room. The red light in the room opposite. The red glow in the shack in Shanghai. All so close to the surface, even now.

She still felt it every bedtime, when they kissed each other chastely and went to their separate rooms. She would lie, heart thumping, dreading the creak of a door, a hand in the dark, a little touch of Ernest in the night.

She searched for the words, and forced them from a dry throat. "You've been so understanding, Ernest. And I'm sorry, I really am. I hope . . ." He seemed content with this. Or accepting, which might not be the same thing.

Maud was not Wallis's favorite subject, but she was relieved when

Ernest brought her up now. Her sister-in-law had agreed to ask her to a lunch. Not especially graciously, by the sound of it.

"She did wonder why you'd never wanted to come to anything before," Ernest added wryly.

Wallis was tempted to point out that Maud had never asked her. Her house was relatively close to theirs and far more splendid, but Wallis had not so much as set foot in it during her entire time in London.

The invitation took its time to arrive. Wallis had almost given up hope by the time the envelope finally dropped through the letterbox. It was a charity lunch and the chosen cause was the General Lying-In Hospital, a maternity facility in Lambeth, one of the poorest parts of London.

Maud, of course, lived in one of the wealthiest parts of London, Belgrave Square. As Wallis walked into it, daffodils glowed in the central garden while the white stucco facades shone against the spring sky. She felt a sharp twist of envy. How had a beady hopping bird like Maud married into this sort of money?

As she approached the pillared Smiley portico, nerves tightened in the pit of her stomach. She pressed the bell and was shown into an imposing marble hallway by a black-and-white-uniformed maid. Between the shining floor and the glittering chandelier lurked a smell that seemed familiar. She paused, sniffed. Was it possible that Mrs. Codshead had entered the service of her sister-in-law?

At either side of the hall were great reception rooms jam-packed with overstuffed furniture, small tables, fire screens, gloomy oils. If it were hers, Wallis thought, she would lighten it all up. Make space, bring in flowers. But it was no surprise that Belgravia was wasted on Maud.

She followed the maid up a magnificent staircase with an elaborate balustrade and portraits. There was one of Maud in court dress, flatteringly elongated in a white satin gown, enlarged black eyes grave and beautiful beneath a headdress of ostrich plumes. Wallis tried to be amused by the lack of resemblance rather than annoyed by the remembered snub.

"Missus Simpson, ma'am," announced the maid from the doorway of a drawing room yet more cluttered than the ones downstairs.

Wallis had expected her home-altered outfit to be easily outshone but saw that her white-trimmed black dress, cheap as it was, cut a positive dash amid the creased tweed suits that had gathered together. The average age was twenty years north of her own; catching a flash of pince-nez, she revised this upward. No doubt someone soon would produce an ear trumpet.

"At last!" Maud rose from their center like a bee from an overblown tweed rose.

Wallis stared. She was punctual to the second. Had Maud deliberately asked her to come late? Maud had turned to the gathering. "May I present my sister-in-law, Mrs. Simpson." Her tone was one of weary forbearance. As a series of names was rattled off at speed, some titles among them, Wallis realized that not all English aristocrats were as glamorous as the social pages suggested.

The sound of cracking knees and a powerful waft of mothballs accompanied the rising of the assembled to their feet for lunch. Served in Maud's heavy, ornate dining room, it was a tasteless slop in which some familiar gristly lumps bobbed about. Recognizing Skeleton Stew with a shaft of glee, Wallis had no doubt now who was manning the stoves.

She hovered at the back of the queue and helped herself to the tiniest amount politeness permitted.

Behind her, at the table, a discussion was in full swing. Everyone seemed very agitated. Wallis recognized the subject as a recent scandal: a group of gate-crashers had tried to infiltrate a grand ball. The titled hostess had thrown them out personally.

Maud was positively bristling in her condemnation. "*Disgraceful* conduct!" Then her eye flicked to Wallis, who was just sitting down. "Don't you agree, Wallis?"

Wallis didn't, as it happened. She had followed the saga in the newspapers and sympathized wholeheartedly with the crashers. No one knew better than she that to be invited in London you had to know people and to know people you had to be introduced and to be introduced you had to know people. She did not in the least blame a handful of youngsters wanting to cut through and have some fun.

She gave her hostess a noncommittal smile, but the subject was not to be dropped. "You don't think, Wallis," Maud inquired with meaningful emphasis, "that the unwanted guest is a problem for the London hostess?"

The insult was clear, but Wallis tried to ignore it. She turned to her neighbor, an old duchess whose blouse was fastened by a jet pin similar to one she had seen at the Victoria and Albert Museum.

The duchess seemed kindly, even so. She raised her lorgnette, the better to inspect Wallis. "I hear you're new to London, dear."

Maud seized the opportunity. "Wallis has spent a long time abroad," she informed the table. "Including in Shanghai."

The room whirled about Wallis. How did Maud know? *What* did she know? She must somehow have got this out of Ernest.

"Tell us about it," Maud invited brightly. "Wasn't it very . . . exotic?"

Wallis's heart raced and her temples were pounding. The eyes of the whole room were upon her. Even ancient duchesses, it seemed, knew about the city's reputation.

"I hear it caters to every taste," Maud went on.

How Wallis hated her at that moment. She searched in vain for a riposte. She thought desperately of her mother. Alice, with her famous wit, would have known what to say.

Quite suddenly, inspiration struck. "Every taste?" She smiled dazzlingly around. "You could get marmalade, if that's what you mean." The line had come out of the blue and could not have been more Alice-like if she had been there herself. *Thank you, Mother.*

The ancient duchess cackled. "Marmalade! How amusing your sister is, Maud!"

"Sister-in-*law*," said Maud, with a frozen smile.

To Wallis's relief, conversation now moved to the ongoing season. But the danger was not over. Maud's malicious black eye was soon on her again. "You do know what the season is, don't you, Wallis?"

Probably better than you do, Wallis thought. "Of course." She smiled. "It starts with the summer exhibition at the Royal Academy, although one doesn't go to see the pictures, of course. Then there's Eton Fourth of June, which is actually in May; then the Eton and Harrow cricket match at Lord's, although no one goes there to actually watch cricket."

Everyone laughed, apart from Maud. But she seemed to admit defeat, at least for the moment. Royalty was the next topic of conversation, and, recalling her efforts at the client dinners, Wallis tried gamely to join in.

"Queen Mary is remarkable," she observed brightly. "She only has to change her coat to start a new style."

Maud looked disgusted. "Queen Mary *never* changes her coat. She always looks the same. That's what's so marvelous about her." She began a long, complicated and apparently aimless tale about how she had, during the last war, hosted a ball. There had been an air raid and the guests had rushed to Maud's cellar, as had several passersby, including a woman called Freda Dudley Ward.

"And Buster Dominguez," Maud added.

"Who, dear?" asked the duchess, leaning in.

"Buster Dominguez. He brought her. Some sort of Latin diplomat."

Wallis was now completely confused. Just where was this story going?

"But it wasn't who brought her, it was who she left with," the thin-haired peeress added knowingly.

It now emerged that the Prince of Wales had been a guest at Maud's party and had fallen in love with Freda in the cellar. Their relationship had been going on for twelve years.

✦ ✦ ✦

Maud tapped a glass for attention. "Ladies. To business. We must now turn our attention to fundraising."

Wallis had quite forgotten this was the reason for the gathering in the first place. No one so far had as much as mentioned the Lying-In Hospital. She waited to hear what form the fundraising would take. Something heart-sinkingly dreary, no doubt.

"At our last meeting we agreed on a pageant," Maud went on.

Wallis perked up immediately. Charity fundraising pageants were exhaustively covered in the magazines and newspapers. They were costumed processions held in theaters, and tickets were sold as for a performance. Wallis had not been to any but enjoyed reading about events such as "The Great London Pageant of Lovers," where Prince Nicholas Galitzine had dressed as Abelard and the Honorable Stephen Tennant as Prince Charming. "The China Shop" pageant, meanwhile, had taken the theme of "Porcelain Through the Ages" and starred Lady Diana Cooper, the most famous of the aristocratic beauties, as "Leeds Pottery." Both productions were by the super-fashionable Cecil Beaton, who must be the best-connected man in London, Wallis thought.

"I could wear a costume," she offered excitedly. She would look a lot better than the rest of them. Her picture might even get in the papers.

Maud stamped on this immediately. "All the parts are cast."

"What are the parts?"

"Fish."

"*Fish?*"

"It's to be a pageant of fish," confirmed Maud crisply.

"I could be a fish."

"She could be a fish," the duchess agreed supportively.

"We've got all the fish we need."

"An American fish, perhaps," put in the peeress.

Maud glared at her. "This is a pageant of *British* fish."

Wallis gave up. It was hopeless. Maud was determined to keep her out.

"Why don't we ask Cecil?" the peeress suggested brightly. "He can decide. He's designing it all."

"Well, he's not here yet, is he?" Maud snapped. "He's terribly late."

"Cecil?" Wallis repeated. "Cecil *Beaton*?"

The best-connected man in London? A living, breathing link with all the glamorous fun she longed for?

CHAPTER TEN

The ladies had returned to the sitting room when the maid appeared. "It's Mr. Beaton."

"Cecil!" breathed Maud.

He shimmered in, a vision in a white summer suit with lilac cravat. He had a long face and dreamy, sloping eyes. "Maudie, darling! Can you ever forgive me?"

Wallis stared. *Maudie?* Moreover, her redoubtable sister-in-law was clearly putty in this man's long, white, beringed hands.

"Don't mention it!" she twittered.

Cecil beamed round. His eyes skated over everyone else, stopped at Wallis, and seemed to focus sharply. "But who is *this*, Maudie? Where have you been keeping her?"

Maudie reluctantly performed the introductions. "My sister-in-law, Mrs. Wallis Simpson."

He kissed her hand. Up close, his pale cheeks looked pink, as if lightly rouged. "*Enchanté*, Mrs. Wallis Simpson."

"*Enchantée*, Mr. Beaton."

"But you are *fabulous*! Where are you *from*?"

"Recently, Shanghai," Maud said acidly before Wallis could answer.

Wallis groaned silently, but Cecil's eyes widened. "Even *more* fabulous!"

"Cecil!" Maud slapped his hand playfully. "You're here to talk about the pageant, remember!"

"Remember? My dear Maudie, I've thought about nothing else! Literally nothing!" Cecil beamed at her dazzlingly. "I've chosen the most *marvelous* music," he told her, spreading his hands for emphasis. "'Forest Murmurs' by Elgar."

"Oh, *Cecil!*"

"The curtains will slowly draw apart disclosing a stage *flooded* with light like a sunset."

"How simply *perfect!*"

"A herald will announce the historic spectacle, and each lady's name will be proclaimed as she wends her way daintily and sweetly toward the footlights and out quickly at either side of the stage."

A few further arrangements were agreed on, including, to Wallis's delight and Maud's barely suppressed fury, the addition of an American fish.

Eventually, everyone rose to leave. To Wallis's keen disappointment, Cecil was first out of the door. She had hoped for a repeat of the interest he had shown in her. A chat perhaps. A glimpse into his glamorous life.

As she was handed her coat in the hall, a movement caught her eye. A large, truculent figure in an apron at the other end, instantly recognizable. Outside was all brightness and birdsong. Something pink approached her from the side.

It was Cecil in a voluminous rose scarf and a broad-brimmed straw hat. The ensemble was completed with a silver-top cane. "I've been waiting for you," he said. "Shall we walk together?"

In the daylight, the extent of Cecil's makeup was clear. His rouge was echoed in the red stain of his lips. His sloping eyes, enhanced with mascara, sparkled as he looked at her. "I'm simply *dying* to speak to you alone."

Delight bowled through her. It was happening at last. He recognized her as a kindred soul. They would become friends, he would ask her to things . . .

"So, Shanghai."

She crashed to earth with a bump. Feeling the familiar panic start up, she groped for Alice's line. She spoke quickly. "Before you ask, it was exotic. You could get marmalade."

Cecil laughed. "I'm not interested in marmalade, dear. Is it true there are more prostitutes in Shanghai than anywhere else in the world?"

Wallis felt ambushed. As the familiar panic rose, she took a deep breath. All the joy had drained from the afternoon. She was back into the dirty old street with the overhanging eaves and Win's strong hand dragging her down it. The women watching knowingly as they passed. The little room with the red paper lantern. Murmurs, laughter, moaning, gasping. The disgust for Win she had felt, and the shame for herself.

Her throat closed. She felt sick and put a hand to her mouth, closed her eyes.

When she opened them, Cecil was looking concerned. "Are you all right, dear? It'll be something you ate. Everyone says that new cook of Maud's is dreadful. I arrived too late for lunch on purpose."

All her tension exploded instantly into laughter. She felt the warmth of the sun on her face and saw the flowers in the square. It was all right. It was all in the past. She took a breath. "They call them flowers, actually," she said. "The prostitutes."

"Are there many of them?"

"Around seventy thousand."

"Seventy thousand!" exclaimed Cecil. "How on earth do they organize themselves? Do they just mill around?"

She hesitated again. But the sloping eyes were expectant. "There's a hierarchy," she told him. "Male opera singers are top of the range."

"How marvelous! I love a good tenor myself. Then who?"

"Then it's first-class courtesans, followed by ordinary courtesans."

Cecil clapped his hands and squealed. "How deliciously deviant!"

Time, she decided, to turn Cecil's interrogative guns back on him. "So do you know lots of Bright Young Things?"

"Millions," said Cecil. "You name them, I know them."

"The Jungmans?" Baby and Zita Jungman, a pair of ethereal sisters, were always in the magazines.

"Yes," said Cecil briefly. "So who's next in the whore's who's who?"

"Um, street flowers, flowers in opium dens, flowers in nail sheds who do it standing up."

"What! Stop! Do it standing up in nail sheds?" Cecil was shouting in excitement. "What's a nail shed?"

"I have no idea, I've never seen one." This was not exactly true. "Then there are the flowers at the wharves. They're called Saltwater Sisters and, um, cater to sailors. They're the bottom rung."

"As it were!" Cecil cackled. "Is that it?"

It was not, not by a long chalk. There were the teahouses and the singsong places, the courtyard bordellos and the flower boats. But she had revealed enough. More than enough.

"So what are the Jungmans like?"

Cecil reluctantly accepted it was his turn. "Like a pair of eighteenth-century angels made of wax!" he declared. "Baby is particularly waxy."

"Do you know the Magnificent Morgans?" They were another pair of society sisters. Thelma Morgan had married Lord Furness, a hugely rich shipping tycoon, while Gloria had married a Vanderbilt from America's foremost financial dynasty.

"Twins, of course," Cecil said with authority. "With marble complexions and silky hair. Their noses are like begonias. They should have been painted by Sargent with a bowl of white peonies nearby . . . what are you laughing at?"

"Noses like begonias?"

"It's quite true," Cecil insisted. "Thelma's and Gloria's noses absolutely *are* like begonias. With full-blown nostrils and lips richly carved, they diffuse an atmosphere of . . . of . . . hothouse elegance!"

Cecil's descriptions were hilarious. She egged him on for more. "How about Lady Diana Cooper?" The famous beauty had been "Leeds Pottery" in his porcelain-themed pageant. Wallis braced herself for the most magnificent opinion of all.

She was not disappointed. Cecil clasped his hands and looked transported. "She is *divine*! One of the most lyrical specimens of humanity of our generation!"

"Is she?" It was hard to keep a straight face.

"She is the fleet-footed Greek goddess! She is a petulant Botticelli Madonna, an arrogant Velázquez infanta, a pensive Charles II court lady! Her features are faultless: the curve of her chin, the stunning attack of her coloring, her rose-petal cheeks, flaxen hair and sky-blue eyes with their wistful look of inquiry!"

"Look out!"

They were crossing Kensington Gore now, and Wallis seized Cecil's arm to steer him. He was ignoring the traffic, seemingly expecting it to stop before him as he continued to rave.

"She only ever wears clothes that suit her to perfection, spontaneously finishing her appearance with a veil, a scarf, a brooch, a knot."

"Or all four!" chortled Wallis.

They had reached Hyde Park Corner station.

"Here I must descend among the masses," said Cecil, kissing her on both cheeks. "But we will meet again!"

"I'd love that," she said, imagining parties with the Jungmans and Magnificent Morgans.

"You must come to my studio and pose for me. I see you looking romantically disdainful. I'll wrap you in gold! You'll look perfect, like a bit of ancient Venice!"

"Hey, less of the ancient."

"You have the repose of archaic sculpture! You are like a Giotto painting with your features and hair!"

People entering the tube were staring.

"I will see you again soon! At the pageant of fish!"

She watched, laughing, as he descended the steps, waving his arms like fins.

"So how did it go?" Ernest asked later, over dinner. "Made some new friends?"

"Mm-hmm." She nodded proudly. "And I've a part in the pageant. As a crawfish."

He paused midway through raising a fork to his mouth. "I've changed my entire existence just so you can dress up as seafood?"

"Yes." She grinned. "Just for that."

She took another bite of perfectly steamed asparagus coated in delicious hollandaise. Lily really was turning out extraordinarily well. "Did Maud ever tell you she introduced the Prince of Wales to his mistress?"

"Really?" Ernest looked surprised. "I had no idea. Maud, a procuress. Who'd have thought?"

His eyes were twinkling. Wallis burst into laughter. "Oh, and she has a famous new cook as well. You'll never guess who."

The Duke of Windsor's Funeral
Buckingham Palace
June 1972

She had been given a suite at the front of the palace. It had huge floor-to-ceiling windows. They gave a view down the Mall but admitted little illumination. There was little to let in now; the day was drawing to a close.

The bed was vast, hung with swooping brocade the color of dried blood. The same thick curtains framed the windows, drawn back by fat silk ropes with tassels the size of a pony's tail. A heavy chandelier had been attached to the coffered ceiling, and from picture rails high on the walls, dark oils in gold frames slumped from chains. It was dreary and gloomy and felt like a tomb; perhaps it was meant to. The host family would clearly like to see her in one.

Grace, popping in from her own room down the corridor, sipped from a tooth glass of vodka. She had brought a bottle in her handbag.

"You should go," she urged. "People will expect you to."

They were talking about the Trooping the Colour.

"There aren't any people." Wallis sipped from her own tooth glass. "No one cares. They've forgotten all about David." She told Grace what Mountbatten had said about the crowds.

"Forgotten?" Grace snorted. "That's ridiculous. You were the most famous love story of all time."

"It's all in the past. People have moved on. Apart from the Windsors, aided and abetted by the Mountbattens. They just want to humiliate me. Get their revenge."

"For what? Lilibet wouldn't be queen without you. If anything, they should be grateful."

"Well, they aren't." Wallis took another despairing swig.

"And it's not true that no one cares," Grace persisted. "Look at the traffic thing."

"Traffic thing?"

"That holding up of the intersections. He said he didn't want you to be stared at. Then he's telling you there's no one to stare. Doesn't make sense."

Wallis studied her friend. "Grace, you're wasted as a countess. Should have been a detective."

The coiffed blond head nodded. "I should. But it's definitely strange. Why hurry a person no one wants to see through the center of a city?"

"Power play?" Wallis shrugged. "Because they can?"

Grace gave a skeptical sniff. "Maybe."

Wallis stood up. It was time to get ready for dinner. Or "family supper," as the footman Lilibet had sent had described it. The contradiction of sending a footman to announce an informal event became more marked when the flunkey advised her, straight-faced, that tiaras were not necessary and day dress would be worn.

"Talk about cutting loose," Grace observed wryly when he had gone.

Grace was not invited to dinner, nor Dr. Antenucci. Wallis felt insulted for her friend and her faithful physician, but Grace calmed her down. "Me and Antenucci, we'll order Chinese." Her hazel eyes sparkled. "We'll get a footman to fetch it! And watch some English TV; there's got to be a TV set somewhere. We'll have a great time, don't worry."

A different footman returned to escort her to the dinner. Like his colleague, he wore a scarlet tailcoat with thick gold edges. Grace had been staggered by the number and the splendor of the servants. Dr. Antenucci, a normally voluble New Yorker, had been uncharacteristically speechless.

"I know," Wallis said to them. "David really did give all this up for me."

"And never regretted it," Grace said stoutly. "Not for a single moment."

The corridor was wide enough to drive a car down. Her low-heeled shoes sinking into the cherry carpet, she followed her escort past a sequence of elaborate state rooms decorated in lavish Oriental style. She remembered what Grace had said about a Chinese takeaway and smiled. She felt quite calm now. With a wave of his doctor's bag, Antenucci had taken away her fears. Which was precisely what he was there for, of course.

Glimpsing a stone balustrade through some windows, she realized it must be the famous balcony. The one on which the family appeared on great occasions. She was behind the scenes of history. But then, she always had been.

At the end of the corridor the polished doors of the dining room stood open. This too was Oriental; huge vases on pedestals, ceramic lions, wall paintings of emperors on thrones with backgrounds of mountains and temples. The central light looked like an upside-down glass umbrella. Beneath it, figures were talking and laughing. She could see Philip among them, sense already his crackling, dangerous energy. But was Elizabeth there? That most dangerous energy of all?

As they all fell silent and turned to stare, Wallis felt she was in some dreadful dream. She must meet the eyes of the woman who had hated her for forty years. *Courage*, she urged herself silently. *Courage!*

Her heart hammered, and the people in the room melted together, became blurred. As a Queen Mother–size figure detached itself and came toward her, Wallis felt she might faint.

"So lovely to see you!" Lilibet wore her usual wide, impersonal smile and a dress of unpleasant mid-green. "Mummie's terribly sorry, but she's not able to join us this evening. She hopes you will forgive her."

Relief choking her throat, Wallis sank into a shaky curtsey.

"Drink?" suggested Lilibet as she rose.

Dr. Antenucci had warned her not to mix alcohol with the sedatives, but she wasn't going to survive this stone-cold sober.

Red and gold glowed at her side. A footman, proffering a tray crammed with glasses of champagne. Wallis took a steadying sip; the world came into focus again.

"Which one are you riding tomorrow? At the T the C?" An attractive blonde had come up to the queen.

"Burmese, of course." Lilibet turned to Wallis. "Have you met my daughter, Anne?"

Anne wore a hideous nylon blouse. After a curt greeting she walked off, tossing her gleaming ponytail.

Charles appeared. "How are you, Aunt Wallis?" The Prince of Wales's smile was warm. "I'm so very sorry about Uncle David. I wish . . ." His eyes flicked uneasily toward his mother. "I wish I had known him better."

CHAPTER ELEVEN

Bryanston Court
London
1930

The flat was finished and ready to move into. She loved everything about it; it was everything Upper Berkeley Street was not. Bright and modern, clean and new, with efficient heating and water systems. And a satisfactorily grand-sounding Ambassador double-two-one-five telephone number.

On the first possible morning she took Ernest to see it and covered his eyes as he entered. "What do you think?" she asked, taking her hands away.

"Amazing," he said, looking round.

"Amazing good or amazing bad?" She genuinely hoped he liked it. While she had been in charge of the project, he had written all the checks. Their finances remained dire, so he had clearly done something. Taken out a loan perhaps. She had not asked, but nor had he offered. Or uttered a word of complaint.

He smiled at her. "Just . . . amazing."

"Good." It had been hard work, tracking down exactly the perfect pale green for the drawing-room walls, the right beige for the carpet, the correct cream for the damask curtains. She had found the long Italian sideboard and the William and Mary cabinet in local antiques shops. Ernest glanced at them; yes, they had been expensive, but she had offset them with sofas and chairs that were cheap but didn't look it.

She saw him swallow at the sight of the flowers, costly tall white blooms in tall glass vases. He seemed most appreciative of the bookcases that filled one entire wall and held his collection of volumes.

"Come see the dining room," she invited. He followed her, and she saw his eyes widen at the mirror-topped table, the white leather chairs and the toile de Jouy wallpaper. Sconces had been fitted to the walls, and glass candlesticks held long pink candles. Reflected in the table, they formed a prettily colored wax forest. They lifted her heart. "Think of how pretty our dinners will look!"

Ernest nodded in agreement. "My business contacts are going to love it."

She rolled her eyes. "We've been through this. You're having those in hotels from now on."

His round brown eyes became apologetic. "Sorry. I forgot. But . . ." The basset hound forehead creased. "Who will we entertain here?"

She smiled at him. "Leave that to me. I'm working on it."

Next was the bedroom with its aquamarine walls, pink curtains and coverlet and bright silver bedside telephone. A wave of awkwardness passed between them as he turned to her, a silent question in his eyes.

In silent answer, she opened the door into the adjoining room, where polished mahogany cupboards and drawers gave a smart, masculine air. It was predominantly a dressing room, but contained a single bed. Ernest gave her a resigned smile. "Much more my sort of thing."

She led him through the guest room, with its circular bed upholstered in oyster satin. "It's quite MGM," Ernest said, referring to the film studio.

"I'll take that as a compliment." She smiled, leading him into the bathroom with its mirrored pillars, sky-blue tub, white walls and white fluffy rugs, as close to the one in the Whigham mansion as she had been able to manage.

"Well?" She smiled.

"You want an honest answer?"

She folded her arms and gave him a mock frown. "Possibly."

"Looks like a cocktail bar in Detroit," said Ernest, grinning.

"Funny you should say that!" She led him back into the sitting room and opened a cupboard. Inside there was an ice bucket, a cocktail shaker, spirits and mixers, glasses and swizzlers. "We're going to have cocktails."

"Cocktails?"

"Remember them?" She looked at him wryly. "Admittedly it's been a while. The bar in Paris?"

"Of course." He looked back at the makeshift bar. "But . . . you mean we're having them now?" He glanced at his watch. "It's only half past ten."

"I mean I'll be holding a cocktail party every night."

"*Every* night?"

Between six and eight." She hastened to explain her idea to him. "You see, I'm not sure that formally inviting people would work yet. I don't know many, and I don't have any clout. But I thought that if people knew they could drop in here on the way to other things, have a cocktail, a hot savory . . ." She stopped, seeing she had left Ernest behind.

"What people?" he asked.

"All kinds of people. Aristocrats, showgirls, diplomats, bankers. That's the secret of a great party. Mix it up." She did not add that, as a navy wife, she had been noted for lively gatherings. It had been one aspect of marriage to Win that had worked.

Ernest had sat down on the edge of the bathtub. He looked pale.

"Don't worry," she told him. "It won't be until after the pageant. I haven't asked anyone yet, and besides, I've got my crawfish to sew."

✦✦✦

Cecil had sketched the design for her: tight-fitting and brightly metallic to show off her slender figure. As all the other participants were either elderly, rotund or both; their outfits were more exercises in concealment. At the many dress rehearsals there was more good humor than Wallis had expected, ancient aristocrats laughing at their appearance.

Only Cecil was not seeing the funny side. He had started to worry about reputational damage and was behaving like a spoiled child. "I'm going to be a laughingstock," he fretted after a rehearsal in which two large tadpoles had collided and fallen over.

"Can't you bring in a few Bright Young Things?" Wallis suggested hopefully. "The Jungmans, for instance? The Morgans?" Cecil had promised to introduce her to both, and here was an ideal opportunity.

"They wouldn't be seen dead doing this" was the unflattering response.

Later, Wallis saw him talking to Maud. Her voice, simultaneously horrified and offended, came floating across the stage. "I'm sure we can find someone under a million, as you so flatteringly put it, Cecil. Let me ask around."

Angela came to the next rehearsal. She was an exquisite twenty-something with bobbed blond hair. Like a beautiful Joan of Arc, Wallis thought. She was also thoughtful and kind, helping some of the more infirm participants through the gloomy, confusing passages of the theater without tripping over the ropes. Cecil had cast her as an eel, and in her silver glittering costume she was often seen steering a staggering scallop or an unsteady goldfish.

One day, Angela brought her mother. Tiny, vividly pretty and beautifully dressed, she caught Wallis's eye immediately. Here was a woman she would like to be friends with. She seized the opportunity. If she was in her crawfish costume, too bad.

Angela's mother was reading on a chair in the theater foyer. Sitting down next to her, Wallis began singing her daughter's praises. The woman's lovely eyes brightened with gratitude. "How kind of you. Angela was delighted to help. My name is Freda, by the way."

Wallis introduced herself. Freda looked at her with happy curiosity. "You're Maud's sister-in-law? How wonderful for you. She's a very old friend of mine."

Wallis tried to look as if it were wonderful while concealing her amazement that dull Maud had a friend like Freda. "How do you know her?"

Freda's laugh was soft and attractive. "A friend and I were walking through Berkeley Square. The air-raid warning sounded—this was during the war—and we ran for shelter to the first place we saw, which was the portico of a large house. It turned out to be Maud's, and although I didn't know her she was terribly kind and let us stay until the raid ended. We've been friends ever since."

Wallis felt something like a landslide inside her brain, a swooping joining up of dots. She realized who Freda was: the star of the astonishing lunch anecdote, the woman who became the Prince of Wales's mistress after meeting at Maud's.

Freda now smiled, rose, said it had been lovely to talk but now she must find Angela.

Wallis hurriedly mentioned the planned cocktail parties. "Do drop in if you can," she added.

"How lovely," said Freda.

Wallis watched her disappear daintily into the auditorium.

Moments later an oyster rushed out of it and up to where Wallis was sitting. Maud's puce face glowered from a hole in the middle of the shell.

"Just a word of warning, Wallis dear. No one in London just asks people to drop in."

Wallis smiled sweetly back at her. "Well, I'm from the United States of America. And I'm doing things my way."

* * *

The day before the pageant performance, she woke with a sore throat. As the day developed, so did her illness, and by the following morning it had ripened to full-blown influenza. Despite aching in every limb, alternately burning hot and shuddering with cold, she insisted on getting up and getting dressed.

"Go back to bed," Ernest instructed, pausing in the bedroom doorway. He had his hat and coat on, ready to go to the office. "The pageant'll have to happen without you."

"It can't. I have to go. Everything depends on it."

"The Lying-In Hospital has been going since the 1760s. It will manage without you dressing up as a crawfish."

She couldn't bring herself to say that that was not quite what she meant. After today she would not see Cecil again. She had mentioned her cocktails, but he had been noncommittal, and once the show was over she would be back to square one. Plus a few geriatric bridge parties if she was lucky.

"I have to go," she muttered, attempting to struggle up before collapsing back down with a groan.

Things became a blur after that. She was in a dark, hot passage where strange sea creatures paraded past. They looked at her and laughed eerie echoing laughs. Her head hurt and it was hard to breathe. She had no sense of time passing but gradually the darkness ebbed and the weight on her chest lifted. She woke up one day to find the room had stopped whirling and the pain in her head was gone.

Ernest was vastly relieved. He gave her shoulder a loving, sympathetic squeeze. "I'm so glad you're better."

She stared tearfully back at him, feeling anything but glad herself. Recovery meant facing failure. She remembered the pageant and the parties she had planned in its wake. But no one had called while she was ill, either in person or on the telephone. What was the point? No one cared.

She stayed in bed for some days after that; what was there to get up for? She lay propped against her pillow, the silver telephone beside her silent, the newspapers and magazines Ernest brought to cheer her up unopened, their gossip and social pages unread. Instead she watched the sky through her bedroom window go through its diurnal motions. The bright light of morning, the flatter light of afternoon, the rich tones of early evening. Evenings were the worst, when her dashed hopes of being a hostess particularly came back to haunt her. To think she had imagined that Cecil would come with the likes of the Magnificent Morgans!

The evenings dragged by, the flat so silent she could almost hear the distant snap of the fire in the sitting room and Ernest turning the pages of his classics volumes. She pictured the cabinet with the ice bucket and the cocktail shaker, the spirits and mixers, the glasses and swizzlers. She had chosen it all so carefully. But it would never be used.

One evening the silence was broken by the distant ring of the doorbell. It was followed by the sound of footsteps in the passage and the sight of Ernest in the bedroom doorway, looking unusually flustered. "You'd better rise and shine, Wallis. There's a Cecil just arrived. Says he's come for cocktails. He's brought some women with him. Thelma and Gloria, I think they're called."

CHAPTER TWELVE

No one had ever got dressed so fast. Wallis was hurrying down the corridor just as the guests had got their coats off. She felt as if she were stepping into a part she had long been rehearsing to play. As Lily came past, arms full of furs, Wallis said, "The sausages, please, Lily. Oh, and the ice."

Lily, also playing her role beautifully, nodded as if this were routine and not the first time it had ever happened. She knew what to do; Wallis had briefed her some time ago.

In the drawing room, Ernest was clearly asking Cecil the usual questions.

"I went to Cambridge, Arnie."

"It's *Ernest*."

"But I have to say it was slightly wasted on me. I never went to lectures. However, I *was* good at acting. I was hailed as 'one of our greatest living actresses' at the University Amateur Dramatic Club."

Seeing Ernest's eyebrows shoot into his hairline, Wallis chuckled to herself. She felt toward Cecil a passionate gratitude. He had done as he promised. She could have kissed his brown-and-white co-respondent shoes.

"I failed all my exams and left without a degree," Cecil blithely continued. "My father arranged that I enter the family firm, but it was soon clear to all that the cement business wasn't for me."

Wallis hurried across the carpet. "Cecil! How wonderful to see you!"

He greeted her rapturously, kissing her on both cheeks.

"How was the pageant? I'm so sorry I wasn't able to come."

"Well, it wasn't quite the same without you, dear. A couple of the tadpoles cried off too. We had to pad out the fish with literary characters. Mrs. Throgmorton came as an Abyssinian maid playing on her dulcimer and singing of Mount Abora."

"*Kubla Khan*," said Ernest immediately. "Coleridge." He took a breath, and quoted: "'Could I revive within me her symphony and song.'"

"Mrs. Throgmorton's symphony and song were, alas, rudely interrupted by the curtain falling down on her and knocking off her wig," Cecil said. "But everyone agreed it was a most artistic achievement."

Wallis turned to the two dark-haired women standing with Cecil, one voluptuous and smiling and one slight and appraising. "Welcome," she said excitedly.

"Wallis, Arnie," said Cecil. "May I introduce the Magnificent Morgans? The Big Apple's most terrific twins? Otherwise known as Lady Thelma Furness and Mrs. Gloria Vanderbilt!"

She felt a swoop of tremendous excitement. These guests, in her drawing room!

She allowed herself a discreet glance at their noses. Were they like begonias? In fact, they were small and tip-tilted. Their lips were richly coated in lipstick and their faces heavily powdered. They had emphatic eye makeup, and their dresses, exposing the voluptuous one's breasts and curves, a little looser on the other, were black. Shaking hands, Wallis thought that Thelma was the friendly one. Gloria seemed more watchful.

Lily entered with sausages and handed them around just as instructed, with tiny plates and napkins. Cecil was in raptures. "Perfection! And I say that as a connoisseur of sausages!"

"And all the flowers, I can see you adore flowers!" chimed in

Thelma. "I always say a room without flowers is like the sky without the sun."

Wallis avoided Ernest's eye. She sensed he was wondering if people were going to exclaim like this all night. He flinched as Thelma shuffled up to him and began to stroke his arm suggestively with red fingernails. "And we have something else in common, Wallis!" She giggled at Wallis.

"You mean we're both from the States?"

Ernest, Wallis saw, was looking terrified.

"No, we're both married to men in the shipping business! All the nice girls love a sailor, is that not so?"

"Yes, and we all know which sailor in your case," put in Gloria waspishly. "It's not dear Marmaduke either. Her husband," she added, apparently for Wallis and Ernest's benefit.

"Lord Furness is an only child, thankfully," supplied Thelma. "Imagine what his mother would have called the others!"

Cecil was looking about him. "What's a girl got to do to get a drink round here?"

Wallis darted for the cocktail shaker and hastily handed the glasses round.

"Do you miss the States, Wallis?" Thelma asked. "I sure do," she went on, without waiting for the answer. "Remember when we first arrived there, Gloria? We were barely seventeen and innocent as newborn babes, but then we just happened to meet nice Mr. Cholly Knickerbocker, who put us in his social column in the *New York American*!"

"And then you just happened to meet the heir to AT and T, who you just happened to marry before you just happened to divorce him to marry someone who just happened to be richer. . . ."

Thelma snatched up a cushion and threw it at her sister. "Do shut up, Gloria."

The impact of the cushion had caused Gloria's cocktail to slop in her glass and spill onto the pale carpet. Wallis tried not to mind the stain that was spreading there. Or that Cecil had smeared sausage grease on the sofa.

"Coco and Bendor are back on again," Cecil observed with pretend weariness. Wallis's ears pricked up. There was only one Coco she had heard of: Mademoiselle Chanel, whose clothes she so admired. She now learned that her lover was the Duke of Westminster, the richest peer in England.

"He's crazy about her," said Gloria enviously. "Sends her boxes of vegetables to Paris from his country estates. With emeralds hidden in the bottom!"

"Lucky her." Thelma pouted. "Duke used to send me baskets of plover's eggs from Holland. But there were never any emeralds in those."

"And of course he's put her initials on the lampposts!" Cecil shook his head in wonder. "Double Cs! In gold!"

Wallis tried to picture a London lamppost. She had never really noticed them. "Why would he do that?"

The three of them burst out laughing. "Because he *can*!" exclaimed Cecil.

"He *owns* Central London!" exulted Gloria.

Wallis hadn't realized anyone did. Or could. It was a level of wealth and extravagance she had never guessed existed. She loved all this high-level gossip. After all her longing, it was happening. It was like being in a wonderful dream.

"So tell me, Wallis." Gloria drained her cocktail. "What do you make of London?"

"I love it," she said firmly. Well, she did now.

"Really?" On the opposite sofa, over her glass, Gloria's gaze was skeptical. "What exactly do you like about it?"

Wallis glanced at Ernest. "The famous historical sites," she said loyally. "My husband's taught me so much about them."

"I like those too," gurgled Thelma.

Gloria pounced on this immediately. "Husbands or historical sites?"

"The latter," said Thelma calmly.

Her sister glanced at her, amused. "Thelma was thrilled to be shown the very place where Mr. Van Cleef and Mr. Arpels sell their jewelry."

"I didn't mean that sort. I meant all the old buildings."

Gloria snorted. "Yes, St. James's Palace has become quite a favorite."

There was a detectable change in atmosphere. Wallis saw her three guests swap significant looks. About what, she could not guess.

The cocktail glasses were empty. Time to get up and make more.

Behind her, Thelma was asking Ernest about his books. "So many! Have you read them all?"

"Yes, actually," Ernest confessed with pride.

"I just love men with brains!"

"Rubbish," snorted Gloria. "You just love men with huge bank balances."

"Well, what about you?" Thelma hit back. "Don't tell me you fell for little old Reggie Vanderbilt for his good looks and charm."

They were like a double act, Wallis thought, exchanging a delighted glance with Cecil. It was so exciting, so amusing. She felt she never wanted the evening to end.

"Actually," retaliated Gloria, "our meeting was very romantic. We met in the snow outside the Plaza Hotel. He took me for a ride in Central Park. The sun shone, the reservoir sparkled, the winter air was like champagne. I was thrilled and flattered and in love."

"With his money!" chortled Thelma.

Placing the four glasses on a mirrored tray, Wallis turned and approached the sofas with them. "Tell Wallis and Ernest how you met HRH, Pops," Gloria urged her sister. "That was the most romantic encounter ever."

The glasses on Wallis's tray were shaking, suddenly. Even Ernest now sat up. HRH? The St. James's Palace reference made sense now. But could they really be talking about the Prince of Wales? Freda Dudley Ward was his mistress. Wasn't she?

Thelma was laughing. "We met in Leicester."

"An interesting city," said Ernest. "The cathedral . . ."

"Pops wasn't in the city," cackled Gloria. "She was in some field outside it. At a cow show."

"A . . . cow show?" repeated Wallis.

"Uh-huh." Gloria nodded. "The very same one at which the heir to the throne was presenting the prizes. Gotta hand it to ya, Pops." She winked at her sister. "You've got ingenuity. You do your research. Who else would have thought to make a move like that?"

Thelma rolled her eyes. "You are a beast, Gloria. As it happened, I was quite brokenhearted at the time. Things weren't going very well with Duke . . ."

"That's Marmaduke," Gloria informed the company, with a smirk. "He's serially unfaithful, but so is Pops, so it evens itself out."

Ernest sat upright and cleared his throat.

"Quite right, Ernest," said Thelma, straightening too. "Gloria goes too far sometimes. She's quite wrong to suggest there my meeting with the prince was premeditated."

There was a disbelieving snort from Gloria.

"As I was saying," Thelma continued with considerable dignity. "I was in need of distraction . . ."

Another snort, this time from Cecil.

"And so I took myself off to Leicester Fair. There was a big crowd round one of the show rings, and I went to see what the attraction was. A young man was pinning a blue ribbon on one of the cows."

"You'll never guess who it was," cackled Gloria. "Anyway, Pops bewitched him with her innocent charms, and now they're inseparable."

Wallis glanced at Ernest. He stared back at her, clearly shell-shocked.

"Bit tough on dear Freda though." Cecil sipped ruminatively.

Thelma laughed. "Oh, the lacemaker's daughter. Well, her time was up, really."

"Lacemaker's daughter?" Wallis thought of the tiny, charming woman.

"Her parents are from Nottingham, apparently."

Lily entered with more sausages.

"I heard," said Cecil, nibbling, "that Freda only found he'd dispensed with her services when she rang up the palace switchboard and they wouldn't put her through. The operator was sobbing. And then of course there's poor Angela." He shook his head, still chewing his sausage.

Wallis remembered the lovely, kind girl. "What happened to Angela?"

"She utterly adored HRH and saw him every day all her life. But now he's abandoned her as well," said Gloria condemningly.

Wallis felt indignant on Angela's behalf. What sort of a man was this Prince of Wales, able to cut such ties so lightly? Then she thought of the figure she had seen in the car, who hadn't looked cruel or thoughtless.

Thelma swigged her cocktail. "Well, you're the expert on abandoning children, Gloria. What about Little Gloria?"

Her sister's dark eyes flashed. "Little Gloria is very happy with Reggie's mother. And I'll be back in New York at the end of this week."

Wallis wanted to pinch herself. Unlike her guests she had drunk practically nothing, but her head was whirling all the same. Here was the inside track. A world of which most people knew nothing. It made her feel giddy, and also afraid, as if her grip on it was so tenuous it would slip away.

"Dumping Freda though, after fifteen years." Gloria thoughtfully studied the sausage on her fork. "Honestly, Pops, don't you feel a tiny bit guilty?"

"Not really," Thelma said genially. "He'll dump me in the end as well. May as well enjoy it while it lasts."

Shortly after this, the three guests rose, somewhat unsteadily. Cecil and Gloria were expected at different dinners and Thelma at the Embassy Club by her royal lover.

"Don't forget you musht come and pose for me," Cecil slurred at Wallis as he clapped on his hat. "Female matador is what I'm thinking now. Or maybe a highwayman's cloak and buckles."

"Do look me up in New York," said Gloria, not sounding as if she meant it particularly.

But it was Thelma who spoke the magic words. "We must have lunch," she said, kissing Wallis warmly on the cheek.

Closing the door behind them, Wallis sank down, sat on the carpeted floor and rested her forehead on her knees.

Ernest appeared in the hall. "Thank goodness they've gone."

She looked up, amazed. "Didn't you like them?"

"Well, they're amusing enough. But all those women seem to care about is money, which isn't very attractive."

She raised a finger to her lips. "Shh! They're still outside, getting the elevator."

"Anyway, I'm going to bed."

Wallis watched him retreat. She couldn't agree that she was glad they had gone. She had loved every moment and hoped desperately that Thelma had meant what she said about lunch. Hearing their laughter outside as they rattled the lift door open, she felt she had been handed the key to a new and gilded world.

The Duke of Windsor's Funeral
Buckingham Palace
June 1972

There were candelabras, printed menus and flowers in those ghastly tight arrangements they seemed to go in for here. At each place was a gold charger with the royal coat of arms and silver flatware extending like wings on either side. Everyone had their own dish with a couple of butter pats, and their own silver salt and pepper pots. For a family supper, Wallis thought, it was toward the more formal end of the spectrum.

Her seat was in the center of the table, with Charles on her right and Philip on her left. Opposite was Lilibet, looking busily about her and talking in her decided voice. Her keen blue gaze darted everywhere, always returning to Wallis as if checking she was behaving herself.

She felt her heart hammering hard. Her mouth was dry; the glass of champagne was long gone. As was the second one. The alcohol was charging around her body, making her feel reckless and light-headed. Antenucci was right; she shouldn't have drunk it. But it was too late now.

She took the menu and stared at it while she composed herself. Soup, chicken, something called Dalmatian ice cream.

Sitting on the other side of Philip, Anne was explaining it to someone. "It's mint choc chips in vanilla ice cream. My mother thinks she's invented it, doesn't realize you can buy it in every ice cream shop in the world."

"I expect you're used to wonderful French food, Aunt Wallis." On her right, Charles sounded apologetic.

"Doesn't look like it," observed the other side. "But then, didn't you once say it was impossible to be too rich or too thin?"

Wallis summoned her strength and gave him a dazzling smile. "I never said that. It's a myth, like Marie Antoinette saying 'Let them eat cake.'"

"Interesting comparison," remarked Philip before turning to the woman on his left.

Under the pretext of reaching over for his pepper, Charles whispered, "Don't take any notice!"

She gave him a game, if shaky, smile.

They started to talk about gardening. Charles turned out to be keen on it, as David had been. She told him one of David's favorite stories, about a new gardener he had encountered at their country house, the Mill, in France.

David: *Qui êtes-vous?*

Gardener: *Je travaille pour le duc de Windsor.*

Duke: *Mais c'est moi, le duc de Windsor!*

Gardener: *Pardon, monsieur, mais je ne parle pas anglais.*

Charles laughed. "That's hilarious!"

"Side-splitting," commented her other side.

She ignored him. She thought of the Mill as it would be now, empty and silent without them. She pictured his garden, the flowers growing all unknowing that their careful attendant was gone. She pictured his bedroom, like something from a barracks. A hard bed, a few shelves for his clothes. He had always taken the worst room in any house. She pictured the barn that David had made his refuge; across one entire wall was a world map on which his travels as Prince of Wales were all marked. Opposite the fireplace stood the desk from which he had made his abdication broadcast. From Fort Belvedere, the bass drum from the Grenadiers regimental band that served as a coffee table. On a sideboard, a set of crystal beakers, mugs and goblets that had been engraved for his coronation. He had never ceased to think of England. It had taken him a lifetime to realize he would never be allowed back. Alive, that was.

The soup plates were now removed, whether they had finished or not. Charles in particular seemed a slow eater. Wallis wondered if the heir to the throne had ever been more than half-fed. As a succession of dishes covered with silver domes replaced the soup plates, and a battalion of footmen stepped forward simultaneously and lifted the lids, Wallis braced herself. She must talk to Philip.

She dabbed her mouth with her napkin and looked about her at the decor. With its huge vases and riotous carving it seemed to her a crude parody of any real Oriental interior.

"Why is this room Chinese?" she asked Philip, who was chewing violently on his chicken, his lean cheeks bulging with meat.

From across the table Lilibet leaned forward brightly. "It comes from the Royal Pavilion in Brighton. Recycling it was supposed to save money, but it actually ended up costing more than new interiors."

Sycophantic laughter greeted this doomed attempt at royal economy. Wallis did her best to smile along with them.

Philip was looking at her. His eyes were wolfish like his uncle's. "You're an expert on the Far East, of course."

"I wouldn't say that." But her insides stiffened. Here were dragons. Her time in Shanghai had been the focus of sensational rumors during the abdication. Philip was telling her that, widow or not, he'd give her no quarter. He would show her, beneath the veneer of politeness, what the family really thought of her. That nothing was forgiven or forgotten.

Later, as they rose to leave, Charles leaned close. "Can I ask . . . I just wondered . . . are you going to the lying-in-state?"

She glanced at him, apprehensive. Was he going to warn her against it too? The empty chapel, the lonely bier?

"I understand that you might not feel able." Charles's voice was gentle. "But I just wanted to let you know, Aunt Wallis, that

I was going to make a private visit myself tomorrow night. To pay my respects. I could take you . . . if you liked. . . ."

His kindness warmed her heart and lifted her spirits. "Thank you," she whispered. That would make two visitors at least.

When the dinner was over and she returned wearily to her room, she found Grace sitting in the same chair as before.

"I waited up. I had to tell you!"

"What?"

"It's not true!"

"What isn't?"

Grace spoke rapidly. "David. He hasn't been forgotten at all. Antenucci and I saw the TV news. Thousands of people have been to Windsor to pay their respects."

"Thousands!" Wallis slumped against a table, clung to its edge.

"Thousands upon thousands. Mountbatten's been spinning you a line. I knew it!" Grace was triumphant. "That's why they stopped the traffic! They want as little attention on you as possible."

Wallis groped her way to a chair. It was too much to take in, especially this late. She felt as if she had been awake for weeks.

Grace leaned forward, her eyes shining. "Everyone remembers Edward the Eighth, Wallis. He'll never be forgotten. Because of you."

CHAPTER THIRTEEN

Bryanston Court
London
1930

Wallis had imagined a long and agonizing wait for a lunch invitation from Thelma, and the ghastly possibility that it might not come at all. To her amazement she received a note the very next day.

She walked the half hour to the Ritz. Given their finances, a taxi was out of the question. At least Thelma, as the inviting person and wife of a multimillionaire, would be paying.

Summer was now turning to autumn. The trees in the streets were shedding their leaves. Between them were the black lampposts that, as Cecil said, bore the interlocked gold Cs of Chanel.

In the Ritz's golden interior, the staff sprang to attention. A manager almost swept the floor in obeisance. "The restaurant? This way, madame. . . ."

She felt a thrill as she followed him across the Palm Court. She had read about this place; it was famous for its dances in the evenings. The decoration was deliciously frivolous; fluted pillars, gold cupids and splashing fountains. Between the eponymous palm fronds, groups of ladies were taking tea; there was the tinkle of spoons, the clink of china, the decorous murmur of conversation. Waiters hurried about.

The ceiling of the oval dining room was astonishingly ornate, flower-painted with suspended bronze swags. The windows gave onto Green Park and a distant view of Buckingham Palace.

Thelma had not yet arrived. A smiling waiter escorted Wallis to a pink-clothed table.

She filled the time by planning possible conversation topics.

They had the shipping industry in common. And living in America. But Thelma's version of both was so much bigger and richer.

"Madame? An aperitif?"

Wallis would have loved nothing more. But it would not be good manners to add to Thelma's bill. Especially when she was not there. "A glass of water, please," she said firmly.

A further half an hour elapsed, and Thelma still had not turned up. Wallis was about to rise and go when there was a commotion in the doorway and a voluptuous figure in a tight black dress came swaying in high heels over the pink floral carpet. "Darling, I'm late!" Thelma called, as if Wallis had somehow not noticed.

She wiggled into the seat the waiter had pulled out for her and tossed off her wrap to reveal an expanse of cleavage. She beamed at Wallis. "So lovely to see you. And such heaven to meet Arnold the other night."

"Ernest."

Thelma was waving at the waiter. Her fingernails were painted purple. She glanced at Wallis's glass. "You're having water?"

Wallis opened her mouth to say that a glass of wine would be welcome.

The waiter arrived and was rewarded by Thelma inclining her bosom at him.

"My usual, please, Jean."

He glided away.

"I just love your adorable little flat!" Thelma got out a diamond-studded compact and reapplied her scarlet lipstick. "Do you know, before Cecil took me, I'd actually never been to that part of London before? I'm not sure I even knew it existed."

She wasn't being rude, Wallis told herself. To someone like Thelma, whose area of operations was exclusively Mayfair, anywhere north of Oxford Street would be alien territory. But a change of subject seemed called for.

"How did you meet Cecil?" she asked.

Thelma looked up from powdering her nose. "He saw me in the street and followed me into a shop. Said he'd always wanted to meet me. Quite strange. But rather fun."

The waiter reappeared with Thelma's usual, a bottle of Pol Roger. She watched avidly as it was opened, downed one glass instantly, and then looked on with satisfaction as it was refilled. Wallis could only look on longingly.

The menu arrived. There were colossal prices beside delicacies such as lobster salad or foie gras. Thelma promptly ordered both and clapped the menu shut.

"A green salad," Wallis said, politely choosing the cheapest possible item at the exact same moment her companion emptied her second glass of Pol Roger.

"I do so love drinking, don't you, darling?" Thelma said happily. "I'm making up for lost time, I suppose. My first husband was an alcoholic, so I had to rather stay away from it then." She took another sip and sighed. "Marrying Junior was a terrible mistake."

Wallis could relate to that, even if she had no intention of saying so. Her problems with Win were not up for discussion.

"Because Junior wasn't anything like as rich as he said," Thelma went on, sounding indignant. "He'd spent all the AT and T inheritance before he even married me. When I discovered that, I felt a complete indifference to him. Nothing is deader than a dead love!" She paused for another swig of champagne.

"And then, just by chance, I found myself in Paris at a dinner of Gloria's. Duke was there. A man with a tragic past."

"Really?" Wallis was surprised. Given his wife was cheating with the Prince of Wales, he sounded more like a man with a tragic present.

The first course had now arrived, and Thelma was forking in a slice of foie gras.

"Oh yes. His first wife had died on board his yacht. As it had no embalming facilities, he'd had to bury her at sea. Can you imagine?"

Wallis couldn't. Embalming facilities? What yacht had those anyway? As for the death and burial at sea, if she were Thelma, Wallis thought, she might avoid sailing holidays. "I think that might have put me off slightly," she admitted.

"Well, I'm a tough girl." Thelma was attacking the foie gras with gusto. "And Duke interested me. He was one of the foremost peers and one of the most brilliant businessmen in England. His every word was legal tender!" She cocked her head to one side consideringly. "Well, the ones that weren't profanities, that is."

"You mean he swears?" Wallis asked. Violent bad language had been another horrible Win habit. Ernest, by contrast, never used it.

"It's a characteristic of unsentimental men," Thelma maintained.

That was certainly one way of putting it.

"And Duke's so shy, as well. His language is a combination of the stables where he breeds his horses, the Yorkshire collieries that make the family fortune and the docks where his ships tie up."

Wallis looked down at the tablecloth, a smile tugging her mouth. The extent to which Thelma saw everything in terms of money was incredible. Even swearing.

"He intrigued me completely!" she went on. "He combined boldness with strength, and frankness with another element, one I had not been close to! Know what it was?"

Wallis shrugged.

"Power!"

Wallis was beginning to wonder, in that case, what Thelma was doing with the prince at all. Perhaps she wasn't. If so, how could she be speaking about her husband so openly, as if this was all perfectly normal? Or was this how the upper classes behaved in Britain? Wallis had never come across this phenomenon before.

The foie gras plate, scraped clean, was now taken away by one waiter while another placed the lobster salad. A tiny bowl of leaves appeared before Wallis. Thelma continued unabated.

"There seemed to be nothing Duke could not do—no one he did not know! It was a whirlwind courtship!" Thelma was jabbing at a pink claw with a silver poker. "Duke took me to the Café de Paris and ordered me whole truffles cooked in champagne!"

Wallis thought that sounded disgusting. What a waste of both truffles and champagne!

"I arrived in England to get married in 1926! Right in the middle of the general strike! Duke sent a fleet of Rolls-Royces to meet me at Southampton! He got out a revolver and placed it on the dashboard, saying, "'Now I'd like to see any bastard stop this car!'"

"Such a romantic," murmured Wallis, but the irony was lost on Thelma, who nodded enthusiastically as she yanked out the lobster meat.

"Our honeymoon was by train to his enormous estate in Scotland! He traveled everywhere with a secretary and two valets!"

"*Two* valets?"

Thelma sighed. "Then, as soon as we got back, Duke starting running around," she said mournfully. "Affairs left, right and center. I was sick at heart and had nowhere to turn. And it was in this state of mind that I met the Prince of Wales."

"At the cow show," put in Wallis.

"Yes! At the cow show! It was a bolt of emotional lightning." Thelma brightened up again and flung her arms out, narrowly missing a passing waiter with a tray. "The strongest physical attraction! We were two people in love who wanted desperately to gain happiness! He invited me to dinner at St. James's Palace. We sat by the fireplace and had cocktails, and afterward we went to the Hotel Splendide for a waltz!"

"What is it like?"

Thelma leaned forward. Part of her cleavage spilled on the table, like blancmange. "Simply marvelous! The admiration in his eyes while we danced, it seemed there had never been a time when we didn't know each other! It all seemed so natural and so right! I was conscious of the fluttering of my pulse, of a vague sense of expectancy . . ."

Thelma was wasted being a royal mistress, Wallis thought. She should write sensational novels. "I meant St. James's Palace."

"Oh." Thelma patted the napkin on her red lips. "You know. Usual sort of thing. Sofas on either side of the fireplace. Desk in the corner. Portrait of Queen Mary covered in diamonds. Huge four-poster bed!" Then her voice dropped suddenly and sounded quite brisk and normal. Her dreamy expression became beady and focused. "And actually, that's what I wanted to talk to you about."

"The prince's *bed*?" Wallis was completely confused. She thought of the round satin one in her guest room. Had Thelma seen it on the way out? Did she think her royal lover would like one?

"What happens in it, to be precise." Thelma leaned further forward, revealing more of her abundant cleavage. "Contrary to what you may imagine," she added briskly, "David's absolutely hopeless. Either he can't get it up at all, or if he does he can't . . ." She nodded, winked and leaned back.

As well as shocked at this unwanted revelation, Wallis was confused. Thelma's husband's name was Marmaduke, wasn't it? And the Prince of Wales was called Edward. Just how many lovers did the woman have? "Who's David?"

"Edward Albert Christian George Andrew Patrick David, to be precise."

Wallis frowned. "The Prince of *Wales*?" She had no idea what else to say. She leaned her elbows on the tablecloth and rubbed her forehead. "Why are you telling me this?"

"Isn't it obvious?"

"Not exactly."

"So you can help me, of course!" Thelma said brightly. "With David and his, erm, difficulties."

"*What?*" Wallis gripped the arms of her chair. "Me?"

Thelma giggled. "It's *advice* I want, Wallis. Nothing else! You're hardly his type. You're much too old, and while you have a certain style you're not exactly beautiful. And obviously you don't have any money or know many people."

Wallis was far too stunned to feel insulted. The conversation had long since passed the bounds of normality. "Advice? What sort of advice?"

Thelma leaned forward again. She licked her lips in a speculative sort of way. "Cecil told me that you worked in a Shanghai brothel. You trained with a madam who taught you sexual techniques that would pleasure the most recalcitrant men."

CHAPTER FOURTEEN

Wallis was staring at the Ritz restaurant ceiling. It was whirling like a merry-go-round, the painted flowers wheeling past, the brass garlands too. *What* had Thelma just said? Wallis, who had never even slept with her husband, was the assumed mistress of Eastern sexual arts?

"It's absolute rubbish," she said, surprised at how calm she sounded. "Cecil's made it all up."

"Cecil makes everything up," said Thelma. "I should have known." She covered her face dramatically with her purple-tipped fingernails. Her voice, from between her fingers, had lost all its breeziness. There was a note of real despair.

"It's all such a fucking struggle, quite literally. And it's not even just the sex. I'm also supposed to organize his social life. Both at my house and at the Fort."

"What's the Fort?"

"David's house," Thelma groaned.

"I thought he lived at St. James's Palace."

"He does. But that's the official residence. The Fort is his weekend home. His private castle."

"I've never heard of it."

"That's the whole point. It's secret. No one goes apart from close friends."

Wallis was silent. Official palaces, private castles. She felt, again, that thrilling sense of being on the inside track. "How wonderful," she said softly, imagining the fun it must be.

"Well, it *was*!" Thelma wailed from behind her hands. "When *Freda* was in charge. The parties were legendary, apparently. She was amazing at everything. No wonder he was always asking her to marry him."

"He asked Freda Dudley Ward to marry him?" Wallis was stunned. "But she was married already!"

"He asks everyone. It's a thing with him. He asked me too."

"But you're married as well. Although, I suppose," Wallis mused, "you could get divorced."

Thelma laughed. "The Prince of Wales, marry a divorcée! If you think that's a possibility, Wallis, you don't know the British!"

"I never said I did." Wallis smiled.

Thelma returned the subject to her parties. "But *I'm* hopeless at them. I always seem to get the wrong people."

Wallis could easily imagine the reason. Freda had charm, tact and insight, whereas self-obsessed Thelma would be clueless about who would go with who. To know this about the prince's inner circle was so fascinating it not only soothed away her shock and fury but made her want to help, to be involved.

"If I could make a suggestion," she said, "I think the secret of a good party is to mix the social lions with a few interesting people from all walks of life. A touch of the unexpected."

Thelma took her hands away. Her face was flushed and her mascara smudged. "Unexpected?" She sounded unconvinced. "What sort of unexpected?"

Wallis ransacked her brain for the most outrageous combination. "Let's say you had a dinner where the prince met Mahatma Gandhi and was served a tasty hamburger on a Minton plate."

Thelma looked derisive, then her eyes widened. "Wallis! You're dead right! He would *love* that! Is Gandhi here?"

"I think he's in prison, actually," Wallis said. Trust Thelma not to know that the ascetic leader of the movement against British rule in India had recently been arrested. The dramatic circumstances, dead of night, at his camp, had been in all the newspapers. "But you get the idea."

The bill came, even huger than anticipated. As it was placed before her, Wallis stared at it in horror, imagining what Ernest would say if she actually had to pay it. She waited for Thelma's purple-tipped fingers to reach over and take it away.

They did not though. The bill stayed where it was, while Thelma tottered off to visit the powder room. Wallis, with a cold, sick feeling in her stomach, found herself scrabbling in her handbag. The entire week's housekeeping money would only just cover it.

As Thelma returned, beaming, and Wallis struggled to rise on her trembling knees, she felt an arm tuck itself in hers. "It would be so wonderful if you and Arnold could come stay at the Fort next weekend."

"Stay with the Prince of Wales? *Us?*" Ernest looked flabbergasted. He had just come in from the office and was hanging his hat in the hall.

"Us, yes!" Wallis was practically jumping with excitement. "Isn't it *thrilling?*"

"Um . . ." He rubbed his face in the way he did when tired. "I'm sorry, Wallis. It's been a long day."

"We've been invited to Fort Belvedere!" she reiterated gleefully. "That's the prince's private castle, where only his friends go!"

Ernest was unbuttoning his overcoat. "But we're not his friends. We've never met him."

She stared at him. Was it possible he had misunderstood her somehow? She had expected him to be as delighted as she was. "But we're friends of Thelma's."

He did not reply to this. He hadn't been impressed with Thelma, she knew. *All those women seem to care about is money*, he had said after the Magnificent Morgans had left the flat.

She folded her arms and leaned against the wall. Ernest was kind and easygoing almost all the time, but very occasionally he could be stubborn. This was obviously one of those occasions. If she was going to save the weekend, deft footwork was required.

"I thought you liked the royal family," she said.

"I do," he said. "The British monarchy stands for decency, fair play and centuries of tradition and service."

"So what's the problem?"

"The Prince of Wales lets the side down. All those mistresses. Married women too." He was hanging up his coat; his wedding band flashed in the light.

She had to concede this was a fair point. "But haven't princes always had mistresses? Aren't you being old-fashioned?"

Ernest stared at her. "I'm surprised to hear you say that, Wallis. You're a modern girl. The prince sounds like something from the Dark Ages. He has an appalling way of treating women. From what Cecil said."

Cecil's voice came back to her. *Freda only found he'd dispensed with her services when she rang up the palace switchboard and they wouldn't put her through. The operator was sobbing.* Then she thought of what Thelma had said too and how Wallis would have agreed wholeheartedly with Ernest had it not been for her own sight of the prince, looking sad in the back of his car. She wondered where the truth about him really lay. "But wouldn't it be better to judge him after we've met him? We're hardly going to get the chance again."

"Well, I don't want the chance in the first place" was Ernest's reply to this.

She thought quickly. "We'll be in some very grand company. Our fellow guests are Lady Diana and the Honorable Duff Cooper."

They had been walking out of the Ritz when Thelma told her.

Already electrified by the invitation itself, she had almost collapsed into the doorman's arms at this extra detail. Lady Diana Cooper. The woman Cecil had described with such passionate admiration as being like not just one famous work of art, but many. She remembered him raving about her faultless features, the stunning attack of her coloring, her sky-blue eyes with their wistful look of inquiry.

But Ernest was frowning. "Who?"

"Oh, *honestly*, Ernest! Lady Diana Cooper! She's a famous beauty. And her husband is something important in the government." She took his arm. "This is the social deep end. We really are in the big league here."

She regarded him eagerly. But he looked just as doubtful as before. "So why on earth ask us?" he said.

"What do you mean?"

"I mean, why invite us? To be with people like that?"

She fought her impatience. "I think Thelma thinks we might amuse people. She likes to mix social lions with interesting people from lower down the food chain."

Ernest stared at her. "*Us*, interesting?"

She nodded determinedly. "Thelma thinks we'll be a breath of fresh air."

"But what would someone like me have to say to the Prince of Wales?"

"Well. Let's think. You have ships in common. And the prince trained as a naval officer. You could talk to him about rigging and hardtack."

Ernest looked scornful. "I don't actually *sail* in the ships at Simpson Spence and Young."

"It was a *joke*, Ernest." She spoke through gritted teeth.

"We're just ordinary people." Ernest returned to his original theme.

"Yes, but that's the *point*, Ernest."

He groaned. "Oh, come on, Wallis. Among all these grand aristocrats, we'll be complete fish out of water. You know what the class system is like. We can't compete on any level, and we'll only make fools of ourselves. It'll be a humiliation, from start to finish."

All her delight leaked away and was replaced by despair. She thought of the dull dinner parties with Ernest's contacts, Maud's spiteful attacks, the cocktail parties that had never happened. And yes, most of all, the impenetrable class system, designed to keep people like her out. Well, it had succeeded. This was her best chance yet, but Ernest seemed determined to destroy it.

"And they're all so rich, and we're—"

"*Poor!*" she burst out. She could not bear it. She had been so excited, and he had killed it stone-dead. "Not just boring nobodies, *poor* and boring nobodies!"

She regretted it immediately. Ernest looked absolutely stricken. He walked to the sofa, sat down and stared at the carpet.

"I'm sorry," he said. "You didn't sign up to be the wife of a poor man. The firm was in better shape when we met. But the crash, you know, it just decimated the business. I'm still trying to turn it round. It is happening, but slowly, and more slowly than you would like, I know."

Contrite, she sat down beside him and took his hand. "I'm sorry too. That was mean. I couldn't wish for a better husband, and you're trying your best, you're working so hard. Besides . . ." She stopped. She had been about to add *there were things you didn't sign up for either.*

"Besides what?" He was looking at her. Had he guessed she was about to say the unsayable?

Silence fell. She willed him to change his mind. Now that he felt guilty, there was a tiny chance that he would. "It's only one weekend," she pleaded. "A one-off."

He rubbed his forehead. The ring gleamed with the movement of his fingers. "You really want to go, don't you?"

She nodded. Her insides were clenched, her fingers curled into fists with the tension of it. "We'll regret it all our lives if we don't."

"We might regret it all our lives if we *do*."

"But what could possibly *happen*?"

"I don't know. Whenever you see the prince in the newspapers he's always falling off horses or falling out of nightclubs. I can't ride, and I don't like nightclubs."

Wallis had guessed by now that behind her husband's objections was fear. This glamorous world scared him, just as it excited her. "He'll just want to talk fashionable gossip," Ernest said. "And I don't know any. I don't even know any *unfashionable* gossip."

She laughed, took both his hands and looked into his face. "Just think of the *contacts*, Ernest! Whatever happens, you'll meet some important people. It will help the business. Really, can we afford not to go?"

She had won, she could tell. His broad chest heaved up and down in a resigned sigh. "Guess I'd better rush out and buy an etiquette book," he said.

But a human etiquette book was on the other end of the phone in no time. Maud, while doing her best to disguise it, was clearly infuriated. How dare the sister-in-law from nowhere be asked to weekend with the Prince of Wales?

CHAPTER FIFTEEN

Winning the battle with Ernest did not mean winning the war. He had planted doubts in her mind that had never been there before. How could they amuse people like Lady Diana Cooper? How would they seem a breath of fresh air to the heir to the throne? What would they talk about?

And there was the small matter of her wardrobe. Wallis rummaged in despair through her clothes. Everything was old or, if new, from the cheapest shops imaginable and altered by her own hand. A real sophisticate like Lady Diana Cooper would see through that immediately.

Hardly enough for a new dress, Aunt Bessie had said of the tiny legacy Alice had left her. But a new dress was what she needed now. Her mother, Wallis knew, would not have wanted her to spend it on anything else. A weekend with the Prince of Wales! Her ostracized daughter. How proud she would have been. What a kick in the teeth that was for snooty Baltimore!

Here was the shop. Wallis stood before it, studying the window, as she had before. Then, imagining Alice looking down with delight, she smiled at the gray London sky and pushed open the door.

Inside was another world quite removed from that outside. All was restrained elegance. There were white walls, oval mirrors, Oriental screens and white-and-gray armchairs. A heavenly perfume rose richly to her nostrils. Chanel's famous N°5, almost certainly.

She approached the rails in an almost trancelike state. She felt like a worshipper at a shrine. Everything was so beautiful, so desirable, it made her head spin. Crepe de chine belted blouses, sleeveless evening dresses in black tulle, cropped tweed jackets with patch pockets and turned-back cuffs. There was a ruby-red coat trimmed with a wide ermine collar. So fine was the velvet, her fingers could hardly feel it.

"You! Down there!"

Wallis snatched her hand away. Her heart thudded with fear. At the other end of the shop, a pair of assistants were looking at her in alarm. Who had spoken?

Instinct made her glance up. Set high in the wall was a balcony with a black ironwork rail. A woman was standing at it, staring at her intently.

It couldn't be, surely. But Wallis had seen photographs, and there was the same sharply beautiful face with curving cheekbones, long mouth, slim arching eyebrows. She wore her dark hair in a tousled bob and a striped fisherman's top under several ropes of huge pearls. On each of her wrists was a thick black bangle studded with large paste jewels.

The excitement Wallis felt was mixed with annoyance that her first encounter with the famous Coco Chanel should be a reprimand for touching her clothes.

"Do excuse me," Wallis said humbly.

"For what?" the Frenchwoman demanded.

"For mauling your blouse."

"I am happy if you touch things, if that is what you mean. It is what they are for. Wait there," she said, and disappeared.

A few seconds later she appeared on the shop floor. Below the fisherman's shirt she wore a pair of beautifully cut loose white trousers and a ballet dancer's flat black pumps. The mass of pearls over her striped shirt were imitation, Wallis now saw with surprise, but the jewels on the bangles were genuine. Fake and real mixed up. Smart trousers with a sailor top and ballet shoes. How clever. How innovative.

"This," said Coco Chanel. Her sharp black eyes were flicking about Wallis's tweed coat. "This is excellent."

"Thank you." Wallis was surprised. The coat was an old one, from New York. But she had always been fond of it. "It's not a very expensive one," she admitted.

The bracelets rattled as an arm was waved. "Expensive has nothing to do with it! The cut, the design is all. It must be sinless! The perfect tweed coat is almost impossible to get right. It requires *reserves* of intelligence!"

Wallis could only nod. But now Chanel was darting forward, grabbing the material and rubbing it between her long fingers. "Ah, but it is not the real tweed! I can tell, just by touching, whether it has been made with the water from the actual River Tweed."

It seemed an unlikely claim, but if anyone could perform such a feat, Wallis figured, then this woman could. "It probably isn't genuine," she agreed. "I bought it in New York."

The dark eyes sparked. "You are American?"

"Yes."

The dark eyes narrowed. "So why do you speak with a British accent?"

Wallis was beginning to wonder if she was imagining it all. First her coat, now her accent. Why would the great Chanel be interested in either? "It's a long story," she said, rather wearily.

"And I would like to hear it! You must come and have a drink with me!" Chanel had turned her back and was walking away toward the little doorway she had appeared from. Wallis hurried after. A helix-shaped flight of stairs wound up to the white space above. At the top was a landing with a small dove-gray sofa.

The designer plonked herself down and patted the cushion beside her.

A girl in a dove-gray dress appeared, scissors round her neck. There was a workroom nearby, evidently. "Tea, madame?"

The Frenchwoman looked at Wallis. "Do you like tea?"

She had certainly tried her best to; it was the quintessential English drink. But the fact remained that it looked and tasted like dishwater. "Not really," Wallis admitted.

"*Moi non plus.*" A hand waved imperiously at the seamstress. "Bring champagne!" She turned her attention back to Wallis. "So, you work in fashion?"

"I thought about doing so once." She had looked into it in New York after the divorce. A magazine competition had offered a position on the staff as a prize.

"So why didn't you?" The designer spoke as if it really were that simple; Wallis just had to want it to do it.

Wallis described the magazine competition. "I stayed up all night polishing my essay, but the editors rejected it."

A snort from Chanel. "Typical. Magazine editors know nothing. It was about what, this essay?"

"Spring hats."

"But what is a spring 'at? It can be anything."

Wallis smiled. "That was my point."

The champagne arrived. Chanel lifted her coupe with her fingers under the bowl. "Champagne for courage!" she declared. "Red wine for endurance, but always champagne for courage!"

"Courage." Wallis smiled, raising her own glass.

"So." Chanel narrowed her eyes. "To business. If you want to make a living with clothes, I could offer you a job."

"A *job*?" She had come in here for a dress.

A shrug. "Why not? You can come back with me to France."

Her matter-of-fact tone sent excitement barreling through Wallis. She felt ridiculously flattered. The great Coco Chanel thought she had some skill, wanted her to work with her. In Paris, the most elegant city in the world. For a second she could almost imagine it. And, of course, had she not met Thelma, had the invitation to Fort Belvedere not been made, she might have been really tempted.

"I'm sorry," she said regretfully.

Chanel said nothing, only got out a packet of cigarettes and applied a bright, licking flame to the bottom of one. "But why not? You do not like London, I can see."

Wallis smiled ruefully. "Is it that obvious?"

A nod, a stream of blue smoke. "You want to fit in with the English. But you are not succeeding."

Wallis felt panic clutch her insides. If this was evident to a Frenchwoman, how much more evident would it be to the Fort Belvedere crowd? Was Ernest right and they would only humiliate themselves?

"What am I doing wrong?" she asked, rather desperately.

"The reason is very simple. It is because you are trying too hard."

"Trying too hard?"

"You are American but you try to speak with an English accent. You correct your American phrases to English ones. This is a mistake."

"Is it?"

"The English," Chanel instructed, "don't like people trying to be like them. They set traps for outsiders. Phrases. Table manners. Names."

Wallis's eyes widened. This was true. She knew it. She had lived it.

"It is impossible not to get caught in these traps. Better to avoid them altogether."

"But . . . how?"

The black eyes gleamed. "I will tell you a story. I have an English lover."

The Duke of Westminster, Wallis remembered. She thought of the lampposts, the boxes of vegetables with jewels in the bottom. Then she thought of what Cecil had said about her. He must have been exaggerating about Chanel too.

"No doubt you have heard of him. The Duke of Westminster." She pronounced it *Westminstair*. "He is the richest man in England.

He put my initials on the lampposts of London. He sent boxes of vegetables to Paris from his English estates. They had priceless gemstones at the bottom of them."

Wallis's jaw dropped. So it was true. "That's . . . amazing."

"*Incroyable*, yes? Do I look like the sort of person who unpacks vegetable boxes?" Chanel pulled on her cigarette. "He takes me into all the best houses, where I am accepted without question. You want to know why? Because I never hide the fact that I am foreign!" The cigarette waved triumphantly. "Au contraire, I exaggerate it!"

"Exaggerate it?"

"Yes! As you should too. Be American! Be proud of your flag and your republic! I myself am always as French as can be!"

"And that works?"

"*Mais oui!* Because I am different! I am not part of their class system. They cannot rank me. They can afford to be nice to me. And so they are."

"That's absolutely brilliant," Wallis said.

The insight was like a lightning strike; it lit up everything around. All was suddenly revealed. This was where she had been going wrong all these years. "Thank you," she said. "You can't imagine how much you've helped me."

She picked up her champagne glass, fingers under the coupe. She felt filled with a new confidence. She raised the glass to her lips, smiling. "*Courage.*"

She left the shop eventually with a perfect black dress and an offer.

"I am going back to Paris tonight," Chanel announced. "If you grow tired of life here, come and work for me there."

"If I do, I will," Wallis promised. "But for the moment, I can't."

A theatrical Gallic shrug greeted this. "Ah well. Perhaps an even greater destiny awaits you. Who knows?"

The Duke of Windsor's Funeral
Buckingham Palace
June 1972

She would wear Chanel. She would look her best for David's lying-in-state. He alone of his family had understood clothes. Jewels too. She touched her shoulder, on which a large brooch glittered. Her austere dress provided the perfect background. He had given her so many. The engagement ring with its huge sapphire. The diamond brooch shaped like the Prince of Wales's feathers. The great cat pieces designed by La Panthère—Jeanne Toussaint, Louis Cartier's mistress. True to her name, Jeanne had produced for Wallis a diamond panther astride an enormous Kashmir sapphire.

Most spectacular of all was the flamingo clip with plumage in emeralds, diamonds, sapphires and rubies. It had retractable legs so as not to dig into her if she bent down. "You think of everything," she had joked when David had demonstrated it. Today, on the thirty-fifth anniversary of their wedding, she wore his present from an earlier anniversary, a diamond-encrusted heart brooch topped with "WE" in entwined emeralds beneath a crown.

A tap at the door. One last glance at the mirror. She touched her brooch.

The door opened, and Charles put his head around. "Ready, Aunt Wallis?"

"As I'll ever be."

"How are you feeling?"

Impatience stirred. How did he think she felt? But then she remembered Grace's account of the crowds at Windsor. It put new heart into her and she rummaged for a joke. "Medicated."

They walked through the palace. Acres of red carpet stretched away between pillars. Vast portraits of Queen Victoria stared challengingly from the walls. Charles's brilliantly shined shoes reflected the blaze of the chandeliers. As before, she found him easy company.

They discussed the Trooping the Colour earlier that day. From her window in the center of the palace front, right under the rippling flagpole, she had had the perfect view over the gray-graveled forecourt and the great black gates yawning wide. Outside, behind a line of policemen, excited onlookers had strained and surged.

The sharp sound of horses' hooves had brought a sudden hush. Then, below her, a red-jacketed figure on horseback emerged. In the uniform of colonel-in-chief of the Grenadier Guards, the monarch was buttoned and braided with shining gold, crossed with a blue silk sash and blazing with medals. A snow-white plume rose from the black regimental cap.

But it had not been Lilibet she had seen. Memory had substituted a slight blond figure for the buxom one with dark hair. "The uniform trousers are hideously tight," Charles said. "I had to lie on the floor to get mine on."

"David's once split right down the side. His valet colored his exposed leg with ink."

"Ha! I'll remember that when it happens to me. A top tip from one Prince of Wales to another!"

They looked happily at each other. Then Charles's face became serious.

"The lament was very good," he said gently.

She had to concede that it had been. The sad melody, floating in the summer air, had been more moving in its sheer simplicity than any number of stirring band tunes. She blinked away the tears. "David always loved the bagpipes. He liked to play them himself. Composed for them too."

"Really? I didn't know that."

"He once played his father a piece he had written. The king admitted it wasn't bad. But then he roared, in that way of his. 'BUT IT'S NOT ANY DAMN GOOD EITHER!'"

This seemed to switch a light on inside Charles. He looked at her eagerly. "So Uncle David didn't get on terribly well with his father?"

"You could say that."

"Why?"

"David once asked him, funnily enough. His father said this." Wallis summoned George V's costive spirit again. "MY FATHER WAS FRIGHTENED OF HIS FATHER AND HIS FATHER WAS FRIGHTENED OF HIS MOTHER. SO I'M GOING TO MAKE DAMN SURE MY CHILDREN ARE FRIGHTENED OF ME!"

"Goodness. That probably explains quite a lot."

"I'd say it explains everything. Once David got over his fear, he wanted to be as unlike his father as possible. He dressed in the exact opposite way. He chose friends his parents didn't approve of. And his attitude to the throne was different too."

"Really? How?"

"Well, his father was considered an excellent king. A hard act to follow if you know what I mean."

"I know," Charles sighed, "exactly what you mean."

She had been expecting a chauffeured limousine, so it was a pleasant surprise to find Charles's silver-blue sports car waiting outside.

"It's an Aston Martin," he said proudly. "Like James Bond drives."

She gave him an amused glance. Was Charles believing his own publicity? She knew from the papers that the awkward prince had recently become something of a sex symbol. Girls raced across the beach to kiss him, and he had been linked with a string of titled beauties. The pressure was on to find a wife.

They zoomed out of the gates.

"May I ask your advice about something?" Charles asked awkwardly.

"Certainly. You're not the first Prince of Wales who's confided in me."

He laughed. "And I'm willing to bet it's about the same thing."

"Which is?"

"Marriage," he groaned.

"Ah. Well, now you're asking."

"I only have to look at a girl and she's on the front pages the next day." His knuckles tightened on the steering wheel. "They follow me everywhere, the beasts."

"Well, they held back last time, I guess."

He looked at her, mystified. "What do you mean?"

"In 1936 there was a press blackout. Beaverbrook, Harmsworth, the newspaper barons. They all agreed not to run stories about my relationship with David."

"Lucky you."

"Don't know about that. Might have been better to have it out in the open." She paused. "Anyway, as they missed the story last time they're going to be twice as keen this time."

"So it's all your fault!"

"I guess. But what isn't?"

They grinned at each other. Then his expression darkened again.

"I want to put it off at least until I'm thirty. Marriage, I mean. Then I'll find some suitable aristocratic broodmare to spend the next fifty years with." He sighed heavily.

"And until then? Someone unsuitable and unaristocratic?"

He glanced at her. "How did you guess?"

She raised an ironic eyebrow. "Let me think. Experience, maybe? Not an American divorcée, is she?"

He laughed. "She's called Camilla. Camilla Shand. I met her last summer and I just can't forget her, Aunt Wallis. She's got this wonderful laugh and this great sense of humor, and she loves horses and hunting. You should hear her screaming when you approach a fence and she's behind you. 'Bloody hell, get out of the fucking way!'"

She could hear the joy in his voice. "Her family are wonderful too, all warm and close, not chilly and formal like mine. And she doesn't care about clothes or makeup or shopping." He was speaking faster and faster, his words falling over each other in his enthusiasm. "Her hair is never brushed and her nails . . . well." He glanced at the perfect buffed ovals on the ends of Wallis's fingers. "Put it this way, Aunt Wallis, she's very different to you."

"She sounds pretty similar, actually. As in they don't want you to marry her."

He shook his head. "She's a commoner. With a history."

"Like all the best people."

Lost in his gloom, Charles did not smile. "And now I've got to go to sea for six months. I'm not sure she'll wait for me. There's this other guy sniffing around. Parker Bowles. Major in the Blues and Royals. Had an affair with my sister."

"With Anne?"

"Oh yes. She might look stern, but she likes a roll in the hay."

Wallis blinked. "Well, I never."

"So what do you think I should do?" Charles sounded forlorn. Then he smiled. "I guess I'm the second Prince of Wales to ask you that question."

"As a matter of fact, no. David never asked for my advice. He knew from the start exactly what he meant to do." Her face clouded.

Charles did not notice. "So what do you think I should do?" he repeated.

"Well. Do you want to follow your heart or your head?"

He knitted his dark brows. "Marriage is too important to let my heart rule my head. Whoever I marry is marrying the monarchy. And I have to secure the succession."

"Oh yes. The succession."

He looked at her. "You and Uncle David never had children, did you?"

She sidestepped this with a practiced deftness. "I always say that David wasn't heir-conditioned."

"Ha ha. Very good."

They were on the motorway now. The sun was lowering in the sky. A rich golden light suffused the roadside trees.

"So should I follow my heart?" Charles questioned. "Marry Camilla despite the opposition?"

"You're asking me that? Me of all people?"

"You of all people have been through it. You know what it means. Whether it's worth it."

"That's a very big question."

"So what's the answer?"

She thought. "It's not quite the same thing. David left his throne. You don't want to renounce your position by the sound of it."

"No . . . but." He gave an exasperated sigh. "I want to be Prince of Wales—king eventually—while being married to the person I love."

"Well, that's your answer then." She smiled at him. "But I'd fasten your seat belt. You're in for a bumpy ride."

CHAPTER SIXTEEN

Fort Belvedere
Windsor

They went by train to Windsor. From there they would get a taxi to Fort Belvedere.

Out of the window, Berkshire spread out beneath the sun. Summer was in full swing now, the trees so thick with leaves that no branches could be seen at all. Great green shaggy hedges bordered every golden field.

They had chosen an empty carriage so Wallis could practice her curtseys. It was hot; as ever in British trains, the windows were stuck. She wore a navy linen dress, but Ernest wore a thick suit, his best, and was sweating profusely. His tight shirt rubbed painfully against the boil on his neck; worry about Fort Belvedere had brought on a particularly bad attack of hives.

"Wallis!" he had kept saying. "This weekend is going to be a *disaster!*"

"No it isn't!"

"But how do you know? How can you be so sure?"

"Because, Ernest, I have a plan."

And with that he had to be content, although "content" was hardly the word.

Now, using the etiquette book, he was trying to coach her on greeting royalty, but the train's wobble and lurch made this a challenge. They stood in the aisle between the seats, clinging to the seat tops with both hands. "The trick," said Ernest, "is to put your left leg well back and behind the right one. Or is it the other way around?" He frowned down at the page in his hand, then staggered forward suddenly as the train made a violent swerve. "Oh, Wallis! How I wish this was over."

"It soon will be," she reassured him. "And then we'll have something to remember for the rest of our lives."

After curtsey practice, they read the newspapers. Wallis checked the Court Circular to see if Fort Belvedere was mentioned. It was not; considerable space, however, had been given to the Duchess of York opening a sale of work. Wallis studied the smiling picture and thought, as ever, that she looked like the cat who'd got the cream.

The front-page story was about a riot at Hyde Park. A march of the jobless from the northeast, on their way to Westminster to present their plight to Parliament, had been intercepted by police. They had used violence, and the photographs were disturbing: gaunt and exhausted men and boys cowering before uniformed men with truncheons.

"Look at this," she said to Ernest, leaning over to show him.

He shook his head. "Terrible."

"It is, isn't it? Didn't they have the right to a peaceful protest? Unemployment's nearly two million now."

Nearer the center of the paper there was a report in which a woman said her husband had had only one year's work in the last twelve. Wallis read it out to Ernest. "They and their five children live on a few shillings' dole a week and a diet of bread, margarine and tea. They live in slum conditions; a broken brick floor, stairs with no handrail, a lavatory shared with two other families . . ." She stopped and bit her lip. She had never lived anywhere quite so bad with Alice. But somehow the possibility had always been there.

Ernest rustled his newspaper irritably. "Wallis, I agree with you that it's awful. But what can anyone do about it?"

"Well, someone must be able to. The government, for instance." She frowned as a thought struck her. "Duff Cooper's a member of it, isn't he? I can ask him this weekend."

"You'd better not," Ernest countered sharply. "Remember what Maud said."

"Oh yes." Wallis squinted her large eyes to resemble her sister-in-law's small ones and bunched her wide mouth in a prissy manner. "There must be *no* mention of politics and controversial matters before royalty!"

It was a really quite excellent imitation of Maud's pompous, affected tones. Ernest managed a faint smile, despite himself.

She thought over the phrase again. "But why *wouldn't* politics be discussed before royalty? The Prince of Wales will be king one day."

"*He* won't be interested in politics. All he cares about is hunting and dancing. And womanizing."

"Oh, Ernest. There might be more to him than that."

"I doubt it. There might actually be less."

She reached over and patted his knees in their thick trousers. "Cheer up. Read out something from your guidebook."

Typically, he had bought one for Windsor Castle and the adjoining Great Park in which Fort Belvedere was set. The park was mostly wild, he now explained, with open land, streams, meadows and lakes. It had been like this from ancient times, when it had been a royal hunting forest. There were huge old trees, one supposedly the oak of the satyr Herne the Hunter.

"Wait, Ernest. Herne the *what*?"

"The Hunter." Ernest consulted his book again. "A terrifying antlered specter," he went on, "rattling with chains and streaming with blue light. It is reputed to haunt the park's shaggiest depths and spirit away the unwary."

Wallis laughed. "I hope he doesn't come to Fort Belvedere!"

Ernest sighed. "He probably will. He's probably there already."

"Don't be so miserable! You never know, you might enjoy yourself."

Ernest rested his guide on his knee and looked at her. "Wallis, so far as I'm concerned, the sooner this weekend is over, the better."

Their taxi bowled through Windsor, a charming town full of quaint old buildings. Through a pair of elegant gates and suddenly they were in a large and manicured park with the great gray range of the castle receding behind them. Wallis stared, wide-eyed, out the rear window. The place was enormous.

Gradually, the park became wilder. At either side of the road, rough grass spread like shaggy carpet beneath trunks twisted into fantastical shapes. There were shades and thickets. It felt different from the sunny expanses farther back. Wallis remembered the ghostly hunter. Amid the dells and dense, dark bushes, Herne seemed much more real. She was struck by the thought that even in protected royal fiefdoms, dangerous forces were at work.

The thought dispersed as they reached a large and beautiful lake.

"Virginia Water," supplied Ernest, from his book.

A warm blue sky shimmered above the trees. Wallis noticed a cluster of towers that she thought at first must be Windsor Castle before realizing that distance and direction ruled that out. These towers were much smaller, and sand-colored, not gray. Nor were they massive defensive barbicans but piled atop one another in a charming, haphazard sort of way.

Was this Fort Belvedere? It would be an appropriate house for the glamorous heir to the throne. There was a magical fairy quality to it. The tower top with its fluttering flag made her think of Camelot.

Ernest was squinting at the flag. "It's not the Prince of Wales's feathers or the royal standard."

Wallis wouldn't have recognized either of those anyway. Or this flag, a triangle of yellow balls against a black background. But she knew he was saying that the castle wasn't Fort Belvedere. She felt disappointed.

Ernest, meanwhile, was consulting his book. "The Duchy of Cornwall," he said suddenly. "Sable, fifteen bezants in a pile. Of course."

"What on earth are you talking about?"

"That flag. It's one of his titles. Duke of Cornwall. The prince."

"You mean . . ." She felt excitement rising again. "You mean that *is* Fort Belvedere?"

"Yes," said Ernest heavily. "I mean that is Fort Belvedere."

The towers disappeared as the taxi skirted the lake. They drove through a little gateway and up a gravel driveway winding in graceful turns through a shady wood.

Ernest read from his guidebook. "Fort Belvedere was begun in the eighteenth century by William, Duke of Cumberland, third son of George the Second . . ."

Around another bend and the building slid once more into view, much larger and closer now but still with its beguiling toylike quality. Wallis clutched Ernest's arm. "Oh!" It was love at first sight. No structure she had ever seen had such a powerful and instant effect on her.

The little castle was of pale golden stone. It glowed in its setting of rich green shrubbery, white-framed windows winking merrily in the sunshine. Whoever had designed it clearly wanted it to look fun, with as many levels, battlements, arrow slits and towers as possible. It was straight out of a fairy tale, like something a child might draw, and filled Wallis with a corresponding childish delight.

"Some eighty years later," continued Ernest, beside her, "the famous architect Wyatville, whom George the Fourth had commissioned to restore Windsor Castle, was directed by him to enlarge the structure. . . ."

"We're 'ere," interrupted the driver as the taxi came to a crunching halt in the gravel. She could hardly bear to get out of the car, because that would be the first step toward it all being over.

Hesitantly, she approached the front door. This was in the studded medieval style, but small and painted white. It was half-open, but because of the bright day outside, nothing could be seen but darkness. No one seemed to be around.

Behind her, Ernest was paying the driver. Doors slammed; an engine started; there was the sound of receding tires.

Wallis had walked to the side of the building. An archway framed wide views over sunny countryside. In front was a large lawned parterre that spread out like an open green fan, edged with a low wall castellated with apertures in which about twenty tiny cannon, mounted on tiny gun carriages, pointed over the green fields into the blue distance.

Toy cannon for a toy fort, she thought, clasping her hands in joy.

Ernest came up behind her. "There's no one here," he said anxiously. "We're too early. When did Thelma tell you to come?"

She felt surprised that anyone could feel anxious in a place like this. "Ernest, relax. You know what Thelma's like. She'll turn up eventually. And it's a *gift* to be here by ourselves! We can look around this wonderful garden!"

She was longing to explore it. Sunlight glittered on the laurel bushes. There were bright herbaceous borders huge with blossom, and paths that led in interesting directions.

"You look," Ernest said. "I'll wait by the front door with the bags."

She wondered who he thought might be interested in their battered suitcases. On the other hand, hers did contain the precious Chanel dress. Leaving him in charge, she set off toward the cannon. And there was another surprise. Directly below the battlements was a big blue swimming pool whose waters sparkled invitingly. It was set into a wide paved terrace on which groups of outdoor furniture suggested sunny gatherings, or gay parties under the stars. All was quiet. The air was hot and scented. The peace was absolute, that thick and settled silence of the perfect summer afternoon.

Quite suddenly, she glanced behind her. A movement? She expected to see Ernest, but there was no one there. The terrace lay green and empty under the sun but she had the impression of someone watching from somewhere. She shook herself. This fanciful place was giving her fancies of her own.

A flight of graceful half-moon steps led from the battlements to the swimming pool terrace. There were rocks to the side in whose crannies small flowers nestled. She bent to examine them, admiring the attention to detail of whoever had planted them. A bee droned by. Birds twittered.

And then, suddenly, her heart was thudding again. She could feel, once more, that watching gaze. But, as before, she could see nothing. A ghost? She thought of Herne the Hunter and shuddered. But he was a creature of the night woods, not the bright daytime garden.

She went down to the terrace. Fresh vistas presented themselves. In one direction was a tennis court and in the other a walk lined with magnificent cedars. White rhododendron and pink azaleas had been planted beneath them. Wallis wandered along it, the fruity, sweet scent of the flowers nudging at her nostrils.

At the end of the walk she saw a wheelbarrow filled with weeds. She realized with relief that there was a gardener nearby; it must have been him she had glimpsed, whose presence she had sensed.

There was a snapping of twigs behind her. She turned to see someone emerging from the bushes with a rake. He was small and slender with a grubby shirt tucked into worn flannel trousers. He had on canvas shoes and a straw hat pulled low over his eyes.

"Can I help you?" he asked politely. He spoke in that London twang she had once found so difficult to understand.

"Oh," she said, flustered. "Do excuse me. I've been asked for the weekend. I thought I'd look round the garden."

"Like it?"

"Oh yes," she said, and was about to elaborate when a movement in the corner of her eye distracted her. But it was no legendary demon; rather, Ernest hurrying up the cedar avenue. "Wallis! I've been looking for you all over!"

"My husband," Wallis explained awkwardly to the gardener. "Well, you've found me." She smiled as, panting, Ernest reached her side.

The sweat stood out on his brow, and he looked intensely uncomfortable in his thick suit. He fished out a handkerchief and mopped his neck, wincing as his fingers touched the boil. "There's no one around," he said to Wallis. "Let's just go back to London."

She folded her arms. "We can't! Thelma might turn up with the prince at any moment. It would look so rude."

"Well, it's rude of them not to be here to meet us," huffed Ernest.

"I quite agree," said a voice from behind. It was light, with a faint Cockney accent. They both turned to the gardener in surprise.

He removed his hat and all was revealed. That famous dazzling grin. That shining blond hair. It could be nobody else. "I offer my sincere apologies. I didn't realize Lady Furness wasn't there when you arrived."

Ernest gasped. Amazement flashed through Wallis. She had expected a buildup to this moment; time to anticipate meeting the Most Famous Man in the World. It would be like an explosion, the blare of trumpets, an electric shock, perhaps all three.

"You must think me terribly rude," he went on in his odd London twang.

Now that she knew it was him, she could see how exactly like his pictures he looked. The tip-tilted nose; golden hair; large, glassy blue eyes. What was unexpected was his height. She had imagined him tall, but he was the same size as she was.

"No, no, Your Royal Highness, our fault entirely, Your Royal Highness . . . we were early, Your Royal Highness . . ." Both Wallis and Ernest almost literally fell over themselves in their bows, curtseys and haste to assume blame.

"You're very kind. And it's just 'sir,' now, by the way. You've done the Royal Highness bit. But as we haven't met before, could you bear to introduce yourselves?"

She sensed Ernest beside her, swallowing and working himself up.

"Mr. and Mrs. Ernest Simpson," she said, taking charge.

"Simpson," said the prince, frowning. "I should know you, of course. But Thelma invites so many people . . ." His voice trailed away. Wallis felt sure he was about to add *and none of them any good*. Her heart sank. This was the worst of starts.

The Duke of Windsor's Funeral
Windsor Castle
June 1972

Windsor crouched on its hill, a crenelated black heap, with glow-ering clouds gathered about it. As Wallis and Charles got closer, the clouds parted like theater curtains to reveal a magnificent sunset. David, Wallis was sure of it.

Don't be afraid, he was telling her. I'm with you.

Thick bands of hot gold like the color of his hair were overlaid with coral like the freshness of his cheeks. Streaks of clear pale blue recalled his eyes. The display was glorious, exuberant.

The grass looked strange. The banks below the castle walls were not the expected green but whitish, dotted with color. As they neared she saw that these were flowers. Bunches of them. A sea of blooms, spreading in all directions.

"Crikey," said Charles. "There must be several entire flower shops here."

She was moved. She wanted to get out and pay tribute to the tributes. She turned to Charles. "Can we stop?"

In the warm air, the flowers smelled heavy and sweet. She stooped over a few, reading messages handwritten on labels and tied with string.

There were modest nosegays "From a Devoted Subject" and cheerful sprays "In Respectful Memory." Small untidy bunches, grabbed from gardens either their own or someone else's, were "For Our Beloved King."

"The white ensign," said Charles, pausing by a grand arrange-ment of red and white carnations and blue cornflowers.

"What's that?"

"The navy flag." Charles was reading the dedication. "From the surviving officers of the first Exmouth term, Royal Naval Col-lege, Osborne, 1907."

He straightened, looking awed. "Gosh. Uncle David's school friends from sixty-five years ago! I can't imagine anyone at my school doing that for me."

"You had a bad time at school?" She tried to remember. "In Scotland, wasn't it?"

He nodded ruefully. "It was like a prison camp with tartan."

People had left other tributes. There was a book, pushed in among the blossoms. *Edward VIII: Our King*. An illustrated biography from 1936, presumably. And here was a newspaper front cover. ABDICATION! KING EDWARD VIII WILL BROADCAST TONIGHT! For a nauseating, dizzying moment she felt herself back there, in the center of that chaotic time, before realizing it was a reprint, sold by some souvenir hawker.

"Second Coming type," she murmured.

"What did you say, Aunt Wallis?"

She gestured at the newspaper. "That very big fat typeface. Second Coming type, only for the very biggest announcements."

They walked up the side of the chapel, past the rippling carving, the stone beasts holding shields. A small group of clergy waited on the porch. Charles went to talk to them. He returned to her side looking awed. "Sixty thousand," he said.

"Sixty thousand what?"

"Came to see Uncle David. Two thousand an hour. At one time the queue was a mile and a half long."

Joy shot through her. David would have been so pleased. But then, glancing up out of the doorway at the fading gold and coral, she wondered if he knew anyway.

Inside the chapel, the last of the sunlight slanted through the stained-glass windows and threw many-colored light on slender pillars and soaring arches. High above, the fan-vaulted ceiling spread like carved-stone lace.

The Garter stalls were in the middle of the nave, the dark oak carved with exquisite delicacy. She remembered them richly decorated with colored silk banners and heraldic devices. But the banners had gone; the place was stripped bare. The focus was on one thing only.

She had imagined her first sight of it, rehearsed it in her mind, imagined being dignified and calm. But something elemental seized her when she saw the coffin. The impact was shattering, exploding like a bomb in her brain, screaming and blaring and juddering painfully to the ends of her fingers. She felt as if something had been ripped away. She clung to Charles, gasping with shock.

It was raised on a catafalque the exact blue of his eyes. A brilliantly colored flag covered it. Around it, pillar candles taller than she was flickered in the dying light. Four soldiers kept vigil, scarlet uniforms dim in the gathering darkness, so still they seemed not to be breathing.

A single wreath of lilies glowed faintly on top and she stepped closer to see who they were from. WALLIS, said the label. She had no memory of sending them. But suddenly, skewering like a rod, came a sense of loss so powerful she wanted to scream. The urge to drop to the floor and beat her fists against the stone was almost overwhelming.

Gradually, she regained control. She stood awhile at each corner, feeling for him in her mind. He was not there. She could not find him. He was somewhere far away. Outside, perhaps, amid the gold and coral stripes of the evening.

She looked at Charles, standing by awkwardly, and said the first thing that came into her head. "He gave up so much for so little." She gestured at herself, her thin little body.

Grace would have warmly assured her that he was glad to. But Charles could only look back helplessly. She turned toward the coffin and rested her forehead against the flag that covered it. "David was my entire life," she whispered, as if to herself. "I can't begin to think what I am going to do without him."

CHAPTER SEVENTEEN

Fort Belvedere
Windsor

The prince was showing them around the gardens. He walked ahead, turning frequently to explain something or show them some interesting feature. The early awkwardness had evaporated in the blaze of his efforts to please. Nothing seemed too much trouble. It was as if the privilege were his, not theirs.

The powerful sun, the unbelievable circumstances, the immense surprise, all combined to give the impression of a dream. The prince in particular cut an otherworldly figure; the way he seemed to dance ahead, his slight, boyish form against the shimmering green, his tousled hair glinting in the sun. He was like some sort of sprite. Peter Pan or Puck, something from another realm.

Wallis wasn't sure how old he was; as the old king's senior son he must be middle-aged. But there was a lightness about him that belied this; he seemed ageless, eternally young. She had noticed that his face seemed unlined; despite being hatless, he did not frown in the sun. With his battered canvas shoes skipping lightly over the turf, he couldn't have looked more different from her husband clumping over the grass in his city footwear, the red boil painfully evident against the fleshy paleness of his face and neck.

The prince had cut acres of laurel with his own hands, he told them. He had cut paths through the woods. He had hacked under-growth, moved shrubs, pruned trees.

"I'm like my father, happiest in the country," he volunteered. "I feel caged in the city. When chance led me to Fort Belvedere, I knew instantly it was the place I was looking for. But it's not a beautiful house, as houses in Britain go."

"Oh, but sir, it *is* a beautiful house," Wallis exclaimed. "I've never seen anything like it. I thought, the moment I saw it, that it's some-where where . . ." She stopped, realizing she was gushing.

"Where what?"

"Where you can just escape from the rest of the world."

He looked at her. He had an odd, darting glance, a flash of bright blue like a glimpse of a kingfisher on a riverbank. "That's exactly right," he said. "It's just that, an escape. I love it as I love no other material thing."

She was amazed how easily he spoke of his personal feelings.

"Wyatville's tower makes a handsome addition," Ernest remarked. "And the flag is the Duchy of Cornwall, I see."

Wallis's toes curled slightly; might the prince think Ernest was pompous? Not at all; he seemed delighted.

"Absolutely! I fly it to show that this is not a royal residence but a private home." He darted another of his twinkling glances at Wallis. "I call it my getting-away-from-people house."

She was feeling giddy with excitement, but the sight of their worn cases at the front door brought her down to earth. Her dismay turned to horror when the prince hurried toward them and picked them up.

"Sir! Let me!" objected Ernest.

The blue eyes flashed at them merrily. "Indulge me! I like to play the porter!"

The entrance hall was small and octagonal with yellow leather arm-chairs and a black-and-white marble floor.

It was like being in a little decorated box.

"I'm afraid there's not a room in the house with the normal number of walls," the prince said wryly.

"But I think that's wonderful," said Wallis.

The blue glance flew at her. "Are you interested in interiors, Mrs. Simpson?"

Ernest chuckled. "So long as everything's white."

"Not necessarily," she corrected, smiling to disguise her irritation.

Still carrying their luggage, the prince led them into another, larger box, a six-sided drawing room where the yellow theme continued, long curtains of daffodil velvet at the four tall windows. She noticed how everything seemed designed with amusement in mind. Two large sofas to sit and chat on. Card tables on which to play. A jigsaw, half-completed, on a long table by the window. For the musician, a gleaming black baby grand, and for the fan of popular music, a gramophone. And over every available surface, crowds of photographs in different-size frames. The walls were paneled in natural pine and hung with colorful paintings of Venice. She realized with awe that they were by Canaletto.

An embroidery frame stood by one of the sofas. She paused to examine it; the work was remarkable. "I didn't realize Thelma could sew," she said, surprised.

The prince guffawed. "Thelma? I'll say she can't. I did that."

"Yours, sir?" Wallis's surprise turned to amazement. The stitches were tiny, the workmanship exquisite. "Where did you learn?"

"From my mother at Sandringham when I was growing up. My brothers and sister and I used to sit around her at teatime. While she talked to us she was doing her embroidery, and because we were all interested she taught us."

It sounded idyllic, Wallis thought, imagining the utter security, financial and otherwise, of a royal childhood.

He gave her one of his flashing grins. "Embroidery is my secret vice. And the only one I'm at pains to conceal. You mustn't tell anyone. If it became widely known, it would shock the country."

The next room was the library. Over the fireplace, a gentleman with a huge white wig looked down with an arch expression. There was an enormous ceremonial drum, strung with silk rope and painted with the insignia of some regiment, which seemed to be doing service as a drinks table. There were bookshelves from floor to ceiling, all with beautiful gold-stamped leather bindings. Ernest edged toward them, pulled as if by some invisible magnet.

"You like reading?" asked the prince, watching him examine the spines.

"Very much, sir," Ernest said reverently.

"My mother and I once visited the writer Thomas Hardy, of whom no doubt you've heard."

Wallis had heard of him too. He was one of the authors whose books Ernest had tried and failed to interest her in. "They're so *depressing*," she had told him.

"I admire Hardy greatly," Ernest eagerly assured the prince. "He's one of the greatest authors in the English language."

"How I wish you had been with us, Mr. Simpson," came the dry reply. "You would have saved me the embarrassment of asking him to clear up a dispute I was having with Mama. 'You see, Mr. Hardy,' I said to him, 'my mother insists you wrote a book called *Tess of the d'Urbervilles*. But I am equally certain that you did not.'"

Wallis stared at the floor. She couldn't look at Ernest. His face would be too much. The story made her shake with the effort of not laughing. It was partly surprise; she had not expected the prince to be funny.

"I don't know what you'll think of the bedrooms," he said, leading the way up a pine staircase with banisters in the Gothic style. Snarling monsters bared their teeth on the newel posts.

"For Wales," he said, seeing her looking at them.

"The symbol of Wales is a dragon," put in Ernest.

"But there's no reason why you should know that," countered the prince. "After all, I don't know what the symbol of Maryland is."

"The oriole. It's a small yellow bird."

"That sounds *much* nicer."

"Sir, do let me take the bags. . . ." Ernest offered. But the cases remained clamped firmly to the end of the prince's tanned and sinewy arms.

They were on the small upstairs landing now, a white paneled corridor hung with a collection of paintings and engravings of the Fort. "It's had quite a career," the prince said, showing them the small, lantern-like building it had begun as and the ruin it was before its present magnificent revival. "My father was surprised when I asked him for it." He drew his brows into a frown and raised his voice. "'I SUPPOSE YOU WANT IT FOR THOSE DAMN WEEKENDS OF YOURS!'"

Wallis laughed. The impersonation of George V, king of Great Britain and Northern Ireland, Emperor of India and the Dominions Beyond the Seas, was as unexpected as it was entertaining.

The prince had turned his back and was opening a white arched door. "This is the Queen's Room."

Wallis had never seen a room so dramatically beautiful. One entire wall, floor to ceiling, was taken up by an enormous arched Gothic window with cathedral-like stone tracery. The light streamed in between swagged red velvet curtains. Before it was a dressing table topped with a thick and ornate silver mirror. It was like a stage set, she thought.

There was a newly installed bathroom. "The devil of a job to get them in these thick walls," he said, pointing out the bath, shower and built-in cupboards. "But I've made sure every bedroom here has one. I like my guests to be comfortable."

"Forgive me for asking." Wallis was no longer able to contain her curiosity and admiration. "But which designer did you use for the Fort? They're clearly immensely talented."

The prince beamed with delight. "You're looking at him!"

More bedrooms followed, each named for a particular color—pink, blue, yellow. "I love color," the prince announced. "I like to mix it up. Stripes with florals, spots with zigzags. I call it chromatic abandon!" He laughed, and she laughed too.

Every bedroom was different, its own little world. The Yellow Room had an antique grotesque panel above the mirror, and flamboyant candelabra on the mantelpiece. In the Pink Room, above a large gold-framed bed in the Marie Antoinette manner, pink toile de Jouy fabric soared to a pinnacle under a golden crown. A pink-fleshed boy god danced in a frame over the fireplace.

"I adore Pan," said the prince. "God of the wild, of shepherds and woods."

There was more than a suggestion of Pan about the prince, Wallis thought. Or Peter Pan, with his ageless charm. The boy who never grew up.

"This is my brother George's room." A door opened onto a riotous wallpaper of bright toucans. He pretended to wince. "All those dreadful birds."

The Blue Room's four-poster had ostrich plumes rising from each corner and was clearly extremely venerable. The canopy curtains and bedcovers, however, were ice-blue chintz and crisply new. There was an air of calmness, light and luxury.

"What a lovely room," Wallis said.

The attention to detail was extraordinary. Every comfort had been thought of, every need anticipated. The small Chippendale desk in the window bay was supplied with writing paper and envelopes. There was a pretty flask of water and tumbler on each side of the bed and a bottle of expensive scented oil by the large bathtub.

"Like it? You can take this one, then." Finally, the bags were put down. The prince looked from one to the other, smiling. "Now, this being your first visit to the Fort, let me tell you about the rules."

Wallis braced herself to memorize a blizzard of timings for breakfast, lunch, dinner. Ernest wore a rictus grin of apprehension.

"There are none." The darting blue eyes were sparkling as he spoke. "Stay up as late as you want. Get up when you want. Do whatever you like."

CHAPTER EIGHTEEN

"What do you think of him?" Ernest asked as they unpacked.

"Hard to say," Wallis replied truthfully. It would indeed be difficult to tell her husband that their host was the handsomest, most charismatic and amusing person she had ever met. That he seemed to her more like a god than a human being. Which was appropriate, as Fort Belvedere was a paradise. She was completely dazzled by both of them. "What do you think?" she asked, turning Ernest's question back on him.

"Well, he's a surprise. I thought he'd be lounging about drinking cocktails and making sophisticated quips. I imagined that awful sort of Englishman who looks you up and down and finds your place in the pecking order with one piercing question. But he couldn't have been less like that. Showing us around his garden and then carrying our bags to our room."

She shot him a teasing look. "Which he's designed himself. Really, who would have thought it? When did he find the time between all that carousing and falling off horses?"

"I was wrong. I admit it. That sewing as well." He frowned, thoughtful suddenly. "You don't think he's . . . ?"

She guessed what he meant. According to Cecil, who ought to know, half of high society was homosexual. Wallis had a completely open mind on the subject. If her first marriage had taught her anything, it was that a supposedly conventional relationship could hide violence and cruelty. But something told her that this was not the case with the prince.

"I don't think so."

"No, he can't be. He's with Thelma."

Dear unsuspecting Ernest, she thought. He had no idea that women existed who covered for homosexual men by feigning to be their wives or girlfriends. But Thelma could not possibly be a beard. If her job was to conceal the prince's true nature, why ask for sex tips, as she had in the Ritz?

"He obviously doesn't get on very well with his father," Ernest went on, "to judge by that impression of him."

"Wasn't that just a joke?"

"If you say so." He finished hanging his shirts. "But I thought he sounded like he meant it."

Wallis examined the little polished desk. The small sheets of cream paper were printed in red with "Fort Belvedere, Sunningdale, Berkshire." The matching envelopes had paper linings. There was also a pot of ink, a pen, a blotter.

It was too much to resist. When would she have the chance again? She took a sheet and began to write to Aunt Bessie.

Dearest Aunt,
   As you will see from the address above, the most unbelievable, unexpected thing has happened.

She sketched out the afternoon's events, reliving each one as she described it.

Love from Wallis in Wonderland, she signed it, and sealed the envelope.

As Ernest rested, she ran a bath. Her husband, she noticed, had put his worn shaving kit on the shelf above the basin. It struck an odd note amid all the expensive shining newness.

As a seemingly inexhaustible supply of hot water thundered from the silver taps, she considered her naked body in the large mirror next to the tub, which itself reflected the mirrors on the other walls. A line of receding naked Wallises stretched away into infinity. It looked like a scene from a Busby Berkeley musical, albeit a rather risqué one.

She looked like a boy, she thought. Her slim, straight limbs. Tiny breasts with a jam dab of nipple. She'd never had what might be called a figure. Nothing further from the voluptuous Thelma could be imagined. As she had somewhat brutally pointed out at the Ritz: *You're much too old, and while you have a certain style you're not exactly beautiful.*

Oh well. She stepped into the bath. Sinking into the perfumed depths, Wallis closed her eyes. She could get used to this level of luxury. But as that wouldn't be possible, she'd make the most of it while it lasted.

She dressed carefully for dinner. The results were more than satisfactory, as the dressing-table mirror confirmed. Her gleaming black hair was arranged in perfect waves, each lash was curled and mascara-coated, and her face was powdered to a pearly sheen. Her bright-red lipstick brought out the deep blue of her eyes. The black bugle beads shimmered on the Chanel frock, whose low-cut back showed off shapely shoulder blades.

"You'll be the belle of the ball," Ernest said, making up in fervency what he lacked in originality. He edged his finger round his shirt collar to ease the pressure on his boil. "I'm so proud of you. You're the finest wife a man could wish for."

She wasn't, of course, in one fundamental way. But the sincere tribute sent a hard ball rolling up her throat. As did the fact that even now, in his evening clothes, he inspired no desire whatsoever.

They were the first in the drawing room for drinks. They stood awkwardly, uncertain what to do. Then Thelma exploded into the room.

"Wallis!" She was crammed into a clinging pale green dress and had a hunted look. "And Arnie! Thank God you're here! I'm having the worst time ever!"

If her rudeness in failing to welcome them had crossed her mind, it clearly hadn't stayed long.

Wallis kissed her cheek, which was flushed and hot beneath the powder. "What's the matter?"

"That *bloody* Diana Cooper!"

Diana Cooper. After the multiple excitements of the Prince of Wales, Wallis had forgotten all about her.

"She's so patronizing," Thelma complained. "And she *hates* me!" As voices could be heard off the hall, her eyes flashed with panic. "Oh God, they're coming! Wallis, you have to help me!"

A tall woman in an elegant pink column dress entered with a short broad man in tweeds. Her blank expression did not change when she saw Thelma. Wallis felt herself seized and pushed forward. "Duff, Diana, may I present Wallis and Arnold Simpson." Thelma sounded panic-stricken. "Wallis, Arnold, may I present Lady Diana and the Honorable Duff Cooper."

Wallis watched Duff Cooper look Ernest up and down with the dreaded cool, assessing gaze. "And what do you do, Arnold?"

Wallis was proud of the cool way Ernest responded. She knew he was nervous, but he gave no sign.

"It's Ernest, actually. And I'm a shipping agent. How about you, um, *Duff*?"

"I'm the financial secretary to the War Office."

Ernest nodded. "Right."

Wallis extended her hand to Lady Diana, feeling a little jump inside as she did. She smiled excitedly as she shook hands, looking with thrilled interest at the faultless features, the stunning attack of the coloring and the sky-blue eyes with their wistful look of inquiry.

It was hard, even so, not to conclude that the look in the sky-blue eyes was less inquiry than complete lack of interest. Lady Diana's hand lay in hers like a limp white fish, and the smile was not re-turned.

The introductions complete, everyone looked expectantly at Thelma, whose expression was that of a rabbit caught in the headlights. "Let's put on some records!" she exclaimed, and began rummaging in the case below the gramophone. As "Tea for Two" started up, she grabbed Ernest and started fox-trotting him around the room.

Duff was at the back of the room, rattling the decanters. "There's hardly anything here," he said irritably.

"That's the servants," announced Thelma as she danced past, dragging a bewildered-looking Ernest. "They help themselves. Their perk, apparently."

"Well, it shouldn't be," said Diana in her deep, rich voice. "You need to put a stop to that, Thelma. Freda wouldn't have put up with it for one second."

Thelma caught Wallis's eye with a *See what I mean?* expression. As she fox-trotted away, she looked despairing.

At the decanters, Duff was despairing too. "Some whisky, a lemon, some sugar and soda," he grumbled. "Though what I'm supposed to do with that, I can't imagine. There's not even any ice."

"Sounds like an old-fashioned to me," said Wallis brightly. "We'll just have to do without ice. Want me to make some?"

"Yes! Wallis is marvelous at cocktails, Duff. Stand aside!"

Duff stood aside, and Wallis set to work, admiring the beautiful glasses and the silver jugs, spoons and shakers. All were engraved with the same symbol: three curling feathers rising from a coronet. Were these, she wondered, the Prince of Wales's feathers? Where was he? Should she make him a cocktail too? Was he coming to drinks or not?

She did, but he did not. Thelma scooped up the spare old-fashioned and, after more hectic dancing, which Wallis and the Coopers, the latter rather against their will, were obliged to join in, the party proceeded into the dining room. The small round table had been set with crystal, silver and white linen. Place cards were held in tiny silver holders, again in the shape of the Prince of Wales's feathers. Rich golden evening light poured in through the windows, giving a glow to everything.

Having been left quite literally to hold the fort, Thelma was making a terrible job of entertaining. The unflappable good humor on display during the evening at Bryanston Court seemed to have utterly deserted her. Perhaps her terror of Diana Cooper was to blame, but whatever the reason, she had drunk rather more than was wise and was saying the first thing that came into her head.

"Corker of a boil you've got there, Arnold," she opined cheerily to Ernest. "Have you tried a poultice?"

As Ernest, crimson with embarrassment, muttered that he hadn't but would, Wallis, almost as mortified, stared at the paintings of horses on the paneled walls. They looked like Stubbs to her; she had spent enough time staring at *Whistlejacket* in the National Gallery to know one when she saw one.

She could hear a strange sound, she realized now. A sort of loud droning, like an enormous bee, coming from behind. She turned and almost fell off the chair. In the doorway stood the Prince of Wales. He wore full Highland dress and was playing the bagpipes.

CHAPTER NINETEEN

The noise was very loud, and made louder by the wooden walls. Thelma was wincing, and Diana was blank-faced, but now Wallis was getting used to it she thought it rather moving. The notes had a romantic, plaintive quality, speaking of loneliness and loss. She had never been to Scotland but knew, as everyone did, of the isolated beauty of the mountains, lochs and forests. She could see them in her mind's eye as the notes poured forth. The prince played with passion and with skill, and with his blue eyes full of melancholy. She sensed that it was important to him, and in performing like this he was revealing something precious and private. He was saying something to them all, but what it was, she did not know.

The first course arrived: oysters on a great silver dish. She watched hers being positioned before her by the white gloves of a red-coated footman. Once, a mere few hours prior even, she would have been amazed at the sight. But what was really amazing was how quickly one got used to it.

"They're from my own oyster beds in the Duchy of Cornwall," the prince explained.

They were prepared so the guests only had to tip them down their throats. The oysters were perfect, so fresh and clean it was like eating the sea. Wallis closed her eyes, savoring the taste. She loved oysters; what it must be to own great stretches of the ocean where they grew.

"What do you think of Mussolini, Duff?" Thelma loudly slurped an oyster. "Duke says he's a Renaissance man."

Wallis was startled. They had had express instructions not to talk about politics, and yet here was Thelma doing it. And that she spoke of her husband in front of her lover seemed almost more extraordinary. Truly, British ways were odd, Wallis thought.

Duff seemed surprised too, although not for the same reason, it turned out. "Renaissance man? I didn't think Duke knew what the Renaissance was."

Wallis slid a look at the prince. He looked tired as he fiddled with his oysters, and seemed a different person from the merry guide of earlier and the passionate musician of just now. She guessed he was pained at the turn the conversation had taken.

Thelma, however, seemed oblivious to her breach of protocol. "Duke says Il Duce's a great all-rounder," she reported. "Rolls up his sleeves and helps with the corn harvest as well as electrifying the railways, playing the violin and governing his country."

Duff raised his eyebrows. "I see. And what does Duke think of Hitler?"

The leader of the German National Socialists, Wallis recalled.

"Thinks he's marvelous too."

Duff took a considering sip of wine. "He isn't disturbed by all the street fighting in Germany? What Hitler's doing to the Communists?"

Wallis glanced at the prince again. He was staring at his oyster shells with what seemed to be weary resignation. She wished Thelma and Duff would stop.

But Thelma just took a great slug of wine and went cheerfully on. "Duke says the Communists are the ones behind it. They're picking on the National Socialists."

Duff put down his wineglass. "That isn't true," he said firmly. "In fact, the reverse is the case. Chap I had dinner with the other day was just back from a visit to Germany. He says Hitler is insane and we should all build battleships while we can."

"Duke says Hitler is Germany's business and no one else's," responded Thelma heatedly. "He says we could do with him here to deal with these so-called hunger marchers."

Wallis remembered the newspaper photographs, the police battering the desperate protestors, and felt indignation rise. How disgusting that someone as rich as Duke held such views. She stared angrily at the tablecloth, wishing she dared say something, not trusting herself to meet anyone's eyes.

"I find that all rather a puzzle, I must say." It was Diana who had picked up Thelma's remarks. "When Duff was an MP in Lancashire we visited lots of industrial areas. Everyone seemed quite happy. The factory girls had the most wonderful pink-and-white complexions because the mills were kept humid for the cotton yarn. And their clogs clattered in quite the gayest manner."

Wallis thought of the gaunt and exhausted marchers and the woman feeding five children on bread and tea. She thought of the difficult times in her own childhood, and hot rage flashed through her. How could someone like Diana know what it was to live on so little? The urge to say so burned on the tip of her tongue. But she caught Ernest's warning eye and bit it back.

The footmen reappeared and took away the oyster plates. A fresh plate, gold-rimmed and monogrammed with the Prince of Wales's feathers, was placed before her. A roast of beef appeared, and the footmen began to busy themselves with serving it.

Duff Cooper, next to Wallis, dabbed his mustache with his napkin and looked at her. "What part of the United States are you from, Mrs. Simpson?"

Be proud of your flag and your republic. Wallis mentally squared her shoulders. "Baltimore," she said with a smile.

"Baltimore," Duff repeated. "I must say, I haven't been there."

"Has anyone?" quipped Thelma, and there was laughter.

Wallis flushed. This wasn't going well.

"What should I know about it?" Duff continued.

Out of nowhere the answer slid into her head. "We eat terrapins."

She could see, in the corner of her eye, Ernest staring at her in amazement.

"Eat *terrapins?*"

"They're the local specialty," she explained. "The men who sell them carry them in burlap bags and have a special call, kind of a high-pitched singsong."

"Do it!" The voice was not Duff's. It came from the other end of the table and had a Cockney twang.

Wallis looked at the prince, startled. "Do it?"

"The special call, do it."

Wallis paused. "Is that a royal command, sir?"

"Yes!" He laughed.

"Okay. It was like this . . ." She sang the notes. The prince nodded, then, to her surprise, tried them himself. He had a surprisingly musical voice. Before long, the whole table was singing the song of the turtle men, and the experiment ended in applause and laughter.

Later, back in the Blue Room, Ernest lowered himself onto the club fender before the fireplace. Wallis sat in the ice-blue armchair opposite. The grate was empty, it being a hot night. Across the room, a soft breeze blew in from the open window. The sky was black, and there was a sliver of moon.

"You were such a success," he said admiringly.

"Maybe a little," she admitted modestly. She had not disgraced herself at least. She had been able to sing for their supper, quite literally.

"The prince loved your terrapin story. I'd never heard that before."

"I'd almost forgotten about them myself." But her mother had

been a great terrapin fan, and Wallis was certain that, from somewhere far away, Alice had supplied the anecdote. She was watching
her, cheering her on.

The clock on the mantelpiece chimed eleven silvery notes. "He's
sent us to bed so early," Ernest said, bemused. "He's supposed to be
the bachelor prince who never turns in before dawn."

"I thought," said Wallis, "that we'd already established he's not all
those things he's supposed to be."

"The only rule is that there are no rules."

"'Stay up as late as you want,'" Wallis quoted. "'Get up when you
want.'"

"I think he means more than just the Fort though," Ernest said. "I
think he means there aren't any rules in general."

Wallis tipped her head questioningly to the side. "In what way?"

"I'm not really sure," Ernest confessed. "It's something to do with
everything being the opposite of what you expect."

"But you said that was charming."

"It is," Ernest hastened to assure her. "It's all great fun. Those nursery
card games after dinner. I haven't played Happy Families for years."

"I've never played it before," Wallis said, remembering the feeling
of the prince sitting by her explaining about Master Butcher and Miss
Grocer. His delight at her progress had been gratifying. "Mrs. Simpson, you're a natural!"

Less comforting was the recollection of the poker that came next.
Wallis had won game after game, to the admiration of the Coopers,
who lost them.

"Where did you learn to play so well?" asked Diana.

Ernest, proudly watching from behind his wife's chair, interpo-
lated eagerly. "China," he said.

Wallis's heart hit the floor so hard she could almost hear the
thump.

"Wallis lived there for a while," Ernest blithely went on. "She paid
her way with poker winnings."

"Indeed?" There was a gleam in Diana's pale eyes. "And what way was that?"

"He played the bagpipes with the full rig on." Ernest broke into her thoughts. "Sporran, skean dhu, the lot."

She stared, not entirely sure what he was talking about.

"I bet that kilt was the Balmoral tartan."

"The what?"

"It was gray and red, checked with black. I'm sure that's the kilt the prince consort designed for the royal family to wear in Scotland. No one else is allowed to."

She rolled her eyes. "The things you know, Ernest. What's your point though?"

Ernest was staring contemplatively at the ceiling. "It's hard to put into words. Something about not standing on ceremony and standing on it at the same time. Like when he got out his ukulele and started to play 'The Red Flag.'"

"That was funny," Wallis chuckled. "He knew all the words."

"But isn't it a little crazy?" Ernest shook his head. "Anyone would think he was a socialist."

"Maybe he is."

"In that case there's going to be a whole lot of trouble when he becomes king."

"Why?"

He looked at her. "Wallis, do you know what socialism even is?"

She gave a defensive shrug. "Not really."

"It's the idea that everyone is equal and has the same opportunities."

"So what's wrong with that?"

"Nothing. But the monarchy's kind of the opposite."

Wallis considered this. "But isn't there a middle ground? Where you could be a king with a social conscience?"

Ernest rubbed his eyes. "Well if there is, the prince isn't. He certainly didn't leap to the defense of the hunger marchers."

Wallis sighed. "No. And he didn't even seem to hear when Diana said that ridiculous thing about the mill girls."

"But none of that's a surprise. Someone who owed his position to birth alone can't afford to care about those less fortunate."

He was right, of course, but it was still disappointing. Wallis decided to put it to the back of her mind and get ready for bed.

She emerged from the bathroom in her nightgown to find Ernest in his striped pajamas under the towering canopy with the ostrich plumes. It made for a comic sight. "I feel like I'm in 'The Princess and the Pea,'" he said.

She slipped in beside him. The linen felt cool and delicious, the bedcovers just the right weight. They pecked each other chastely on the cheek, then turned onto their sides, backs facing as usual. Before long, Ernest's gentle snores announced that he was asleep, but Wallis lay awake, the events of the day playing in her mind like an endless loop of film.

She tossed and turned. The soft pillows and fine linen did not help in the least. Beside her, Ernest stirred. Damn it, she had woken him. His hand now made contact and started to caress. She gasped and stiffened, and the hand swiftly withdrew.

"I'm sorry," came Ernest's muffled voice.

"It's all right." Her chest was rising up and down, panic rushing around her body.

"I just thought . . . you know . . ."

She did know. He thought that the novelty of a strange house and the oddness and excitement of royal company might have made some of the barriers come down. But they hadn't. Possibly the reverse had happened. Poor Ernest.

She turned her head in his direction and spoke into the dark. "Forgive me," she said gently, guiltily. "I'm not quite ready."

He emitted the softest of sighs before replying, "I understand, Wallis."

CHAPTER TWENTY

They were awakened by a tap on the door. It was a maid with a breakfast tray. Ernest went to get it. "She says the prince went into the garden an hour ago," he reported above the clinking of china. "I guess that means we'd better get out there too."

Wallis, still snuggled down in the pillows, opened a sleepy eye. "Why? The rule is that there are no rules, remember."

"Maybe," said Ernest, approaching carefully with the tray. "But as I wasn't quite the success you were last night, I feel I ought to show willing. Go out and pull up some dandelions."

She sat against the pillows as he placed the tray across her lap. It was a work of art. Every single item was monogrammed. The silver spoons on the saucers were placed at exactly the same angle. There was marmalade in a silver dish and creamy yellow butter in another. Her eyes widened at the plenty of it. She really was going to miss this.

It was only nine o'clock, but the day outside looked already bluer and hotter than the one before. She watched Ernest button the waistcoat of his stiff suit and shrug on his jacket. "You're going to *melt!*" she exclaimed.

He gave her a resigned smile and ran a finger round his collar. "I'll see you later," he said, and headed out of the door.

Wallis ate her breakfast leisurely and bathed and dressed as slowly as possible. She wanted to savor every minute in the beautiful room, commit every detail to memory so she could get it out and look at it later. Finally ready, she checked herself in the mirror. Her dress was from a market stall, although it did not look it. The material had been good, a dark, heavy linen. She had altered it, changed the buttons to white, added a slim white belt. She packed hers and Ernest's bags, ready for departure after lunch. Her final act, before she went downstairs, was to slip into the top of her bag a single tiny monogrammed silver teaspoon from the breakfast tray. She knew she shouldn't but could not resist. Along with the letter to Aunt Bessie, which she placed on top of her clothes, it would serve as a souvenir of an unforgettable, unrepeatable weekend. Proof that Wallis in Wonderland had actually happened.

She descended to the drawing room, which was empty in the way she was starting to get used to. Before long though, Thelma entered. She held a hand over her eyes, as if shielding them from some glaring light. "I blame *you*, Wallis," she moaned.

"For what?"

"My condition. Those old-fashioneds were lethal."

Wallis forbore to remind Thelma that she had drunk at least a bottle of white wine on top of the cocktails. Which of them had contributed to her hangover was a moot point. Thelma sank onto one of the sofas, narrowly missing knocking over the princely embroidery frame. "And that *wretched* Diana Cooper," she added.

"What's she done now?"

"This dress!" Thelma swept an aggrieved and glittering hand down her plump form. "It's actually by Molyneux. But I just saw her on the landing and she looked at it as if it were something from a market stall! Can you imagine?"

Wallis did not reply.

"She'll say anything to show me up," Thelma complained. "I don't know who she thinks she is. Her father's not a duke at all, just some philandering journalist her mother had an affair with."

Wallis's eyes widened.

"Yes, really. Didn't you know? And that's not all," Thelma added. "Duff's terribly unfaithful too. But Diana forgives him every time. Know what she says about all the other women?"

Wallis shook her head. Thelma struck a comically melodramatic attitude. "They are the flowers! But *I* am the *tree*!"

She was facing the doorway, and Wallis saw her expression became dramatic in quite a different way. "Diana! Duff!"

The Coopers came in. It was not clear how much they had heard. Duff did not look as if he cared. Green-faced, he collapsed into an armchair and closed his eyes.

Diana, meanwhile, looked as if she had spent the night on a bed of roses being watched over by angels. She wore a pale-blue suit the same color as her eyes and a straw hat whose gold matched her smooth, bright hair. Her pink-and-white complexion was as fresh as a milkmaid's. Or the happy mill girls she had referred to at dinner, Wallis waspishly thought.

She nodded at Thelma and smiled at Wallis. "I love your frock. Where did you get it?"

There was nothing else for it. "From a market stall, actually," Wallis admitted. "I altered it myself. Changed the buttons and put a new belt on."

As she had expected, the pale-blue eyes widened in surprise. As she had not expected, Diana smiled in delight. "But I love market stalls! I get all my clothes from there and alter them like you do!" She touched her hat. "I got this just the other day. For a shilling!"

Duff nudged his wife affectionately with a crumpled tweed shoulder. "Diana even made her own wedding dress when she married me," he said proudly.

Diana bestowed on him what seemed a genuinely loving smile before returning her attention to Wallis. "So much better than spending vulgar amounts of money on expensive things that don't suit one! Don't you agree?"

She did not look at Thelma, but there was no doubt at whom the shaft was aimed. Wallis looked down to hide her smile.

Now something passed the window and caught everyone's eye. It was a figure in flannels and a dirty open shirt, blond hair tousled and carrying a billhook. Ernest followed in his wake, wielding an ax and sweating profusely in his heavy suit.

"Everyone outside!" Thelma struggled up from the sofa. "David wants us to help him cut the laurels."

"I thought we could do what we liked." Duff, from the armchair, sounded exasperated. "No rules, that's the rule."

Thelma threw him a look. "It's not exactly a royal command. But put it this way, I've never known anyone to refuse. And the harder you work, the more popular you'll be."

"Popularity," Duff said, "is overrated."

They stumbled outside into the brilliant sunshine. Wallis, who enjoyed heat, was not unduly disturbed by it but felt sorry for Duff, stumbling unsteadily around with his face screwed up, and amused by Thelma, diamonds glittering in the sunshine and high heels sinking into the turf. Only Diana seemed cool and collected under her broad-brimmed market-stall hat. Like Wallis's, her heels were on the low side.

"Come on!" urged the prince. He was standing by the little row of cannon, grinning, a cigarette clamped between his teeth. "It's good to see so many recruits! I have sworn to annihilate the laurel even if it costs me my last guest! Ladies and gentlemen, choose your weapons!" He gestured at a pile of fearsomely sharp-looking garden implements, their blades glinting in the sun. Besides them was a random pile of rubber boots and gloves. The entire contents of the Fort Belvedere gardeners' shed seemed to have been emptied onto the lawn.

Wallis felt Ernest at her side. His face was glistening with sweat and there were mud smears on his cheeks. "He's a man obsessed," he whispered. "He's built an entire rock garden by himself. He's been telling me all about it. There's a dam below Virginia Water, and the water gets pumped up." He shook his head in wonderment.

The prince, fizzing with energy, led them down the cedar walk and into a plantation of birch. After the scorching garden, the woodland was airy, shady and cool. From what their host was saying over his shoulder as he marched gaily ahead, Wallis gathered it had been choked with laurel until recently.

"Like this," the prince laughingly added, as the path they were following ended abruptly in a dense wall of bush.

"You mean," Duff sounded faint, "that we're to cut all that down?"

The prince nodded, beaming. "It's the last bad stretch, I promise."

He parceled out the sections. Wallis was allotted one at the wood's outer edge. As there was no point in getting them ruined, she kicked off her shoes and peeled off her stockings. The feel of the earth beneath her feet took her back to her childhood in Maryland. One of her relatives had had a farm and Wallis and her mother had gone for summers when she was very small. It was one of her few entirely happy memories.

She had chosen a saw, as it seemed smallest and most manageable. While the method was elusive at first, she was soon cutting through laurel twigs like a knife through butter. She had never been much of a gardener, but perhaps that, she now thought, was because she had never had much of a garden.

There was something intensely satisfying about the simplicity of the work, the physicality, the peppery perfume of the laurel leaves mingling with the smell of a distant bonfire. She worked away, looking up from time to time to see Diana pushing a wheelbarrow in the distance. She did it with the same calm competence she seemed to do everything.

Lunch was a delicious buffet, served outside on the terrace beneath a wall of roses in full pink bloom. There was cold roast chicken, a fresh green salad and hot roast potatoes with a hint of truffle. Looking up at the blue sky above the castellations, Wallis wondered if she had ever seen anything lovelier or more perfectly English. Footmen in little red jackets hovered with champagne. She ate slowly, dreading it ending. After this they would have to go home. She must leave Wonderland and return to the real world.

The prince was talking animatedly about a forthcoming trade visit to South America. "I'm the empire salesman!" he joked. She listened as he described his itinerary. "My ostensible purpose is to open a British Trade Delegation at Buenos Aires. But as I am among friends I can reveal my real mission, which is to recapture for British commerce the great South American markets into which the competition of the United States has made deep inroads!"

He flung a smiling blue glance at Wallis as he said this, and she felt breathless to be so singled out.

"You must come back sometime," Thelma said vaguely as Wallis and Ernest climbed into their taxi after lunch.

"We'd love to!" Wallis gasped. She was about to ask when, but Thelma had already turned away.

"Why did you say that?" Ernest groaned in the back of the car. "I don't want to be asked back, once was enough for me!"

She looked at him, his face sore from the sun, his best suit ruined. She could see his point of view, but she could not share it. She longed to go back already, and they weren't even at the bottom of the drive. She had adored the luxury, the glamour, the gossip. That feeling of being right at the heart of things.

But most of all, she felt fascinated by the prince. She had not, as she had imagined, found out the truth about him at all. Unless the truth was that there were many truths. The sides to his personality seemed as numerous and distinct as the Fort Belvedere bedrooms. The national idol and empire salesman was also the jolly joker, the energetic gardener, the interior designer and the passionate musician. But it was more even than that. A sense that beneath the charm, charisma and showmanship something was buried. Something sensitive and shadowy that few people guessed at. Something she had seen, that one time, in the back of the car at St. James's when he had thought himself unobserved.

She turned away and stared out the back window. Blurred by her tears, the enchanted fort shone in the sun, its gold-and-black flag rippling. And then they turned the corner and it was gone.

The Duke of Windsor's Funeral
Buckingham Palace
London
June 1972

A glimmer at the edge of her eyelids. Morning. She shrank from it, tried to burrow backward into the night. It had been a long one; endless hours of darkness with the wind wailing tragically in the chimneys. It had been like listening to her own misery.

He would be buried today and then she would be alone. She had no relatives, only friends. All with their own lives and priorities, even Grace. No one ever again would devote themselves so completely to adoring and protecting her as David had done.

She imagined returning to the empty house in Paris. The bed he would never again sleep in. The suits hanging in his wardrobe. The sharpened pencils on his desk. The golf clubs, the shoes, the smiling photographs in silver frames. That was all that she had left of him.

She buried her face in the pillow. Her heart was as heavy as a stone. She tried to weep but she could only groan. She thought of the day ahead, watching him sink into the earth. How could she possibly survive it?

She would want to howl and rend her garments but would be required to stand and watch without expression. That was the Windsor way. The stiff upper lip showed self-discipline; mastery over feeling. Easy when one had no feelings in the first place.

Elizabeth. The Queen Mother. There was no avoiding her now. Hers would be the second car, after her own, to arrive at St. George's Chapel. Every major participant in the day's drama was being separately conveyed, and in order of precedence. As the least important, she would arrive first, at 11:00 a.m.; Elizabeth at 11:02; Lilibet at 11:03.

Grace had been shocked that even now, at this final stage, there was no question of company or support. That the Windsor women would be divided to the last. It was, she said, so cold.

Was it ever. "Ice-veined bitches" was how David had referred to certain female relatives.

There was a tap at the door. "It's me," came Grace's concerned voice. "Are you okay? Antenucci said you had a bad night."

The doctor had come in once or twice. He had given her something, and after he left she had seemed to see King George and Queen Mary glaring down at her with their cold Hanoverian eyes.

Grace walked to the curtains and tugged them back. The wan June light tiptoed in. "Do you want me to help you get ready?"

Her funeral outfit was by Givenchy, the only one able to make it in time. The impeccably plain coat and dress had been created in just one night, an unparalleled feat in haute couture. Her only decoration would be earrings and a single string of perfect pearls. She would wear a black veil over her face.

"Thank you." Wallis took a breath. "But, Grace, I want to go by myself."

Grace had offered, loyally, to accompany her. Now she looked dismayed. "Go alone to Windsor? But why?"

"Something I decided during the night. A visit I want to make."

"Who to?" Grace almost wailed.

"David."

Grace sat back down on the bed again and took her hand. "You've visited him already," she reminded gently. "At the lying-in-state."

"Yes, but he wasn't there." Wallis pressed her friend's hand, willing her to understand. "But there's somewhere else. If David's anywhere, he'll be there."

She asked for her car to be sent a little earlier. She affected not to hear the murmured objections of the courtier dispatched to deal with her. As he persisted, she pretended not to be in her right mind. "I'm the widow," she declared, staring with intensity. "This is my day."

In the end he had watched stiff-faced as she glided off from the palace entrance, a good ten minutes in front of schedule. Seated in the back, veil-faced and back straight, she felt a tiny spark of triumph.

"Can we go via Fort Belvedere?" she requested, once they were safely out of the palace precincts.

She had never forgotten it, the miniature Georgian castle, that perfect pile of towers and turrets at the end of a curving path. *My getting-away-from-people house*, David had called it. He had renovated every inch, inside and out. They had talked about it often over the years, always longingly. It was where they had expected to live, where he had expected to die.

Since his death, she had visited it every day in her memory. And here she was back in the actual place, entering through the little Gothic doorway, across the hexagonal hall with its black-and-white marble floor and into the elegant drawing room, where they danced to the gramophone. She saw the dining room sparkling with silver and crystal and ringing with merry voices; the paved pool terrace where summer weekend after summer weekend had passed in a haze of cocktails and the latest dances, guests in bathers and sunglasses on cushioned recliners. The laughter when a sudden rainstorm meant grabbing the cushions and rushing inside. They had been like joyous children who had no idea what clouds were gathering, what storm was about to break.

She stirred, confused. She had been asleep, she thought. They were out of the city now and in a park with trees. The car was slowing. They must be near Fort Belvedere. She strained eagerly for the sight that had always lifted her heart, the silver water, that first glimpse of towers over trees, the flag flying from the topmost like a vision of Camelot.

She frowned, puzzled. She could not see it. She asked the driver to do the approach again. Still nothing.

"Trees might have got higher, madame."

Might they? It was nearly forty years after all. Trees kept growing, presumably. As did the bushes over what might once have been a gateway, with an old metal gate, detached from its hasps, lying at an angle.

As she stared, silent, the driver took the initiative. "I don't think there's anyone here, madame. Looks like it's been empty for a while. Shall I drive on, madame?"

"No, I'd like to get out. Just drive around for five minutes, can you?"

The driver got out and opened the door. He looked worried. She guessed what he was thinking. If she arrived late, after both queens, it would be a catastrophic breach of protocol for her. For him, the consequences could be rather worse.

She raised her heavy black veil and looked at him imploringly. "Five minutes. Please. I need to look for something."

For David, in the place that had been most dear to him. Where their story had properly begun. She slipped by the rusting gate and pushed past the rhododendrons. The drive was near invisible. She had last gone down it in 1936, on a dark December night, headlights off to fool the press, rushing to the ferry that would take her to France.

This bend coming up, it was where she got the first glimpse. Where the little fort first showed itself. She rounded it, picking through the debris, the twigs snapping beneath her feet.

The view was partly obscured by bushes but was anyway almost unrecognizable. Mold and damp stained the once-pristine walls. Grass grew in the gravel over which gleaming cars had crunched, the door that had opened to so many glittering figures was padlocked. The once-glowing windows were now broken and showed nothing but empty darkness. From among the weeds on the crenelated roofline, the pole from which the flag had merrily flown poked emptily into the sky. Not a trace remained to suggest a king had once lived here. It was as if it had never happened, so completely had it gone.

Hearing a syncopated strain from long ago, she caught her breath before realizing it was sparrows quarreling. The silence thickened again, and beat in her ears.

Standing there in her veil, she felt like some black-swathed ghost from the past. Some unquiet spirit condemned to haunt the site of ancient revels, the last one left. She glided slowly forward to the most broken of the windows. She could smell damp and rot, and see, in the murky interior, fingers of cold, pale daylight poking disgustedly in the dust. She could see rubbish in empty fireplaces, empty walls where pictures had hung. The furniture had completely gone.

"David?" she called into the gap. "Are you here?" Her voice echoed emptily back at her. From somewhere above she heard the caw of a raven.

Not there. Perhaps he was in the beloved garden he had created from scratch. She walked a few steps round the side of the house, then stopped. It was like being stabbed through the heart. The wreck was total. The once-elegant elm walk, now full of scrubby undergrowth. And was this wasteland of weeds really the rock garden? She thought of him building it, heaving the stones with his shirt off, thin chest straining with the effort, cigarette ever-present at the corner of his laughing mouth.

She would not go farther. Her five minutes would be up and, anyway, it was too easy to visualize the ruined herbaceous borders, the broken tennis courts, the pool that had been green and sparkling but was now cracked and stagnant. No doubt the tiny cannon from the terrace had gone too.

She bent her veiled head in tribute. She thought of Sleeping Beauty's neglected castle, surrounded by a thicket of thorns. But in that story the princess revived with a prince's kiss. In this one, the prince lay dead across the park.

As they drove away, she did not look back.

"Did you find it, madame?" the driver asked. "What you were looking for?"

She shook her head; the heavy veil moved with it. "It wasn't there anymore."

CHAPTER TWENTY-ONE

Bryanston Court
London
1931

For months, not a peep had been heard from Thelma. Summer became autumn and then winter; 1930 turned into 1931. But of the suggested invitation there had been no sign.

Wallis told herself that there were reasons. Initially, of course, the prince was away in South America. She followed his progress in the newspapers. The "Empire Salesman" was receiving an ecstatic reception. In Buenos Aires, hundreds of thousands of Argentines crammed the streets shouting "*¡Viva el príncipe!*" and singing "God Bless the Prince of Wales," the words to which they had laboriously memorized. Clouds of doves were released from high buildings, their wing tips dyed red, white and blue.

On the prince's return, the wait for an invitation resumed. It did not come, but again, there were reasons. The newspapers now revealed that he was spending his weekends hunting. Photographs of him falling off horses had started to appear again. According to the appointments listed in the Court Circular, his weekdays were mostly spent laying foundation stones, visiting factories and attending banquets.

To start with, Ernest was amused to see her reading the royal diary so avidly. "You used to joke about it," he reminded her.

How could he not understand? she wondered. The weekend at the Fort had changed everything. She had been shown round fairyland by the fairy prince himself. Stardust had been flung in her eyes; she would never be the same again. And her impression that she had seen something in him, something sensitive and complex that no one else had, had only grown within her. She longed to go back to see if she was right. In the meantime, she treasured the silver teaspoon with the Prince of Wales's feathers, and Aunt Bessie's amazed letter of reply.

"Do you think the prince will ever ask us back?" Wallis asked anxiously one evening over dinner. It was oysters; she had taken to buying them whenever she could, despite them not being Ernest's favorite. She was also crushingly informed by the fishmonger that Duchy of Cornwall ones were not available in ordinary shops. "Be honest," she added.

Ernest looked troubled. He had been quite happy to resume ordinary life and disappear back to his office. He was unsurprised by the lack of follow-up, having never expected anything else. "I doubt it."

"But Thelma *said*!"

He sighed. "Thelma's not the most reliable. She's probably found some other people to ask. Put it out of your mind, Wallis. You know more people yourself now that Corinne's in town."

Wallis toyed with her oyster. It was true that the arrival of her cousin had opened up a new area of London social life. Corinne's latest husband was a military attaché at the American embassy; the Simpsons had been asked to several parties and dinners as a result.

"Yes," she admitted.

"So what's the problem?" Ernest probed.

The problem was that it was Corinne who had introduced her to Win. She was married at the time to the commander of the Pensacola naval base, and it was with her that Wallis had stayed after the death of Grandmother Warfield. It was into Corinne's house that Win had walked, dashing in his aviator's uniform, and walked out afterward with Wallis's nineteen-year-old heart and her peace of mind for the rest of her life. Corinne brought bad associations with her, but Wallis preferred not to explain all this to Ernest. She would rather he thought her whiny and spoiled, which he increasingly evidently did.

"What's it about?" she asked, finding a novel called *Madame Bovary* by her dinner plate one evening.

"It's a tragedy about a woman whose life is ruined by her exposure to high society."

She was indignant. "Ernest! My life isn't ruined!"

Dismayingly, he let some seconds elapse before replying. "No," he said as Lily entered with yet more plates of oysters. "But I think you need to stop moping now. It's not as if we were regulars in the royal set anyway. And frankly, we can't afford to be."

Wallis heard the love and worry in his voice. She recognized that he was trying to help her. But she could not relinquish her dream. She would not.

"Diana Cooper isn't rich, Ernest," she pointed out. "She buys her dresses from market stalls too."

"Yes, but her father's a duke. You can wear dresses from market stalls if your father's a duke. Just as you can play 'The Red Flag' on the ukulele if you're the Prince of Wales."

Wallis felt the tears prick. His words brought it all back, that magical, wonderful night where she had held the table spellbound and been applauded by the heir to the throne. She dropped her oyster fork and covered her face with her hands.

"Oh, Wallis! It's not so bad! Try to look on the funny side," suggested Ernest.

"There's a funny side?" she said disbelievingly through her fingers.

"Well, there might be! Maybe he didn't like my poem or something."

The air seemed to go still, suddenly. Wallis peeled her hands from her face. "What?"

"My poem." Ernest suddenly didn't seem to be meeting her eyes. "What poem?"

"I wrote one of my little verses. To say thank you." His voice was uncharacteristically high, his smile uneasy.

Wallis's oyster began to churn within her. "You didn't say anything to me about a poem."

"I wrote it in the office, that's why. Sent it straight from there. But I've got a copy. I always make a copy of my poems." He got up and hurriedly left the room.

She stared after him, struggling not to admit the possibility that Ernest had written some of his terrible doggerel and sent it to the Prince of Wales. And yet it was all too believable. Ernest was so sensible in so many ways but suffered in that one respect from an incurable vanity.

He reappeared, holding out a sheet of paper. The poem was typed, and as she took it Wallis imagined what the secretary at Simpson Spence and Young must have made of it.

> Bear with me and do not curse
> This poor attempt at thanks in verse
> Our weekend at Fort Belvedere
> Has left us both with memories dear
> Of what in every sense must be
> Princely hospitality
> Too soon the hours stole away
> And we, who would have had them stay
> Regretful o'er that fleeting slyness
> Do warmly thank Your Royal Highness
> But with your time I make too free
> I have the honor, sir, to be
> (Ere too long my poetic pencil limps on)
> Your obedient servant
> Ernest Simpson

Her head was ringing with one single high, clear note. It was an inward screaming. All was explained, all hope lost.

"Oh, *Ernest*!" She got up, ran out of the room and burst into tears.

He tried to distract her with a trip to Stavanger, where certain business partners were based. But the prospect of Norway left Wallis, in every sense, cold. There was only one place she wanted to go, one person she wanted to see. But there was no chance of that now.

Her appetite dwindled. Beneath her nightgown, her ribs were almost as prominent as the prince's in his gardening shirt. She would run her fingers over them at night and think about him. It felt like a connection, of sorts.

The year marched relentlessly on. The months passed and winter came round again. The cold bit, the daylight disappeared and the rolling, choking fog filled the streets. Then, one morning, the silver telephone by her bed rang and there was Thelma on the end of it.

"Lunch at Claridge's?" repeated Ernest when she excitedly told him that evening.

"Yes! I've never been." Wallis was thrilled at the prospect. The Mayfair hotel was grand and famous. Everyone who was anyone had their parties there.

"It's very expensive," Ernest said dubiously.

"Well, I'm sure Thelma will pay." While Wallis was privately sure of the opposite, she didn't care. She had managed the hole in her budget last time, juggling the bills, begging for credit. She could do so again. Thelma was her only connection to the enchanting world of the Fort.

"But what does she want?"

"I don't know, she didn't say. She might not want anything. It might just be a social occasion."

Ernest snorted. "And pigs might fly. Thelma always wants something."

Wallis felt irritated by his superior manner. "Yes, Ernest. She might want to ask us back to the Fort."

Alarm skittered across Ernest's round face. He looked as if he were about to say that he hoped not but then thought better of it.

Claridge's modern chic was very different to the baroque opulence of the Ritz. It was luxurious and glamorous in a way that made one feel bold and snappy. The foyer's marble checked floor made her instantly think of Fort Belvedere. Floor-to-ceiling silver grilles of modernist design decorated the walls, and there was a lot of monochrome.

The restaurant had cleverly positioned tables allowing proper conversation. As Thelma, inevitably, was late, Wallis chose a table with banquette seating by a marble fireplace containing a large and heartening blaze.

A waiter supplied her with a copy of the London *Evening Standard*. She leafed through it, looking up from time to time. People were coming and going across the foyer, but no Thelma.

She perused the social pages. The craze of the moment was treasure hunts. Bright Young Things in Bentleys and Rolls-Royces sped through nighttime London in search of tableaux that would point them in the right direction. These were elaborate and labor-intensive: a headsman in black at Traitor's Gate; a "corpse" in an alley in Whitechapel. The Hovis bakery had produced special loaves with clues inside, and there had even been an edition of the *Evening Standard* with clues buried in the features.

Wallis felt there was something rather demented and desperate about all this. Going to such effort and expense for a mere evening's amusement seemed a waste of time to her now. Once, she knew, she would have envied these wild scions of the aristocracy, but that was before she discovered that the most glamorous possible way of spending a weekend was to be barefoot in a laurel grove, or singing along to a ukulele.

Oh, where was Thelma? Even by her own impressive standards she was late. Thirty-five minutes, so far. Wallis was deep in a newspaper report about some Cambridge scientists splitting the atom when something suddenly interrupted her. "Darling!"

Thirty-seven minutes late, Thelma was swathed in thick furs. She peered at Wallis from the depths of them. "Goodness, aren't you *skinny*?" She didn't sound particularly happy about it.

Thelma shoved her furs in the direction of a passing waiter, ordered the inevitable champagne and flopped theatrically back against the banquette. "I'm exhausted! Utterly worn out. Far too many parties." She waved a limp and glittering hand. "You know what this time of year is like."

Wallis tried to look as if she did.

"I'll get straight to the point. I want some advice."

So Ernest had been right. Thelma did want something. "Advice about what?" Hopefully not sex again.

"The new thing." Thelma drained her champagne glass. "The rage."

After six months of hearing nothing, this was the reason for meeting? Oh well. So be it. She thought of the social pages. "Treasure hunts, you mean?"

"Hardly." Thelma's tone was derisive. "They're completely old hat. But quite fun, even so. So *fast*. Lois Sturt got fined six guineas and had her license suspended. She was furious with the policeman. Told him she didn't know there were such things as speed limits."

Wallis could hardly believe she would have once thought this impressive.

Thelma watched the waiter refill her glass. "I'll have the chicken pie," she told him. "You should too, Wallis. Duke swears by it."

Duke swore by everything, of course. Wallis smiled at the waiter and nodded.

"Fancy dress," Thelma said.

"They're the new rage. Fancy-dress parties."

Well, they were old hat to her, Wallis thought. Costume parties had been a popular feature of navy base life in the Corinne days. Thelma now explained that she was going to a particularly grand one, held by the young, fashionable and extremely wealthy Bryan and Diana Guinness.

"But what do you think I should go as? You're clever at this sort of thing."

"Am I?"

"According to Cecil. He was the one who said I should dig you out and ask you."

Really, it was just too flattering. The carelessness with which these people picked you up and dropped you. On the other hand, this was no time to feel aggrieved. "How very sweet of him," Wallis said.

Two waiters now arrived with the food. Plates edged in pretty turquoise stripes were placed before them, along with snowy napkins and silver cutlery. An elaborate performance now began whereby the top of the pie, browned and shining, was lifted off and laid on the plate. The steaming interior was then spooned out on top, so the pie was effectively turned upside down. The smell was so delicious it awakened even her dormant appetite.

Thelma dived into the pie. "Bryan and Diana Guinness are awfully clever, so it needs to be something no one else has thought of." She was chewing rapidly. "And believe me, Wallis, everyone's thought of everything."

Wallis racked her brains. The color of the Claridge's plates and Thelma's not-very-clean teeth gave her a sudden idea.

"How about toothpaste? You could go as Odol. A tube dress of blue oilcloth at the bottom and a silver oilcloth yoke and a silver cap. With white Odol letters across the front."

"Yes! Yes! And the dress could be very tight!" In her excitement, Thelma was spraying pie crumbs everywhere. "Brilliant! I knew you'd come up with something. And now you need to think of one for David. I thought an unemployed miner might be amusing. So many of them about at the moment."

Wallis felt her jaw drop.

Thelma was looking at her closely. "No? Possibly it would be unsuitable. Too dirty. So, something else." She pressed a chipped purple fingernail contemplatively into her plump cheek. "A clan member?"

"A kilt, you mean?"

Thelma giggled. "Not *that* sort of clan, silly. I mean the one with the pointy white hood!"

Wallis took a deep breath. "I'm not sure that's a very good idea."

Racial tensions in the American South were clearly beyond her companion's frame of reference. As was any understanding of her lover's personality. The prince was complex and sensitive; did Thelma really think he would find something so crass amusing?

"How about a pint of Guinness," she suggested brightly. "As the party is being thrown by the Guinnesses?"

Thelma clapped her hands. "Perfect! Now I have to go." She flung her fork back on the plate, stood up and started gesturing for the waiter and her coat. Wallis stared, astonished. Was that *it*?

"Where are you going?" She had been pumped for advice, had produced what was needed and now she was to be thrown aside like some old dishrag?

Thelma looked at her as if she had already forgotten who she was. "Shopping for the wretched Fort," she said distantly. "Oh, good, here's my coat."

Wretched? Picturing the enchanted place, that brief, blessed interlude, Wallis wanted to scream. It was all so *wasted* on Thelma. "What sort of shopping?"

Thelma rolled her heavily made-up eyes. "I've got to buy all David's dreadful servants Christmas presents."

"*What?*" It was so unexpected, Wallis almost wanted to laugh. "But why?"

Thelma was discontentedly pulling her gloves on. "As *maîtresse-en-titre*, I'm supposed to run the blasted place, but, as dear Diana so kindly pointed out, I'm not any good at it. Unlike dear Freda, who of course not only found everyone the perfect gift but also tied each present with the most darling little bow into the bargain."

Longing swirled within Wallis. She loved choosing presents.

"But now it's all down to me," Thelma complained. "I have to go to the shops, Harrods, Harvey Nicks, the army and navy, whatever, and buy every single last housemaid a hanky. *And* wrap it up!"

Wallis stared at her. An idea was forming in the back of her mind. It was probably crazy, born as it was of desperation, but it might just do. "I could do it for you!"

Thelma laughed sarcastically, then her small dark eyes widened. "*Would* you?"

"Just give me the numbers, the budget, and I'll take care of it. You're so *terribly* busy, Thelma!"

"Yes," sniffed Thelma, "you're right, I am. Well, if you're sure you don't mind, that really would be a great help. I'm hopeless at buying presents for servants, I never know what people like that would like." She bestowed on Wallis a patronizing smile. "You'd be *so* much better at it."

"My pleasure," Wallis said smoothly. She was about to be left with the bill, as well as her uneaten chicken pie, but she didn't care. "And where would you like them delivered? The Fort?"

Under the table, her fingers were crossed hard. Such was Thelma's tactlessness; if Ernest's poem, or any other reason, had rendered the Simpsons personae non gratae, it would be revealed now.

"Good idea," said Thelma. Several agonizing seconds went by before she added, as an afterthought, "And why don't you and Arnie stay the weekend again, while you're about it?"

CHAPTER TWENTY-TWO

Really, Wallis! Was all this strictly necessary?" Ernest, humping the boxes of presents onto the Windsor-bound train, was sweating with the effort. "I was worn out by my last Fort visit, and this time I'm exhausted before I've got there."

Wallis, positioning another package carefully on the luggage rack, beamed at him. Her heart was light as a butterfly; she was happier than she had been in months. "We're doing our bit for king and country, Ernest! Well, prince and country."

"I hope he's grateful," grumped Ernest, closing the carriage door and collapsing into a window seat.

Wallis knew that if he was, the credit would go to Thelma. Who, predictably, had made minimum effort, initially just sending a list of retainers in her indecipherable, slapdash handwriting. She had been surprised when Wallis rang for more details. "You've got three Osborns here, for example. Are they men or women?"

"What difference does it make? They're all dreadful."

"Well they might be less dreadful if they get a nice present. Look at it as an opportunity," Wallis said briskly.

"I'm not sure Osborn's an opportunity. He's the butler," Thelma said. "He's the one who thinks ice is an abomination."

So that was why there had been none for the old-fashioneds.

"He also hates butler's trays, which is quite strange when you think about it. He was David's batman during the war."

"His what?"

"Kind of a soldier-servant. They were on the Western front together, so Osborn finds flowers and menus a bit of a comedown."

Portrait of HRH in army uniform, in a silver frame, Wallis wrote down for Osborn Senior. Thelma was now describing his wife, the cook, who suffered from a mysterious ailment. "It's 'melegs' this, 'melegs' that," said Thelma. "Everything's 'melegs.'"

"Oh I see. She has varicose veins," said Wallis, finally working it out. "How awful. She might like a nice handbag to cheer her up."

"A *handbag*!" echoed Thelma, in the Lady Bracknell manner. "Isn't that extravagant? She's only the cook."

"But a good cook," Wallis pointed out, "is worth her weight in gold."

"That'd be a lot of gold in Mrs. Osborn's case," Thelma huffed.

Next it was the housemaids, headed by Ms. Moppett. "Not her real name, no," Thelma said. "I call her that because she mops a lot." It was becoming clearer to Wallis why Thelma didn't command the high levels of service she wished to.

Wallis decided on manicure kits for worn hands, and gold brooches and silk stockings for glamour. She knew more than most how a little glamour went a long way. The night watchmen would, she felt sure, appreciate warm cardigans. Socks, handkerchiefs and scarves were bought for everyone else.

Now, each item personally wrapped and ribboned, all sat in boxes on the luggage racks. To collate all the presents had taken two weeks of solid shopping. But shopping was something Wallis loved, and at which she excelled. And it was all worth it because she was now going back, to the little castle at the center of things. And its mysterious, multifaceted master.

It had been hot and shaggy summer the last time they had made this journey, but now it was cold and sparkling winter, the trees bare against a pale sky, the frosty fields lit by a milky sun. But the train rattled and swayed just as it had the first time. She smiled, remembering the curtseying practice. Ernest had brought his guidebooks along, just like last time. Even the newspapers sounded a similar note to before.

As then, hunger marches dominated the front pages. Recently, two thousand men and women had walked to London from the most poverty-stricken areas of Scotland, South Wales and the North of England. Wallis studied photographs of men in caps with sunken cheeks, and raw-faced, hatless youths carried banners reading "Lancashire Youth Contingent, Fighting Against Starvation." The position of the poor had recently been made much worse by the hated "means test" law. This gave local authorities the power to investigate a whole household's income before granting relief to any unemployed person in a family.

The newspaper photographs of policemen riding at the marchers on their horses, or battering them to the ground with long sticks, cast a shadow over Wallis's sunny mood. "Who's protecting these people?" she asked Ernest. "Baldwin and his Conservative government seem to be doing exactly nothing about it."

"Well, this guy Mosley thinks he has the answer," Ernest replied, showing her an item in his newspaper. "But I don't like the sound of him." Wallis now learned that Oswald Mosley, who had previously been both a Labour and a Conservative MP, had recently founded the British Union of Fascists in the belief that the repressive methods of Mussolini in Italy were the answer to the country's woes.

"It's all getting pretty nationalist," Ernest said, adding that the Irish Free State had just elected a president, de Valera, who intended to break from Britain. Meanwhile, in Germany, Chancellor Kurt von Schleicher was losing ground to the increasingly powerful Adolf Hitler and his Nazi Party. "It's not looking good," Ernest concluded.

By contrast, in America, the reforming Franklin Delano Roosevelt had recently won the presidential election on a ticket to unify the country and set it back on its feet. He had polled twenty-five million votes to J. Edgar Hoover's sixteen million. "The country demands bold, persistent experimentation!" Ernest read, quoting the victorious president-elect. "A New Deal for a New World." He looked thoughtful. "It sounds a lot different to the place we left. I wonder if we shouldn't go back there."

Wallis tried not to look as horrified as she felt. "Go back to the States? *Now?*"

They were on the final run into Windsor. The color of the sky had become richer, first a thick gold and then a blaze of coral against which the branches of the trees stood out in silhouette.

"Well, what is there for us here? America's the future. England is the past."

"Well, there's *this*," Wallis said as, right on cue, crouched on its hilltop, black against the sunset and bristling with towers and turrets, Windsor Castle appeared.

Thelma had promised a car to meet them; unexpectedly, it was actually there. Wallis's heart leaped to see the magnificent gleaming Daimler parked outside the station, its silver fittings glinting beneath the streetlamps. The uniformed chauffeur who had met them on the platform settled them in the back and then put the parcels carefully beside him on the front seat. Wallis thought happily of the set of silk handkerchiefs that had been wrapped for him.

The car smelled deliciously of leather and had a low, powerful purr to its engine. It could not have been more different from the rattling taxi stinking of pipe smoke that had conveyed them to the Fort on their first visit. The vehicle glided through the streets of Windsor, then took the turn into the park she remembered from before. A glance through the back window gave the same view of the receding castle, but this time as a black mass with a romantic castellated roofline and pierced with golden illuminated windows. She wondered what was happening in those rooms, whether the king and queen were there. This led to happy musings on the Fort. Who would this weekend's other guests be? Would they be in the Blue Room again?

The Great Park was dark now. Thick, gnarled tree trunks flashed by in rhythmic sequence, briefly blasted by the light of the head-lamps. Looking out into the blackness between them, Wallis found herself suddenly remembering the legend of Herne, the ghostly hunter who rattled his chains and streamed blue light. As the car lights suddenly showed up antlers between the trees, she clutched Ernest and let out a yelp of fear.

"It's just the deer in the park, ma'am," said the chauffeur.

"Of course," Wallis muttered, and felt rather silly.

They were at Virginia Water now, she guessed, as the trees suddenly gave way to a stretch of lake reflecting the very last and highest of the daylight. Her stomach tightened with excitement as they passed a pair of gateposts and began the gentle climb up a curving drive. And there, suddenly, it was, that most romantic of buildings, not lit by the sun as she had last seen it, but bathed in the soft glow of concealed floodlamps. A shadowy, mysterious mass of differing levels with a scatter of yellow-lit windows surmounted by a soaring tower. On its top she could just make out the gently waving flag. She felt a burst of pure pleasure.

"If you wouldn't mind taking the parcels round to the rear, please," she asked politely as the car crunched to a halt.

"Yes, ma'am," said the chauffeur deferentially.

The front portal of the Fort now swung open and two red-coated footmen issued forth. One disappeared with the parcels while the other took their brand-new luggage. Ernest had been less than de-lighted to see his battered old suitcase replaced by a shining one with his initials on. "I prefer the other. It's like a friend," he objected.

"You've got a new friend now, Ernest," was her firm reply. He had a new shaving kit too, she had made sure of that. She, meanwhile, had a new dress. It was not Chanel; that had been a once and only purchase. But she had recently happened on a seamstress who could copy couture convincingly enough to fool almost anyone and who had persuaded Wallis into something close-fitting in a color different from her usual navy and black. With the delightful prospect of the Fort ahead, and remembering the chromatic abandon, Wallis happily surrendered to the long, tight scarlet frock with sheer and sparkling sleeves.

As they followed the footmen across the hallway with its gay yellow chairs and lively checkered floor, she felt the choice had been a good one.

They were put in the Pink Room. Above the fireplace was the painting of Pan, dancing into the woodland followed by his band of acolytes.

As the door closed, and Ernest went over to the bed and lay on it, Wallis stared at him. "What are you doing?"

"Having a rest."

She glanced at the clock, a large elaborate gold one on the mantelshelf. "But it's nearly six. We'll be late for cocktails."

"I'm tired though. And we can do what we like here, remember. The rule at the Fort is that there are no rules."

Wallis took a deep breath. "Ernest, get ready. We're going down for cocktails. I don't want to miss a minute."

Ten minutes later, they were ready. It was Ernest's first view of her new red frock.

"You look incredible, Wallis," he said as she twirled for his inspection in the pink surroundings of the bedroom.

She felt like the center of a flower, the heart of a rose.

"You're always the most stunning woman in any room," Ernest went on. "Much more attractive than Thelma. Honestly, I can't think what the prince sees in her. Makeup applied with a trowel, and a cleavage you can jump down."

Wallis snorted. "I think you've answered your own question, Ernest. Makeup applied with a trowel, and a cleavage you can jump down."

Hearing loud jazz music as they approached, they expected Thelma at the drawing-room record player. They were surprised to find, alone in the room, a tall and strikingly handsome young man with large black eyes and thick black hair.

Wallis recognized him immediately. It was Prince George, younger brother of the Prince of Wales. When she had seen him before, he had been in uniform or in some other official capacity as the third son of the king-emperor. Now he wore a baggy suit of a startlingly bright check and was dancing wildly by himself in the space between the sofas.

"Hallo!" he said when he saw them. He flashed a wide and wolfish grin displaying very large white teeth. She was reminded, momentarily but startlingly, of Win. "David's just taken delivery of a box of new records. I was just giving them a whirl."

"Your Royal Highness," murmured Wallis, sinking into a curtsey and nudging Ernest to make a bow.

"Never mind all that!" exclaimed Prince George. "Come and Charleston! I could do with a partner!"

CHAPTER TWENTY-THREE

Prince George was a dervish. He whirled about the room with furious energy, his great black eyes blazing with a wild excitement. He was a very good dancer. It was as much as Wallis could do to keep up, especially given the restrictions of her tight-fitting dress.

Ernest sat watching in an armchair, his expression reflecting the slightly surreal nature of the proceedings. But Wallis was beginning to feel the strain. When Prince George stopped to change a record, she seized the opportunity for a break. "Sir," she gasped. "Won't the Prince of Wales be coming?"

This elicited a loud shriek of laughter. "No doubt!"

"So oughtn't we to stop?"

"He's with Thelma. They'll be a while yet." Before Wallis could fully take in the implications of this he had dropped the needle on the record and off they went again.

Such was the sound and fury; it was not until the Charleston had concluded that Wallis, laughing and collapsing on a sofa, realized someone else had come into the drawing room.

Two more, in fact. A thin, tired-looking man was standing with a tiny woman. She had a wide creamy face and soft dark hair, but there was a cool force to the violet stare with which she was fixing Wallis.

Wallis shot to her feet immediately. Ernest was already up. He had recognized them too, obviously. After the Prince of Wales and the

king and queen, these were the best-known members of the royal
family. Prince Albert, Duke of York, the king's second son, and the
Duchess of York, his wife.

"Your Royal Highnesses." Wallis swooped into a curtsey for the
second time in half an hour. Rising back up, she caught her reflection
in a mirror and was horrified to see how red her face had become,
how untidy her hair.

The large violet eyes had not softened in the least. They reminded
Wallis of two hard amethysts. "And you are?" The Duchess of York's
voice was high and precise. She wore a dress of unflattering pale green
with a shapeless cut, which, Wallis guessed, was to hide her plump-
ness. The duke's suit was equally understated, a restrained hounds-
tooth check.

"Wallis Simpson, ma'am. And this is my husband, Ernest."

"You're quite a dancer, Mrs. Simpson." The violet eyes were wan-
dering over her dress in a manner suggesting its wearer was the whore
of Babylon.

"Thank you, ma'am." Wallis kept her smile unwavering and re-
called Coco Chanel's advice. *Be proud of your flag and your republic!*
"I was born not too far away from Charleston, in the Blue Ridge
Mountains. So it kind of goes with the territory, I guess."

But the duchess's attention seemed fixed on her brother-in-law,
who was dropping the needle on another record. Another loud burst
of jazz music followed.

The duchess winced and looked meaningfully at the duke. Looking apprehensive, he put a hand to his thin throat, around which his
tie, Wallis noticed, looked almost throttlingly tight. "I s-s-say," he
began, weakly. "C-c-can we put something a little less r-r-raucous on,
George?"

However rule-free the Fort so far, Wallis thought, regulations had
now clearly come into force. Ernest was looking uncomfortable, and
George, having wrenched the needle off the record, had moved to the
back of the room, where he was relieving his feelings by violently

clanking the decanters. It was, Wallis realized, up to her to rescue the situation.

"How are the little princesses, ma'am?" She smiled, hoping to strike the match of conversation into light.

"Well, thank you," the duchess said briefly. The silence resumed.

"Here," said George, thrusting a cut-glass tumbler at Wallis. "Sorry there's no ice. Osborn doesn't believe in it."

"So I understand." But with any luck Osborn would have a change of heart after his Christmas present. She sipped cautiously at the concoction. "What is it?" It tasted like a particularly strong negroni.

George laughed his high-pitched, unhinged laugh. "Everything!" He waved extravagantly at the decanters.

"No thank you," said the duchess firmly as she was offered one. The duke accepted, but under his wife's eye clearly didn't dare drink it. It seemed, even so, to have given him the courage for conversation. "You m-m-must miss central heating, M-M-M-Mrs. Simpson?" he ventured.

She met his exhausted eyes. They were blue like the prince's, but duller and with dark heavy bags beneath. *Miss central heating?* He obviously thought she was fresh off the boat from the United States, where she had enjoyed every last mod con.

"On the contrary." She smiled at him. "I've grown to like your cold English houses."

"R-r-really?" He seemed at a loss for a rejoinder.

The duchess stepped in. "But surely, Mrs. Simpson," she unsmilingly inquired, "you cannot love our dreadful London fog?"

Wallis considered. "I don't love it, exactly. But I've grown to find it interesting. It's almost a living thing, the way it prowls about."

The duchess sniffed. "You sound like Mr. Eliot. He writes poems about fog, I believe. He's American too, I think," she added, as if this settled it.

Ernest sprang into life immediately. "Yes, one of our finest poets," he said eagerly. "Have you read *The Waste Land*?"

"No. He read it to us. Came to the palace. Completely incomprehensible, we thought, but at least it made Lilibet giggle."

"Good evening, good evening!" The Prince of Wales was in their midst, as suddenly as if he had appeared by magic. A cigarette was clamped, as always, in the side of his grinning mouth.

A violent flash of excitement went through Wallis. She felt the energy in the room change immediately. Everything seemed sharper, more vivid. Amid the evening shadows he seemed to blaze like a firework. He was wearing a bright yellow jersey beneath a suit of check so exuberant it made Prince George's look positively muted. His baggy trousers sported the usual enormous turn-ups.

"Bertie! George!" She watched him shake hands genially with his brothers, clapping them both affectionately on the back. Even more than before, he seemed a magnetic force, pulling everything toward him.

She noticed how his sister-in-law, now being kissed on her creamy cheek, seemed to melt on contact. There was obviously affection there. Perhaps something more. The previously cold eyes had a new warm glow, and the chilly tones had become teasing.

"Oh really, David! What *are* you wearing?"

He looked himself up and down, mock-indignant. "Can't a grown man dress as he likes? You sound like Papa!" He pulled his laughing features into a frown and looked sternly around. "IS IT RAINING IN HERE, BOY?"

"Raining, Papa?" The comic falsetto was Prince George, now at the decanters at the rear of the room. "No, Papa."

"THEN WHY TURN UP ONE'S TROUSERS IN SUCH AN ABSURD MANNER EXCEPT TO CROSS PUDDLES! YOU'RE THE WORST-DRESSED MAN IN ENGLAND, BOY!"

Wallis glanced at Ernest. He had been right. The prince really was not overfond of his father. As Prince George brought his brother's cocktail over, he pretended to start at his shoes, fashionable brown-and-white brogues. "YOU'RE IN THE GRENADIERS, ARE YOU NOT?"

"Yes, Papa," said his brother meekly.

"SO WHY," Prince George roared, "ARE YOU WEARING COLDSTREAMER'S SPURS?" Wallis could not help laughing. The prince now swung his blue gaze her way. "Mr. and Mrs. Simpson!" He sounded gratifyingly delighted. "How very good of you to come back!"

"Sir." Wallis channeled her excitement into a deep and graceful curtsey.

"Mrs. Simpson is a friend of Thelma's," the prince announced. "She's an American," he added, as if this were something agreeably exotic.

Bertie nodded. "Y-y-yes. We've just been talking about it, as a m-m-matter of fact."

The prince drew on his cigarette. "I love the States," he said. "When I was in New York I got a ticker tape welcome. It was thrilling beyond description. I rode on the back of a motorcar bowing and waving like an actor who has been summoned by a tremendous curtain call."

Wallis could easily see it, the blond figure moving through canyons of buildings, blurred by blizzards of paper, acclaimed by roaring crowds.

"America *is* wonderful," the prince went on. "So modern and invigorating. I feel at home there in a way I never do in this country."

Wallis was startled. Had the Prince of Wales, heir to the British throne, really just said that he didn't much like England? But perhaps it was a joke. George was laughing, even if Bertie and Elizabeth remained stiff-faced.

The prince smiled at Wallis in a way that made her feel giddy. "I love the way Americans talk. Hot diggity dog. Okey-dokey. You take life so lightly. You seem somehow to have the knack of being young."

"We know how," she agreed happily. "And the older we get chronologically, the greater and more apparent becomes the difference between our ages and our maturity. My mother used to say that emotional maturity in the average American adult arrives at age twenty-nine and lasts for an hour and twenty-seven minutes."

She had meant it as a self-deprecating joke to disarm the Yorks, but it seemed to have misfired. Bertie looked awkward and Elizabeth unsmiling.

The prince looked delighted though. "Is that what they say? Capital! But what I appreciate most about Americans is they are not in the least bit impressed by my title."

"Well, sir. We are a republic, after all."

"But I think," Ernest put in hastily, "that America lost something irreplaceable when it got rid of the British monarchy."

The prince's smile faded. "Oh really," he said. "Is that what you think?"

Thelma burst giggling into the drawing room, babbling excuses and managing several wobbling curtsies. She looked somewhat disheveled and was crammed as usual into a dress several sizes too small for her. Wallis waited to see Elizabeth of York treat her with the same rudeness and disapproval she had experienced herself. Thelma was the prince's married mistress, after all.

But to her surprise, the two women embraced with every appearance of warmth and began a lively discussion about the little princesses. Wallis looked down, puzzled. What on earth was going on here? Why was Thelma acceptable while she herself was not? Was it some impenetrable British behavior thing, or was there something about her that Elizabeth of York really didn't like?

CHAPTER TWENTY-FOUR

As last time, dinner began with a performance on the pipes by the Prince of Wales, again in his full Scottish rig. Wallis stared at the kilt. Was it the Balmoral tartan, as Ernest claimed?

She found his playing more moving even than before. Further proof that beneath the gay and joking exterior was a thoughtful and sensitive person. When the prince sat down, somewhat red-faced, to applause, she was clapping the most enthusiastically. She could feel Elizabeth's sardonic stare but concentrated instead on the bright-blue flash of gratitude.

"I composed that one myself," he said.

"Oh yes, I remember," chortled George, nodding to the footman to refill his glass. "You played it to Father at Balmoral. He was amazed, he didn't know you could play the pipes." He drained his glass in one go and frowned deeply. "'IT'S NOT BAD! BUT IT'S NOT VERY GOOD EITHER!'"

The menu was the same as last time: oysters and beef. Having hit on a winning formula, the prince clearly wasn't inclined to change it, or perhaps this was Thelma's responsibility. Personally, Wallis thought, she might have been tempted to vary it.

The duchess was telling a story about Princess Elizabeth, who, earlier that day, had been confused about an engagement her mother was leaving for. "I was opening a fair for the unemployed and Lilibet thought that sounded great fun," the duchess told the table in her high, decided little voice. "I had to explain that it wasn't really that sort of a fair. It was to raise money for poor people."

Thelma laughed loudly. "Hilarious! The things children say!"

Wallis didn't think it was hilarious at all. She glanced up the table to see what the prince was making of it, but, as last time, he was not paying attention. He seemed to be having a private conversation with his neighbor, his brother Prince George, who seemed already the worse for drink.

"I just cannot imagine what we are to do with our middle-aged unemployed." The duchess sighed. "I fear that a lot of men will be workless all their lives." Shaking her head so her diamonds glittered in the candlelight, she raised her crystal champagne glass to her pink-painted lips.

"No doubt you are right," said the duke. "But what can one d-d-do about it?"

"They will never have jobs unless some women give up theirs," the duchess declared.

Wallis stared at her. Women give up their jobs? They had only just—in any meaningful way—started to enter the labor market.

"Women," the high-pitched voice went on, "can be idle quite happily. They can spend hours trying their hair in new ways or making last year's black coat into this year's jumper."

Deciding that she could not let this pass, Wallis opened her mouth. But Ernest, to her surprise, got there first. "I think," he said, in calm but firm tones, "that the winning of the vote put an end to that. I don't think you'd ever get women to go back to dyeing their hair and their jumpers as a full-time occupation."

The duchess put down her champagne glass.

"Is that what you think, Mr. Simpson? Well, I think it a crime for women to take jobs that men can do as well."

"Yes, like being queen!" shouted Prince George, who was waving his glass at the footman.

The prince finally seemed to stir himself at this. "As a matter of fact," he pointed out mildly, "there have been some excellent queens. Elizabeth and Victoria made better monarchs than most kings."

The duchess smiled at him. "Well, that's hardly relevant now, is it? You're next in line. And then your children."

The prince did not answer, but there was a shout from George. "To the top, man, come on!" he roared at the footman, who jumped with shock. The red wine spilled over the glass rim and ran down George's fingers. It looked like blood, Wallis thought.

Afterward, there was dancing in the drawing room. But it wasn't long before an excitable George had dragooned the company into performing a conga through the Fort. With him at the front and a clearly reluctant Elizabeth bringing up the rear, they danced through all the bedrooms including the prince's own on the ground floor. Gathering every detail she could in the few seconds she was in it, Wallis noted that it seemed simpler than the ones upstairs. A large regimental flag stretched across the wall above the bed, and a thick fur rug was thrown over it. The bathroom contained both a steam bath and a purple lipstick.

The conga route then went through the kitchens, where the staff had hastily sprung to attention, only to be told by George to join the end of the line.

Finally back in the drawing room, he swooped on the box of jazz records. "I say, David!" he yelled, getting one out and inspecting it. "It says on here that they're unbreakable. Shall we put them through their paces and see?"

Without waiting for an answer he hurled the heavy black disk across the drawing room into the wall. It did not smash but, having narrowly missed a Canaletto, thudded to the floor. More records were flung after that. The pretty Yellow Room, so carefully arranged for conviviality, now filled with flying black objects, accompanied by George's shrieks. His large eyes blazed with a manic black fire.

She found a rare common cause with the duchess by crouching behind the sofa to avoid the sharp-edged platters that otherwise threatened to behead them. Elizabeth said nothing, however, just stared at the floor. Around them, the room was loud with George's raucous laughter, Thelma's screeching, Bertie's stammering objections. There was a thud of lamps falling over, a clatter of photographs shooting off tables. It was only when one record knocked over the prince's embroidery frame that a halt was called. But it proved merely temporary as George now demanded they take the records down to the swimming-pool patio, where they could be hurled against the stone walls and smashed with impunity. It was at this point that the Yorks took their leave, Elizabeth's face tight with contempt.

"Party poopers!" George yelled after them as he wove unsteadily toward the swimming-pool terrace with the records in his arms, his elder brother holding his arm to steer. Thelma, in her high heels, a fur hastily thrown over her shoulders, tottered, giggling, in their wake.

Wallis felt someone take her arm. "Come on," said Ernest. "We're going to bed. And first thing tomorrow, we're leaving. I'm too old for all this. Come to think of it, so are they."

When they reached the Pink Room he opened the door and stood aside to let her in. Her heart sank as she entered. The pretty chamber, formerly so tidy and comfortable, looked like a whirlwind had hit it. As the conga had passed through, George had decided it would be fun to throw their clothes about. Silk stockings dangled from open drawers, and other intimate garments were scattered over the bed. There were cocktail glasses on the dressing table, one smeared liberally with Thelma's purple lipstick.

Ernest surveyed it, head shaking. "I can't believe that members of the royal family behave like this. They're rude about the king, violently self-indulgent, completely uncaring about the conditions most subjects live in and snobs into the bargain. It's outrageous. I told you we should never have come back."

Wallis did not reply. It was true that the fairy kingdom had been violated. But she could not agree that they should leave next morning. The evening had been strange and alarming, but her impression of being at the center of things, of edging ever closer to discovering who the prince really was, was stronger than ever. She hoped that, by the next day, Ernest would change his mind.

CHAPTER TWENTY-FIVE

The next morning, Wallis opened the curtains on a landscape of blue and silver. A fall of snow in the night had covered the fan-shaped lawn in brilliant white and painted with diamonds the trees and bushes that edged it. Under a bright early sun, everything danced and sparkled. She was filled with a childish joy and seized with the urge to go outside.

In the great pink bed, Ernest was still asleep and snoring. She decided not to wake him. His threat to leave first thing was undoubtedly real. As they had drifted off to sleep, the shrieks from the pool terrace could still be heard; their room faced that way, after all.

She got dressed quickly. Her eye caught the little desk, on which a letter to Aunt Bessie remained incomplete. She had left space to describe the evening, but the paper would stay blank. Upright, no-nonsense Aunt Bessie was unlikely to be impressed by the events of the night before. After a few lines about the sparkling weather, she scribbled a sign-off of "Wallis in (Winter) Wonderland," pushed it into the envelope and dropped it in her bag.

Next, she took Ernest's big overcoat and slid her arms into it. It was much warmer than her own. It would look strange, but it was early and there would be no one about to see her. She took her gloves and tied a white silk headscarf over her dark hair.

Huddled in the coat, she crept out of the bedroom and down the stairs. Silence reigned. The Fort was in any case almost empty; the Yorks were back in Royal Lodge, their home nearby, and Thelma, of course, would be wrapped up in the fur rug with her prince. The thought gave Wallis a sudden, strange sensation, one that instinct told her to steer well clear of examining.

Downstairs, the servants had not yet begun clearing up. The dining room remained as they'd left it. She stood on the threshold, surveying the wax-encrusted crystal candlesticks, the tipped-over glasses, the red wine soaking into the white linen tablecloth. Its thin, vinegary smell, mixed with that from the overflowing ashtrays, laced the air.

Wallis wondered why Thelma allowed this. Personally, she would have made sure the place was shipshape by now. She could not resist going in to straighten a Canaletto askew on the paneled wall. Gently righting the frame, she looked at the bright, engaging scene. There was sunshine, boats bobbing on bright waves, little dogs. She could almost hear the slap of the water, the chatter of the people, the seagulls whirling above. She bent to pick up a pile of framed photographs on the floor. The king and queen, he frowning, she stern, glared back at her. The glass across the two of them was cracked.

"Not my fault," Wallis said to them as she replaced them on a table. The last thing she did before she left the room was straighten the embroidery frame. She thought of what the prince had said about his mother, how he had learned to sew at her knee. He had a happier relationship with her than with his father, obviously.

She let herself out the front door and felt the freezing air rush in her lungs. She felt like the first person awake in the whole world. No foot had yet trodden on the wide curving lawn. It was all hers to possess.

Turning back to regard the little castle, she smiled with sheer pleasure at the sight of it. Amid the glittering trees, the powder-blue sky stretching above, it had a beguiling innocence. The prince's words came back to her.

I love it as I love no other material thing.

The Fort was his paradise, his dream. She felt it represented something noble and good, even if last night there had been bad spirits abroad. She hoped the good would triumph, but the prince was going to have to assert himself more, she thought.

She walked across the snow, savoring the satisfying crunch beneath her soles, noticing the little pile of snow atop every tiny cannon. Nature was so thorough; it paid such attention to detail. No branch was without its sparkle, no spider's web without its string of tiny frozen diamonds.

The pool terrace made her pause and sigh. Black circles, evidence of the night's debauchery, lay scattered over the frosty paving. She stooped to look at the labels. *Moon over Dixie* by Duke Ellington, *Night and Day* by Fred Astaire, *All of Me* by Louis Armstrong. That such romantic songs had received such violent treatment seemed a pity. But none were smashed. Love had survived.

The box, somewhat battered and half-covered with snow, was nearby. She stacked the records carefully inside and continued on her way, humming the tunes as she went. *Night and day, you are the one . . .*

Pulling Ernest's coat tightly about her, the cold pinching her nose, she walked down the winding drive between the rhododendron bushes and recalled, a few months ago, marching along in the heat behind the merry prince, ready to battle encroaching laurel. She had known him for half a year, but it was hard now to imagine life without him. She reached the entrance gate and went out into the Great Park itself. There was an immediate feeling of openness, of crossing from a small, self-contained world to another, much larger one. Here, too, all was silent. The path was frozen and unyielding beneath her shoes. Virginia Water, as she passed it, had the solid look of thick ice.

She remembered the bitter Maryland winters, when as a child she had been an excellent skater. Even the impecunious Alice had been able to afford a pair of skates. It sparkled in her memory, something lovely amid all the difficulty. How she had relished the speed and freedom that the blades had given her, the glide and the glitter, the thrill of long curves, the leaping and landing, the rushing cold.

She walked on, her hands pushed deep into the huge pockets of Ernest's coat. The great oaks in the park were dashed with snow; it picked out every bulge and twisted branch. Between were mysterious snow-weighed dells and hollows that made her think of Herne the Hunter and how Prince George had something of that same wild, demonic spirit. And then, with a blinding clarity, it hit her.

How could she not have seen it? Because it was too unexpected? Because members of the royal family did not suffer the same weaknesses as ordinary mortals?

Prince George was exactly like Win. And his brother was trying to cope, as she once had. She recalled the prince's tense expression as George drank glass after glass. How often had she looked on helplessly in just that way as his companions poured more drink into Win? The smiling determination with which, during the conga, his brother clung to George reminded her of the many times, with a similar rictus grin, she had physically dragged a reluctant Win from some party, the dead-drunk weight of his body threatening to pull her down too.

The memories roared back, wave after sickening wave of them. Hiding bottles, begging Win to stop, to see a doctor. She had no doubt that, in George, she had seen the same terrifying specter of addiction.

And in the prince, she had seen herself. She had walked quite a distance, she realized. She had reached the point in the path where the magnificent rear vista of Windsor Castle spread before her, windows twinkling in the bright winter sunshine. Her shadow stretched before her across the snow, long and black on the sparkling white. There was a movement; another figure. Someone was behind her.

"Mrs. Simpson, isn't it?" The Prince of Wales had paused and was looking at her quizzically.

It was extraordinary. She had been thinking of him, and there he was. He looked exhausted, she thought. Heavy mauve pouches swelled beneath the famous blue eyes. She remembered the struggles with Win, the sleepless nights, the violence, the sapping exhaustion, the despair and misery of it all. She felt passionately sorry for him.

He was looking at her with surprise and she thought how eccentric she must look in Ernest's vast greatcoat. The prince was dressed immaculately in a handsome camel coat over a suit more sober than the one last night. But there were still bright touches: an azure silk tie of extraordinary thickness; his rumpled golden hair and shoes polished to an almost liquid gleam.

"Good morning, sir." She sank in a curtsey.

"Out for a walk, are you?" A flash of a slim silver monogrammed case, the click of a lighter. "I'm just coming back from church, myself."

"From *church*? *Sir*," she added hastily.

He looked amused. "You seem surprised. But it rather goes with the territory, if you're me. Defender of the Faith and all that."

"I guess so," she laughed. "Sir," she added.

"Are you a churchgoer, Mrs. Simpson?"

"Oh, sir, call me Wallis, please. And, yes, I go sometimes. Not as often as I should. And if I'm honest, usually only when I need . . ." She paused. She had gone most frequently when things with Win were at their worst.

"Need what?"

"Well, help, I guess. There have been times in the past where a little divine intervention would have been pretty useful."

She could hardly believe she was saying all this. And to the Prince of Wales, of all people. But it was crowding her mind, and so out it had come.

"It's the same with me," he said. "I sit there confiding to the Almighty the most urgent of the matters in which I need his guidance. Quite a few, I can tell you."

His tone was rueful, sad even. She felt certain he meant his brother and longed to say something that, if it didn't quite comfort him, at least showed that he was not alone in his difficulty.

Did she dare? There wouldn't be another opportunity. She might not see him again after this; Ernest would be ready to leave just as soon as she got back.

"Sir," she said suddenly. "Your brother. Prince George."

"Oh, yes? Quite a character, isn't he?" His grin, clamped round the eternal cigarette, looked distinctly uneasy.

"I've known characters like that, sir. I was very close to one . . . once." She paused. "What I wanted to say, sir, was that I know how terrible it can be."

He looked at her then, and it was no darting glance. It was as if he was seeing her properly for the first time. She had a powerful impression that she was looking into a sort of mirror. That somehow, somewhere, she had always known him.

"Oh yes," he said. "It can be terrible, all right."

CHAPTER TWENTY-SIX

They were walking along together now. "I had to be doctor, jailer and detective combined," the prince said. The words made clouds in the sparkling air. "I couldn't turn my back for a second, in case he got into trouble again."

She nodded. "I know exactly how that feels."

"He's a lot better now, but there's always the danger of relapse. I try to keep what's in the decanters to a minimum."

Thelma had blamed this on the servants. She wondered if Thelma even knew about it. But why would the prince confide in her, and not his mistress?

"So he's an alcoholic?"

"Yes. But only partly."

"How do you mean 'only partly'?" She hoped he wasn't one of those people who refused to accept the full extent of a problem.

"I mean that the drink is only part of it. There's also the drugs. *Then* the women. *Then* the men."

"What?" Wallis's hand flew to her mouth. "Jeez Louise."

He gave a rueful smile. "Jeez Louise indeed. But actually, Kiki was the start of it all. Kiki Preston."

"What did she do?"

"Gave him heroin. She was known as the Girl with the Silver Syringe. I threw her out of the country along with all the other hangers-on."

His pace had increased such that she had to hurry to keep up. "How did George take that?"

"Not well, it has to be said." Another cigarette was lit. "He was on the brink of suicide. But I managed to pull him back."

She wasn't sure exactly where in the park they were now. As with the conversation, she was in uncharted territory.

"I moved George into St. James's Palace with me," the prince went on. "I put him in my room and literally sat by his bed during the whole awful withdrawal. It was the worst thing I've ever been through, and I say that as someone who served on the Western front." The hand that held the cigarette was trembling.

"I've been through it too," she said gently. She thought of Win shaking, sweating, threatening and roaring for alcohol. Lashing out, cursing, throwing whatever he could lay his hands on.

He glanced at her. "Yes, you were close to someone, you said. Who was it?"

"My husband."

Amazement swept his face. "But he seems such a steady chap."

The urge to laugh pressed wildly within her. "Not *Ernest*. My first husband, Earl Winfield Spencer."

"Earl who?" Then his face cleared. "Oh, I see. Like Duke Ellington."

She could not help laughing now. The idea that Win was some sort of senior aristocrat.

He laughed too. "So you're divorced?" he said.

"Yes."

He stared at her for a moment, then turned away, drawing on his cigarette. "So that's why I took up needlework. To soothe my nerves. Something to do while I was sitting in the sickroom."

They were back on Prince George, she realized. She frowned. "In the sickroom? You told me your mother taught you. You said you learned at her knee, at Sandringham. Round the tea table . . ."

He shrugged his shoulders in the beautiful camel coat. "I could hardly tell you the truth. Not at that stage, anyway."

"Your mother and father . . . ," she began. It had just occurred to her that the rigid king-emperor and his marmoreal queen, those personifications of dignity and correct form, were also the parents of George. "What do they think about it all?" she asked.

"My father is aware that if the matter became public it would be a terrific scandal."

There was an edge to his voice. She realized what he was saying.

"You mean that's all that matters to him? But George is his son."

"My father is not a sentimental person. And he is terrified of scandals. It was to avoid a scandal that he once unsentimentally refused to let his cousin come to England with his family. That was the Romanovs."

"The ones who were shot in the cellar by the Bolsheviks?"

"The very same. I learned at an early age not to expect much from my father, but it seemed that Nicholas the Second thought differently. A mistake."

How horrible, she thought. How cold, unfeeling and cruel. "But what about your mother?" Surely she had wanted to help. What mother wouldn't?

"My mother blocks out anything she might find difficult. When I was small it took her two years to work out that my nanny was torturing me."

"*Torturing* you?" It got worse and worse. The perfect royal childhood she had imagined had been the exact opposite. No wonder George had gone off the rails.

"I'd rather not go into details, if you don't mind. But one of her favorite tricks was to pinch me very hard at the exact moment she handed me over to Mama. So I was always crying, and Mama always handed me straight back."

She felt dreadfully sorry for him. She could see the small, unhappy, bewildered boy so clearly. She could see it now, in his eyes, as she looked at him.

"Are you all right?" he asked. "You look a bit tearful."

"I'm fine," she said, dragging out a large, Ernest-size hanky. "It's just . . . so sad. Your childhood. Your parents."

"They're the king and queen first and parents second." He seemed quite dry-eyed and pragmatic. "That's just the way it is. We can't all grow up in the Blue Ridge Mountains of Virginia, on the trail of the lonesome pine."

He was quoting a popular song, and she laughed. "Sir, I can assure you that growing up in Baltimore wasn't that much fun either."

He seized on this immediately. "Really? In what way?"

"You can't really want to know, sir."

"Oh, I do. I do. And please stop calling me sir. It's David."

"Well, David." Speaking his name felt strange and exciting. "I guess I was pretty lonely."

He seemed animated in a way he had not been before. "I know what that's like! Why were you lonely?"

"People left me out of things. I had only one friend, really. Mercer Tolliver. She had golden hair in these thick sausage curls." She laughed, then slid the prince an uncertain look. "You can't really want to know."

"I do! Tell me more about Mercer Tolliver."

"Is that a royal command?"

"Yes."

"Okay, well, Mercer was the only person who ever asked me to a party. But her mother crossed my name off the list because my mother was looked down on by everyone."

"Why?"

She decided not to go into the Uncle Sol story. "We were poor."

His eyes lit up. "Poor?"

"My father died of TB when I was a baby. There was even a stigma attached to that: it was the poor people's disease. We lived in a one-room flat, and my mother sewed to make money. She even tried cooking in a boardinghouse. But it was a disaster, as she had no idea about budgeting and fed them all best steak. It cost her far more than it did them."

The prince laughed. "Go on."

"There's not much to say. It was pretty miserable, generally. I didn't have a proper coat, so I went to school in winter with my hair wet. My legs were blue with cold. Everyone felt sorry for us in a contemptuous sort of way. I can't remember a time when I didn't feel ashamed." She looked down, feeling tearful suddenly.

She heard him exhale. "For me, too, everything has always been bound up with shame."

She looked up. "It put me off ever wanting children of my own." She stopped. He would be shocked.

"Yet another thing we have in common," he replied lightly.

She must have misunderstood, she thought. Having children was part of his job. Elizabeth had said as much the night before. *You're next in line. And then your children.*

He walked on. She followed, wondering if she had gone too far. They were in a very secluded part of the park now. Between the snowy trees, a plain little house could be seen. There was a blankness to the windows, which suggested it was empty and that no one had lived there for some time. The prince paused and looked at it for several minutes. She had the impression he was paying his respects, as at some memorial. Something had happened here, obviously. Something sad.

When he turned to her, she saw his eyes were bright and glinting, as with tears. Now he was moved.

"This was where my brother lived," he said. "My brother John."

She thought quickly. The prince's brothers were Bertie and George. There was another one, but he was called Henry, wasn't he?

"He died when he was thirteen," the prince said. "Here, as a matter of fact. He was an epileptic and did not live with the family. He lived alone with his nurse, and my parents visited him occasionally."

"They sent away their own child?" She looked at the blank windows of the house, imagining a small face peering out of it. She felt outraged, disgusted. These people were barbarians.

Her evident emotion seemed to please him. "His behavior was a problem. My father could not cope with anything but absolute obedience."

She fumbled for her handkerchief again. "Poor John. Poor, poor John."

The prince smiled faintly. "He was a sweet little boy. Very friendly." Then he looked back at the house. "And he is one of the several reasons why parenthood is not for me. Do I want to be a father? Am I equipped to be a father? Do I have good fatherly examples before me?" He took a drag on his cigarette and blew the white smoke up in the air, where it curled like a Prince of Wales feather. He threw her a darting glance. "What do you think?"

They returned through the park. She wanted to assure him that what had been said before the little house would remain there, but she gradually sensed it was not necessary. For some reason, he trusted her.

Soon they were back at Virginia Water, and she could hear voices. There were figures on the ice, shouting to one another, clinging to chairs for support. One was in the bearlike fur coat that Wallis had last seen Thelma in at Claridge's.

"Are they the hall chairs from the Fort?" The prince sounded incredulous. "How on earth have they got them there?"

The answer was in the small group of servants at the ice's edge, prominent among which was Osborn, arms tightly folded in his butler's black coat. Even from this distance Wallis could see how blue his nose was.

"David!" Thelma waved wildly at him, then screeched and clutched her chair. She pushed toward them, followed by another yellow chair piloted by the fur-clad Duchess of York. The duke brought up the rear; he was the only one who could actually skate unaided, it seemed.

"Where have you been?" Thelma yelled over the fence of frozen reeds and bulrushes that separated them.

"To church," called back the prince.

"With Wallis?" Thelma chortled, looking at her. "I didn't realize you were so devout!

"Elizabeth and I are having such fun," she went on before the prince could reply. "I always say that if I lived in a little backstreet somewhere and pegged out my washing in the yard, the person I'd most like to live next door to is Elizabeth York. Then we could gossip over the wall together as we pegged!"

Wallis looked down to conceal her laughter, both at the thought of Thelma pegging out washing in a backstreet and Elizabeth of York's unimpressed face at the vision being laid before her.

The prince was smiling broadly too. "Have you brought any skates for me?" he asked. "I love skating on Virginia Water. It was about the only thing I really enjoyed as a child."

Thelma bent down and picked something up. Two pairs of blades flashed in the sunshine. "One was supposed to be for Arnie, but he couldn't find his coat."

"Because his wife is wearing it," observed the Duchess of York coolly.

Thelma giggled. "So you are, Wallis. How strange you look. Can *you* skate, by the way? Shame to waste them when we've gone to all the trouble of bringing them!" She waved the skates, which swung in her hand.

Wallis glanced at the servants in their livery, who had carried the heavy chairs and were waiting to take them back. They were openly shivering now.

She stepped onto the ice. She unlaced her brogues and slipped her feet into the skates, adjusting them to fit. She stood up, pushed forward, and it was as if the intervening years had never been. She was the small Bessiewallis again, gliding easily, light as thistledown, picking up speed all the while.

As she swung into a long curve she was aware of someone behind her, a figure in a camel coat who was equally fast, his blond hair glinting in the sun, eyes as blue as the sky. He smiled at her, she laughed back at him, and they sped away together, relishing the rushing cold, the exhilaration, the impossibility of not smiling, of not being joyful.

The Duke of Windsor's Funeral
Windsor Castle
June 1972

On the castle's great round tower, the Union Jack flew at half-mast. There were television vans and souvenir stands. The lawns were even thicker with flowers than before.

The town that had been so empty when she visited with Charles was now packed. Thick crowds lined Windsor's pavements. They peered into the limousine with unabashed curiosity. Their faces seemed close, and doubt gripped her; perhaps, after all, these people still hated her. Perhaps they still thought she was the wicked witch, the scheming gold digger who had stolen the fairy prince away.

Fearing hostility, she shrank back into her seat, glad of the thick veil over her face to protect her from angry eyes.

"It's 'er! Mrs. Simpson!"

She hadn't been that for nearly forty years. The crowds, the stares, they brought it all back, the days of letter bombs and broken windows, of slogans daubed on walls. Heart hammering, she waited for the jeers.

None came, however. Rather, they watched her pass with a sort of quiet respect, as if she were some grand old actress from a once-famous drama long since settled into legend.

They arrived at the chapel at eleven exactly. Waiting on the wide golden steps was a familiar elegant figure. She was clearly the job Mountbatten had been allotted.

On the porch, the detailed stone carving, the dark intensity of the stained glass, gave her a feeling of claustrophobia. A bell was tolling. A group of clergy stood about, magnificent in miters and copes. How David would have hated it, she thought. He had loathed churchmen, the archbishop of Canterbury most of all. A sanctimonious old snob, he had thought him.

The bell, doleful, heavy, boomed in her skull.

"Such a noise," she murmured.

Every clang seemed to press her nerves together, fuse them to the point of hysteria. She felt she might scream, or burst into crazed laughter.

"The curfew bell," said someone in a black-and-gold cape. "It weighs two tons and rings only for the birth of a prince or a royal marriage or a Garter service or the death of a sovereign."

A quip forced its way to the front of her scrambled mind. "So you can guess what it's for when you hear it and have a twenty-five percent chance of getting it right?"

The cape stared at her.

"May I present the archbishop of Canterbury," murmured Mountbatten.

"Archbishop Lang?"

Still, after all this time? *Auld Lang Swine*, David had called him.

"Archbishop Fisher," corrected the man.

Mountbatten led her off. The royal family, he told her, were gathering at the deanery, next to the chapel. Several members were already there.

Panic drummed in her chest. She clasped the sleeve of his overcoat. "Do I have to? How can I face them alone?"

It came out as: "How will I recognize them all?"

He patted her hand and gave her a wolfish smile. "I'll help you."

There was, she supposed, a first time for everything.

The deanery was wood-paneled and full of people in dark clothes. In their well-bred English way they all pretended not to stare. But she felt the furtive glances, and a curiosity that, while as intense as that outside, was different. While, for the crowd outside, she was a player in a dead entertainment, for the crowd inside she was the living embodiment of embarrassment.

The notorious Mrs. Simpson. A legend made flesh. Powerful, selfish, heartless. After a few seconds' silent protest, she surrendered to the part. Why not? It would be easier for everyone, especially her. It offered a framework for thoughts that were otherwise formless anguish. She took a deep breath, steeled herself, became powerful, selfish, heartless.

"Eddie and Katharine Kent." Mountbatten presented a tall bald man and a small fair woman.

Wallis nodded, shook hands, summoned up some heartless thoughts. Well, the Duke of Kent was certainly different from his father. Prince George had lots of hair. An extravagantly handsome man with a great lust for life, and certain other things too. His wife, Princess Marina, had been haughty and distant, but this new duchess, Kate Kent, had a pure blond beauty and looked kind. That wasn't going to end well. A capacity to feel was no advantage in this family.

Mountbatten was moving her on. "You remember Alice Gloucester."

"Oh yes." The wife of Prince Henry, Duke of Gloucester, had been as bad as Marina in her time. But now, looking into the faded eyes, Wallis struggled to think heartless thoughts. Alice had suffered greatly; Henry had had several bad strokes.

"Prince Henry is very sorry he can't be here," Alice told her, in the formal way she always talked of her husband. "Especially as he's the only sibling left. George, Mary, Bertie and now David, all gone."

And John, of course, Wallis thought. But no one ever talked about him.

"The Ogilvys, Alexandra and Angus."

Just like her mother. Princess Alexandra had Marina's face. Angus looked ancient beside his wife, but Windsor women liked

it that way. Take Princess Mary and the Earl of Harewood. Geron-
tophiles, the lot of them.

"Olaf of Norway . . . the prime minister, Mr. Heath . . ."

Interesting, she thought. In a room of those who only consid-
ered themselves powerful, a genuinely powerful person at last.
She placed her narrow black-gloved hand in Heath's. "The last
British prime minister I met was Stanley Baldwin."

"Yes, I suppose it would be, ma'am."

"We got on rather well, considering."

She felt herself steered away by Mountbatten.

"Margaret and Tony Snowdon . . ."

Wallis stared into Margaret's eyes, violet like her mother's,
and remembered the child she had been. Curious, naughty, delightful. But life had not treated her well, or rather, the family
hadn't. The Peter Townsend business. Not being able to marry
the person she loved. No wonder Margaret's pretty face had a
petulant, bitter cast these days. She was still tiny but plumper, in
a rather tight-fitting black coat and a hat like a black chrysanthe-
mum. Her husband, Tony, looked like a dog; a restless, impatient
dog at that.

"Edward and Andrew . . ."

Lilibet's younger boys. Dark-haired Andrew was evidently
aware of his good looks but of little else, she suspected. Edward
seemed more intelligent but had the vast Windsor teeth.

"And Anne and Charles . . ."

"Aunt Wallis!" Prince Charles kissed her while Princess Anne
just nodded, making it clear she was there under sufferance.

Someone had entered at the door behind her. The atmosphere in the room had changed; the attention momentarily
switched from the notorious widow. "Granny. At last," muttered
Anne. "Why does she always have to be so late?"

To steal the show, thought Wallis. The room was now pin-
drop silent; the company held its breath. The queen-forced-

to-be was meeting the queen-who-never-was. As if to underline the drama, the bell now fell silent.

Wallis armed herself by picturing that cool stare, head tipped appraisingly to one side. She drew a deep breath, then turned slowly.

Her first reaction was laughter. Elizabeth's hat was so unbelievably hideous, still sporting that wartime brim with what looked like a white plastic arrow stuck through it. She fought the instinct; she did not want to seem crazy. She thought instead of all the selfishness and heartlessness, all the spites and revenges over the years that bore the prints of the plump little fingers now extending themselves toward her. Over the money, the HRH title, the blackening of their name at every opportunity, the barring of David from his homeland. The latter was supposedly in case he cast her own husband into the shadows.

But the real reason, Wallis thought, *was that she hated we were happy.*

The powdered cheek neared and didn't quite touch Wallis's own. There was a fine down on its wrinkled surface, a gust of lavender scent. A gloved hand lightly took hers, accompanied by a sympathetic murmur loud enough for all to hear. "My dear, I know exactly how you must be feeling. After all, I've been through it myself."

Having delivered her blow, Elizabeth gave her the sweetest of smiles. Wallis smiled warmly back.

Something had changed, she realized. Perhaps she was acting so well she was convincing herself, but her pressed nerves had eased, as had the tightness in her head. She realized that with David gone, this woman no longer had power over her. Wallis had always been the target, but only her husband had ever been hurt.

"Wonderful, isn't she?" Charles was at her side, watching his grandmother talking to Canterbury, who looked starstruck.

"Granny has this amazing effect on people. It's charm, pure and simple."

Wallis looked at him. Charles was kind but delusional. He really thought it was the person, not the position.

Lilibet had now arrived and came over in her brisk way. "I believe," she said brightly, "that the service is about to begin."

CHAPTER TWENTY-SEVEN

Chelsea
London
1933

Every window of the great house blazed with light. The wide black door, flanked by burning torches, was open to admit a queue of people in elegant evening dress. In the fading sunset of early spring, diamonds glittered, pearls glowed, dresses shimmered and shoes gleamed. The air was full of perfume and laughter. The legendary London hostess Lady Colefax was holding one of her parties.

Wallis, in the queue with Ernest, remembered the times she had stood outside this very house and watched the cream of London society entering the famous portals. It felt unreal that she had become one of them, that, on the pavement opposite, people were gathering to watch *her* go in.

It had been, in the end, so very simple. Just a telephone call. "Sibyl Colefax here," an assured voice had informed her one morning.

Wallis had been so amazed she had almost dropped the silver receiver. Ernest, predictably, was less excited. "Why is she asking us?" he wanted to know, after Wallis had patiently explained who Lady Colefax was. "We don't know her."

"Try to be pleased, Ernest. It's the hottest ticket in town!"

"We can't afford hot tickets, Wallis." Money had never been tighter at Bryanston Court. There was even talk of getting a lodger.

A new frock out of the question, she wore her Chanel dress. She felt, as always when wearing it, that Coco sewed some of her own indomitability into her clothes. She felt no nerves, only a happy curiosity, and looked about her excitedly, trying to spot people she recognized from the social pages. "Wallis!" It was Cecil.

She squeezed his arm in delight. "How wonderful to see you!"

"Likewise, my dear." The sloping eyes looked her up and down. "You're quite the talk of the town."

"*I* am?"

"Well, you and Arnie." Cecil's smile took in Ernest, who gave him an irritated nod and muttered "Ernest!" under his breath.

"But why?"

"Small matter of having stayed two weekends at the Fort. To stay once is interesting. But to stay twice, fascinating." He nudged her. "You're on the radar now, baby. An official FOP. Friend of the Prince. You've arrived. And to think I knew you when you couldn't get to the opening of an envelope."

"Thanks for reminding me, Cecil." She spoke lightly, to disguise her surprise. That they were invited because of the prince had not occurred to her. But even if he was right, many weeks had passed since the visit, and nothing had been heard from anyone. Having arrived, had she already departed?

If so, it would be a bitter disappointment. What the prince had revealed on the walk through the park seemed more astounding every time she thought about it, which was more or less all the time. She had said nothing about it, not even to Ernest. But it had hummed inside her, like an engine, ever since.

Having sensed that he was mysterious and seen some of his many faces, what lay behind them had amazed her. She had never suspected anything of the kind, had never even imagined it. She felt honored by his confidences, moved by his vulnerability and shocked by what he had endured. Their common painful experiences seemed to bring them together while setting them apart from everyone else. She felt that she understood him in a way few people could. It was like being shown a startling truth.

But perhaps he had decided, after all, that he had said too much. It was understandable that he would regret speaking with such candor, especially to someone he hardly knew.

Cecil was brazenly inserting himself into the queue beside her, much to the annoyance of the woman behind. "Hello, Emerald," he beamed over his shoulder. "You're looking utterly wonderful tonight."

"Silly old bat," he whispered as he turned back around. "She's actually called Mavis, but a numerologist told her she'd have better luck being called Emerald."

The queue moved forward. Wallis could see the house through the open door now: a beautiful marble mantelpiece with a mirror over it, and beyond it a large and lovely room with French windows. Cecil nudged her again. "So come on! What's the Prince of Wales really like?"

"He's very pleasant."

He looked disappointed. "Is that all?"

"That's all."

They were in the house now, and all was movement. Waiters wheeled past bearing silver trays of champagne flutes. Maids whisked by with perfume burners, leaving a trail of scent. Somewhere a jazz band played. Wallis stared round, taking in the details. This, then, was how to give a party.

"Cecil!" exclaimed a deep, rich female voice. An elegant blonde in long white gloves was sashaying toward them. "Viscountess Castlerosse," Cecil murmured as she approached. "*Grande horizontale*."

Ernest leaned in. "What's one of those?"

"A ceiling expert."

Viscountess Castlerosse held a cigarette in a holder and wore a white column dress pinned with jewels. "So you're Mrs. Simpson," she said to Wallis, looking her up and down with what seemed friendly interest.

The ignored Ernest asserted himself. "And you're an interior designer," he said. "A ceiling . . ."

He stopped as something dug him hard in the ribs.

"No one's as extravagant as Doris," twittered Cecil nervously. "Her idea of economy is to buy just the twelve couture gowns per season. Isn't that right, Doris dear?"

"You misrepresent me, Cecil." The viscountess was looking at him suspiciously.

Cecil's face, always pale, was drained entirely of color.

"I'm a very serious person," Doris went on. "No one loves the written word more than me. Especially at the bottom of a check." She burst out laughing and sashayed off.

They followed the crowd through a series of elegant eighteenth-century rooms. Chandeliers with real candles were flickering on the gilt edges of clearly important paintings: mythical scenes with fleshy goddesses and horses rearing and plunging. Elsewhere there were dogs looking dolefully upward, a child holding a bird and a man going for a pee in the corner of a Dutch interior. Ernest was studying them all intently.

Cecil leaned over to Wallis. "Someone needs to tell Arnie that no one looks at paintings at parties."

"Well, Ernest does."

They moved on over shiny lacquered floors, past walls of deep-green brocade bordered with shining gold filets. There were long pedestal clocks of beautiful wood festooned with scrolled gold decoration, enameled white faces, and wood and gold pendulums moving behind a panel of glass. There were vases and marble busts everywhere, atop elegant wooden cabinets.

"There's Diana," said Wallis, recognizing a sleek and shining blond head at the far end of the room. She waved, glad to see another friendly face. A pale and elegant arm rose in reply.

"Like the Lady of the Lake holding Excalibur," said Cecil reverently. He pointed out various people. "There's Chips Channon. Cocteau said his eyes were set by Cartier." They certainly had a glitter, Wallis thought, taking in Channon's sleek hair and dapper appearance. "That's Lord Berners he's with. He dyes his pigeons pink and patrols his estate wearing a pig's head mask."

"Why?"

"To discourage sightseers, of course," said Cecil, as if it were obvious. "And there's Edwina Mountbatten. Her grandfather was the king's banker, and she inherited a Mayfair mansion, four Van Dycks and works by Reynolds, Raeburn and Frans Hals."

Wallis burst out laughing. "Sorry," she said as Cecil looked affronted. "All that wealth. It's just ridiculous."

"If you say so. But look, here's a poor person," he said, indicating a tall blond youth with a Roman nose. "His name is William Walton. He's a musical genius who lives with the Sitwells and has the most amusing Lancashire accent."

Wallis turned to him. "You're such a snob, Cecil."

"I don't deny it. And there's Evelyn Waugh, who's even worse than I am. He actually thinks it's common to look out windows."

"To look out . . . ?" repeated Ernest. His expression was a mixture of appalled and exhausted. Wallis sensed he would not last much longer.

"Which one is Lady Colefax?" she asked.

"You mean you don't know?"

"I've never met her before."

Cecil looked about. "Sybil," he declared authoritatively, "will be the plainest-dressed woman of all. She is the epitome of pared-down elegance. Be at your best when you talk to her. She's a master of the art of touching off verbal fireworks."

Ernest groaned. "I'm not sure I'm up to verbal fireworks. It's been a long day at the office. Just fetch me when you're done, Wallis. I'm going to sit down somewhere." He took a glass from a passing tray and went off.

Seconds later, the epitome of pared-down elegance appeared.

"Sibyl!" exclaimed Cecil as a tall, handsome woman with iron-gray hair came up to them. "May I present Mrs. Wallis Simpson? She pays her way with poker and knows all about the brothels of Shanghai."

The pit of Wallis's stomach fell away. She realized at once that this was payback for not telling Cecil what he had wanted to know earlier. Face flaming, she searched for the words. What words though? She could not deny it. But, like Doris, she had been misrepresented. Thank God Ernest had gone to sit down.

Sibyl, however, looked delighted. "My dear, that's just too price-less!" Her voice was a low, warm gurgle of approval. Then her eyes rolled over Wallis's shoulder to the people behind. The audience was over.

Wallis turned furiously on Cecil, but he had disappeared. She grabbed a glass from the nearest tray and drank it in one. It had a kick like a mule and made her reel slightly. She should eat something. Trays of tiny sandwiches were being borne past by smiling maids. Wallis took one and derived what comfort she could from the rich taste of foie gras.

"How was the Fort?" It was Diana. "I hear you were there last weekend."

Everyone had heard, evidently. She wondered if Diana was jealous, but her wide pale eyes gave no such hint.

"You must be getting to know the prince quite well now," Diana said lightly.

Wallis gave a noncommittal smile. If Diana was fishing, she was determined to give nothing away.

"Not that anyone ever really does, of course," Diana went on. "He's a mystery, but central to his charm is his ability to make people think they're the only ones who understand him. It's a way of making people feel special. And one of the most powerful."

She wafted off, and Wallis looked after her. Diana had no idea what she was talking about. There was no possibility that what the prince had revealed to her was anything but the painful truth, told by one suffering human being to another.

She decided to go and look for Ernest. The evening had lost its sparkle; she wanted to go home. As she left the room, Diana raised her white arm again in a wave. Cecil was with her, and it now occurred to Wallis where his poker information might have come from.

She found Ernest, predictably enough, in the library. He was sitting in a corner with a pile of volumes on his lap and looked completely happy. *Possibly the happiest person in the room*, Wallis thought. Most of the faces she looked at seemed discontented and strained beneath the jewels and makeup. One face looked particularly strained; familiar too. With a stab of surprise Wallis realized that it was Thelma. Her heart suddenly burst into life; was the prince there too?

Their eyes met, and Thelma hurried over. She looked better than usual, in a loose rose crepe de chine dress with a matching long coat. Her hair was bound up in a rose crepe turban. "Wallis, am I glad to see you!"

This was a surprise, after so many weeks without communication. But then again, this was Thelma.

"Hold on to your hat," she murmured. "Here's Steamboat Willie."

A short, slight man came up. He had a rodent-like face, red hair and a combative air.

"Wallis, darling, meet Duke," said Thelma. Wallis was fascinated. This was the famous Marmaduke Furness, multimillionaire shipowner, unsentimental swearer and fan of truffles in champagne. "Duke, darling, meet Wallis Simpson."

"Who the bloody hell's Wallis Simpson?"

She looked down, lips twitching. Lord Furness more than lived up to his billing. He was so rude it was almost funny.

Ernest was beside her, she realized. He had stopped examining the books and come over.

"This is Mr. Arnold Simpson," Thelma said. "He works in shipping as well."

Furness's pale, protuberant gaze now raked over Ernest, lingering on his worn evening suit. "Oh, really? What's the firm called?"

"Simpson Spence and Young."

"Never heard of it."

His expression, as he turned on his heel and pushed away through the crowd, was one of disgust.

"So that was Duke," said Wallis, looking after him. She felt as if a bucket of cold water had been poured over her.

"Lovely, isn't he?" said Thelma dryly. "But now he's gone, I need to ask you something."

Hope sprang through Wallis. She might be meeting the prince again after all. She looked inquiringly at Ernest, whose expression was resigned. "I'll be over there," he said, nodding toward the bookcases.

Wallis smiled at Thelma. "So how can I help?"

"We can't talk here," Thelma said, looking about her in a hunted sort of way. "It's rather a delicate matter. Are you free for lunch tomorrow?"

CHAPTER TWENTY-EIGHT

I t's Gloria," said Thelma, twisting the stem of her champagne glass.

She had chosen the Ritz for their lunch. Wallis had not been back there since the first time. The cupids and fountains were all the same, but something had changed. The previously triumphant Thelma seemed at a definite low ebb. She had not, most uncharacteristically, even finished her first glass of champagne.

"What's happened to Gloria?" asked Wallis, who, even more uncharacteristically, had been poured some champagne of her own. She lifted the glass to her lips.

Thelma looked up. Her face was puffier than usual, and her eyes smaller with great dark shadows under them. "They want to take Little Gloria away from her."

"Her daughter?" Wallis replaced her glass suddenly. She knew that Gloria's husband, Reggie Vanderbilt, had died suddenly some years ago. So why take the child from her only remaining parent?

The answer was shocking. "Reggie's mother says that Gloria's an immoral person. There's a court case coming up. . . . She'll be accused of dreadful things." Thelma grabbed her glass.

"What dreadful things?"

A waiter proffering a bottle appeared immediately, but Thelma, in contrast to her old indiscreet fashion, waited for him to go before continuing. "Of being caught in bed with someone."

Wallis blinked. "But Reggie's dead. What's Gloria supposed to do?"

"The someone wasn't a man."

"I see," said Wallis evenly. She sipped her champagne.

"You're not shocked and disgusted?" Thelma sounded surprised.

"What people do in bed is their business. So long as they don't harm anyone else. Don't you think?"

Thelma was married to the brutish Duke after all. He was hardly a poster boy for heterosexual relationships, any more than Win had been. Moreover, she was conducting an adulterous affair with the Prince of Wales. Thelma, more than most, might be expected to have a flexible attitude.

She was shaking her head, however. "What I think is that it's inconvenient. I've got to drop everything and go over to New York to prop her up." She took another swig of champagne.

"Well, she is your sister," Wallis remarked, unimpressed by Thelma's disloyalty. Had she a sister, she felt she would support her, even one like the brittle and watchful Gloria.

"Oh, we were always more rivals than sisters," Thelma said dismissively. "Mamma set us against each other from the start. We were to marry rich men. She used to cut our eyelashes to make them grow back thicker and made us sleep in gloves with cold cream on our hands to make sure they stayed white and soft."

Given how spectacularly Gloria's pursuit of wealth seemed to have imploded, Wallis wondered what Mamma would think now.

"Anyway," said Thelma as the waiter handed her a menu. "I didn't ask you to lunch to talk about Gloria."

Ask you to lunch. Would Thelma pay for this one? She hoped so. The Simpson funds really wouldn't support another. But just in case, she ordered her usual small green salad.

Thelma snapped the menu shut. "Tournedos Rossini," she added, to the waiter. "Medium rare. And more champagne."

As the waiter glided off, she leaned forward, revealing the usual expanse of cleavage. "I want you to do something for me while I'm away."

Wallis eyed her cautiously. "What?"

Thelma lifted her glass and giggled. "Look after the little man for me."

"Little man? Who's that?"

"David, of course."

Things seemed to slow down suddenly.

"Look after him?" she asked faintly. "Me?"

"Yes, dear. He seems to have taken rather a shine to you. You had a good chin-wag the other day, he said."

Chin-wag was one way of putting it, Wallis supposed. On the other hand, she doubted even Thelma knew what the prince had told her. The thought that he had taken a shine to her made her glow inside. He didn't regret it after all.

"We did," she acknowledged, hoping Thelma wouldn't ask what the chin-wag had been about. She seemed entirely uninterested, however.

"He does bang on a bit, I find," she remarked. The food had arrived and she sawed off a piece of steak. "I let it go in one ear and out the other."

Wallis, forking in a leaf, found it blocking her throat suddenly. She had to swallow forcibly.

Thelma watched her with amusement. "Dangerous things, salads. Better to stick to the old goose liver." She poked the foie gras atop her steak with her fork. "Anyway, sweetie, as I was saying, look after the little man for me, will you? Make sure he doesn't get into any mischief."

"What sort of mischief?"

Thelma was chewing. "Other women, mainly," she said with her mouth full. "When you're in my position, you can't turn your back without someone else leaping into his bed. Mind you"—she grinned—"they'd be disappointed if they did. I call him the little man for a reason. As you might remember."

Wallis looked down at her plate. She felt she hated Thelma for speaking of the prince in this callous way. She seemed neither to understand nor to love him, nor did she seem to feel any loyalty. Her interest in him was entirely self-serving.

"All right," Wallis said. She would be a friend to him. He clearly needed one, prince or not.

"Good. He'll be safe with you," said Thelma, glugging her champagne. "He's hardly likely to find you attractive. You're much too old and skinny!"

"Tell me you're joking," said Ernest. He had just come back from work and was gray with exhaustion. "The Fort, again?"

Her husband was probably the only person on the planet who regarded this particular invitation with dismay, Wallis thought. On the other hand, it was why she respected and liked him so much. Ernest was no snob. He was a man of absolute integrity.

"It's just while Thelma's away," she assured him. "And there won't be many other people there. Just the Fruity Metcalfes."

Ernest, on the sitting-room sofa, had taken a swig of whisky as she said this. He coughed. "The Fruity Metcalfes?" His eyes were streaming. "Who in God's name are they?"

A car was sent for them. So luxurious and comfortable was it that Ernest fell asleep instantly and snored all the way from Marble Arch to Sunningdale. Wallis, excited, waited for the wonderful moment the Fort towers appeared above the treetops. Her heart soared at the sight of it, the fairy castle with its flag rippling in the sunset.

They were in the Queen's Room, with the huge cathedral-like window taking up one entire wall. "We've been promoted," said Ernest.

The long sleep seemed to have done him good. His tired eyes looked brighter, and if he wasn't exactly cheerful, he seemed at least resigned. "Now for the Fruity Metcalfes," he said. "I wonder who's fruity, her or him."

Him, it turned out. Fruity was a tall man in violently loud mustard check. He stood before the drawing-room fireplace in a familiar manner. "I'm the original wild Irishman!" he informed them in booming tones.

Wallis and Ernest were quickly apprised of the fact that he had known the Prince of Wales for a very long time. "We met in India in the twenties. Been leading him astray ever since! The king's always thought me a very bad influence!"

There was something oddly competitive about him, Wallis thought. She sensed that he regarded each newcomer to the royal fold as a potential threat and was keen to warn them off.

"Drink?" Fruity was busying himself proprietorially with the decanters. To her surprise, Wallis heard the clink of ice cubes alongside that of the crystal. Osborn must have had a change of heart. Was it anything to do with his Christmas present?

Fruity's wife was as restrained as her husband was overwhelming. Dark-haired and dark-eyed, she sat languidly on one of the sofas regarding Ernest and Wallis, but particularly Wallis, with an appraising stare not unlike that of the Duchess of York.

Wallis smiled back in her usual friendly manner while wondering what exactly gave these women the right to be quite so rude.

Her name was Lady Alexandra, but she was known as Baba, a nickname from her childhood in India, Wallis gathered. The Curzon family, from which Baba was descended, were aristocrats and colonial bigwigs, although exposure to different cultures and countries did not seem to have broadened their minds.

"You've probably heard of Baba's brother-in-law," Fruity said, from where he stood before the fender with his legs apart. It was as if he wanted to occupy as much space as possible. "Tom Mosley."

Baba smiled to herself at the name, Wallis saw. A private, feline smile. Ernest looked up. "As in Oswald Mosley?" he said. "The British Union of Fascists?"

"The very same," Fruity confirmed in his Irish burr, which sounded, in Wallis's ear, both too Irish and too burry. "Good chap, just what the country needs, don't you think?"

Ernest regarded him steadily. "As a matter of fact, I don't," he said. "The British Union of Fascists seems to me to have unfortunate tendencies."

Baba was staring coldly at Ernest. "Oh, really?" said Fruity in an aggressive manner.

"Really," said Ernest, swirling the ice cubes in his whisky tumbler. "I find the way they go into the East End and pick fights with Jews very unpleasant indeed."

"You don't think Britain is for the British?" said Fruity. His wide, easy grin had become a sneer. "You're American anyway; what business is it of yours?"

"Well said," put in Baba spitefully.

Wallis sat on the opposite sofa to Ernest, holding her breath. The mood had turned ugly very quickly. She wondered why the prince had picked such unpleasant people as his friends. She found herself, for once, in agreement with the king. Beneath their comical nicknames, Baba and Fruity were anything but funny.

She had expected Ernest to subside, but instead he placed his glass carefully on a side table and stood up. He was very tall, and while Fruity was tall, Ernest had the advantage. He was also broader, and looked more so in the sober gray suit that, beside Fruity's silly checks, had an air of quiet command.

"Actually," Ernest began, "I'm only half-American. My grandfather was Jewish, from Warsaw." He paused, before continuing, with quiet pride, "His name was Leon Solomon and he came to London during the pogroms. Then he moved to Plymouth, where he worked in the docks and started the family shipping business. My father was one of twelve children, and when he left to seek his fortune in the States, he changed his name to Simpson."

Absolute silence fell on the drawing room. Baba looked horrified, Fruity angry. Wallis wanted to applaud. But the pride and delight with which she gazed at Ernest contained a considerable amount of surprise.

The prince appeared, suddenly as always, and as always it was as if the entire company were blown up into the air and then floated slowly back down to earth. He wore a gray pin-striped suit with wide lapels and baggy trousers. The look was finished with a wide lavender silk tie and black-and-white brogues.

"Well," he said, accepting a drink from Fruity and darting a swift glance round. "How are you all? What have you all been talking about?"

Wallis was in first. "The weather." She smiled sweetly.

Back in the Queen's Room, she closed the door and leaned against it. "You never told me that about your grandfather!"

"You never asked." Ernest raised his eyebrows. "Does it bother you?"

She shook her head. "Of *course* not. On the contrary. He sounds quite a guy. Why bring it up now though?"

He turned away, hands in his pockets, and walked toward the magnificent window. A maid had been in while they were downstairs, and the vast red curtains had been pulled across the tracery. Ernest pulled them back.

"That's better," he said. He turned to her. "To answer your question, I kept my background to myself because I wasn't sure it was a particular advantage. But the way things are going, pretty soon we're going to have to pick a side."

CHAPTER TWENTY-NINE

To her surprise, the dinner menu had changed. Lightly smoked salmon preceded chicken in a delicious tarragon sauce. She wondered if Thelma's absence had something to do with it. The staff wanted to show what they could do.

Another surprise was that the prince did not play the bagpipes before dinner. He seemed tired and looked, after his earlier bright appearance in the drawing room, rather dejected.

Fruity was eager to supply the explanation. "We've been up to Yorkshire today, visiting workingmen's clubs in the most horrible little towns and villages."

"Oh, sir, how boring for you." Baba shuddered. "Aren't you terribly tired?"

The prince ground out his cigarette in the silver ashtray next to his untouched salmon.

The atmosphere felt uncomfortable. Someone, Wallis realized, had to take charge and direct the conversation, and in the absence of Thelma, the duty fell to her. She was to look after the little man, after all. Deftly, and with the apparent artlessness at which she was now so practiced, she guided the talk toward America.

Metcalfe's predictable contempt for Roosevelt did not bother her in the least. It was to be expected from someone who believed that to run a state was to crush people rather than empower them. Finally the conversation landed where she intended, on Baltimore.

"Baltimore, Ireland?" sneered Fruity. "In County Cork, on Roaringwater Bay?"

It was a competition, she recognized. Fruity was using his Irishness as she used being American.

"Baltimore, Maryland," she said equably.

"Never heard of it," sniffed Baba.

"That's a shame. It's a very interesting place. Want to hear our state anthem?"

She looked brightly round the table.

The prince had perked up, she saw. There was color back in his cheeks. "Yes," he said, nodding his shining head.

She saw Ernest look down, smiling. He knew what she was going to do, she sensed, and why she was doing it. She took a deep breath and launched into "Maryland, My Maryland."

As any Fascist might, Fruity looked astounded and Baba appalled as the melody of the hymn to international Communism filled the room. The prince's face was creased with amusement. "It's the same tune as 'The Red Flag'!"

Wallis reached the end and grinned at him. "Yes, sir. And it sounds so much better on a ukulele!"

The prince laughed. He was sitting up now. Vitality and humor radiated from his face. "Do tell us another of your wonderful Baltimore stories, Mrs. Simpson."

Fruity and Baba looked at each other in alarm. "I can tell you some wonderful Baltimore stories," Fruity boomed. "There was a time, on Roaringwater Bay . . ."

The prince looked at him impatiently. "Not now, Fruity."

Wallis smiled around the table. "I'd like to tell you the story of Betsy Patterson."

"Betsy *who*?" sneered Baba. "I've never heard of her."

"Patterson. Otherwise known as Napoleon's sister-in-law. I take it you've heard of him?"

The prince and Ernest laughed at this. Ignoring Baba's glare, Wallis tapped her glass with a spoon for silence. She enjoyed telling stories and did so with flair. It felt like a long time since she'd had an audience.

"It's 1803," she began. "Betsy is the belle of Baltimore. Young Prince Jérôme Bonaparte, Napoleon's brother, meets Betsy, falls in love and marries her."

"How romantic!" exclaimed the prince.

She looked at him mock sorrowfully. "Not for long, I'm afraid. Jérôme was a minor, and his brother, the emperor, refused to recognize the marriage."

"Party pooper!" said the prince.

"Wasn't he?" agreed Ernest.

"It doesn't get much better. When Jérôme returned to France in 1805, Betsy was forbidden to land."

Ernest and the prince booed loudly. Fruity and Baba were having to adjust their hostile expressions.

"So she came here to England . . ."

Cheers greeted this.

"Where her son, Jérôme Napoléon Bonaparte, known as Bo, was born."

More cheers.

"But the following year, Napoleon issued a state decree of annulment to end his brother's marriage."

Boos.

"And poor Betsy lived unhappily in exile in Paris for the rest of her life."

The prince and Ernest elaborately mimed tears at this unfortunate ending. Then there was applause and laughter. Wallis glanced at the Metcalfes. They wore stiff, unwilling smiles.

❖❖❖

"Let's play Frank Estimations!" Baba suggested as they sat on the so-fas after dinner.

The prince and Fruity greeted the suggestion with enthusiasm, although it was not a game Wallis was familiar with.

"It's very simple," said the prince. "We all get a piece of paper on which we give each other marks out of ten for certain qualities. It's all anonymous though. No one knows who's given who what."

Wallis nodded. "And what are the qualities?"

"Sex appeal, good looks, charm and sincerity."

Wallis was unsurprised, when the lists came out of the hat, to find herself being graded one out of ten on all counts by half the players. The bigger surprise was getting ten out of ten on everything from someone whose handwriting was not Ernest's. For his part, the prince was appalled to be given low marks for sincerity, again by half the players.

"*Two* out of ten?" he exclaimed, his comically outraged expression flickering in the firelight. "I consider sincerity my most important quality!"

Wallis had given him ten out of ten for that.

Later, Wallis could not sleep. She tossed and turned, the events of the evening churning in her brain. She particularly regretted making en-emies of the Metcalfes. But it had been unavoidable; they had been hostile from the start. Why so defensive? she wondered. Fruity had known the prince for ten years, she and Ernest for barely ten months. What threat could they possibly be?

But it was the prince who occupied the center of her thoughts. The evening confirmed what had been building up for some time: what she felt for him was more than sympathy. She found him powerfully attractive; she even desired him. She had never thought to want a man again, but she wanted this one. Something long buried was stirring. However, as Thelma had pointed out, he was unlikely to want her. *You're much too old and skinny!* And even if he did, what about Ernest?

Abandoning all attempts at slumber, she got up. The carpet felt soft and thick under her bare feet. She opened a window and leaned out into the dark. The air was cool and fresh. Above her soared the towers of the Fort, excitingly floodlit, the flag waving on the topmost. She thought of the view from up there, looking toward London. She imagined Herne the Hunter out in the park, rattling his chains and streaming blue light. She shuddered.

There was no moon, but a scatter of stars. She stared at them, trying to identify the constellations. The hoot of a distant owl broke her reverie. Or perhaps it was something else. She now caught a whiff of cigarette smoke and realized she was not alone. Someone was beneath the window, a mere few feet below, sitting in the dark. She knew with a sudden certainty that it was the prince. He hadn't been able to sleep either.

"Sir!" she whispered. "Is that you?"

"Yes! But call me David, remember?"

She was seized by the dizzying possibility, the wild hope, that he had chosen her window on purpose. That he wanted to talk to her.

"What are you doing?" she asked. She could hear him draw on his cigarette and could make out the top of his head a couple of feet below the windowsill.

"Thinking."

"About what?" Thelma? Perhaps he was missing her. Misery twisted within her at the thought

"America."

Definitely Thelma, then. Wallis was silent. The smoke from his cigarette drifted up to her; she inhaled it. It was the nearest she was ever going to get to him.

"If America can suddenly reinvent itself as a laboratory for social change, why can't Britain?"

"What?"

He repeated the remark. He was talking about Roosevelt, she realized. His reforms, his plans for social change, to kick-start the economy and bring it out of recession. His New Deal, in other words.

"Well, Britain can, can't it?" she asked.

"Can it?" He sounded suddenly frustrated and unhappy. "The level of poverty here is appalling. Some of the housing conditions I see send me back to the Fort almost ill."

Amazement flashed through her. Royalty did have views on politics, and vehement ones too. "So why do you never say anything?" she asked.

"Say anything?"

"I mean at dinner. When people are making snooty remarks about hunger marchers, mill girls, workingmen's clubs and so on."

Her questions seemed reasonable to her, especially given the previous frankness between them. And the reminder to call him David. But perhaps she was assuming too much, because now he was silent. Then, to her relief, he laughed.

"Wallis. You are one of those rare people who speak truth to power. Let me explain. I'm surrounded by people like my dinner guests, people with whom there is no point in arguing. Either their reprehensible views are set in stone or they are naysayers and gloomsters who think the forces that cause all this misery are worldwide, economic and beyond a prince's scope."

"But *are* they beyond your scope?" she questioned. "Can't you do anything about it, really?"

He blew out a stream of smoke. "Sadly, royal power in British politics is limited to the power of suggestion. I wish it were otherwise. I wish there was a way of bringing the monarchy closer to the people."

"Can't you find one? You're the Prince of Wales."

He did not reply but got up. She could hear the gravel crunch as he paced about the path.

"I try, Wallis. I really do. I go to these former coal-mining villages and industrial centers that aren't very industrial anymore. My father wanted me to wear a top hat and ride in a Rolls-Royce. I had to refuse. I wanted to go in a plain car and wear an ordinary bowler. When he saw the photographs he went wild."

"You were right though," she said steadfastly.

"Yes, I was. What else could I do? How could I expect these wretched people to relate to me otherwise? And these places I meet them in. They're utterly bleak and absolutely bare.

"I have to walk through these rooms, past benches crowded with unemployed men, and all I can hear is the creak of the floorboards beneath my weight. I am expected to talk to the men, but it is hard to know what to say."

"So what do you say?"

He sighed. "All the usual stuff. I sympathize with them in their hardships and remind them that the government is trying to help. They seem to appreciate it and take my appearance as a sign that the monarchy hasn't forgotten them in their misfortunes. But, oh, Wallis, I feel so dreadful afterward."

She was moved by his predicament, his frustration. "It sounds terribly difficult."

"It *is*. And I want so badly to help, you see. Something must be done. And I don't see *why* I shouldn't do it. I *can* be a prince with a social conscience."

"You can," she agreed. "In fact, I don't see how you could be anything else."

"Do you really think so? Really?"

"I do."

"You know, Wallis, you're the first woman who has ever shown any interest in my work. Because, to be honest, I don't know what any of it means or even why I'm doing it."

She leaned farther out. "David, what you do is important."

"Well, it doesn't make me feel important. It makes me feel like an idiot."

He was completely beguiling. This self-doubt, there was something pure about it, a shining innocence. "You just care, that's all."

She saw his cigarette tip glow in the darkness. "You know, Wallis, the first time I met you I felt immediately very drawn to you."

"Did you?" She could hardly speak over the beating of her heart.

"Yes. And whenever I've seen you since, I've always felt so pleased."

She clutched the windowsill. She felt she might faint.

The cigarette tip glowed again. "I wonder what you thought about me."

"I liked you very much," she said, unhesitating. "You're so charming and attractive. But what's really charming and attractive is that you don't act as though you're even aware of it. Your title, your position. You're so unassuming about it all."

He laughed. "Don't be deceived. It's lack of confidence. I can never believe it when someone likes me. No doubt it comes across as charisma and disarming modesty."

The glowing tip hit the ground and was stamped out. "Good night," he said abruptly, and walked away. It was only when she turned round that she remembered Ernest was in the room with her, snoring away in the pink bed.

CHAPTER THIRTY

Thelma's stay in New York had extended into several weeks. Her sister Gloria's court case for custody of her daughter did not seem to be going well. The latest development was that her own mother had given evidence against her.

Wallis had not warmed to Gloria Vanderbilt on the one occasion they had met. But she felt sorry for her now. She remembered Thelma's account of Mamma pitting the sisters against each other in the race for a rich man. Her suitability to rule on whether Gloria was a fit mother seemed doubtful.

But, in the meantime, Thelma's absence certainly had its upsides.

A week or so after the Simpsons had returned from the Fort, the doorbell of the Bryanston Court flat rang loudly. "I was just passing," the prince explained, smiling, "and I thought I'd drop in and tell you about my new scheme in South London."

She sat opposite him in a dream, hurriedly mixing cocktails, as he outlined a plan to turn some Duchy of Cornwall land in Kennington into housing for workers.

His eyes glowed blue with excitement as he spoke. "I had talked about doing it before," he said, "but I met with the usual lack of interest. Your encouragement"—he smiled at her—"made me determined to try again."

"That's wonderful, David."

Her voice was steady, but she was shaking internally at this proof that the conversation outside the window really had happened. Because the morning after, the prince had given no sign, any more than he had after the conversation in the frozen park. It was beginning to form a pattern, one step forward, two steps back, and this suited her, because that way there was no repercussion to what was said, however intimate. She was a sounding board—that was all. And what else could she be? She felt dazzled, infatuated by him, but only in the way one might love an unattainable film star. She was married to Ernest; the prince, meanwhile, seemed firmly attached to Thelma.

He spoke about her often, and in unabashedly romantic terms. They had been on safari together in the early years of their relationship, and the memory seemed a particularly dear one. "I had a little Puss Moth airplane to scout for lions," the prince recalled fondly. "Every morning I used to buzz Thelma's tent to wake her up before soaring over the bush in search of game."

"David?" whispered Ernest as she went to the kitchen for more ice. "Since when has he been David?"

She shrugged and smiled. "You know how he hates formality."

The prince seemed in no hurry to go.

"I'm starving," Ernest whispered, catching her in the corridor again.

She smiled at him. "Well, let's have dinner."

"But he's still here!"

"He can eat with us. We'll just have to hope he likes beef stew."

A week later, he appeared again. And, a few days after that, again. Ernest found it baffling. "He could spend his time with anyone; why us?"

"Because he likes us. He likes our conversation."

"Well, yours, certainly," Ernest agreed. "You're always egging him on about that workers' housing."

"Yes, because it's a good idea. He wants to do something with his position and needs a bit of encouragement. I don't think people do, on the whole."

Ernest yawned. "Yes, but do you have to encourage him until four a.m.? Some of us real-life workers have to get up in the morning."

She smiled at him. "Relax, Ernest. Once Thelma gets back, it'll all be over. We're just looking after him while she's away. He's missing her very much."

Absence certainly seemed to be having the celebrated effect on the royal heart. "I wish she would come back," he would sigh. "I feel quite lost without her."

But as Gloria's court case continued to make ever more lurid headlines, Thelma remained in New York. The Vanderbilts' maid had now testified that she had seen her mistress kissing the marchioness of Milford Haven, a British aristocrat.

Yet even as word about Gloria's difficulties crossed the Atlantic to Britain, news of the prince's interest in the Simpsons seemed to be going the other way. Aunt Bessie, from Washington, got in contact and sent a handful of newspaper clippings sprinkled with their names. Wallis wondered whether her gossipy cousin Corinne had something to do with it. There could have been talk in embassy circles; certainly, Corinne had been more than usually insistent with her invitations of late.

"Oh, do come, Wallis," she would plead, of some dinner party.

"I can't."

"You mean you have another invitation?"

"No, I'm having a quiet night in."

"You seem to be having an awful lot of those at the moment," Corinne remarked.

Mary Raffray, her old friend from New York, seemed also to have got wind of something. Recently divorced, she proposed a stay with them in London. She needed the distraction, she explained.

"Does she have to?" groaned Ernest. "There's hardly room in this place to swing a cat as it is."

"Don't exaggerate," Wallis rebuked him. "You'll just have to stop spreading out your books all over the sitting room, that's all."

Ernest had recently developed a passion for deciphering the hall-marks on silver and had amassed several volumes on the subject.

"Besides, we owe her," Wallis went on. "She's been very kind to me in the past, and she introduced us, remember."

"But what about your friend David?" Ernest asked.

He had a point, Wallis knew. Now the prince was in the habit of coming for personal talks and to have Wallis encourage him, she could hardly have Mary sitting there too.

"Will you take her out?" she asked Ernest. "Show her the sights, take her to the theater? Mary loves opera," she added artfully. "Which is more than I do."

Ernest didn't need asking twice. Once Mary had arrived they spent several nights a week in the cheap seats at Covent Garden, taking in everything from *Tristan* to *Tosca*. Wallis, meanwhile, continued to provide a sympathetic, encouraging ear for whatever the prince wanted to talk about.

It might be the housing project, or a design for a new planting at the Fort, or a scheme for promoting a British trade drive somewhere, or even the latest American jazz record. She was delighted to hear all of it and remained confident that what she felt for him was idealized and remote, a twentieth-century version of the courtly love that medieval knights entertained for fair ladies. What the prince felt for her was never again referred to, although she dwelled on it every night before sleep.

One morning, Ernest appeared in her bedroom. He was dressed for work and was waving a brown envelope. "Telegram for you," he said.

She opened it and felt a violent jolt. Eventually she looked up at

Ernest and said brightly, "It's from Thelma. She sails for Southampton today."

"How funny," Ernest responded. "Mary's sailing for New York today. They can wave at each other in the middle of the Atlantic."

Wallis felt something break inside her. She knew that the prince would now stop coming, just as suddenly as he had started, and with as little explanation or warning. She was no longer needed, not on that urgent, intimate level.

She would never forget being taken to the very heart of his confidence. It had been thrilling and flattering and the most profound event of her life. But she must accept that with Thelma the cat returned, Wallis the mouse must scurry back to her hole and hope for the occasional invitation to the Fort. It had been a golden time while it lasted.

Mary's visit had done Ernest good, and seemed also to have provided Mary with her distraction. She rang frequently, and Ernest could be heard carrying on a long and jokey conversation before the receiver was finally handed over to Wallis. "She's gotten really interested in silver hallmarks" was Ernest's explanation. "She's been telling me about the ones she's seen in New York."

Mary's conversations with Wallis centered around the possibility of visiting again. "But she's only just gone back," she complained to Ernest. "I'm not sure I could cope with her again so soon."

He raised his eyebrows. "I've got a business trip to New York coming up. I guess I could call in and see her."

"Would you?" Wallis said gratefully.

Gradually, everything returned to the way it had been. They even went back to doing household accounts on a Tuesday evening. Wallis stared at the columns of figures in despair. After all that had passed, was this really the future?

"Does beef mince really cost so much?" Ernest was asking one evening, when Lily appeared at the door of the dining room in a state of considerable fluster. Her eyes sought Wallis's in panic.

"It's His Royal Highness, ma'am."

With a muttered exclamation Ernest rose to his feet and began closing the account books. Wallis, meanwhile, fled to the sitting room, where the prince was pacing up and down, clearly angry. She decided not to ask, just mixed her stiffest cocktail.

"There," she said, handing it over. She looked at him as she did so, and his expression startled her. It was full of such terrible misery she thought the worst immediately. "Your . . . father?"

He stared at her, then gave an exasperated snort. "I'd hardly be this upset if it were. He'll go on forever anyway. He's indestructible."

"So what is it?" His mother? George?

"Thelma," he said, all choked up again. He looked as if he was going to cry.

"Her ship . . . ?"

As he nodded, she gasped. Had it gone down? There had been nothing about it on the radio. Perhaps royalty heard these things first.

She led him to the sofa and sat down next to him. She could feel his whole body trembling. The hand that held his drink was shaking. She waited as he struggled with the words. "Prince Aly Khan."

She was completely confused. "The Aga Khan's son, you mean?"

"He's on the s-same s-s-hip," the prince said unsteadily. "They're spending every night together."

Understanding hit her like a slap. Aly Khan was the disaster at sea. Handsome, fast-living, very young and very rich, he was well known for his womanizing. It wasn't hard to see what had attracted Thelma, whose virtue was always easiest around great wealth.

While some hurt and indignation were to be expected on the

prince's part, his complete devastation was surprising. He looked less like a man nearing forty than a boy a quarter that age. He began to sob, with such abruptness that it sounded like a burst of laughter. He cried openly, without putting his hands to his face, like a child.

"He filled her s-s-stateroom with roses. They d-d-danced on the d-d-deck in the moonlight." He flung himself to the floor and sobbed on her knee.

His tears soaked into her dress. She could only murmur her sympathy and stroke his soft, fair hair. She thought how vulnerable he was, how sensitive and easily hurt. She was not sure how long she sat there. The yellow evening sunshine that had poured through the windows became the rich copper of sunset and eventually the street-lit gloom of night. The prince wept on. Once or twice Ernest opened the door, stared in with raised eyebrows and closed it again as she shook her head.

"I loved her," the prince wailed into her knee. "I truly loved her."

"I know," Wallis soothed, while wondering how he possibly could have. Feckless, idiotic, greedy Thelma was the last person on earth to deserve this level of devotion, especially from a man who was the idol of an entire empire. But as she knew more than most, love did not conform to logic.

"I can't bear it," he howled. "It's too painful."

"I know, I know," she soothed. "It's like being shot in the stomach."

He raised his head. His eyes were red and swollen. "Yes. That's it exactly."

She nodded. "Like being alive and dead at the same time."

"You know!"

"I know, all right."

He rummaged for a handkerchief. "Oh, Wallis. I only feel better when I'm talking to you."

It made her ache inside. She resisted the urge to hold him tightly, to kiss him.

"I feel so stupid," he said.

"You shouldn't. Anyone can love anyone. We just close our eyes to their flaws, ignore anything that doesn't fit our image of them and away we go."

"Do you really think so?" He was looking at her intently.

"I really think so."

Finally, late in the evening, he raised his wet and swollen face, muttered his gratitude and was gone into the night.

Next morning, the telephone rang. It was Thelma.

"I'm back!" she announced brightly. "Let's have lunch!"

CHAPTER THIRTY-ONE

Sardines!" Thelma exclaimed, wincing at the Claridge's menu. "I simply could *not* face them! The day that beastly maid told that story about Gloria and Nada Milford Haven, we had sardines for lunch. They have painful associations!"

Wallis fought the urge to laugh. It took a type of crazy genius to connect the Vanderbilt scandal with a sardine. She wondered if this was what the lunch was about, to let off steam about the trial.

Thelma looked messy and tired and her makeup was smudged. Wallis tried not to dwell on the most likely explanation: a passionate reunion with her royal lover. Presumably the whole Aly Khan business was now smoothed over. Thelma no doubt had her methods, and a man in love would want to be convinced.

Wallis watched her greedily scanning the menu. "Caviar," she snapped at the hovering waiter.

Wallis ordered her usual green salad. "Still dieting?" Thelma frowned at the thin white arms revealed by her companion's dark sleeveless dress. "You're fading away, Wallis."

Ernest had said much the same thing several times lately. She ate little these days, it was true. Far less than she once had. Her undressed weight was around a hundred pounds.

"David didn't come to see me last night," Thelma said. "It's the absolute silliest thing, but I think he might be cross about something."

Wallis looked down to disguise her surprise. Had they not made up after all?

Thelma took a thoughtful swig of her champagne. "It's so odd. He's been looking forward to seeing me so desperately. He rang me every day while I was in New York, several times, telling me how much he loved me and that he could not live without me."

Wallis continued to stare at her napkin. She held her breath.

"I'm just the tiniest bit concerned"—Thelma toyed with the stem of her glass—"that he might have heard the silliest rumor about Aly Khan. Has he said anything to you about it?"

Wallis wished she had her companion's ease with a casual lie, but the truth was her only option. She raised her head and looked at Thelma. "He did mention it," she said reluctantly.

The dark eyes flared. "Really? And what did he mention, exactly?"

"He'd heard something about roses. And dancing."

The eyes narrowed. "Anything else?"

Wallis sighed. "He might have heard something else. Why don't you ask him?"

"Because it's all so utterly *ridiculous*!" But something flickered across her face that might have been fear.

The caviar arrived. Thelma shoved the silver spoon into the pile of glistening gray-black eggs. She seemed to be weighing up something. "Wallis," she said eventually. "I'll let you into a secret."

Wallis wished with all her heart that she wouldn't. But Thelma was leaning over the table toward her, her expression slyly conspiratorial.

"Aly *may* have visited me in my stateroom," she whispered. "He may even have made love to me. And, oh, it was *wonderful*, Wallis! Nights unlike any I have known!" She closed her eyes and wriggled with remembered ecstasy. "He was *insatiable*! He knows *exactly* how to please a woman. Unlike certain princes I could mention," she added with a giggle.

Wallis, who had automatically leaned forward too, jerked backward in disgust. It wasn't just the vulgarity; it was the disloyalty. How could Thelma be so treacherous? She felt outraged for the prince. He had loved her so much but deserved so much better.

Thelma slid the spoon into the eggs again. "But it was only fun, of course. It didn't mean anything. I'm devoted to David, obviously."

Wallis did not reply.

"I'd hate there to be . . . How shall I put this?" Thelma cocked her messy head to one side. "A misunderstanding."

Wallis wasn't sure what was meant. What was there to misunderstand? It had happened, and Thelma had admitted it.

"For David to take it, well, *seriously*." An expectant silence followed this.

"I think he was . . . rather hurt, possibly," Wallis admitted.

Thelma leaped on this immediately. "Hurt? He's a fine one to feel hurt! What about all the people *he's* hurt? Freda, for instance."

Who you replaced, Wallis thought. What a hypocrite Thelma was. Wallis picked up her fork and began to poke at her salad with it.

After the waiter had refilled her champagne glass, Thelma resumed her former light tone. "Did you *talk* to David much, while I was away?"

"A bit," Wallis admitted. "You did ask me to look after . . . *him* for you." She could not bear to say "the little man." It was patronizing and demeaning. Thelma's gaze was steady. "What did you talk about?"

"It was quite wide-ranging," Wallis replied evasively.

Thelma raised an eyebrow. "And where precisely did it range?"

"Well, the unemployed, for instance. He told me how worried he is about them."

She was surprised by the response, which was a snort. "Oh *yes*," said Thelma. "He's *terribly* worried about them. Sleepless nights, I should think."

"What do you mean? He seemed very concerned about it."

"Oh, he is! Those poor people! He can't get enough of them! Four families in one room, shared lavatories. Always banging on about them."

"But . . . aren't they worth banging on about?"

Thelma picked up her glass. "Don't ask me, I don't know the first thing about shared lavatories. Neither does David."

"He sounded utterly miserable about them."

Thelma drained her champagne. "He *likes* the idea of being utterly miserable about them. But if you ask me it's a sort of vanity hobby. Something he does to be different from the rest of his family."

Real anger welled up in Wallis. "How can you say that? He wants to modernize the monarchy. Bring it closer to the people."

Thelma laughed. "Believe me, baby, David's idea of modernizing the monarchy is to fly his own plane and install a few bathrooms."

Wallis could feel how red her cheeks were getting. How the blood was burning up her neck all the way to her ears and forehead. Trust Thelma to trivialize the prince's concerns. Just because she cared only about money didn't mean everyone had the same selfish views.

"Well, he sounded convincing to me," Wallis said defiantly.

"Oh, he *sounds* convincing. He's the consummate actor—they all are in that family. But he never actually *does* anything." Her eyes sparkled merrily. "Still, just as long as you didn't encourage him. That's the single worst thing anyone could do."

Wallis balled her hands into fists and breathed deeply to calm down. The blood was thundering in her ears, so it was difficult to hear the words that now floated over from Thelma.

"What?"

Thelma smiled her sweetest smile. "I asked whether you and Arnie would like to come to the Fort this weekend. You can help me convince David that nothing happened with Aly."

CHAPTER THIRTY-TWO

T hey arrived at the Fort to find their hosts nowhere to be seen.

"This is so awkward," Ernest hissed as they unpacked in the Queen's Room. "You can cut the atmosphere with a knife."

It had been harder than ever to persuade him to come. He thought the Aly Khan story ridiculous, but the prince's hysterical sobbing had not impressed him either. Wallis knew he felt she was getting too involved, that it was getting too complicated.

"After all, whose side are you on here?" he asked her. "Thelma's invited us, but it's David you sympathize with."

Seeing him get out a pile of office papers, and as it was a warm early-summer evening, she went out into the garden. It was a good way to avoid Thelma, who never went outside if she could help it, and it was interesting to spot what improvements had been made since the last visit. There was always something.

And of course, part of her hoped she might see, in the distance, a familiar figure armed with a rake, a ready smile and tousled blond hair shining in the sun.

On the swimming-pool terrace she found blond hair and a ready smile, but they belonged not to David but Diana Cooper. She wore a white swimming costume and round dark glasses and was sitting on a long padded chair with her slim white legs stretched out in front of her. She looked like a very modern Greek goddess.

"How lovely!" Diana said, placing her book down on the warm flagstones. It seemed to be some large volume of history, about Henry VIII. Wallis grappled briefly with her usual feelings of inadequacy when in the presence of this poised, beautiful and now, it turned out, educated aristocrat.

"Do sit down," Diana invited. "Duff's off playing golf with the prince. Sir looks quite the fashion plate today," she added. "Plus twenties with vivid azure socks!"

Wallis smiled, sat down and looked over the dancing waters of the pool. She thought of the time in the snow, picking up records thrown by Prince George. He had not been mentioned lately. Hopefully the worst was over on that front.

Diana broke into her thoughts.

"I find the Fort simply enchanting, don't you? It only needs fifty red tin soldiers to stand on the battlements to make it into a Walt Disney colored symphony toy. Which is appropriate, if you think about it."

"Is it?"

"Yes, because we've all been invited to keep peace in the nursery this weekend. Between sir and Thelma." She smiled.

Wallis had no intention of discussing Thelma and the prince. But Diana obviously did and had, in her roundabout way, steered the talk to where she wanted it.

Diana adjusted her sunglasses. "I see you don't know, so I'd better fill you in. Thelma's made a bad mistake, and I rather fear she's going to pay the price."

Wallis still did not reply.

She was glad when Diana reached down and picked up her book again. For a few moments there was no sound but the turning of pages and the high, sweet piercing notes of a bird.

"What's the book?" Wallis asked, grateful for a chance to change the subject.

"It's Duff's actually, a sort of general British history. "I'm just reading about Catherine Howard."

Wallis dug about in her memory. "One of the wives of Henry VIII, wasn't she?" *Divorced, beheaded, died, divorced, beheaded, survived.* She had no idea which category applied to Catherine Howard.

"That's right. One of the beheaded ones, poor thing."

Wallis remembered now. She had visited the Tower of London one dark, cold winter day. There had been no one else around. She had stood on Tower Green looking at the cobbled area surrounded by a chain railing where the scaffold had once stood. There had been a plaque with the names of women. Lady Jane Grey. Queen Anne Boleyn. And, yes, Queen Catherine Howard. "What happened to her?" she asked Diana.

"Rather a sad story. She was much younger than Henry was, only a teenager, and not terribly bright. She had an affair, which the king found out about. He had been very much in love with her, and he was furious at the betrayal. There was a terrible scene when she ran screaming along the corridor begging him to forgive her. He was in the chapel at the time, praying." Diana sorrowfully shook her head.

Wallis shuddered. Diana had brought it vividly to life. She could hear the terrified girl, see the vengeful old man. "And I'm guessing that he didn't stop praying in order to forgive his foolish teenage wife?"

"He cut her off, in every sense. You didn't get a second chance with Henry."

"Same story with Anne Boleyn, right?"

Diana tipped her head back and stared at the hot blue sky. "Up to a point," she said. "What happened with Anne Boleyn was a bit more complicated. She gave Henry the excuse to reinvent the monarchy to suit himself."

"But didn't she just want to be queen?" Wallis thought she had read as much somewhere.

"Well, that's the usual version. But I think it more likely that she didn't realize quite what she was getting into. It would have been wonderful at first. Henry was so powerful, and being his favorite must have been intoxicating." Diana stretched in the warmth beating down from the blue sky. "Like sunshine all day long."

Wallis studied her. "You've really thought about this, haven't you?"

Diana nodded. "I'm interested in history, and in women who get bad reputations. It's usually terribly unfair."

Skimming across Wallis's mind came something Thelma had said about Diana. *Her father's not a duke at all, just some philandering journalist her mother had an affair with.* Was there a personal reason for this interest? "Unfair?" Wallis asked.

"Almost always there's a reason why someone wants to blacken their name," Diana explained.

"What sort of reason?"

Diana sat up and clasped her knees. "Well, in Anne's case, she took the blame for Henry defying church and state, which was far more about power and money than love. It must have been terrifying for her. Everybody hated her; she was abused whenever she appeared in public; she was called a whore and a witch. I'm sure in the end that being queen was the very last thing she wanted. But by then it was too late."

Wallis was fascinated. "I had no idea about any of that," she said. "Poor Anne."

Diana nodded. "Henry was completely ruthless. People think he was blinded by passion, but it was really all about control. Once he wanted her, that was that. She was trapped. She had to surrender; she had no choice. She must have known it would all go wrong in the end, but what could she do?"

A cloud had passed over the sun. Wallis shivered. Time to go.

"Thank goodness kings are different these days." She smiled, thinking of the plus twenties and the azure socks.

Diana opened her book again. It seemed to be her turn not to reply.

◆ ◆ ◆

Later, they arrived in the drawing room for drinks to find Thelma looking distinctly *distrait*. She was skittering around, clanking the decanters with shaking hands. "Remind me how to make those old-fashioneds, Wallis."

"I'll do it. You sit down."

Thelma sat down, but almost immediately bounced up again and came to the back of the room. "David's hardly speaking to me. You've got to help me, Wallis!"

Wallis swirled the cocktails with a silver stick. On top were the three princely feathers. "Help you how?"

Tears were pooling in Thelma's eyes. Dried ones were already visible amid the makeup coating her cheeks. Her purple bottom lip trembled. "Tell him I didn't have a fling with Aly!"

"I can't tell him that!" Wallis looked back at her almost as pleadingly. "It wouldn't be true."

"Yes it would!" Thelma wiped away a tear with a hand whose nails were bitten down to the quick. "What happened wasn't *meaningful*."

It had been meaningful for the prince, Wallis thought.

"It was just one tiny mistake . . ." Thelma was weeping now: shuddering, messy sobs.

"I don't know what to say," Wallis said helplessly. Despite everything, she felt sorry for Thelma.

An arm now shot out and grabbed hers. "But you'll say something, won't you?"

"But why would he care what I say?"

The clinging fingers increased their pressure to a painful grip. "Come on, Wallis," Thelma urged. "You like coming to the Fort, don't you? If he dumps me you won't be able to stay again either. Think of it that way. Whoever replaces me won't ask *you*. Will she?"

Fortunately, just then, the other three inhabitants of the Fort arrived in the room. The prince was in his Highland outfit, and the dagger in his sock gleamed in the lamplight. He did not look at Thelma but made a great fuss of Ernest and Wallis. He then sat down at his embroidery frame and began stabbing the needle swiftly in and out.

As Thelma hurled herself next to him, Wallis was unprepared for the prince to look up at her, smile and suggest she sit down too. She reluctantly inserted herself into the space he had rather forcibly created between his mistress and himself.

As, not long afterward, he paraded around the dining table with his bagpipes, his cheeks inflating and his face red and his eyes fixed and stern, the tune sounded less like the usual tragic lament than a declaration of war. He placed Wallis on his right side and Diana on his left while Thelma was positioned out of his eyeline, her face a picture of misery. She said little, but drank glass after glass of wine.

There was the usual dancing afterward, although, claiming a headache from too much sun, Diana excused herself and Duff. Thelma, drunk, lurched about with Ernest while the prince fox-trotted with Wallis. Then, suddenly, he declared his intention of going to bed and disappeared from the room immediately. His remaining guests stood looking at one another. The record ended, and the needle lifted.

"And then there were three," remarked Thelma sarcastically.

Ernest yawned. "Actually, I think I'll turn in as well."

Wallis tried frantically to catch his eye. She did not want to be left alone with Thelma, especially in her wild-eyed and unhinged state. Anything might happen. But Ernest picked up his jacket and left.

"I'd better go too," Wallis began, intending to dive out after him.

"Oh no you don't!"

Wallis stood where she was, and Thelma started to pace around her, unsteady on her heels, her gaze icy.

"I want to talk to you, Wallis Simpson." She sounded angry, threatening. "Looked after the little man rather better than I imagined. Didn't you?"

"Thelma, that's not fair. I don't know what you're suggesting, but . . ."

"You don't *know* what I'm *suggesting*?" Thelma stopped pacing, put her hands on her hips and laughed bitterly. "What do you think I'm suggesting? When the cat's away, that's what I'm suggesting."

"No, Thelma, you're wrong," Wallis protested. Although a better word would be delusional. Thelma had deceived her lover, with whom she was already deceiving her husband. She, Wallis, had deceived nobody.

"You deny David's been coming to see you?"

"David has been coming to Bryanston Court, yes. But only while you were away."

The face with its smudged makeup came closer. "Oh. It's *David* now, is it?"

Wallis tried to ignore this. "He was very upset," she began.

"Don't tell me," Thelma snarled. "Collapsed on the floor and started sobbing, did he?"

"Yes, as it happens," Wallis said levelly. "I don't think you quite understand what you did to him. I don't think you understand the first thing about him."

"And you think you do?" Thelma stared at her. The fury had died from her eyes; her expression had grown calm, even slightly pitying. "Baby, have you any idea of what you're getting into?"

Then she picked up her handbag and left the room. There was the sound of the front door closing, and a car engine starting up. A crunch of tires on gravel.

Just like that, Thelma was gone.

CHAPTER THIRTY-THREE

The next morning was soft and sweet with some hints of mist. The air rang with singing birds, and as Wallis entered the Great Park, wildflowers of all colors glowed in grass sparkling with dew. Rabbits loped about, and squirrels scurried up tree trunks. There was a fresh, earthy smell, and the sun had a latent brilliance that promised a beautiful day. As she passed Virginia Water it shone like polished silver.

If he dumps me you won't be able to stay again either. . . . Whoever replaces me won't ask you.

Thelma had gone for good, she knew. But Wallis had no intention of spending what might be her last morning at the Fort exchanging languorous quips with Diana in the drawing room. She wanted to walk, take one last lingering look at it all.

She had started with the Fort gardens, but then the Great Park had called to her. It was where she and the prince had had their extraordinary conversation, when she had drawn so close to him they had briefly seemed almost the same person. But he was about to become remote once more—someone she saw only in newspapers. She would be like Cinderella after the ball, but no one would come looking with a glass slipper. She told herself that this was just as well and reminded herself to be cheerful. It had all been far more than she had ever expected.

She had dressed carefully for this last walk; it felt ceremonial. She chose a black-and-white polka-dot frock and a broad-brimmed white hat. When she looked in the mirror, at her glossy black hair and her white-pale face, the only color was her lipstick: the usual bloodred. She smiled at herself, picked up her coat and closed the door. Ernest was still snoring, the papers he had been reading before he fell asleep scattered on the carpet beside him.

A large equestrian statue marked the point in the park where the view toward the castle began. She stood by it for a moment, admiring the distant prospect, which, in this slightly milky light, reminded her of the Turners she had seen in her gallery-haunting days. Days now poised to return, she thought with a sigh.

What a magnificent place Windsor Castle was, sprawling and ancient, built over so many centuries. Like the British monarchy itself, she thought. She smiled, imagining how many people had stood there and drawn the same parallel. From then on, she would be seeing the Crown from the outside, as they did.

All the same, she knew a little of what the heir to all this felt about it, how he intended to change it when he was on the throne. Something about the sheer scale, weight and might of this age-old building hinted at what he might be up against. He would need all the help and encouragement he could get. So whoever replaced Thelma would hopefully be equal to the task.

She walked on. The castle got closer. She left the park and entered the town. She was at the fortress's formidable entrance now and decided, on a whim, to go in. A bell was calling the faithful to the chapel inside. On another whim, she decided to join them.

She walked quickly over the cobbles under the cold and shadowy portcullis and out into the sun-warmed lower ward, with its clipped lawns and the chapel rising like a cliff of carved stone, all spires and sparkling glass. It was the second-most beautiful building she had ever seen, the first being the Fort.

The inside was a dream of Gothic loveliness. Bright morning sunlight slanted through the stained-glass windows and threw many-colored shadows on carved pillars and soaring arches. She slipped into a seat in the nave and looked at what she knew from Ernest's guidebook to be the carved oak stalls belonging to the Knights of the Garter, an ancient English order of chivalry. Each stall, actually an elaborate seat, was hung with the bright heraldic banner of its current occupant and surmounted with carved devices from their coat of arms: swords, helmets, crowns, curling vegetations and fantastical heraldic beasts, all gilded and brightly painted.

Elderly men, contrasting with the dashing promise of the swords and flags above them, occupied a handful of the Garter stalls. They all looked asleep to Wallis, but she saw now that among them was a young man, almost invisible in the shadows beneath his carved canopy. It was the prince, she realized, and felt an excitement mixed with longing.

His face was still and contemplative, quite lacking the animation she was used to. She wondered if he was talking to the Almighty as he had told her he did. He was looking up at one of the windows, and as she watched, the sun outside threw a beam whose colored rays, falling on his pale and perfect profile, imbued it with an ideal noble beauty.

It was as if the same sunray was shining on her heart. As the high, pure voices of the choir rose up to the carved ceiling, she felt that if this was her last moment on earth, she could die happy.

An insect buzzed by her and broke the spell. She saw that the church had filled up since she had sat down. In a pew very close to her were some familiar-looking people. Bertie, Elizabeth and their two small daughters, the famous little princesses. And next to them, the king and queen.

Wallis was glad of her hat, which threw a useful shadow over her face. While Their Majesties had never met her, she doubted Bertie and Elizabeth would be pleased to renew the acquaintance.

Queen Mary looked even less the loving mother than her son's stories suggested. Her air of rigid humorlessness was offset by a cartoonishly enormous bust that spread across her front in a continuous swell, its size amplified by the inflated Edwardian sleeves of her pale mauve coat. A matching and equally Edwardian toque hat, tall, vaguely turban-like and so covered in flowers it seemed she was wearing a planter on her head, rose above a fringe of gray curly hair reminiscent of a sheep. Even from a pew away Wallis could see this fringe was false and attached with pins in the Victorian fashion. She could completely understand how this woman's eldest son, in his behavior, his dress and his choice of friends, wanted to place himself as far as possible from this vision of unbending, unappealing antiquity.

The king was frailer than the terrifying figure she had anticipated. His watery eyes gave him a lachrymose air, but the bright-red cheeks suggested a temper. Most of his face was covered with a beard and mustache heavily yellow-stained with nicotine. Smoking clearly ran in the family. Next to his father in the pew, Bertie looked gray-faced and as tense as ever, while Elizabeth, also as ever, exuded soft femininity and cat-with-the-cream contentment. Wallis wondered again what it was she had done to deserve this woman's instant dislike. And what Thelma had done to deserve the opposite. Did the Yorks know what had happened with Thelma yet?

The little girls were adorable, she thought, dressed identically in white hats and gray coats. She guessed Margaret, the smaller, to be about four and a livelier, naughtier character than her elder sister, who exuded a calm propriety. They were looking about them curiously, and when they chanced to look at her, Wallis could not resist a broad wink. To her amusement, the two pairs of blue eyes widened in amazement. Then, to her delight, they smiled back. Elizabeth had a particularly winning one, a great, broad monkey grin.

The first hymn began. The king and queen sang surprisingly loudly: she with a German accent and gratingly off-key and he, the ex-sailor, with a quarter-deck roar that seemed to echo round the chapel. But then they were, Wallis reflected, Defenders of the Faith: a faith that had, moreover, obligingly put them right at the top of the social heap. Were she in their position, she would probably defend it too. She glanced at the prince; his lips were hardly moving. It occurred to her to wonder why he wasn't sitting with the others.

The preacher mounted to the lectern: short, old and with a shiny bald head. The sermon he began was soporific in the extreme. She looked at the princesses, anticipating fidgeting and planning to tip them an understanding wink. She wanted to see the monkey grin again. Both were sitting still, however, their attention apparently riveted on the vicar.

Glancing back at the preacher, Wallis realized why. The bee that had jerked her from her contemplations was now flying round the priest. Its fat black form appeared intermittently against the carvings to his rear. It seemed to be getting lower, and the circles it was describing, more restricted.

The vicar droned on, oblivious. The bee was now revolving around only his head. It seemed that it would, any minute, settle on the gleaming center of the vicar's bald pate.

Would it sting him? Would he shout? Swear? The thought was enough to send bubbles of laughter up her throat.

The princesses were evidently also following the drama closely. She could tell that both were riveted to the bee's every twist. The gently buzzing spiral was now narrowing; the supreme moment was at hand.

And then it finally landed, and in just the bald spot anticipated. The little girls' eyes were vast with disbelief, their mouths round red Os. They glanced at Wallis, saw she was looking too, and the monkey grin flashed again. Margaret, meanwhile, snorted, and at this Wallis's mirth overcame her. Burying her face in her handkerchief, she attempted to disguise it as a cough.

This attracted the duchess's attention. She looked at Wallis, and at her giggling daughters, then back at Wallis again. While her expression did not change, there was ice in the violet eyes.

When Wallis next glanced at the girls, their expressions seemed carved in stone.

CHAPTER THIRTY-FOUR

She was among the first out of the chapel afterward and back in the park. It was time to turn her thoughts toward the rest of the day, the rest of her life. She had left a note for Ernest, asking him to pack. But would there be lunch, or would they just go? She did not know.

The sun was more powerful than it had been earlier. She removed her coat and felt the breeze on her sleeveless arms. She would miss the freedom and space of Windsor. Of course, she could come back; the Great Park was open to all. But she doubted that she ever would; it would hardly be the same.

While it was hot on the path, the air felt cool between the trees. She glanced into the woodland and remembered the legend of the dark and turbulent spirit Herne. Never in all her visits had she seen anything of the spectral hunter with his chains and his horns and his streaming blue light. It was all baloney, as Ernest had said.

She was almost at the statue of the man on horseback when she heard a roar behind her. It was a car engine, approaching so rapidly that she barely had time to leap out of the way. It had an open top, and she scowled at the driver, rude and careless idiot that he was.

He screeched to a halt and grinned back at her from under his wide tweed checked cap, his face hidden by goggles and his body concealed in a greatcoat. Brown leather gauntlets covered his hands.

Then he pulled off the cap to reveal bright hair and pushed up the goggles so a familiar blue beam blazed out. Her heart turned over.

"David!"

"Like it? It's my new American station wagon!" Proudly, he stroked the padded leather back of the passenger seat.

The magnificent cream roadster was long and roofless, with ribbed leather seats, shining spokes, gleaming headlamps and glittering chrome fittings.

"It's beautiful."

He turned off the engine, opened the door and got out. "I saw you in the chapel," he said. "I looked for you afterward, but you'd gone."

I looked for you. She felt a ripple of delight.

"It's a beautiful place," she said. "Historic."

"It's that all right. Vindsor is vun big history lesson! The St. Chorge's Chapel! Henry ze Eight is buried there. Ant Chane Seymour!"

She realized he was imitating his mother. And now he was drawing his brows, to assume the character of his father.

"AND SOME OF QUEEN ANNE'S CHILDREN AS WELL! TALK ABOUT A MIXED GRILL. FUNNY OLD BUSLOAD TO BE GOING THROUGH ETERNITY TOGETHER!"

She laughed. "I just saw your family in the chapel."

"So did I. Worse luck." He twisted to look up at the statue above him and clapped one of the horse's great bronze legs. "This is George the Third. The king who lost America. Know what my father says about this statue?"

"That he shouldn't have lost America?"

"Hardly. My father hates America. If it hadn't been lost already he'd have given it away himself. No, my father's objection is that George was dressed up like a Roman." He drew his brows again. "'DAMNED FOOL, DRESSING UP LIKE THAT! PRETENDING TO BE SOMETHING HE WASN'T! SHOULD HAVE THANKED GOD HE WAS BORN AN ENGLISHMAN!'"

She laughed again.

"But do you know what's really funny about it," the prince mused. "George wasn't English; he was German, and so, more or less, is Papa. And while we're on the subject, if anything more perfectly encapsulates the condition of royalty than dressing up and pretending to be something we're not, I can't think what it is."

Had something happened in the chapel? Was that why he had sat apart from his family?

"What's the matter?" Wallis asked gently.

He sank down with his back against the stone plinth. "The usual one," he said, stretching his legs out on the grass. "My father. And for the usual reason too."

"Your clothes?"

He stared at her, then laughed. "My wife."

The world seemed to stop for a moment. Her legs seemed suddenly weak. She lowered herself, trembling, a few feet from where he sat, curling her legs under her, reaching for a daisy as a distraction. "Your . . . wife?"

Her mind was rioting. Surely he couldn't mean *Thelma*?

He asks everyone. It's a thing with him. He asked me too. Hadn't Thelma once said that, at lunch at the Ritz? Had they somehow made up?

Queen Thelma? Was that even remotely imaginable?

He had got out his cigarettes and was flicking his lighter. "My father thinks it's high time I got married. He's even got my cousin Louis Mountbatten to draw up a list of suitable European princesses for me to choose from."

He pulled in a lungful of smoke. "There are seventeen of them and the youngest is Thyra of Mecklenburg-Schwerin. She's fifteen. I'm nearly forty, by the way."

"That's quite an age gap," Wallis agreed. While relieved that the bride wasn't Thelma, she could see this was little better. He frowned, stubbing his cigarette out on the grass.

"But I don't want to pick a wife from a stable of aristocratic broodmares and lead one of them up the aisle of Westminster Abbey." He made a mocking *clip-clop* noise, and a gesture like holding reins.

She grinned. "No."

"It's all so ridiculously old-fashioned. Society's changed. Women have changed. They vote, go to university, train for professions, fly around in airplanes even." He lit another cigarette.

"You want a wife who can fly a plane?" Amy Johnson and Amelia Earhart had both made record-breaking flights recently.

He looked puzzled, then grinned. "Ha! Wouldn't that be something? No, I mean the blasted monarchy should keep up. A modern king should be able to choose a wife who's an equal partner, someone who can support, encourage and advise."

"Absolutely," she agreed. "Like Eleanor Roosevelt and FDR." The wife of the new president was rumored to be as interested in social reform as her husband.

His face lit up. "Exactly! As an American, you can see that. It would be a whole new way of being queen. Changing a thousand years of royal history."

She felt excited. It was a radical vision, but she could see the sense in it. "I think that's a brilliant idea."

He blew out a stream of smoke. "Well, it's the only way I can see myself becoming king, that's for sure."

She looked at him closely. "How do you mean? You will become king, won't you?"

He was regarding the distant castle with narrowed eyes. "I suppose so. But I increasingly wonder what the point is. Surely, in the modern age, the time of kings and princes is past. They seem so incredibly out of date to me."

He had said something like this before to her. *I don't know what any of it means or even why I'm doing it.* But this seemed to take it a stage further. This was the family business he was denigrating. His own destiny he was doubting. "You can't say that. You're the Prince of Wales."

"Yes, but I'm entirely the wrong person. I *hate* it! I can't tell you how utterly *sick* of it I am. I absolutely fucking *loathe* it."

She was grappling with her disbelief. "But you have all your wonderful ideas. A prince with a social conscience."

"Wallis, you are amazing. You're so can-do, so full of New World positivity. You say to me the things I say to myself, but you make it sound as if it could actually happen!"

"But why can't it?" she demanded. "You've started your housing project now, haven't you?"

He groaned. "Yes, but it hardly scratches the surface of what needs to be done. Which most people don't want me to do anyway."

"But when you're king, you'd be in charge!"

"You're so delightfully American. Do you know what a constitutional monarchy actually is? It means they'll block me at every turn. I'll be reduced to dressing up and poncing about as usual."

She had known he was frustrated, but not that he harbored such violent loathing. "But you're so wonderful at poncing about," she said. "Everyone loves you."

He couldn't help laughing at this. "Well I don't love *them*. I'm sick of being yelled and shrieked at. I get clapped on the back until I'm black and blue, and my hand is shaken until it swells up like a football. They stab me as well."

"*Stab* you?"

He nodded.

"*Who* stabs you?"

"The old ladies." He sounded quite matter-of-fact about it.

"Old ladies *stab* you?"

He squinted up at the burning sky. "After Armistice parades, when I'm meeting the veterans. There are always widows hovering about. They come up to me, and as they get close I see them going for it."

"Going for it?"

"The hatpin. Usually they keep it in the crook of their elbow. They whip it out and then shove it into me hard wherever the nearest point is. My arm usually."

Her mouth had dropped open. "But . . . why?"

"Why?" He removed his cigarette and looked at it. "Because their sons or husbands or brothers, or all three, were killed in the war. They're mad with grief, and who better to take it out on than the person who symbolizes what the whole of that appalling and point-less carnage was supposedly about. King and country."

She stared at him. "Don't you do anything about it? Couldn't you have them arrested or something?"

"Probably. But I don't want to. I don't blame them at all. In their shoes I would do the same." He raked a hand through his bright-blond hair. "This might sound strange, but it feels like the only occa-sion where my presence as a royal does any actual good."

He stood up and stretched. "Well, Wallis. What a conversation. I haven't known you long, but I've never come across anyone I find so easy to talk to. It's as if we've known each other forever." He smiled, holding her in the blue spotlight.

"I feel that too," she replied simply.

"I can't tell you what a relief it is to have someone who under-stands. No one else does. Papa finds fault at every opportunity. Com-plains about me to everyone else too. The other day he told the archbishop of Canterbury that once he's dead I'll ruin myself in a year. Charming, eh?"

She gasped. "How unfair! He should be proud of you. Your ideas are wonderful."

"He wouldn't see it that way. Papa only looks backward, never forward. The entire twentieth century is anathema to him." He blew out a column of smoke. "He's not interested in progression or mod-ernity in any form."

"So that's why he hates America?" The remark had puzzled her since he had said it.

"Yes, and because he knows I love it. If I'm honest I bought an

American car partly to annoy him." He glanced at the gleaming roadster with a sort of defiant pride. Then he sighed and seemed to deflate. "It feels like such a struggle. This wedding thing. Sometimes I feel tempted to give in and to marry whoever they want me to. Just for some peace."

She was getting up too, striking the grass from her dress. "But you can't! You should marry the person *you* want to. How can you be a good king if you're not happy? You can't be the right sort of king with the wrong sort of wife."

He was staring at her. "That's true," he said slowly. "I can't be the right sort of king with the wrong sort of wife."

Then he beamed at her, started up the engine and patted the seat beside him. "Hop in, Wallis. We're going on a journey!"

CHAPTER THIRTY-FIVE

She had never in her life driven as fast—the road was a single gray blur and the trees a rush of green. A great roaring filled her ears. She clasped her hat with one hand but had nothing to steady herself with the other. He glanced at her, grinning beneath his goggles.

"Hang on to me," he shouted as they rounded a corner.

He changed up a gear and went even faster. A pair of low white entrance lodges shot past. Then a drive bordered with rhododendron in full bloom, brightly colored. Ahead was a pale-pink house of vaguely Oriental design. It looked like a cake, she thought.

He roared up to it and turned in a semicircle. A wave of gravel lifted in his wake. He stopped, turned off the engine and smiled. "I thought we'd pay a call on Bertie. Show him the new car."

So this was Royal Lodge. How funny that two such serious people lived in such a trivial-looking building.

The front door, at the top of a flight of wide, shallow steps, was pale green. It now flew open, and the eldest princess appeared, still in her coat. They must only just have gotten back from the chapel. "It's Uncle David!" Elizabeth hammered down the steps to greet the newcomer.

He pressed the horn and laughed. "Lilibet! Oh, and Margaret too!"

The younger princess had appeared and ran down the steps after her sister.

"Uncle David! Uncle David!"

He was clearly a great favorite, Wallis saw with surprise. Not all relations with his family were terrible, then.

She was still clinging to the prince, she realized, as the duke and duchess appeared. She sprang away as if he were burning hot, but it was too late. The cold violet stare was on her.

"D-D-David!" exclaimed the duke. As usual he looked and sounded harassed. "To wh-wh-what . . ."

"Do we owe the pleasure?" put in his wife smoothly, placing on his arm a hand that was yet gloved from church. But the glance that she slid Wallis hinted that it was no pleasure at all, not in her case.

The prince drummed his gloved hands on the steering wheel. His goggles glinted in the sun. "Thought you'd like to see my new wheels! Come and try it out, Bertie!" Wallis felt fear churn within. Surely he wasn't intending to leave her here with Elizabeth.

The duke looked doubtfully at his wife, then longingly back at the gleaming car. Lilibet and Margaret were dancing excitedly round it.

"Poop poop!" Margaret was shouting, pointing at the big brass horn. "Poop poop!"

Wallis laughed. "I'm guessing you've read *The Wind in the Willows*."

Lilibet looked up from examining the car with her sister. "You're an American," she said with surprise.

"That's right. I am."

Wallis was hoping for the great monkey grin, and there it came, transforming the princess's serious face.

"I know you!" Lilibet exclaimed. "You're the lady who winked at us in the chapel!" She turned to her mother. "Mummie! This is the lady I told you about!"

Wallis's heart sank. Her fame had gone before her, it seemed. Elizabeth did not reply, just took her daughter's hand and steered her firmly away.

"You can honk it if you like," the prince was telling Margaret, demonstrating the device's mighty blast. The younger princess squeezed the great black rubber bulb and squealed with delight at the noise it made.

"Come on, Bertie!" urged his brother again gaily.

The duchess's gloved hand pressed her husband's arm. "Go on," Wallis heard her mutter. "Get it over with. I'll show her round the garden."

This broke the deadlock. The duke bounded over, and Wallis was obliged to get out. Her heart was beating so hard it thumped in her ears. She could even hear it over Lilibet's honking. The car roared away, and as the engine faded, it seemed to Wallis that never had silence been quite so silent.

Another woman had appeared on the steps. Wallis thought she recognized her from St. George's Chapel, sitting behind the Yorks. She was young and exceptionally tall, with lovely skin and chestnut hair. She had intelligent eyes either side of a large nose, and there was about her, as she looked at the duchess, an air of apprehension.

The duchess ushered her daughters toward the newcomer. "A walk in the woods, perhaps, Crawfie?" Crawfie did not need to be told twice.

"Where are we going?" Lilibet could be heard asking indignantly as she and Margaret were marched toward the trees. "We never walk at this time of day, Crawfie! *Crawfie?*"

Elizabeth smiled at Wallis. It did not quite reach her eyes, or anywhere near them. "Would you care to see the garden?"

Elizabeth was a fast walker. Her legs were short, but they were quick. Whenever Wallis drew level she managed to move ahead to oblige her to follow a few steps behind, rather in the manner of a lady's maid.

"Dahlias," Elizabeth said, sticking a hand out at one side.

"Roses," she added, gesturing with the other.

The two royal gardens formed a striking contrast, Wallis thought. Whereas the Fort's was carefully contrived to look natural, the opposite was the case at Royal Lodge, where the flower beds were laid out in squares like a box of chocolates. The colors, as she had noticed on her way up the drive, were glaring and assertive, rather than the Fort's subtler shades.

She tried to make friendly remarks about the weather, but these were pointedly ignored. It seemed the Duchess of York asked the questions.

"And how is *Mr.* Simpson?"

Wallis blinked. "Oh. Ernest's very well, thank you. He's back at the Fort."

The duchess bent to pull up a weed by the path. "He didn't go with you to church?"

Wallis smiled. "Ernest's not much of a churchgoer, I'm afraid."

The violet eyes looked at her sharply. "And you are?"

It was unmistakably an attack. Wallis looked round her brightly. Time for a change of subject. "You have a very nice garden here."

"My husband is an expert gardener. His particular passion is rhododendrons. Do you admire rhododendrons, Mrs. Simpson?"

"Well . . . ," Wallis began. Rhododendrons had never struck her as especially attractive, with their leggy, woody branches and dark, dusty leaves. She certainly couldn't imagine being passionate about them.

"Bertie once wrote a very amusing letter to our friend Lady Stair," Elizabeth went on. "He substituted the names of rhododendrons for certain words. For example, he thanked Lady Stair for giving him an agapetum time."

Wallis looked back at her blankly. "Agap . . . ?"

"Agapetum. It's a variety of rhododendron. The name means 'delightful.'"

Understanding dawned. "Oh, I see! Agapetum time, delightful time." As jokes went, it seemed on the labored side.

"And Lady Stair wrote back and said she was timetum to have received his His Basilicum Highness's letter. 'An honor' and 'royal,' respectively," said Elizabeth crisply.

"That's . . . ingenious. I wish I was such an expert in gardens as you English are."

"As a matter of fact, I'm Scottish. Do you know Scotland?"

"Not really," Wallis admitted. "But I've heard it's beautiful."

"Do you fish?"

Wallis had never seen the point. Stand up to her thighs in cold water when she could order from a good fishmonger? She knew better than to say so, however. She shook her head, smiling.

"Stalk?"

Wallis decided she had had enough of Elizabeth's peremptory manner. She would have a little fun. "As in the bird?"

"As in the *stag*," Elizabeth snapped. "Those animals with big antlers. Perhaps you don't have them in America."

"Oh, we do. But at home we call them elk."

There was a roar from the front of the house. *Rescue*, thought Wallis. She smiled brightly at Elizabeth. "Sounds like the boys are back."

"Their Royal Highnesses very possibly are," corrected the duchess stiffly.

"Enjoy yourself?" asked the prince as he and Wallis drove away.

"Very much," she said diplomatically. "The garden's lovely."

"Think so?" He cast her an amused look through the goggles. "I find it awfully stiff. All those blasted rhododendrons."

"Agapetum." She grinned to herself.

"What?"

"Nothing. The girls are very sweet."

"Yes. Lilibet's a regular Shirley Temple."

"Which," Wallis chuckled, "makes Elizabeth Mrs. Temple Senior."

He laughed so hard the car almost veered off the road. "Mrs. Temple Senior!" He honked his horn with delight.

She wanted the drive to last forever but there already came Virginia Water. The towers of the Fort showed above the trees, the view she loved most; it blurred with tears as she looked at it, committing it to heart this one last time. Other people than her would be coming here from now on, the friends of the new favorite, the wife even.

"Wallis!" He was looking at her. She forced a brave smile.

"David?"

"Don't suppose you'd fancy coming to the Fort next weekend? You and Ernest? It's Ascot, so feel free to bring some friends."

CHAPTER THIRTY-SIX

The course at Epsom Downs was as green as emerald under a bright-blue sky. Bright-red buses were packed with merry people; bookmakers were yelling their odds; bands played; there were brilliant feathered hats, pearly kings and queens.

The real king and queen were several carriages ahead, and the prince and his brothers were with them. Wallis was still quite unable to believe she was actually part of a royal procession, albeit right at the end and right at the back. Trotting through the narrow, shady lanes to reach the racecourse, they had run the gauntlet of lines of onlookers, all of whom had cheered as the royal family went past. First Their Majesties with the Prince of Wales, then the Yorks with the other two princes, then various cousins, uncles and aunts.

The enthusiasm of the onlookers had dwindled in proportion to the dwindling fame and importance of those in the subsequent landaus. By the time the carriage containing Wallis, Ernest, cousin Corinne and her husband brought up the rear, the crowd's mood had become critical.

"Look at 'er 'at!" they snorted at the yellow side-tipped number that Corinne was sporting.

Corinne did not mind. She had been in a state of awed and amazed excitement since arriving at the Fort the evening before. They had had cocktails by the pool, a bright wall of roses and delphiniums and polyanthus behind them. Corinne was beside herself to meet the prince, yet had enough presence of mind to make jokes. There had been one about the Fort and turrets syndrome which had had David in stitches. Wallis could see him thinking that here, at last, after all the dull people and those of doubtful views, was some actual fun.

Following the prince as he conducted his usual tour, carrying, as usual, the bags of his guests, Corinne had turned to Wallis with widened eyes. "Who would have thought it, cousin of mine, back in the days of Pensacola naval base?!"

"Not me, for sure," Wallis replied.

"You were running a married quarters flat then," Corinne reminded her. "And now you're running this place!"

Wallis frowned at her, a frown intended to remind her that Ernest was close behind and that Corinne was mistaken anyway. She had already explained that her role as de facto mistress of Fort Belvedere was an interim position. Sooner or later she would be replaced with a new favorite, or even a wife. But until then, she was delighted to organize the smooth running of the house she loved above any other. And the man she loved above any other, albeit in secret, certainly seemed to appreciate her doing this.

"You take such trouble," the prince would say of her efficiency and attention to detail. His praise made her feel like a flower in the sun. Even if her role was mere glorified housekeeper, it was enough just to be near him.

But it was true that she had improved his life. Under her command, things at the Fort had improved radically. The staff, in response to the habitual courtesy with which she treated them and obviously glad to see the back of Thelma, were infinitely more obliging. There was about the place a new sense of ease and efficiency, as if the windows had been thrown open and a fresh and invigorating breeze was blowing through.

Tacitly and humorously, she had tackled the Fort's master too. She had suggested he should drink less, certainly smoke less, try harder to be punctual. To her relief, he had taken this in good part.

"My father's the only other person who's attempted to impose standards on me." He chuckled. "You're a good influence, Wallis. An inspiration."

They were out on the racecourse now; there was a smell of horses and harness, a sweeping view of green bends and white-painted rails. But the main thing was the noise. Clapping and cheering filled the air; the crowd in the stands had spotted the approaching royal carriages.

While the king and queen raised languid hands in acknowledgment, there was no doubt who was the real focus of the excitement. The prince sat opposite his parents, facing backward down the course, his top hat shining in the sun. As he removed it and waved it at the crowds, the spectators erupted in a roar.

Corinne leaned forward. "My God! They're crazy about him!"

Wallis nodded. It was the first time she had been with the prince at a public event, and the degree of adulation, while she had known it existed in theory, was an altogether different matter when encountered in the flesh.

The crowd was like a great force: noisy, hot, adoring. Its intensity and fervor were both thrilling and frightening. She understood suddenly how real and direct was the relationship of the British with their kings. These people identified passionately with their prince; he was part of their lives and was in their hearts. And he dealt so lightly with this crushing expectation. Proudly, admiringly, she watched him rising to it all: smiling, waving, seemingly as delighted to see them as they were to see him. You would never know, she thought, that he had ever expressed a vehement dislike of it all, let alone that he felt violently nauseous.

"Riding backward in that carriage always makes me feel sick," the prince had told her earlier. "I suppose," he had added wryly, "that one of the few advantages of promotion to king will be that I'll be able to see the course coming toward me for once."

She felt certain that his doubts about assuming the throne would be overcome eventually. How could they not; he and the people seemed made for each other. He would be the most popular king in history.

In the members' enclosure, a familiar tall and handsome figure approached. Wallis smiled at Corinne. "May I introduce you to His Royal Highness Prince George?"

As the curtseying Corinne nearly fell over with excitement, Wallis noticed how much better George looked. His big dark eyes had lost their crazed look and the air of manic energy had faded too. Thanks to the devoted care of his brother, the evil influence of the Girl with the Silver Syringe seemed to have been banished for good. George was now engaged to be married, to the beautiful Princess Marina of Greece.

"You know *everyone*, Wallis!" Corinne gasped afterward.

But she had it the wrong way round. Wallis had always known who everyone was. The difference was that now, everyone knew who she was. She was asked to parties, dinners, receptions. A succession of people now nightly rang the Bryanston Court doorbell. The cocktail hour she had tried and failed to launch had taken off of its own accord. Even as Wallis admitted one group into the hallway, the rattle of the elevator from below announced more arrivals at the front entrance.

Everyone suddenly seemed to have decided that between the hours of six and eight it was open house at the Simpsons'. Wallis would find herself sitting before a low table in the Bryanston Court sitting room mixing drinks and handing them out to a circle of people, some of whom were familiar and some not.

"Who are they all?" Ernest would whisper when they passed in the corridor. She would be dashing to the kitchen to order more food from Lily while he hurried in the opposite direction with fresh ice.

"Well, tonight we have Chips, Emerald, Lord Sefton, Mike Scanlon from the US embassy. And Cecil, of course."

Who, she had been sure to warn, was never to raise the subject of Shanghai again. Thankfully Sibyl Colefax seemed to have forgotten about it; when she had come, their decor had absorbed her completely.

"Wallis, how long is it all going to go on for? We can't afford to entertain the whole of London."

He was right, she knew. The promised turnaround in the fortunes of Simpson Spence and Young had not only failed to materialize, but things seemed to be turning in the other direction. As it was, their lack of staff apart from Lily meant that every evening before six Wallis was rushing around the flat with a duster and checking all was straight in the bathroom. They were, Ernest warned, only days away from watering down the gin.

"People will lose interest in us when David finds someone to replace Thelma," she reassured him.

"I hope you're right," said Ernest, who began to disappear into his study when he got home, pleading work. It was left to her to run the parties, and run them she did, throwing herself into the gatherings, giving full rein to her entertaining talents. It was one of the things she was best at, and she knew it. She loved the feeling of being at the center of things, of hearing all the gossip.

The Duke of Westminster had married an earl's daughter. "You should see her in the Westminster tiara," sniffed an unimpressed Cecil. "She looks like a jeweled nippy."

Everybody laughed at this unkind but accurate comparison. There was definitely something of the harassed Lyons waitress about the wan-faced new duchess.

"Why didn't he marry Chanel?" Wallis asked. She often thought of Coco with affection. Coco had helped Wallis at a crucial time. The duke must be crazy to give her up.

"I heard that they had terrible rows," someone offered. "*He* gave her rubies to make up. *She* chucked 'em off his yacht. I'm not sure I believe it."

Wallis pictured glittering red stones floating down through clear blue water and landing on a bed of golden sand. It was the maddest but also the most glamorous thing she had ever heard. And she completely believed it. Such bravado would be typical of Chanel.

"I heard that she wouldn't leave Paris," Cecil said. "He wanted her to move to England. Offered to bring her staff over and set up an atelier for her in Eaton Hall. But she said *non*."

"That's *her* story," someone else butted in. "But a French dressmaker was never going to be Duchess of Westminster. The English upper classes don't marry foreigners from nowhere."

CHAPTER THIRTY-SEVEN

Weekends at the Fort started to be supplemented by nights out in London. Wallis had not seen this side of the prince's life before. After a day of official events, or "stunting," as he called it, he played hard at the best clubs in town.

They went to Ciro's and Quaglino's, where the famous Leslie "Hutch" Hutchinson sang "These Foolish Things" and "Where the Lazy Daisies Grow." Sweeping up to the entrance of the Embassy Club with the heir to the throne, Wallis remembered how desperately she had longed to come here during her early months in London.

Afterward, Ernest was appalled. "Do you know how much that cost?"

As the prince carried no money, they had had to tip the staff. Wallis reminded him of the glamour of it all, how Luigi the maître d' had shown them to the prince's special table, commanding the best view of the room. How champagne had appeared immediately, swiftly followed by the king of Spain and Winston Churchill. How dazzling the decor had been, how gilded the mirrors and red plush the banquettes. How wonderful Ambrose the famous bandleader was. If the prince applauded after a dance, the orchestra played it again; if he didn't, it didn't.

"He's going to ruin us," Ernest lamented. "We can't go on like this, Wallis."

"We have to!" she told him. "What else can we do? Until he finds someone else, he needs us, Ernest."

"By then I'll be in a debtor's prison. Doesn't he realize we don't have the money?"

She sighed. "I honestly don't think it's crossed his mind, Ernest. I don't think he's ever had any poor friends before."

An idea struck her then, so obvious she was amazed it had not occurred to her before. "I can ask Aunt Bessie."

"Your Aunt Bessie! But she's an old lady! I can't borrow money from an old lady, Wallis!"

"Nonsense. I'm her only niece. I'll call her."

Aunt Bessie, as anticipated, was happy to help. But she also had questions, and with her usual candor came straight to the point.

"There's been some gossip in the newspapers here saying you've taken the place of Lady Furness."

Wallis was genuinely surprised. "That's crazy. How could that possibly be true? I'm ancient and ugly. And he has his pick of the most beautiful women in the world."

"Beauty," remarked Bessie, "is in the eye of the beholder."

Wallis laughed. "Well, I don't think any beholder could say that about me. I'm the prince's friend, that's all. He likes me because I cheer him up and encourage him."

"You're sure there's not more to it?"

"You're right, there is. He appreciates that I always speak my mind. He values that because everyone else is so sycophantic and false."

But her aunt was right. Her love for the prince was a wild, sweet, secret indulgence, its object remote and distant as the stars. But there was no possibility that he reciprocated it. There was a doubtful sniff from the other end. "Well, I hope you're not neglecting Ernest. He's a good man, as I've told you before."

She meant at Alice's funeral. It seemed like centuries ago. "But wouldn't Mother have loved it all?" Wallis said. To see her daughter the confidante of royalty, the eye of a glittering social storm. She would have been thrilled. Delighted, proud and also vindicated. And, hopefully, watching it all from somewhere.

"Ernest is a good man," she agreed. "And I'm not neglecting him."

"Or he neglecting you," Aunt Bessie warned from the other end. "If you're concentrating on the prince, he might look elsewhere."

"Don't be ridiculous," Wallis said. "He's devoted to me. He's always saying so." Although, now she thought about it, most recent conversations with Ernest had been hasty exchanges as they rushed back and forth from the kitchen.

"Well, don't take him for granted. Ernest is a patient man, but he's not a saint."

Wallis felt a prick of unease. It was true they had little time together these days. Might Ernest, weary of the lack of attention, wearier still of celibacy, start to look elsewhere? "Anyway, none of this is going to last. There'll be another Thelma along any minute. Or even a wife."

For the moment, however, the parties and dinners went on. The days that had once dragged now whirled. The telephone that had once been silent now rang so much that the company insisted on installing another. "They said they had too many complaints about the line being busy," Wallis explained to a baffled Ernest. Both now rang constantly by her bed at once.

"Who are all these people? What do they want?"

"That was Maud. She wants an invitation to the Fort." Wallis tried to sound matter-of-fact and not hint at how richly satisfying these increasingly desperate requests from her sister-in-law were.

"But in general what they want is the prince. They think that if they ask me I'll bring him too."

Day blended into night; it was night most of the time. Mornings disappeared; days started at lunchtime and were short, too-bright and bleary interludes before it all began again. Soon there was hardly a great house in Mayfair that Wallis did not know intimately. She discovered a surprising variety behind the stucco facades. Some were large and bare, like Emerald Cunard's. Others were spectacularly ornate, like the Channons' blue-and-silver baroque dining room.

As Ernest increasingly found reasons to avoid it all, their lives began to diverge. Often she would come in from a party to find Ernest at the breakfast table about to go to work. She would collapse opposite him in her evening dress, starry-eyed, heart racing, and give him a breathless account of the night's proceedings. "It was Lord Derby's party. . . . The champagne was so wonderful that he had taken the label off."

"Why?" asked Ernest.

"Because the vintage was so marvelous and exclusive no one else could possibly afford it."

Ernest frowned. "Isn't that the reason you'd want to keep the label *on*?"

Wallis shook her head excitedly. "No! He didn't want to embarrass his guests, you see. That's what David said, anyway. He thought it was very chic."

Ernest raised his eyebrows. "And this is the man who worries about the unemployed."

Wallis leaped to the prince's defense. "But he *does*! He spent ages tonight telling me about his new campaign for pithead baths. Apparently the mine owners don't want to install them."

"Let me get this straight." Ernest replaced his coffee cup in its saucer. "You were drinking champagne so expensive that the label had been removed as some bizarre act of social one-upmanship. While talking to the heir to the throne about the ablutionary arrangements of *miners*?"

"Yes, and what's wrong with that?"

"Wallis, doesn't it strike you as a little weird that he always wants to discuss the poor while surrounded by the privileges of the very rich?"

"Not at all!" she blazed back. "Where else is he supposed to discuss them? He's the Prince of Wales. That's his life."

"My point exactly," said Ernest, picking up his briefcase and leaving the room.

But the prince's life, the more she saw of it, seemed less a privilege than an imprisonment. The long arm of the king was ever present. He had complained to his son about his nightclub habits.

"He always goes to bed at eleven, and so he thinks staying up beyond that is immoral," the prince ruefully told Wallis. "The Embassy's perfectly respectable, but he's never seen it and so he thinks it's dissolute."

"It's crazy." Wallis shook her head. "You're not a boy anymore. And how does he even know where you are?"

The blond brows darkened. "Spies. Charles Cavendish tells his mother, who's Mama's Mistress of the Robes. Smarmy as be damned, both of them."

Wallis sighed. "You need to get away from all this. Take a holiday."

He nodded. "Yes, but that will just set off Papa again. He hates my jaunts abroad."

"He never leaves the country though," Wallis pointed out. "But someone in the royal family has to. On the mystery shopper principle."

"The what?"

She raised an eyebrow teasingly. "You wouldn't know about such things, lofty as you are. But in the States they're a method of research in department stores. I applied to do it, once."

He brightened immediately. He found her job-seeking stories amusingly exotic. She suspected that he had never had a friend who had had to look for one before. "Tell me!"

"Well, I didn't get the position, obviously. But the idea is that someone from a marketing company goes into a shop to see it as shoppers do. See what's right and what's wrong."

He shook his golden head in wonderment. "I never knew. But what's it got to do with the royal family?"

"I would have thought it was obvious. Royal family members should go to other countries occasionally and view Britain as foreigners do. Hearing their criticisms can be more important than their compliments."

He drew excitedly on his cigarette. "Wallis, that's genius."

A few days later, she and Ernest met at the breakfast table again. Wallis collapsed happily into a chair and poured herself a coffee. She had some news.

"David's taking a house in Biarritz in August. He wants us to come and stay."

She expected Ernest to brighten, but he did not.

"Good timing, I'd say," she added. "You've been working so hard. You deserve a rest." She stretched out a placatory hand and patted his arm.

He looked at the hand. "I don't think so," he said. Something in his tone made her gather herself and sit up, tucking her evening dress beneath her. She waited.

He took a breath and raised his head. "I'll be in New York in August," he told her.

"Again?" She was puzzled. "But you've only just been."

His round brown eyes, so open and friendly usually, had a look she had not seen there before. Guilt, with a touch of defiance.

She touched her forehead. "Mary," she said. "Of course." How could she not have realized? There had been more than one visit to New York since Mary had been in London. Many telephone calls. They couldn't all have been about silver hallmarks, Wallis thought now. But in the whirl of her new lifestyle, she had not realized. Perhaps she had not wanted to.

"Have you actually slept with her?" she asked.

He covered his face with his large hands. "I'm sorry, Wallis."

She shook her head. "You have nothing to be sorry about." She meant it. What sort of a wife had she been to him? She smiled at him. "You deserve some happiness." She paused and swallowed before asking, "Do you want me to divorce you?"

There was a silence. The prince skittered across her mind. He could not remain friends with a twice-divorced woman. But the dread now gathering within her was entirely about losing Ernest. His steady companionship and comfort. His sanity and gentle humor. His great good sense. Life without it was unimaginable. She loved him dearly, in her way. But her way was not enough, obviously. How could it be?

Ernest was looking at her sadly. "I don't want you to divorce me. I would hate that. But I can hardly expect you to want to remain married to me."

Her hand shot out and clasped his. "But I *would*, Ernest. I *do*!" She looked at him pleadingly. "It's all my fault anyway. I've never been a normal sort of wife."

His eyes were wet with tears. "I didn't marry you because you were normal, whatever that is. I married you because I loved you. And I still do."

"You've been a wonderful husband to me," she assured him. "And once all this is over"—she raised a hand in the air, which took in the Fort, Mayfair and Mary—"we can grow old together. Look back on our memories." She went over to him and put her arms round his broad chest. He felt firm and solid, reassuringly real.

He put his arms around her and drew her tight. "I couldn't bear to lose you," he said into her hair.

She clung on to him, feeling anchored. "Nor I you."

CHAPTER THIRTY-EIGHT

B oulevard de Prince de Galles, avenue de la Reine Victoria, avenue Edouard the Seventh. I'm guessing"—Wallis smiled, shading her eyes from the powerful sun—"that you're not the first member of your family to come to Biarritz."

"Apparently Queen Victoria used to come and drive round in a donkey cart. But I'm the first to stay *here!*"

The villa was built in the modern style, low, boxy and white. The material seemed to be concrete.

"It looks kind of like a factory," Wallis mused, following the prince up the steps.

"It *is* a factory. A fun factory. And fun is what we're going to have." He looked over his shoulder. "Once we get away from that lot!"

He meant the bevy of palace officials who the king had insisted accompany his forty-year-old son on holiday. A couple of disapproving palace equerries, Trotter and Aird, were supplemented by the military establishment in the form of a Lieutenant Commander Buist and his unprepossessing wife, Gladys. Given this degree of supervision, Aunt Bessie, whom she had invited along as chaperone in the absence of Ernest, was hardly necessary.

And yet it was a comfort to have her. Wallis watched fondly as the elderly lady moved up the steps to the villa with an agility belying her near-eight decades.

Beyond the wide arched doorway a marble-floored hall was dominated by a curving staircase rising to the rooms above. In front, a vast white salon led onto a huge white terrace. The views across the bay were spectacular. Wallis went to the balustrade and looked over. Out at sea, white sails plowed leisurely through the blue. The wide stretch of ocean made her feel restless. She had the impression she was on the edge of something more than merely land.

The prince appeared behind her. "Let's slip off for supper on our own." His blue eyes were sparkling. "Some simple bistro on the seafront with rough wooden tables and candles stuck in bottles."

And so they did, he slight in shorts and sandals, she slender in a shirt and skirt. "We could be any ordinary couple on holiday," he beamed as the waiter, who had evidently recognized him, showed them to the best of the rough wooden tables.

Part of her felt she should point out that they were not a couple, ordinary or otherwise, nor could they ever be. But a greater part was profoundly thrilled. And so she did not correct him. Instead she sipped her drink, a dark orange liquid with a powerful kick.

He stared into the flickering flame of the wine bottle candle. "They were so dismal, these cottages on the riverbank." He was talking about a recent visit to Newcastle. "I met a man about forty, poorly but cleanly dressed and with an honest face. 'What is your trade?' I asked him. 'Foreman riveter,' he answered. 'How long is it since you have worked?' 'Five years, sir.'"

He paused to split a langoustine. "Five years without work! Can you imagine? And what was I supposed to say to him? That he just had to be patient?" He drained his wineglass and thumped it back down on the table, eyes burning.

Recognizing the signs, she sought to distract him from his fury. She had grown adept at managing his moods. She saw that she needed to act or he would just drink more and become more angrily despairing. "I once tried to get a job in the steel industry," she said.

His face lit up at once. "Did you, Wallis?"

She nodded. "A friend in Pittsburgh, whose husband owned a steel firm, thought I could sell tubular scaffolding."

He snorted into his drink. "Tubular scaffolding!"

"Actually, I rather fancied the idea," she went on. "I saw myself in my best suit, heels and hair perfect, but with a head full of rock-hard figures."

She saw that his face had lost its stiffness and was mobile and lively again. "And what happened?"

"Well, I went to Pittsburgh and saw my friend's husband. 'Know anything about construction?' he asked me. I had to admit that I didn't. Then he asked me if I'd ever studied engineering. I told him never."

The prince was laughing loudly.

She frowned, taking on the personality of the steel factory owner. "'Can you use a slide rule?'" she growled. "'Can you do calculations on the spot?'"

"No, sir!" the prince protested in a falsetto meant to be her.

She shook her head sadly. "The world of the steel tycoon was not for me, it turned out."

"And thank goodness it wasn't!" the prince exclaimed. "I'd have never met you otherwise!"

They ordered more wine. Music struck up, some folk band with violins. It was melancholy, the notes drawn out and sobbing, reminding her of the way he played the bagpipes. She thought of all he had endured, all they both had. His mood had dipped again too. "I can't imagine it, being free to look for work," he said glumly. "I'll never have that opportunity. I've had a job waiting for me all my life."

"Yes, but you can do such good with it!" she reminded him, as always when the talk reached this point. "You can help so many people when you are king."

He gave a determined sort of nod. "Yes, I can, can't I?"

"Of course you can! You'll bring the monarchy close to the people. Make it relevant."

He nodded, happy again. "What would I do without you, Wallis? No one else believes in me."

The water was silver beneath a pearly sky. Yachts had moored for the night. Wallis narrowed her eyes to see the name of the nearest. *Rosaura.*

"Isn't that Moyne's?" The prince drew on his cigarette. "Didn't realize he was here. I was at Oxford with him. He's one of the Guinnesses and quite staggeringly rich. His mother was worried about him *under*spending his student allowance. Nice problem to have, I always thought."

She stared at him, a thought starting to form, but then he laughed, fixing her with his blue eyes so everything else dissolved, and she laughed back. "Wonder if he'll lend it to me for a couple of days," he added, looking speculatively at the boat, then back at Wallis. "One can get tired of Biarritz."

Whatever his real feelings, Lord Moyne was only too delighted to hand over his yacht to the heir to the throne. The chaperones at the villa were less than delighted to hand the prince his freedom, but the yacht's small size and the resident crew meant a strict limit on passengers. Wallis found herself plowing through a sparkling but choppy sea with her euphoric companion manning the wheel and setting the course down the coast. She settled herself in the most sheltered spot she could find and watched the red rocks of the west become the golden bays of the Riviera, always with the steep and snowy mountains behind.

They disembarked at Saint-Jean-de-Luz, where they wandered the Old Town's narrow, shady streets and explored the cool and ancient churches with their incense and Madonnas. The market with its wealth of flowers and food amazed her. Beneath the striped awnings

of the stalls was astonishing abundance and variety: tomatoes, potatoes and onions of every size, shining green zucchini, marbled mauve
eggplant, sea-fresh silver fish.

"Do you know what I'm pretending?" he said as they walked
along.

"No, what?"

"That we're just an ordinary couple doing the shopping."

She smiled at him. "A lovely thought."

"Isn't it?" There was real yearning in his voice. "I would so adore
to do just normal dull everyday things with you, Wallis. Live a normal life."

She caught his mood, and briefly imagined a world without Win,
without Ernest, without all the mistakes and complications. To start
all over again with a clean slate. With him. She looked up at him, and
he tilted his head toward her, and for a second she thought he was
going to kiss her, and then for a second he did, grazing her lips with
his for the briefest moment.

It was like a bomb going off. The shock flashed along her nerves,
roiled in her stomach. She felt no revulsion or terror. Only desire and
want and need.

Her lips burned and seemed to swell like something budding and
bursting into bloom. She felt herself open up like a flower. She wanted
to be touched again, kissed again. She breathed fast, shallow breaths,
struggling to regain control.

"This is the best holiday of my life," he said, looking straight into
her eyes as if swearing a sacred oath.

She had now recovered enough to speak. "Mine too."

"Let's not go back! Let's run away together!"

"Ha! We can't do that! I haven't got any clothes."

"We can buy clothes wherever we end up! Where should we go?"

There was a wild light in his eyes; he really meant it.

"David," she said gently. "We can't. Not in real life."

He groaned. "I can't bear it anymore."

"Bear what?"

"I'm not entirely sure how to live without you."

The sky seemed to tilt and the surroundings to blur. She reminded herself fiercely that he must have said the same things to Thelma, to Freda. The thought was like treading water, keeping her head above the surface. "You lived quite well without me before you met me," she said.

"Yes, but it's killing me now."

"Don't say that. Be sensible, David." But even as she spoke she felt the water closing over her head.

"I can't bear to think I could have gone my whole life without meeting you."

"I'm a dime a dozen." And yet there was the sense that she was below the surface now, sinking, sinking.

They sailed back under a great yellow moon. They stood on the deck and studied the rippling path of light that it cast. It stretched brightly to the horizon, dancing with promise. He stood close but did not touch her, and the warm air between them seemed to crackle with desire. She felt the stars pulsing above them and the ocean swelling beneath the boat. When he moved closer to her, she held her breath. His mouth met hers, at first lightly and then more urgently.

"Are you sure?" he murmured into her shoulder.

"No. I've had bad experiences at this sort of thing."

He laughed. "So have I. But shall we give it a go anyway?"

They lay on the deck and explored each other. He was slow and careful. He stroked her like a frightened animal might be stroked, delicately building trust. Rigid at first, she gradually relaxed. She had not realized that what Win had done so brutally could be done so gently. Afterward, they clung together. He was so gentle, she thought. She held on, so he could not float away.

"There," he said. "That wasn't so bad, was it?"

"No."

"Shall we do it again?"

"Let's."

"I love you, Wallis," he told her. She smiled back at him, sure that he didn't mean it but grateful for it to have happened. He had freed her. She felt full of a new joy.

On their return to the villa she found a concerned Aunt Bessie on the terrace. She snapped shut her book and got straight to the point. "Bessiewallis, what's going on?"

"Going on?"

"These old eyes aren't so old that they can't see. What on earth happened on that boat?"

I realized what I had been missing all these years; he restored a part of me I thought gone forever. I found joy.

Wallis turned and looked into her aunt's anxiety-creased face. "You don't have to worry about me. I'm having a marvelous time. It's all great fun."

"That's exactly why I'm worrying," the old lady flashed back. "If you let yourself enjoy this kind of life, won't it make you restless and dissatisfied with everything you've ever known before?"

"I know what I'm doing," Wallis said testily. She was nearly forty, after all.

Bessie sighed. "Have it your own way. But I tell you that wiser people than you have been carried away, and I can see no happy outcome to all this. If it goes on, something terrible will happen."

"Like what?"

Aunt Bessie sighed. "Let me be blunt. This liaison could wreck your marriage and leave you high and dry at the end. If Ernest divorces you and the prince moves on, what then?"

Wallis stared back out to sea. She could hardly tell Bessie what she and Ernest had decided between them. Let alone that Ernest had a mistress of his own. "The prince will move on," she said. "He has to get married." But she knew even as she spoke that she felt differently about it all. The prince finding a bride would be more complicated now.

Bessie opened her book again. "The sooner he gets a wife, the better."

The Duke of Windsor's Funeral
St. George's Chapel
Windsor Castle
June 1972

On entering the chapel she caught that same gentle scent of orange blossom. Somewhere an organ played softly. Sitting at the end of one of the pews in the nave was an impeccable old man who seemed familiar. As she passed he looked straight at her; beneath the waved silver hair, tinted a slight blue, were the familiar long face and dreamy blue eyes. Cecil. It had all begun with him, and now here he was to see the end.

Her seat was in the choir, nearest the altar. The coffin was gone, along with the soldiers. She no longer dreaded its return. For David's sake she was playing a part he would have relished; she who had never been crowned would outqueen the queens with her display of dignity. The alternative was to keen and rend her garments, which in this company was unthinkable. If she mourned among the Windsors, she would mourn alone.

She wished that Lilibet, who sat beside her, would not pat her arm in that nanny-like way. Meanwhile, up the nave came Elizabeth, milking the moment, nodding and smiling to all.

"Oh, do come on, Mummie," Lilibet muttered.

Wallis watched from behind her veil. If she no longer feared Elizabeth, still less did she envy her. Her position was now strange, even ridiculous. She and David had observed, amazed, from afar as the accession of her daughter had made her own role redundant and forced the formerly grand aristocrat, strength and stay of a wartime nation, to accept the demeaning pantomime part of Queen Mum. The nation's favorite granny, a jolly old gin-swigger who liked a flutter. For someone so conscious of position, this vulgar characterization must be torture.

The organ struck up the hymn. Before Wallis could even open her order of service Lilibet had whisked it away, found the place and passed it back. "The King of Love My Shepherd Is."

Ironic, surely. For whom among these people had David been the king of love? Apart from her. As something started inwardly to collapse she pushed the thought aside. She would not keen or rend. Mop and mow. Not in public, not here. She would be bold and resolute. Selfish and heartless.

As the singing ceased, there was a movement from the chapel's west end. The funeral procession had begun. A black pit opened within her but she straightened her back, raised her head beneath its thick veil.

The archbishop intoned the psalm. "'For a thousand years in thy sight are but as yesterday.'"

Especially in the world of British royalty. This could be five hundred years ago, easily. She watched the procession of Garter Knights, old men with plumed hats under their arms. Then the choir: little boys with shining eyes in snowy surplices. The clergy in their copes and miters. Then, most medieval of all, the Kings of Arms, like playing cards from Alice in Wonderland in tights and tabards embroidered with the heraldry of the United Kingdom. Their spectacles looked all wrong, but that was the trick. The glasses were in fact right; it was the costumes that were anachronistic.

The heralds each held a blue velvet cushion: the ribbons and cross of David's Order of the Garter in the center, his field marshal's baton on another, and on the remaining one his other decorations. The gold and silver, the jewels and enamel, picked up and threw back the colors in the glowing windows. What remained of David was light, she thought.

For all her composure, the sight of his coffin blindsided her. A great agony rose within; the force, she felt, would split her. The absolute impossibility of his death fought violently with the reality of what was now passing by, draped with the royal standard, borne by his own soldiers. The boots of the Prince of Wales Company, First Battalion the Welsh Guards, squeaked and scraped in the hush. She felt as if her entire life had shrunk to this point, had always been leading up to it. She could see nothing before or beyond.

She held herself still. If she didn't move, it could not touch her, could not be happening. It helped that behind David marched Philip. The sight of him restored her self-control, as displaying emotion before him was out of the question. Men such as he thought sorrow was weakness, that feelings were something to be manipulated and exploited. Various expressionless kings, princes and dukes followed, among them Charles and his brothers. Bringing up the rear, inevitably, was Mountbatten.

David was placed on the bier and she stared at the flag, at the bared teeth of a lion, as Mountbatten mounted the pulpit and began to read the eulogy.

"When I married fifty years ago he was my best man. More than my best man, he was my best friend all my life . . ."

Wallis kept her eyes on the lion's snarl. She imagined David turning in his coffin, as he could not yet turn in his grave. Mountbatten had been nowhere near as close as he was claiming. Perhaps when they were both young, but long before David met her.

"An attractive American woman changed the course of his life. Indeed, changed the course of history."

He had not said her name, she realized. She sensed that this was deliberate. She gave a tiny shake of her head. While she was used to the Windsors' implacable hatred, its infinite variety surprised her every time.

"I remember the dreadful day of the abdication."

As Mountbatten's voice broke, Wallis kept her scorn hidden behind her veil. Elizabeth was not the only old ham present. Wallis tried not to listen, concentrating on the windows, the stall carvings, all the while talking to David in her head.

I am here, I am here, I am here.

"His brothers and myself . . . were trying to dissuade him. I was bitterly opposed. . . . It made no difference to our friendship. What a great debt the people of this country . . . We shall miss him, but nobody more than myself."

Disgust swirled through her. She could see Grace, across the aisle, trying to catch her eye as Antenucci looked on anxiously. She knew what they were telling her as clearly as if they were saying it. She may be half-dead, her other half lying in the box before her, but what a life she had lived. And when she was entirely dead, it would be her that people remembered. Her, and David.

The coffin was placed on its bier before the altar and the Garter King of Arms stepped forward. His voice echoing impressively against the ancient stone, he began to proclaim the ancient style and titles:

"Knight of the Most Excellent Order of the Garter. Knight of the Thistle. Knight of St. Patrick. Knight Grand Commander of the Bath. Knight Grand Commander of the Star of India. Knight Grand Cross of St. Michael and St. George . . ."

As he paused for breath she could almost hear the collective sigh as all present considered all David had given up, her own slight black figure providing an equally slight reason for such sacrifice. She knew they were musing on opportunities lost, talents wasted, a heritage thrown away. Of the much he could have done and the little he did. But what did they know? And what had they done, anyway?

"Military Cross. Admiral of the Fleet. Field Marshal of the Army. Marshal of the Royal Air Force . . ."

She closed her eyes beneath her veil. She had heard these words before. On a sharp, chilly morning when bright sunshine bounced off polished trumpets and picked out gold threads in the lion, the unicorn, the dragon and the harp. It was January 1936, and she was standing at the window of a room in St. James's Palace, looking down on the courtyard where her lover was being proclaimed. He had given all of it up, for her.

"The most high, most mighty and most excellent monarch King Edward the Eighth, of Great Britain, Ireland and the British Dominions Beyond the Seas, Emperor of India, Defender of the Faith."

Again, through her veil, she caught Grace's steadfast eye. Reminding her that for all the heartache of ostracism and exile, David had never ceased to feel that his happiness was worth a throne.

CHAPTER THIRTY-NINE

London
1935

The country was celebrating the Silver Jubilee of the king and queen. The streets were red, white and blue; flags hung across every thoroughfare, garlands brightened every building; there were gold lions, oversize Britannias, ribbons and streamers, portraits and pageants in towns large and small across the nation.

The royal couple rode daily about their capital in open horse-drawn carriages polished to a mirrorlike gleam. Taking a different route every time, they were cheered as wildly by the poor of the East End as the rich of the West. Delighted crowds roamed the streets. Thousands slept all night along the route to St. Paul's Cathedral, where the great Thanksgiving Service was to be held. Potentates, prime ministers, maharajahs, tribal chieftains and sheiks flocked from the farthest corners of the empire to pay tribute to the ruler of four hundred ninety-three million subjects. The great buildings were floodlit; there were river processions, state dinners, balls, church services and celebrations. It was an enormous, flamboyant outpouring of love for a monarch whose style was anything but exuberant.

The old king-emperor broadcast his gratitude, laced with an obvious surprise, to the nation "for all the loyalty and—may I say?—the love with which this day and always you have surrounded us."

"Well," said Ernest, turning off the radiogram in the Bryanston Court sitting room. "It doesn't sound to me as if the British Crown has a lot to worry about."

Wallis, fixing her earrings in the mirror, looked at him. "How do you mean?"

Ernest picked up *The Times*, whose front cover showed George V, ablaze with feathers and gold braid, delightedly greeting a ragged small Cockney child. "The king may be old-fashioned, fuddy-duddy and all the things that David says, but the people love him nonetheless. More than that, they seem to adore him."

Wallis finished attaching the second earring. "That's because they don't know him. This is a man who routinely bullies his children and belittles his wife. He despises his heir, ignored the fact one of his sons was a drug addict and cast another into the wilderness for being an epileptic. If the British people knew all that they would have a different view."

"But they *don't* know that, do they?" Ernest turned the page. "So far as they are concerned he's the old man who's steered a steady course through the last half century. Just listen to this." He raised the newspaper and began to quote from it. "'The bonds have never been closer between king and country—'"

"The king doesn't know the first thing about the country," Wallis cut in. "All those places that David goes, the derelict valleys, the silent mills, he's never seen any of them."

Ernest went on. "'The king is the repository of universal trust. In the twenty-fifth year of his reign he is the very essence of the unity of the British Commonwealth of Nations. His selfless devotion to duty, high purpose in all things, understanding of his fellow man and simple honesty of character—'"

"Ridiculous," Wallis impatiently interrupted. "This is the same honest man of high purpose who ruthlessly abandoned his cousin and young family to be murdered in a cellar by the Bolsheviks. Any selfless devotion there was entirely to the cause of his own survival. The people are deluded."

Ernest lowered the paper. "I daresay. But it seems to me that when it comes to the royal family, the British are happy to be deluded. Deluded is what they want."

"David doesn't think so. He wants to bring the monarchy closer to the people. Modernize it. Make it—"

"Relevant," interrupted Ernest. "So he keeps saying. But do the people want it to be modern or relevant? Does David need to invent a new way? Why not stick to the old way? Much easier."

"Well for a start," Wallis replied, exasperated, "David doesn't even know what the old way is. Do you know that this great king, with his honesty and understanding of human nature, doesn't show his son and heir a single state paper? He's the Prince of Wales, he'll be king one day, but he's never allowed to be at audiences with government officials, or even to see inside a red box. He knows no more of what the king does all day than you or I. Is it any wonder he's having to make up a whole new approach?"

Ernest looked surprised. "I didn't know that."

"No one does. The great British public least of all."

The doorbell rang. "That'll be David. I'd better go." She gathered up her bag and the fur wrap that lay over the sofa arm.

"Where tonight?"

"Dinner at the Channons'. Then dancing at Quag's."

"It's something, to be royal favorite," said Ernest affectionately. "Still, you know where to come when it's all over."

"I certainly do," she said, dropping a kiss on his head as she passed him on the way to the door.

His words lingered as she went down in the lift to the car. *When it's all over.* But it was showing no signs of ending, even so. Nor, increasingly, was she sure that she wanted it to. Sleeping with the prince had changed everything. He had lit something inside her; it glowed in her eyes, shone in her hair and streamed off her skin. Ernest could hardly fail to have noticed it. But then, he seemed happy enough himself, enjoying a similar arrangement with Mary.

And he was right, being royal favorite was something. It was a glamorous whirlwind with luxury and privilege at every turn. Doors opened. Corks popped. There were witticisms, famous faces, rooms full of flowers, pieces of glittering jewelry. There was perfume and laughter, tea on terraces, cocktails in nightclubs, rolling parkland through the windows of beautiful houses.

And at the center of it all was the prince with his overwhelming charm and seemingly magic power; his slightest wish was translated instantly into the most impressive kind of reality. Trains were held; yachts materialized; the best suites in the finest hotels were flung open; airplanes stood waiting. All brought about without apparent effort, a murmured request here, a telephone call there, underlined by the calm assumption that this was the natural order of things and always would be. That she, little Wallis Warfield of Baltimore, Maryland, was part of this enchanted world was a source of such constant amazement and required such constant energy and effort there was little left over to do anything but accept it and enjoy it. Was there a danger in that?

If you let yourself enjoy this kind of life, won't it make you restless and dissatisfied with everything you've ever known before?

It was not the pampering and privilege she enjoyed most; rather, the weekends at the Fort when it was just the two of them or very few guests. She felt so happy then, and that it would last forever. But then the hours would melt away and the moment of separation would approach. The wrench was an almost physical pain. She dimly recognized that attachment to this intimacy was more dangerous than attachment to the glitter and glamour. The latter was mere luxury, the former was love.

But it had already lasted far longer than she ever thought it would, and when it finally ended, what then? A world without David was unimaginable. She felt a clutch of sickening fear, and the downward swing of the lift seemed to echo the uncertainty of everything.

The excited doorman swung wide the ornate glass-and-cast-iron front door. As she glided out, the rear door of the gleaming limousine opened to receive her. David gathered her into his arms and kissed her passionately. The sickening fear left her and the world righted itself.

"How are you?" she asked him, laughing as she wiped her lipstick from his mouth. It had been some days since she had seen him. On behalf of their father, the king's four sons had toured the four kingdoms. Bertie to Scotland, George to Ireland and Henry to the English provinces. David, naturally, had gone to Wales.

"Feel my muscles." He thrust his arm at her. "I've got biceps like dustbins. All that waving."

He produced an envelope. "I've got something for you. An invitation."

"To what?"

"The Jubilee Ball at the palace. The big culminating number of the whole bang shoot."

She shook her head. "I can't, David. It's an official occasion. All your family will be there, the whole world." She thought of the sheiks and chiefs and maharajahs. "It's out of the question."

"Not if I want you there," he said, looking petulant. "I can invite who I want."

She felt a ripple of exasperation. "Would you really want to put me through that?"

"Well, it wouldn't be just you. Ernest is invited too, naturally."

That was hardly the point. She lay her cheek on his coat and sighed. "David, dear. Doesn't your love for me reach to the heights of wanting to make things a little easier for me?"

He sounded bewildered. "What do you mean? I'm inviting you to a ball. I thought you'd like it."

He had not the slightest idea that, to her, it might seem that she was entering the lion's den. It had felt just like that when, the previous November, he had asked her to the wedding of Prince George to Princess Marina at Westminster Abbey. She and Ernest had sat in the nave, in the best seats, and everyone had stared at them. While the occasion had been beautiful and impressive, it had also been intensely uncomfortable. "I heard someone behind me talking about the Un-importance of Being Ernest," Ernest said ruefully afterward.

The prince was still talking. She tuned in, suddenly.

"What did you say?" she asked sharply. She could not have heard properly. Something about wanting his family to meet his future wife.

He was holding her close and speaking into her hair. "I want to marry you."

She pulled away and stared at him in shock. Was he joking? But his face was serious, profoundly so. He was looking straight into her eyes.

"I mean it," he said. "I really do. You've changed me. I've never been loved the way you love me. I've never met anyone who could save me before you."

Ernest was not initially keen to accompany her to the palace ball but allowed himself to be persuaded on the grounds that such an event came along only once in a lifetime. "And, of course," he said, "it'll be something to tell Mary about. I'm storing up memories for her too, for when it's all over."

Ernest was so content with the arrangement, Wallis thought. It was so simple for him. He was enjoying his affair, but there was never any question of falling in love with Mary, or preferring her over his wife. She wondered how Mary saw it. For understandable reasons, it had not been discussed.

Her own situation was becoming more complicated by the day. The prince's proposal had been a shock, not just on its own account but because it had seemed heartfelt.

She wished he had not asked her, even so. She needed no false as-surances. Things were complicated enough already; lines everywhere were becoming blurred. She was married. And yet the longer the affair went on, she felt less anchored to reality. It was one of the reasons why she had insisted Ernest come to the palace.

He looked magnificent in his red Guards uniform, while she, in a green lamé dress with a purple sash, looked eye-catchingly bright. Perhaps too bright, but the dress was beautifully cut and the designer had pressed it upon her. Many people pressed things on her these days. Having had so little for so long, it was hard to resist.

The palace was enormous, far bigger than they had both expected, and fantastically ornate.

"You're Wallis in Wonderland." Ernest smiled, leading her between the pillars and marble statues.

Everything was red, cream and gold. The ceilings bristled with carving and dangled with massive chandeliers. Grand portraits hung on every wall.

The prince had sent a car for them, expertly timed so they were among the first in the great red-carpeted entrance hall. Pouring into the great wide space behind them came a chattering river of guests. The men looked rather better than the women, Wallis thought, admiring braided uniforms, fringed epaulets, feathered headdresses, sweeping robes, breeches and gold-buttoned tailcoats. She thought of Chanel, who would have launched a whole collection on the back of this, perhaps several.

They were swept in the crowd up a magnificent double staircase edged with a delicate gold balustrade. An imposing pillared doorway led into a huge cream-and-white room. An orchestra was playing waltzes, and the warm air was heavy with scent from enormous flower arrangements.

At the far end of the room, under a tall, fringed red canopy, a pair of golden thrones stood under the royal coat of arms. Seated on them were two familiar figures. Pride surged through Wallis. She thought of Alice, and of those old Baltimore snobs who had shunned and belittled her. But here was her daughter, meeting the King of England.

The king and queen looked different from the grumpy old people they appeared in the newspapers. Crowned, sashed and glittering with jewels, they were grandeur personified. King George wore full dress uniform, Queen Mary a beaded evening dress and more jewels than Wallis had ever seen on one person. Across the breast of each was the blue silk sash and sparkling diamond star of the Garter. It was quite literally a blaze of glory.

Ernest bent to whisper in her ear. "I'm not sure how you update all this, Wallis."

She nudged him. But he had a point. How possible was it to modernize a monarchy where spectacle seemed to be everything?

Diana Cooper glittered into view, a silver column of loveliness. As Duff greeted Ernest, she inclined her head. "Quite the life you're leading at the moment, Wallis. The prince is mad about you; everyone says so. You're the talk of the town."

Alarm shot through her, followed by delight and, finally, surprise. She still could not believe she was the object of anyone's interest. She, who had been so obscure for so long.

"Just be careful, Wallis," Diana went on unexpectedly.

Wallis stared. "Careful? You sound like my old aunt."

"Your old aunt's a woman of good sense, I hear."

So Aunt Bessie was being talked about too.

Diana's pale eyes were serious. "Look, Wallis, I'm only saying this because I like you so much. I don't like many people, especially women, but I do like you. You have a good heart."

It was hard not to be touched by this. And flattered.

"I don't want to see that good heart being hurt," Diana went on. She glanced over to Duff, now greeting several other people. "This is going to have to be quick," she said. "But just try and take it all with a pinch of salt."

"Oh," Wallis assured her, "I am. Absolutely."

"He's very charming. And volatile. There's something very vulnerable about him, which is quite irresistible."

Wallis felt uncomfortable. Diana could be unnervingly accurate. *He's a mystery, but central to his charm is his ability to make people think they're the only ones who understand him.*

"But you know why, don't you?" Diana was looking at her. "You know what it's all about?"

She was hot, then cold. What did Diana know? Was it possible that the secrets the prince had shared with her, about his childhood, his brutal nurse, one brother's addictions and another's cruel ostracism, his unfeeling parents and his doubts about the monarchy, had been shared with everyone? Or if not everyone then at least with this aristocratic sphinx? She felt she could not bear it if so. She lifted her chin. "Tell me, Diana. What is it all about?"

"His mother." The red lips curled triumphantly. "It's all about his mother."

"His *mother*?"

The golden hair, immaculately marcelled, nodded. "It completely explains how he is with women," Diana went on. "Every encounter is another chance to repair that relationship with that central figure who rejected him."

Wallis looked away. The urge to laugh was twisted with profound relief. Diana knew nothing after all. Far stronger, deeper and darker reasons bound them than Queen Mary, who David actively disliked. She glanced over at the marmoreal, jewel-laden figure, complete with pinned-on wig. "You've been reading too much Dr. Freud, Diana."

Diana shrugged. "You may be right."

"Wallis!" Suddenly the prince was at her side, blazing away in a uniform that made Ernest's seem plain and restrained. Conscious of her husband, and of a certain stir in the crowd, she tried to greet him calmly. But the excitement in her eyes gave her away, she knew. She felt gripped by a childish glee, and wanted to jump for joy.

He looked her up and down with pride and delight. "There is no question about it. You are wearing the most striking gown in the room. And now, come and meet the old monsters."

It's all about his mother. Ha! thought Wallis. A likely story. "Do you think that's a good idea?" she asked, even so.

"Don't worry, they'll hardly notice. On these occasions, my mother's main concern is to persuade ancient cousins to return various items Queen Victoria lent them. It's an obsession with her. Come on, Ernest. You too."

Ernest raised his eyebrows. "If you say so."

As the three of them moved forward, people melted away, as if before something white-hot. But she could feel them, the cold, jealous English eyes. She held her head high and met each gaze. Most looked down, or aside, but one pair, deep violet in color, was fixed and steady. Wallis paused, smiled and sank into a curtsey. "Your Royal Highness."

Elizabeth gave an icy nod. Next to her was Princess Marina. Londoners had taken George's beautiful Greek wife to their hearts, copying her hats, admiring her warm spirit, but for Wallis now there was only cold disdain. She noticed, even so, that both women looked at David with a reverent adoration.

They moved on. Soon they had reached the thrones. The king was nodding amiably, and Queen Mary's whiskery face was creased into something approaching a smile. "Remember zose missing candlesticks from ze Cumberland silver?" she was asking a bent old lady directly in front of Wallis.

The prince darted forward. "Mama! Papa! Allow me to introduce a very great friend of mine."

"Vere do you sink I fount zem? Among poor cousin Lilly's things, of all places!"

Still apparently occupied by the candlesticks, the queen put her hand forward absently.

Her husband was a different matter. Rising from her curtsey to him, Wallis met, above the nicotine-stained beard, an expression of cold menace. She saw him lean forward so his head was close to his son. She heard his voice, low and vicious. "I told you not to invite your mistress!" The king rose, suddenly, his swords and medals jangling. The queen looked up in surprise, then rose hurriedly too.

The noise died away. All was silent.

"That woman in my own house!" the king ground out through his beard as he stomped off the dais and through the private door at the back. In the still and silent room, the slam seemed to echo.

It hadn't been his mother but his father, she thought. She felt winded, as if someone had punched her. It was like a bad dream; it could not possibly be real. But Ernest's eyes, round, kind, concerned, angry, told their own story. He came forward and gently took her arm. As he piloted her out of the room, she looked up only once, to meet the triumphant gaze of the Duchess of York.

CHAPTER FORTY

The other guests were down on the swimming-pool terrace. But Wallis had pursued the prince into his study at the Fort, determined to impress upon him how humiliated she had felt. The faces of the scoffing courtiers still loomed in her dreams, Elizabeth's most of all.

"I was and still am terribly upset," she told him. "You only think of what you want and act without the slightest thought for others."

He sat on the arm of a leather sofa and looked at her wretchedly, his eyes so full of sorrow that her heart twisted with pity. "I'm so sorry, Wallis."

"Elizabeth's face, you should have seen it. She loved every minute." The blue eyes narrowed. "Mrs. Temple Senior! That fat Scotch cook! Why worry what she thinks? She's only jealous. She wanted to marry me but had to accept B-B-B-Bertie."

Surprise bloomed within her, and a spike of triumph. She had suspected as much. "Well, now you're on the subject of marriage, we need to talk about yours."

"Yes, to you." He turned upon her his blazing grin.

She looked away to avoid its power. It had a way of immobilizing her, stalling objection, making her forget what she wanted to say. "You know that's madness," she said.

"Love is madness," he said cheerfully.

She sighed. "I've been thinking about this. We don't need to stop seeing each other once you're married. We can still be friends."

He looked at her quizzically. "Friends?"

She nodded even though she didn't really know what she meant precisely. This was uncharted territory.

The prince was much more decisive. "Wallis, you and I have never been friends."

She turned away in despair. It was like arguing with a stone wall.

"I've transferred my entire heart over to you," he beseeched her.

"I never wanted you to do that." But she knew she did.

He came over, nuzzled her neck. She shuddered with pleasure at his familiar touch. "You're angry with me," he murmured.

"Yes, because you won't accept the truth." She felt close to tears. "We can't get married."

"Wallis, please don't say that to a boy," he said in a low voice. Particularly in letters, he had recently started referring to them both in the third person. He was "a boy" and she was "a girl." Collectively they were WE. To him, who had invented it, the combined initials symbolized the union of the two of them. But to her it was the opposite: they were West and East, which could never meet.

"I love you more and more each and every minute and miss you so terribly when you're not here." She saw his eyes were brimming with tears, like hers.

His vulnerability stirred her, as it always did. The hurt, lonely and unhappy little boy he had been could always speak to the hurt, lonely and unhappy little girl she had been. She decided to drop the subject. Any marriage between them was impossible; she had satisfied herself of that.

Or, rather, Ernest had. Earlier that week, before leaving for New York, he had moved to calm his wife's fears. Apprised of the prince's rash promise, he had researched the matter with the relish and thoroughness with which he approached any historic subject and had returned from the library with pages of notes and opened them on the mirrored dining room table.

"Don't worry, Wallis. There are at least four enormous obstacles in his way."

She looked at herself in the table's mirrored reflection. She had lost yet more weight, and her dark eyes were huge and apprehensive. "And what are they?"

As Ernest set about explaining, she tried to gather her scattered wits to concentrate. "Well, the Royal Marriages Act of 1772 forbids a member of the royal family to marry without the consent of the sovereign. And on the evidence of that Jubilee Ball, it's fair to say that His Majesty looked less than keen."

Wallis watched her reflected face flinch with the horror of the memory. The monarch's icy stare, her own hot rush of shame, the shocked silence, the slammed door, the gasps and barely suppressed giggles.

"And then," Ernest went on, "there's the Church of England, of which the monarch is head and which is completely opposed to divorce. A divorced woman would be the last person on earth they would permit the sovereign to marry. And you'd have to divorce me as well, so that would be two divorces."

"It's so hypocritical," Wallis mused.

"Hypocritical?"

"I'm just remembering a conversation I had with Diana, about Henry the Eighth."

"About Henry the Eighth?" Ernest looked amazed. "And there was me thinking you girls just talked about clothes."

Wallis was staring into the mirrored surface. "Henry defied the Church of Rome to marry Anne. He divorced his first wife, and the Church of England was the result. Meaning that the church that now forbids royals to divorce was created itself by a royal divorce."

Ernest nodded. "Good point. I hadn't thought of that."

Her dark eyes gazed back at her. She remembered what else Diana had said, how hated Anne had been, how she was abused when she appeared in public, how she was called a whore and a witch. "Diana thinks Henry was cruel and ruthless and that becoming queen was the very last thing Anne wanted. But by then it was too late."

"Thank goodness David's not on the throne, or we might be dealing with all that too." His tone implied he was joking, but Wallis felt nausea whip through her.

"Ernest, please. Not even in jest."

"Don't worry. The king's obviously going to last forever. By the time it's David's turn we'll be long gone. We'll be sitting on the veranda looking at our scrapbooks."

"Promise me we will, Ernest," she said fervently.

He reached over and patted her hand. "Of course we will. We're not divorcing anyway. We've decided that."

"Absolutely. I don't want to divorce you."

"Well, quite. So that's impossible as well. And then there's Parliament, whose permission would be needed. Very likely, as the monarch is also emperor, the various dominions would have to be asked for their view; they might have to vote on it," said Ernest.

She shook her head. "I don't know how he could even mention it. It's so ridiculous it's not even funny."

Her husband smiled at her. "And I haven't finished yet. To marry a divorced woman, the prince would have to withdraw from the line of succession. He could not be crowned king and Defender of the Faith if married to someone he had taken from her husband. Meaning," Ernest added, "that he would lose the bulk of his income and York House, even his beloved Fort."

"Lose the Fort?" Wallis lifted her whisky tumbler. That settled it. She had been worrying about nothing; it was all hot air. There was no possibility that the prince could be serious. Now, in the Fort, she stood by his desk, riffling idly through the papers that were on it.

Spotting something, she drew it out. It was a wedding invitation. The bride and groom were Angela Dudley Ward and a Lieutenant Robert Laycock.

"Angela's getting married," Wallis said, remembering with pleasure the lovely girl at the long-ago pageant rehearsals. The prince had been close to her, she remembered. They had met daily, when he visited Freda. He had watched her grow up and she felt glad that they were still in touch. "It sounds like a splendid match."

The prince, who had been standing at the window with his hands in his pockets, turned. "What?"

She waved the invitation, realizing as she did so that the date was months past. "You didn't go?"

He looked surprised. "Why should I? I never see the family anymore."

"Did you send a present?"

"Of course not," he said, visibly irritated.

This was how it was, she thought. When the prince wished to end a relationship, a shutter slammed down and you were cut off completely, as if you had never known him. It was ruthless and final and it happened to everyone, even people who thought they were close. She had seen it happen to Fruity, and a couple of other equerries the prince suspected to not approve of her. She had never said a word about them herself. It would be like that for her one day when his attentions dwindled, right out of the blue. That day must surely be coming soon.

In the meantime, it was like being swept down a very fast river. The phones shrilled; shoals of invitations poured through the letterbox. Life became almost exclusively nocturnal and Wallis felt increasingly detached from reality. Time was losing its meaning; things just happened, one after the other, and at such a speed she could not reflect during or remember afterward. When, as happened less and less, she and Ernest coincided in the flat, he would ask her where she had been and she found it hard to say.

Christmas came as something of a respite: David was obliged to spend it with his family at Sandringham. "Most boring place on earth," he complained.

"It can't be that bad," she said reasonably.

"You're right, it's worse. Ugliest house in the known universe."

She had seen pictures of it in the newspapers, a great dark building bristling with gables, chimneys and towers. It was true that it was not attractive.

"It's even got its own time zone, did you know that?"

She listened in astonishment as he described how, by order of George V, the Sandringham clocks were all half an hour fast in order to extend the shooting day.

"But the actual effect is to confuse everyone so we're all in a permanent state of terror about being late and incurring the royal wrath."

"He cares about punctuality that much?"

The prince looked rueful. "You've no idea. My youngest brother, Henry, was away once for six months, and when he came back he was a minute late for lunch. Papa was utterly vile to him."

"Well, hopefully the new Duchess of Gloucester will help with that," she said comfortingly. Prince Henry had recently married a Scottish aristocrat called Alice Montagu Douglas Scott. On the basis of previous experience, Wallis and Ernest had refused the prince's invitation to the wedding.

"Well, it won't help with anything else." He groaned. "I'm the only one not married now. I'll get my ear bent all Christmas."

She smiled at him and said, with determined lightness, "Well, you know what the answer to that is." She handed him her gift, which was a cigarette case decorated with a map of their summer travels. "Open it now," she urged.

The fair head shook. "I'll open it with the others. On Christmas Eve."

"Not on Christmas Day?"

"Ridiculous, isn't it? The royal family don't even open their *presents* at the same time as everyone else."

She smiled, but felt a clutch of concern. "David," she said, "please don't open it with the family. Open it now."

He unwrapped it and gazed at the engraved map for a long time. When he finally lifted his head, his expression was resolute. "I'm going to talk to Papa."

"About what?"

"About *you*. I'm going to tell him that I'm going to marry you."

She swallowed. "David, you mustn't. Your father isn't well." The old king had been ailing for some weeks.

"Oh, he'll recover. He's indestructible." He flashed her a dazzling blue-eyed grin, which she resolutely did not return.

He went—in his private plane. Letters flowed from Sandringham. "It really is ghastly here. The worst Christmas ever. Oh God, the boredom . . ."

"A boy does miss a girl so terribly. I love you more and more every minute and no difficulties can possibly prevent our ultimate happiness. . . ."

"You know your David will love you and look after you so long as he has breath in his eanum body." "Eanum" was a word he seemed to have invented; she didn't know where it came from; it meant "small." "Let's not bore ourselves with others on New Year's night. Oh to be alone for ages and ages and then—ages and ages! God bless WE, sweetheart. I'm sure he does—he must."

The telephone shrilled constantly. "You'll never guess," the prince shouted gleefully down the crackling line from Norfolk.

"David! You haven't . . . ?"

"Told Papa? Don't worry, Wallis, not a word. But it seems a little bird might have told him anyway. Or that blasted archbishop of

Canterbury. He's staying here, the snobbish old sneak, and apparently my father said to him the other day that he hopes to God I never marry and have children and that nothing will come between Bertie and Lilibet and the throne."

"What?"

"If only he knew how much I'd like the same thing myself. Bertie and Lilibet are more than welcome to it so far as I'm concerned. They'd both be better at it than me."

"You can't say that!"

"I just did! Hot diggity dog!"

New Year 1936 brought the prince back. As he had wished, and with Ernest in New York, they spent it alone at the Fort. They were gardening under a cold winter sun when a car drew up in a spray of gravel. The prince shoved his fork into some just-turned clods and went to investigate. He reappeared with a letter in his hand. "It's from Mama at Sandringham. About Papa."

Wallis's hands flew to her face.

"She says that there's no immediate danger. But says I should propose myself for the coming weekend. I'm to be very casual about it so Papa doesn't suspect."

Wallis lowered her hands, relieved. "Well, that sounds fine. Panic over."

The prince snorted. "Hardly. You don't know my mother. That's Mama-speak for come immediately, he's at death's door."

She met his despairing gaze with a sympathy that hid her relief. Finally, the end was in sight.

Driving away from the castellated building was like an escape. It was snowing thickly as she looked through the rear window up the whitened drive. In the past, this view had wrenched at her heart. No longer.

At Bryanston Court, Ernest was just back. She ran to him and hugged him tight. How sensible, solid and dependable he felt after so much that was impossible and impermanent.

He took one look at her exhausted face, her thin and wilting form, and put her straight to bed. She slept for twenty-four hours. When she got up, she suggested they go to the cinema. She felt desperate to do something ordinary, anonymous, inexpensive.

As the nearest one was at Marble Arch, not far away, they walked arm in arm through the snow. She felt unburdened, relieved. Never again would she complain about the dullness of life. Being at the center of things was exciting but relentless. A type of imprisonment, even. She was glad that it was finished and she was free.

There was a newsreel before the film began. Behind decorative wrought-iron gates, the bulky facade of Sandringham flickered across the screen. There were crowds outside, huddled against the cold, their winter coats black against the white. A distant factotum was coming down the snowy drive, his gloved hand holding a long envelope. There was silence in the cinema as it was opened and the message framed and hung on the gate.

"The king's life is moving peacefully toward its close."

She closed her eyes. Poor David. The hour of his destiny had come. She would always love him, and their time together was the defining moment of her life. But now, finally, they must go their separate ways.

The Duke of Windsor's Funeral
St. George's Chapel
Windsor
June 1972

The last notes of the Last Post faded into the stonework. The service had ended and she watched as everyone leaving gave a solemn bow to the casket. Mountbatten's took about five minutes. She was the last; worn by the strain, she could manage only the briefest of nods. She felt David would understand; hers was sincere, at least.

The mood, she felt, seemed less one of sorrow for a lost leader than relief at reaching the end of an uncomfortable chapter. Everyone was impatient for it to be over so they could be off.

But perhaps not everyone everywhere. Later she discovered what had been said in the House of Commons by Prime Minister Heath.

"There must be men and women on Tyneside, and in Liverpool and South Wales, who are remembering today the slight, rather shy figure who came briefly into their lives, and sometimes into their homes, in those grim years . . .

"I have no doubt that the duke by his conduct as Prince of Wales and as king had paved the way to a form of monarchy, which today is more in tune with the times than would have been thought possible fifty years ago."

David had achieved his aim. He had modernized the monarchy, enabled it to go on. Not that any of them seemed especially grateful.

Outside, the sun was fierce and bright. Something David had once said came back at her, about needing sunshine for a pageant. He had the sunshine, if not quite the pageant.

The light knifed her tired eyeballs, even beneath her veil. Grace materialized, furious, at her side. "Did you realize that your name wasn't mentioned once, not once, throughout that entire service?"

Oh yes, she was about to say, but felt Philip take her arm. It seemed they were going to the castle for lunch.

The other guests followed, loud and jovial as if leaving a wedding. She told Philip how kind Charles had been in supporting her. The reply was a dismissive snort. "Damned boy needs to get married. That's his job now."

Lunch was in a glittering gold-and-white room. There were several round tables. Mountbatten, inevitably, had been placed on one side of her. On the other was Philip. She suspected a pincer movement; they wanted something.

Louis had made several trips to the house in Paris. "Who are you going to leave that to?" he would ask, picking up a figurine. "I think it should go to Charles."

"How dare he," David had exclaimed after one such visit. "He even tells me what he wants left to him."

For the first course Philip made what, for him, was small talk. He complained about the separate royal households, how they ran them these days. Everyone had different addresses and offices that failed to share information, apparently.

During the lamb, Louis broke ranks. He asked her what she meant to do with the duke's uniforms and orders. "I think you should hand them over to the queen. Not as his niece, but as the sovereign. That would be the dignified thing to do."

She looked at him musingly. His speech in the chapel came back to her, in which she had not been named. Philip's rudeness, Elizabeth's jibes. "The dignified thing to do," she repeated.

Over dessert, the two Battenbergs, mouths full of rice pudding, moved in for the kill. "Have you thought about the will?" Mountbatten nudged.

She toyed with her spoon. "The will?" she said innocently. "What about it?"

Philip was unabashed. "Perhaps making out a new one? In favor of the duke's family?"

Part of her wanted to laugh out loud. But another part of her paused for thought. She was tired, ill, old and lonely. This bitterness had gone on for too long. Perhaps throwing them something might make it all easier.

"I could give my jewelry to Charles," she suggested. "His future wife could wear it."

An intake of breath from Louis. "But weren't all your best things stolen?"

She winced at the memory. There had been a robbery—in 1946. Her jewelry box had been refilled many times since. But Mountbatten's rude dismissal annoyed her.

"You're right," she said lightly, shelving the idea and along with it any hope of the future Princess of Wales ever wearing her magnificent pieces. She would auction them for charity, for the Institut Pasteur, and if the Windsors wanted anything, they would have to bid for it. Served them right.

Philip, on her other side, was inquiring, none too subtly, if she proposed to return to spend her last years in America. She looked him full in the face.

"Don't worry. I shan't be coming back here, if that's what you're thinking."

CHAPTER FORTY-ONE

St. James's Palace
London
January 1936

On the first stroke of ten, trumpeters in golden sleeves raised their instruments in a double fanfare. The sound rebounded from the age-worn redbrick walls of St. James's Palace. It was joined by another, deeper, sound: the guns in the park behind. On a balcony draped with scarlet stood the Garter King of Arms, the ceremonial figure responsible for proclaiming a new monarch.

Resplendent in plumed bicorn hat, tights and a stiff tabard magnificently and colorfully embroidered with the devices of the United Kingdom, he seemed to Wallis like a figure from the Tudor court, not the one of the new King Edward. As he raised a large parchment scroll, this impression intensified. The pageantry was beautiful in its ancient splendor and moving in its seriousness. This was how things had been done for hundreds of years, in an unbroken line of tradition of which the prince was now part. She was watching history in the making.

She thought of how this same palace had been the scene of much carousing, a lot of it in recent weeks. But that must all be put aside now, along with the prince's old life. She had not expected to be asked to the ceremony now underway; he would not be here himself. Tradition dictated that a monarch never witnessed his own proclamation.

Perhaps it was by way of a final leave-taking. That had been Ernest's view, which was why he insisted she go alone. "He wants to show you he's now king and has work to do." When he had called her from Sandringham on the morning of his father's death, his obvious devastation had twisted her heart.

"I can't do it, Wallis," he had gulped, clearly on the verge of tears. "I'm the last person on earth who should be king."

"No," she insisted. "You're the perfect person."

"I can't face it. I hate everything about it. Courtiers, palaces, debutantes, receptions, paperwork, ceremonies, the Established Church. Oh, and did I mention stultifying routine, unvarying tradition, ancient hierarchical apparatus, attendant bishops and the seasonal peregrinations between royal palaces and estates?"

"That's exactly why you're perfect," she told him. "You have a vision. So go on, do it your way. Modernize it. You've talked about it for long enough. Now's your chance to make it happen."

"Do you really think I can?"

"Absolutely!"

"You believe in me, Wallis?"

"Yes!"

The next time they spoke, he had sounded almost triumphant. "Guess what my first act as king was? To turn those blasted clocks back to the right time."

"Well, that makes sense," she agreed. "Sandringham's the center of the British Empire now. Synchronicity is very important."

There was laughter on the other end. "Well, yes. All that. And it threw that wretched archbishop's Sunday service right out of whack as well."

His second act had been to fly his plane back to London, the first king in history to do so. This thoroughly contemporary gesture made a dramatic contrast with the medieval scene before her. But he had always intended to bring the modern world to the ancient one.

Indeed, he had already started. He had told the nation that he would "follow in my father's footsteps and work, as he did throughout his life, for the happiness and welfare of all classes of my subjects." His first tour as monarch would be to the Glasgow slums. She felt proud that he was putting his plan into action, making it clear that helping the needy and unfortunate was his priority. The naysayers were wrong; even Ernest was wrong. The monarchy could be modern and relevant.

The King of Arms raised his voice to lift it above the sound of the booming guns. "Prince Edward is with one voice and the consent of tongue and heart proclaimed our only lawful and rightful liege lord Edward the Eighth. . . ."

He raised his magnificent feathered hat to reveal a head as bald and white as a peeled egg, which made her smile. With his glasses and mustache, the formerly imposing ceremonial figure now looked like a dressed-up bank manager.

"The king! The king!" cried the other people in the room with her, raising their hats in unison. She did not know them, but they knew her. She had been aware throughout the ceremony of the scrutiny of two in particular: a pompous sandy-haired short man in uniform, who was obviously a courtier, and the disapproving woman with him, a thin-haired, thin-blooded aristocratic type, equally obviously his wife. Wallis felt heartily glad that this was the last occasion on which she would encounter such people.

And then, quite suddenly, he was there, lighting up the shadowy room, sweeping like a sudden wind through people bowing and dipping in curtsies. He hurried straight across the room to the window where she stood. Delight rushed through her. Rising from her curtsey, she admonished him in laughing astonishment. "Are you *supposed* to be here?"

He beamed at her, teeth clamped round a cigarette as ever, blue eyes dancing. "I was going to stick to the tradition. Then at the last moment I asked myself what was so wrong in seeing myself proclaimed king? So here I am."

And why should he not, she thought. He seemed so glowing, youthful and vital in these gloomy surroundings, against a backdrop of such ancient tradition. "'Nice customs curtsey to great kings,'" she said. "*Henry the Fifth*," she added, as he was looking quizzical. She had learned it at school but no line had ever come back before now.

He laughed again. "Cripes, Wallis, don't come over all literary on me. Last thing I need just now!" He suddenly spotted the sandy-haired man and his wife, both of whom clearly thought there was quite a lot wrong in overturning the tradition. Their expressions, which combined outrage with obsequiousness, were so comical that Wallis turned away, smiling, to the window.

"Alec! Helen!" The king went over to greet them, his heels sharp on the polished floor. She was still peering out of the window into the court below when she heard her own name called. "Wallis, come and meet Alec Hardinge. He's my private secretary. And this is Helen, his wife."

Extending her hand to the Hardinges, she thought how apt their name was. They both looked flinty to the core. The chill glint in their eyes reminded her of Elizabeth. "Congratulations on the new appointment." She smiled to Alec, whose mean little mouth bunched up even further.

The king clapped him cheerfully on the back. "Oh, it's not new! Alec's one of the old guard. He was PS to my father, but as he knows the ropes I thought I'd keep him on. He's already hard at it, arranging this visit to Glasgow. Right, Alec?"

The man's small, pale eyes flicked uncertainly to his wife before returning to his sovereign. "Sir, I'm glad you brought that up, because—"

But the king was waving at someone else now. "Tommy! Come over and meet Wallis!"

"Is it really the case that you want to go into every single tenement flat in the whole place?" Hardinge was so clearly appalled.

Wallis wondered, with a prick of concern, whether it had been a good idea to keep him on. Surely the new king with his new approach needed a new guard, not the old one. The ropes Hardinge knew might not be relevant now.

"Yes, yes, man, of course I do, we've already been through this." The king threw him an amused glance. "Ah, Tommy," he exclaimed as a tall saturnine figure appeared. "Wallis, this is Alan Lascelles. Deputy private secretary."

Wallis held out her hand. "Tommy or Alan?" She smiled. "You appear to have two names."

The expression of utter contempt that now crossed the gaunt features was so brief she wondered if she had imagined it.

"He's Tommy to his friends and Alan to his nonfriends," the king explained merrily.

As Lascelles inclined his shining dark head, Wallis felt relieved that she would not have to find out which category she belonged to. Not that it was hard to guess.

"Lascelles has form," the king went on.

"*Form?*" This freezingly disdainful figure had a criminal record?

A royal shout of laughter. "Ha, not *that* sort of form! He worked for me before, back in the twenties. Went on many a tour together, eh, Tommy?" He gave Lascelles a playful punch. "America, Canada, Canada again, Africa; you name it, we went there."

A smile that seemed more of a grimace briefly spasmed the deputy private secretary's thin mouth. "We did indeed, sir."

"But then Lascelles sacked me. Left my service in 'twenty-nine, the old so-and-so. Thought I wasn't up to the job, eh, Tommy?"

The king laughed good-naturedly to demonstrate bygones were bygones. Lascelles responded with a diplomatic smile.

"But then my father took him on and now he's back with me, poor bugger! And he and Hardinge are going to help me become Edward the Innovator. Throw open the windows and let in some fresh air! Make the monarchy more responsive to the changed circumstances of these times. Stand up for the young against the old and well-established! Eh?" The king lit another cigarette, apparently delighted with himself.

Wallis watched Hardinge and Lascelles exchange a horrified glance and felt another shaft of anxiety on the king's account. Why, when he could have asked anyone, had he picked as close advisers people who so clearly disapproved of him and were so obviously out of step with his aims and interests? There was music coming from the courtyard now. She leaned toward the window. Soldiers in red and gold were playing "God Save the King." The small area amplified the noise to an almost unbearable level. What was this, she thought, if not hierarchical apparatus and ancient tradition? Could he really change it? Did anyone want him to?

He seemed to her so noble and brave, with the entire weight of the centuries against him. How would he manage alone? The sooner he found a wife who could help him in his work, the better.

She felt that never had she loved him more, now, at the supreme moment of parting. She realized how terribly she would miss him and her eyes swam with tears. He came up beside her and she saw that the earlier jocular mood had gone and there were tears in his blue eyes too. She tried to smile and say, calmly and brightly, "How very different your life is going to be." But it came out high-pitched and hysterical. She pressed her hand to her mouth, overcome.

He gently took her arm. "Wallis, there will be a difference, of course. But nothing can ever change my feelings toward you. You are all and everything I have in life and it will all work out all right for us." Then he smiled his dazzling smile and was gone.

She stared after him in disbelief, the people still rising from their bows after he had passed. He could not possibly mean it.

CHAPTER FORTY-TWO

Everything had changed. But the king was acting as if things were exactly the same. He came to Bryanston Court, just as he had before. "It's so lonely," he told her. "The responsibility is overwhelming. I need you, Wallis."

"What you need is a wife," she said quickly. It was almost a mantra with her now.

Irritation swept the boyish features. "Well, I haven't found anyone yet."

"You haven't looked, that's why."

"I won't marry without love," he said, petulant as a child.

She said nothing. What could she say? That she had thought the same once and it was a disastrous illusion?

"You are the only person I trust, who I can talk things over normally with," he told her. He begged her to come back to the Fort; it needed decorating, he said. He wanted her to help him and even offered her a salary.

"It's a job," she told Ernest, who looked at her darkly.

"One of the oldest jobs, I understand," he said. It was rare for him to attack her and it stung. But the question of intimacy preoccupied both men now.

"Are you sleeping with him? I can't bear it!" the king would rage. She wasn't, as a matter of fact. But slipping straight back into the king's bed seemed out of the question too. Things couldn't go back to the way they had been, but where did they go from here?

"But I'm going to marry you," the king insisted, describing again what he had seen when his father's body had arrived at King's Cross from Sandringham. Accompanying the flag-draped coffin, on which the crown sat on a cushion, the new king had looked up at the station front. The cold January sun had glinted on the weather vane. "And do you know what I saw, Wallis? WE, bright gold, against a blue sky. If that isn't a sign, what is?"

She didn't mention the other sign. As the gun carriage on which the coffin was resting went over a jolt, the diamond cross on top of the crown had fallen off and rolled in the gutter. "Bloody hell," the new monarch had exclaimed, scrambling to rescue it. "What next?"

What next indeed. She had expected him to renounce her; he had not. And while she had no intention of renouncing Ernest, his expectation that things would now return to the way they had been before royalty had entered their lives was not being met. The atmosphere in Bryanston Court was strained. Things had been settled; now they were up in the air again.

"David just needs to get used to it," she told Ernest. "It's all happened so suddenly. I'm a shoulder to lean on, someone he can trust. He's so worried about everything. He doesn't yet have the confidence to put his ideas into practice without encouragement."

Ernest rolled his eyes and sighed. "He doesn't seem to lack confidence to me. He milks those crowds like a showbiz pro. Milks you too, Wallis. He knows exactly what he's doing."

Relations were strained between the king and his family too, she gathered. He complained that Bertie was avoiding him.

"It's the opposite way round," she explained gently. "You're asking me for advice when you should be asking him."

He had started to consult her about what to put in his speeches.

"How should I know?" she asked.

"Well, should I put in jokes, for instance?"

"Jokes?" she echoed, incredulous.

"My father hated them. I used to try to lighten up my speeches when I was Prince of Wales, and he would hit the roof. 'I'VE NEVER PUT A JOKE IN A SPEECH IN MY LIFE!'"

He would pass her papers from his boxes to read. She had nothing to contribute there either but would point out when he had plonked his whisky glass on some Foreign Office letter that required a signature. It would go back covered in drinks rings. Hardinge and Lascelles would glare at her as if it were her fault.

When she suggested he consult them instead, he brushed her concerns aside.

"You want me to do my job well, don't you?"

"Of course."

"Well, you're essential to me, Wallis. I need you by my side *all the time*."

She felt desperate. It was a circular argument. "But you need someone else by your side, someone more suitable," she pleaded. "You must let me go."

She consulted the *Almanach de Gotha* and *Burke's Peerage* and left the social pages lying around so he could see them. He never so much as glanced at them. "You don't love me!" he accused.

"On the contrary," she placated. "I love you far too much. But I must develop the strength to survive without you."

He drew on his cigarette. "But you help me drink less and make me more punctual and do all the boxes and so on. You're a good influence, everyone says so."

This surprised her. "Really?"

"Really." He nodded. Pleasure filled her, all the greater for being so unexpected. She tried so hard, not just with the drink and the time but also his expenses. He showed her the accounts, almost as Ernest had. Her practiced eye meant she could spot immediately how bloated was the administration of the palaces, and where people were taking advantage. How wonderful that someone had noticed and was grateful.

"Who says I'm a good influence?" she pressed. His mother? She had heard that Queen Mary had insulted her, called her an adventuress. The unfairness had cut her to the quick. But perhaps it was not true, after all.

He waved his cigarette vaguely. "Oh, everyone. And it's true. You even go to these damned dinners for me."

"Well, you can't go yourself." He was officially still in mourning for his father. And so invitations to small official dinners with politicians, civil servants and diplomats had started to come her way and now sat on the Bryanston Court mantelpiece along with the summonses to balls and parties. "We'll need another mantelpiece soon," observed Ernest.

The lunches were tricky. She could not venture any opinion in case it was assumed the king shared her view. And she was ruthlessly lobbied by people whose intentions she was ill-equipped to judge. Robert Vansittart, a mandarin at the Foreign Office, was relentless in pushing his pro-Italian policy. It was while trying to escape from him that she found herself facing a young German with fair hair and close-set eyes. "Joachim von Ribbentrop," he said, kissing her hand. He was Hitler's principal adviser on foreign affairs.

Out of the frying pan, into the fire, she thought. The recent Anschluss, which had absorbed Austria into an ever-expanding Germany, and, preceding it, the annexing of the Sudetenland, had revealed the führer, as he called himself, as ruthless in his ambition. Yet Ribbentrop, who had an oily manner, was keen that the king prioritize a visit to Germany.

"An interesting idea," she replied neutrally, knowing it was out of the question. The king could not give the impression that he supported Hitler's expansionism.

"Isn't it?" Ribbentrop seemed delighted nonetheless. "His Majesty is half-German, after all!"

Wallis stared at him. "But one hundred percent a British patriot."

Ribbentrop's smile became knowing. "Madame. A great many of

your British patriots are now visiting Germany to see for themselves
the führer's transformations. The Olympic Games are proving a particularly big draw." He bowed, clicked his heels and withdrew.

As Wallis looked after him, her insides churning with dislike, she
became aware of a presence at her shoulder. A jowly figure with lowered brows and a pushed-out bottom lip stood there. She recognized
him: Winston Churchill, a formerly prominent minister now rele-
gated to the backbenches. He was a dated figure for most people, but
the king was fond of him for just that reason. They had been close in
his youth. She smiled. "Mr. Churchill."

"He was a champagne salesman, you know," Churchill growled.

"Excuse me?" Many thought Churchill to be as eccentric as he
was irrelevant. It seemed that they were right.

"Ribbentrop." The bald head indicated the direction of the just
departed. "Used to sell German champagne, whatever that is."

"It sounds terrible," said Wallis.

"I agree. Give me Pol Roger any day. But now Ribbentrop sells
something much worse."

"And what is that, Mr. Churchill?"

"The ideology of the Nazis. Lethal stuff. But no one wants to listen when I warn them about Germany's rearmament and its insatiable appetite for territory." He stopped and shook his head. "But they
will have to, eventually."

While Wallis agreed, and remembered that Duff Cooper did too,
she said nothing.

Churchill, in any case, did not seem to require a response.

"I'm told," he added musingly, "that Ribbentrop's the Nazi even
the Nazis can't stand. Quite an achievement if one thinks about it."

She changed the subject to the king, of whom he was clearly both
fond and proud. "I think he will make a great king of a new era, and
I believe the country thinks the same." Then they talked about the
United States. She was surprised to hear that he was half-American.
"Like me!" she exclaimed, delighted.

He looked at her twinklingly. "And like yourself, Mrs. Simpson, I have a high degree of administrative capability. One of the most valuable and misunderstood of all the arts, I always think."

She looked at him thoughtfully. "And you're good at speeches too, I hear. Perhaps you should come and see His Majesty. He's struggling with them at the moment, rather."

The collaboration was a great success. "Winston says it's fine to put in jokes," the king reported one day over lunch. "But only at the beginning, to warm people up before the serious stuff at the end."

She nodded. "That sounds sensible."

"He's shown me this great trick too." He demonstrated it. "You turn a bowl upside down like this, then put a glass on top and balance your speech on the glass. Like an instant lectern."

Churchill duly drafted a speech for the king to deliver at his first Trooping the Colour. He insisted Wallis be present, and she in turn used its military nature to appeal to Ernest's old-soldier instincts.

It was a fine hot June day and they sat in their reserved places in the stands on Horse Guards Parade. The park was in full leaf; the sun shone; the air was warm and six battalions of guardsmen, magnificent in scarlet tunics and bearskins, their bayonets flashing, formed three sides of a square in front of the king, his natural glamour considerably augmented by the dress uniform of the Grenadiers' colonel-in-chief. To the young ensigns who came to kneel before him he passed the colors two by two: the king's, of bloodred silk embroidered with his cipher, and the regiment's silken Union Jack with its battle honors.

Wallis watched, remembering the king's grumbles about the impossible tightness of uniform trousers and dutifully listening as Ernest explained the buttons system that allowed the distinguishing of one household regiment from another. She felt tired, heavy and weary. The king then delivered Churchill's brief but moving speech and then remounted to lead the battalions down Constitution Hill toward the palace, where he would take the salute.

They had just moved off when something flew out of the crowd like a bright metallic bird, clattered loudly beneath the king's horse and skidded under the generals riding behind him.

There was a gasp from the crowd, some shouts and a few screams. Horror flashed through Wallis and juddered painfully to every nerve ending. She clung to Ernest. "What was that?"

"Well, if it's a bomb we'll know in a moment."

It was not a bomb but a loaded revolver. An alert policeman had knocked it from the would-be assassin's hand just as he raised it. They watched him being led away between two policemen, a thickset man dressed with somewhat surprising formality in a three-piece suit with a watch chain. One rumor had it that he was an Irish Republican; another, a journalist with a grudge. What was indisputable was that he had failed. But mixed with Wallis's sobbing relief was the guilty knowledge that had he succeeded, he would have saved her a world of trouble.

CHAPTER FORTY-THREE

"Thank God," the king said from where he stood at the palace windows. It had been a day of debutante presentations, but a storm had cut everything short.

Wallis straightened from the box she was unpacking. "Don't say that. Those poor debutantes had been practicing for weeks. It was their big moment."

She really did feel sympathy for them. They had filed in front of him, dipping curtseys in the sticky grass, while he slouched on a gold-framed chair looking as spectacularly bored and resentful as he looked spectacularly handsome.

"Perhaps you should have had the presentations in the palace ballroom like your parents used to."

"I'm breaking with tradition," he said. And indeed he had dispensed with the medaled military uniform, the sword and sash, in favor of a suit. "Besides, the electric light in the ballroom always made the women look so ghastly."

"You think a downpour made them look better?" She recalled the drooping feathers, the mud-soaked white gowns, the expressions of bitter disappointment. If part of the point was to bind the aristocracy to the monarchy, she doubted the event had succeeded. But that might well have been the point.

"I thought doing it in the garden would make it quicker," he said, arranging a picture on the wall. "And I was right!" He laughed, flashing her a blue-eyed grin, which, as usual, went straight to her heart.

"There might have been a future queen of England among those girls," she said, battling hard. But as always when he smiled at her, it was like swimming against an impossibly powerful tide.

He had been king for six months now, but had only just moved into Buckingham Palace. He refused to take his father's old rooms, partly because his mother still remained in them. Queen Mary was in no rush to leave her home of twenty-five years. He seemed content with the small adjoining rooms on the floor below, a rather bare and gloomy old guest suite whose decoration badly needed updating. She had arranged for some things to come from the Fort, to make him feel more at home. But whenever she visited, the boxes had still not been unpacked.

"Queen of England?" he said, still smiling at her. "Why should I look for one among those silly debs? The perfect candidate is right in front of me."

She had been unwrapping a vase; it fell and exploded on the wooden floor. She looked at her trembling hands, the broken pieces. Her mind was a white, ringing void, wiped of all thought.

She remained so for what seemed like hours but was probably only a few seconds. When finally she raised her head and looked at him, his expression remained bright and encouraging. "Queen?" she repeated. "*Me?*"

This was it, she thought. Proof positive. He was mad. The events of the last few months had turned his brain. He had made light of the near assassination, calling it the Dastardly Attempt and going off to play golf afterward. But perhaps it had had an effect after all.

"Yes, you," he said. "Why not?"

"Well, there are a few reasons." She tried to sound sane and steady as she counted them off on her fingers. "The Church, the government, the empire, the people, your family. The fact I'm foreign, ancient and once divorced already. Need I go on?"

"No, that'll do," he said equably. "I'm not saying it will be easy, Wallis. But I'm quite determined."

She bent, holding on to the edges of the empty box to support herself. She stared into the dusty void. She had no idea how to cope with this.

"If in doubt, go to Paris," Ernest advised. "You know how you love the place." A week away would make all the difference, he said. He even offered to buy her a dress.

She had expected the king to make difficulties, but, to her surprise, he was encouraging too.

"Where will you stay?" he asked.

"I don't mind. Honestly, I'd be happy anywhere."

"Well, you can't stay just anywhere. What about the Meurice?"

That was the name of the hotel she had visited on honeymoon with Ernest, the splendid place with braided flunkeys and glorious cocktail bar. She laughed. "I can't possibly afford that."

"You don't have to." The king summoned Lascelles. "Book Mrs. Simpson the best suite," he ordered the unwilling courtier. "And mind you get a good rate."

The morning after her arrival she made her way across the gray cobbles of the Place Vendôme. Past the mighty column Napoleon had erected to himself, along the facade of the Ritz and into the rue Cambon.

Halfway down the narrow but affluent street was the shop she sought: No. 31. Chanel.

Inside were the same white walls, oval mirrors, Oriental screens and white-and-gray armchairs as the London shop. The same heavenly perfume rose to her nostrils. The rails here, as there, were hung with beautiful, covetable clothes.

The voices of shopgirls floated over; Wallis cocked her head to catch the language. It did not sound like French.

"Russian," supplied a voice from behind, unmistakably French-accented. "Dispossessed countesses. But thanks to the Revolution, now modeling and selling for me!"

She turned. Chanel wore a white sailor hat fixed with a large jeweled brooch, a striped belted jacket overlaid with ropes of pearls and a pair of dark trousers. She nodded in recognition and the sharp black eyes swept Wallis before swinging crossly in the direction of the dispossessed countesses.

"They want a pay rise," the designer complained.

"And you don't want to give them one?"

"Why should I pay them more? Don't they realize that working for Chanel gives them opportunities to meet rich lovers?" The black eyes swung back to her. "But you have a rich lover already. The richest."

"You've heard."

By some miracle, or so it seemed to Wallis, nothing had yet appeared about her in the British papers. But the American press was a different matter; Aunt Bessie had written several times in concern.

Keep the newspaper clippings for me! Wallis had written back, in the spirit of reassurance. *They can amuse Ernest and me in our old age!*

Now it seemed she was all over the French press too.

"*Mais oui!*" The dark eyes flared with laughter. "And so I think you have not come here to work for me. I once offered you a job, if you remember."

I am going back to Paris tonight. If you grow tired of life here, come and work for me there.

Wallis nodded. "I remember. You gave me some good advice too."

"Not just good, it was excellent! I told you how to enter British society. And now you are at the very top of it!"

A hot rush of tears made Wallis drop her head. She blinked hard and glanced back up to see Chanel looking at her steadily.

"And now, of course, you want to escape."

Wallis was amazed. "How do you know?"

"Because it is the other half of the story. The half I did not tell you." She turned her back. "Come."

Wallis followed her through a door in the wall and up some stairs to a workroom with mirrors and tailor's dummies. Chanel had already slung some scissors round her neck along with a tape measure and was beckoning her inside. In a matter of moments she had flung a length of beige silk over Wallis and was on her knees, fussing about the hem.

"I have an idea for a dress, and you are the right shape to try it on," she announced, a pin clenched in her teeth like a rose. "This beige silk, it is perfect, no? I love beige."

"What do you mean?" Wallis asked.

"Beige, it is natural, I take refuge in it. You must choose and mix your fabrics like an artist mixes paints."

"Not beige. What you said downstairs. About the other half of the story."

"Did I say that? I talk nonstop. It's because I'm terrified of being bored by other people. If I ever die it will be of boredom."

Wallis was beginning to feel exasperated. "Yes, you did say it. You said there was a half you did not tell me."

"Oh yes! I meant that I sympathized. That I know exactly how you feel."

But Chanel had been abandoned by her own aristocratic lover. As the whole world knew and had discussed at length, another woman had become Duchess of Westminster. Wallis felt that she had the opposite problem.

In the mirror the dress was already taking shape: an uneven hemline and a collar like a crossed scarf. "British aristocrats," the designer muttered. "They are so controlling and possessive. It took me an age to get rid of mine."

"Get rid of him?"

Chanel looked up. "Oh yes. People think Westminstair got rid of me but it was the other way round." She sat back on her heels. Her vivid little face was thoughtful.

"I fell for Westminstair because he was so simple. The simplest person in the world. He did not know the meaning of the word 'snobbery.' It would never have occurred to him. He was so high above it all, he was simplicity itself, as simple as a tramp."

"I know that feeling." Wallis said, remembering the prince darting ahead in his ragged gardening clothes.

"He had a quality of wholeheartedness, which was irresistible. There was no holding back. When the British are really in love, they give everything."

The lump in Wallis's throat prevented her from replying. She could only nod, hard.

"And so at first," Chanel said, "it was like being in a dream world. I had never seen such extravagance. I met Westminstair at the Hôtel de Paris in Monte Carlo. He invited me on board his yacht for dinner. Just me and him and an entire symphony orchestra." The hard black eyes softened with wonder for a moment.

Wallis thought of the time the prince had taken a party to Quaglino's and insisted that the club's celebrated singer Leslie "Hutch" Hutchinson come back with them and perform privately at York House. It had happened so often after that that Hutch claimed his songs were stored in the walls.

"And I loved his vulnerability. He was autocratic one minute and the next positively forlorn. Powerful and dependent at the same time. I adored it."

Wallis sighed. She knew that feeling too.

Chanel's face, which had been radiant, now clouded over. "But after a while I started to feel like his mother and his nanny as well as his lover."

Wallis bit her lip.

"I started to feel . . . enclosed. I could never be unwell or have a migraine because Westminstair would instantly summon the most famous doctors from Harley Street. It was the same with everything. I only had to express a wish for it to be granted."

Wallis said nothing. She knew what it was like to be given everything too.

"And how I hated the stately homes of England. They are so freezing! So inconvenient! No guest of mine will ever be expected to trot along a chilly corridor at night to visit the bathroom or wait for a maidservant to struggle upstairs with boiling water for a hip bath."

Wallis laughed. Once, staying at Knole in Kent, they had been unable to sleep due to the bone-chilling cold of Thomas Cranmer's bedroom.

"And to think," Ernest had observed of the Tudor archbishop and builder of the magnificent house, "that he ended up being burned at the stake."

Chanel was working on the hem of the dress again. "We went to Westminstair's stately home every weekend. It was so boring. The nearest post office was twenty miles away. One would do knitting, change clothes several times a day, go admire the roses in the park, roast oneself in front of a huge open fire in the salon, freeze the moment one moved away from it. That's all a weekend at the stately home consisted of."

Wallis was silent. She had once loved the Fort so much. But there had been weekends recently that bore a close resemblance to this.

"The only thing I liked was the suit of armor on the staircase. The helmet especially. Whenever I went past I would say hello and shake its hand. But it came to seem sinister. I would shudder when I passed it."

A memory came back. They had been returning late from a party through the darkened Great Park. Something darted out from between the trees, something huge and antlered. She cried out in terror, and the prince soothed her. "It was just a stag, Wallis."

And perhaps it had been. Perhaps she hadn't seen a blue light or heard the rattle of chains.

Chanel was twitching at the sleeves now. "These British men, they are very controlling. Westminstair wanted to be the center of my life, and for me to be the center of his. He wanted to own me."

"Own you?"

The black bob nodded. "I wanted to learn English. I could not speak it then. But he would not let me."

"Why not?"

"Because I would then understand all the stupid things he said. He gave me a checkbook full of signed blanks. I gave it back. I make my own money. It was suffocating!" She made a fanning gesture with one long, slim hand.

Suffocating. Wallis had felt it on the way here, on the boat across the Channel. The king had been at sea as well, attending a naval review. He had sent her a ship-to-ship telegram from the destroyer. "I feel so eanum not having talked to you today. Are you missing me as much as I am you?" She had winced, imagining what the navy telegraph officer had thought.

"Westminstair set up a couture room for me at Eaton Hall, his house, and brought over my staff. But couture belongs to Paris, and he could never make me stay away for long. And the House of Chanel is the love of my life and I could never give it up for any man!"

Oh, to have work like that. She had imagined hers was to help the king, encourage and sustain him. Now Wallis only wanted someone else to do it.

"I was desperate to escape," Chanel went on. "I was miserable in a life that from the outside seemed magnificent."

The phrase echoed in Wallis's head.

"So what did you do? To get rid of Westminstair . . . Westminster?"

"I began to behave badly, on purpose. I began to pretend I cared when he saw other women. He would give me jewelry to make amends and I would throw it off the deck of his yacht." Chanel looked rueful. "That was the only really difficult bit. There was a wonderful ruby necklace once. I looked at it for a few moments and then let it slide between my fingers into the sea. Another time he gave me a perfect pearl bracelet. I hurled it overboard into the depths. . . ." She sighed, then brightened. "But it worked. We parted then, and he married Loelia Ponsonby. I hear she looks like a waitress," Chanel added gleefully.

Wallis tried and failed to imagine throwing the king's presents into the sea. It was equally difficult to imagine behaving badly toward him. Neither were in her accommodating, easygoing nature, whereas the volatile Chanel was clearly different. "I have to get away," she said. "But I don't know how."

Chanel sat cross-legged at her feet, lighting a cigarette. "This is what I think." She blew out a plume of smoke. "Just run."

"Run?"

"Yes! Jump out of the window if you're the object of passion."

But her passion for the prince had been the high point of her life. She covered her face. "But I don't want to run or jump. I don't know how to give him up. I need him."

Chanel pulled her hands back down, tsking with irritation. "Stay still! I am working on the sleeves."

"I've never loved another person as much as I love him," Wallis cried. "I'm madly in love with him."

Chanel sighed and looked up at her. "*Cherie*, passion is the worst of all worlds."

"But *why*?"

"Because even grand passion is not love. Love is warmth, affection, patience, tenderness, decency."

Love is warmth, affection, patience, tenderness, decency. That was Ernest, Wallis thought.

She felt calmer, suddenly, as if the clouds in her mind were parting and she could see a clear way forward. She would go back to her husband, once and for all. And then they would leave, go back to America. She looked down at the great designer at her feet. She searched for the words to thank her.

Chanel pulled the hemline irritably. "Can't you stand still even for a minute?"

Wallis must find a way out and the answer struck her. She and Ernest should return to America.

But when he met the boat-train at Victoria, Ernest's kindly face was grim. He looked as if he had not slept for several nights; there was even stubble growth on his chin.

"Whatever's happened?" she asked, alarmed, as he hurried her down the platform.

"I can't tell you here."

He said nothing in the taxi either, and her apprehension had built to screaming point by the time the rattling vehicle drew up at Bryanston Court. Inside the flat, he poured them both enormous whiskies and sat her down in the drawing room. She was still wearing her coat and hat.

"David summoned me to the palace," Ernest began. He was clearly extremely agitated; his voice shook, his lip was trembling. "While you were away."

"Why?"

"To command me to give you a divorce."

CHAPTER FORTY-FOUR

She could not believe what she was hearing. She stared at her gloved hands, on the knee still covered with her outside coat.

"It's all arranged," Ernest told her. "Mary is coming over."

"You've arranged it?" she gasped. "Without even talking to me?"

"The king has arranged it. He's attended to everything. Mary and I are to go to the Hôtel de Paris in Bray and have a maid bring us breakfast in bed."

Her panic was rising. Perhaps, she thought wildly, it was just a nightmare. David would never be so devious in real life. He would never encourage her to go away just so he could work on Ernest. And even had this happened, Ernest would never have capitulated, as he seemed to have done so easily here. He was telling her that the hotel maid would testify at the divorce hearing.

"You are to divorce me for adultery," Ernest went on. "The king has arranged for his solicitor, a Mr. Allen, to represent you. He has even decided the assumed name that Mary should use at the hotel. He wants her to call herself Buttercup Kennedy."

"*Buttercup Kennedy?*" A wild urge to laugh possessed her, followed by a wave of complete despair. She thought of the years she had known Mary. How on earth had it come to this?

"The maid will discover us in an adulterous situation, and after that I'll move out of Bryanston Court and into the Guards Club."

It was all real. She could never have dreamed this. "No!"

Ernest sighed. "There's no point fighting it, Wallis."

She looked about the sitting room, where the king had come so many times. She felt, now, that she regretted every single one of them. She looked at Ernest. The carpet seemed to stretch between them.

"Why?" she asked. "Why isn't there any point?"

"He made it perfectly clear to me. He means to make you his wife, come what may."

"But I'm married to *you*," she cried.

They looked at each other.

"We had an arrangement," she reminded him. "Once it was over, I would come back to you."

He hunched his shoulders and stared at the carpet. "But it was never going to be over," he said. "For a long time now, I—" He stopped.

She felt terrified, as if everything anchoring her to the land was letting her go. "Ernest, talk to me. For a long time what?"

"I feel like I lost you ages ago," he said quietly. "I don't think you could come back to me now, even if you wanted to. Too much has changed."

She gasped, about to argue. He was right, and yet he was wrong too. "Can't we stop it?" she whispered.

He looked at her sadly. "You have no idea what is ranged against us. The resources of an entire empire. He will fight to the end. He will do literally anything to make you his wife."

"But I don't want to be his wife!" She went to him, took his hands and knelt on the floor before him. "Please don't let me go, Ernest! I'm frightened!"

He held her close and kissed the top of her head.

She started to sob into his sleeve. "Why does he have to destroy our marriage?"

"Because he can," said Ernest.

She lifted her hot, tear-streaked face and tried to think straight.

"It's impossible for him to marry me. I'd be twice divorced. The Church would never allow it, as you said. And the government, the empire, the rest of it. They'd all refuse to let him."

She looked distractedly about the sitting room. There had to be a way out of this. What was it? Spotting the copy of *The Times* by Ernest's chair, she saw something gleam in her mind, a bright straw of hope. She clutched at it wildly. "The newspapers!" she exclaimed. "What happens when the story gets out? The people will hate it. They're not going to want me as his wife, still less as queen!"

A great rush of relief filled her. But Ernest's face remained gray and tense. "All part of the plan. The king has an understanding with the newspapers. They have agreed not to print anything until after the wedding."

"He's gagged the newspapers? Can you *do* that?" The strange reticence of the British press. She had never dreamed that this was the reason.

He shrugged his broad shoulders. "Well, he has. That's the sort of power we're up against. We don't have a chance."

She felt sick. She could not accept that she was already trapped. That things had been planned and arranged without her knowing and events were already moving. She could hear the clang of prison doors, the rattle of chains.

Determined, she went to the palace to make one last supreme effort to break things off. The king greeted her with delight and showed her the new shower he had installed, happily turning the water on and off.

"I've always hated baths, you see," he said. "They remind me of my childhood. That hateful nanny, putting soap in my mouth. And all the other beastly things she did to me."

"Stop manipulating me!" she cried.

He looked hurt. "Why do you say that? I thought you sympathized. We've been through all the same things."

Guilt flooded her, and love, and all the other usual passionate, protective feelings.

"Abuse, violence, addiction," he reminded her.

She turned away, to the window. It had not been cleaned for some time. "Yes," she said. "And now we're addicted to each other."

He said nothing to this, but merrily started to talk about the cruise he was planning, which they would go on together. She touched his arm. "David. You know it can't happen."

His blue eyes creased with amusement. "Now, I know *exactly* what you're about to say! I know what your concerns are, and I have devised a brilliant solution."

She felt the wind conclusively leak from her sails. "You have?"

The golden head nodded gleefully. "Yes! You're thinking that we can't go via Italy as planned because of Abyssinia!"

"Abyssinia," she repeated. The tensions in Europe arising from Mussolini's African invasion had gone right to the back of her mind. The Foreign Office's pro-Italian route had proved controversial; foreign secretary Samuel Hoare had lost his job because of a secret pact with the French to divide Abyssinia between Italy and Ethiopia. He had been replaced by the suave Anthony Eden.

"But we are going to avoid Italy altogether and join *Nahlin* at Šibenik, which is in Yugoslavia. Isn't that clever?" His face was full of a bright expectation.

"Narling? *Who's he?*"

"It's the name of the boat. Duff and Diana are coming, and Tommy."

As he continued, humming, about the room, she took a deep breath and tried again. "David . . . Marriage is out of the question for us."

He continued to hum, removing items from boxes, regarding them with his head to one side. "You know how much I love you and always will." He bent to open another box, humming all the while.

"David, please. I have to go back to Ernest."

He stopped unpacking but did not look up. It was so painful, so difficult. More than she had imagined. She pushed on, even so. "In a few months' time you will have forgotten me completely. You'll be so busy, and you'll go on with your job, doing it better and better each year." She forced herself to smile. "And you'll be relieved not to have me nagging you anymore!"

His face remained hidden, still.

Tears stung her eyes. She rummaged for a handkerchief. "We have had such beautiful times together, David. And I am so thankful for them, and I will never forget them. But you are better off without me. You and I would only create disaster together."

Still he said nothing.

"David . . ." Her voice had a pleading note. "More than anything I want you to be happy. Please believe me when I say that. But I feel sure I can't make you so and I honestly don't think you can me."

She waited. Her thumping heart seemed to fill the room. Still no reaction.

"I shall always read about you in the newspapers—believing only half! But please, David. No more talk of marriage."

She stopped. Both voice and nerve were breaking under the strain.

He looked at her, his eyes full of hurt. "What have I done?" he asked, as a child might.

It was like talking to someone in a language they didn't understand. "Destroyed my peace of mind!" she cried. "Now you want to destroy my marriage. Why do you have to marry me?"

"Because you are everything to me," he replied simply. "Everything depends on you."

"But we can remain friends! Lovers even! We don't have to marry! Why can't you take no for an answer? You asked those other women; they all said no."

He smiled. "On the contrary, they all said yes. But I didn't mean it with them."

She took a moment to absorb this. "So why do you have to mean it with me?"

"Because I love you."

"You loved them too! Remember how devastated you were about Thelma?"

He shook his head. "When I met you I had only experienced passion. Love, never."

Love is warmth, affection, patience, tenderness, decency.

She hid her face. "Please don't do this. We must learn to live without each other."

"Why?" Again, like a child.

"Because the alternative is worse."

"No, Wallis, what you propose is worse."

A kind of terrified despair had filled her. She lowered her hands and looked at him. "But you can't marry me and make me queen."

"David can. And he will."

At this infantile use of the third person, all calmness deserted her. "What if I go away?" she cried, desperate. "What if I leave the country?"

"David will follow you," he said simply.

CHAPTER FORTY-FIVE

Ernest duly spent the night with Buttercup Kennedy at the Hôtel de Paris in Bray. As arranged, he was discovered "in an adulterous situation." A few days later he left Bryanston Court and moved to the Guards Club. Wallis was not at home when he went. But when he went to his room and looked out of the window, across Piccadilly to the Green Park opposite, he might have seen, sitting alone on one of the benches, a slender figure in black sobbing her heart out.

The king's solicitor filed her divorce petition. With the king and his party, she went to join the yacht *Nahlin* in Yugoslavia.

Local dignitaries and peasants in costume crowded the quay. They stood waving as the boat sailed out, shouting.

The king waved cheerfully back, his pale bare chest gleaming in the strong sunlight. Diana came up. "Tell me, Wallis," she said in her musing way. "Do you think it might be at all possible to get His Majesty to at least put his shirt on until we get out of sight of all these people?"

Wallis laughed. What on earth made anyone imagine she had the smallest influence on the king? She turned to Diana, trying to keep her tone light. "Feel free to ask him yourself. But it's my experience that when it's something he doesn't want to do, he has a wont of iron."

Diana's pale blue eyes widened. "*Wont* of iron?"

"As opposed to a will of iron."

"Ha! That's a good one."

The king was in high spirits throughout the voyage. Wallis's own mood lurched wildly from one extreme to the other. She would go from a determination to resist him, to find a way to break free even now, to a feeling of overwhelming love. She was full of wild energy one minute, and utterly drained the next. She was brilliant at dinner, holding the table in thrall, the stories and wisecracks following in quick succession and everyone admiring and amused. Then she would go to her cabin and weep from sheer frustration. The king had now abandoned all pretense of caring what anyone thought. At night, he would take her off to his cabin in a highly public manner, and more than once, in the morning, he appeared at breakfast with her lipstick smeared on his face. She sat sipping her coffee, cringing inside.

"How could you?" she stormed at him afterward. "It's so indiscreet!"

The king maintained his benign smile. "Discretion," he remarked, almost proudly, "is a quality which, though useful, I have never particularly admired."

When they arrived at Athens she refused to leave the ship. He wanted to take her to meet the British ambassador, but the thought of His Excellency's official disdain was more than she could bear. She spent the day swimming, floating on her back in the clear cool water and fighting off the urge to strike out to the horizon and never return.

One evening, as the *Nahlin* lay at anchor off a tiny fishing village, Wallis stood at the rails looking at the mountainsides that rose straight out of the sea. She could just make out the tracks cut into the rocky sides, tracks that, presumably, peasants had used for centuries to make their way down from the villages to fish.

The sun was setting behind the boat. Crimson spread across the water. Wallis thought of Chanel and her rubies. She doubted that if she hurled the whole of the crown jewels overboard now that it would make any difference. She should have taken the designer's advice: run, jumped. But she could not. Despite it all, she loved him. Then fear would consume her; what they were doing was madness. It would end badly and she must escape before it was too late. And round and round her thoughts went, chasing one another from one extreme to the other.

The red in the sky deepened. The ocean had a sanguineous gleam. The mountains now loomed in a shapeless mass but something caught her eye, a flash of something.

"What's that?"

The king, as ever, was at her elbow. They both stared across the bloodred water. A moving snake of light was rippling up the side of the mountain. She realized that on the trails she had seen, thousands of peasants were now standing carrying flaming torches.

The king held up his hand. His signet ring gleamed red in the sunset. "Listen!"

Music could be heard. Echoing from the cliffs came refrains of folk songs, sometimes sad and sometimes gay. "*Živjela ljubav.*"

What are they saying?" Wallis wondered.

"*Živjela ljubav.*"

"And what does that mean?"

He turned to her, smiling. "I believe that it translates as 'Long live love!'" He raised her hand and kissed it. "These simple peasants know a king is in love with you."

Wallis stared at the glimmering cliffs. That their relationship had touched these remote people seemed to her extraordinary. They clearly saw it as some epic romance; perhaps it was. She thought of all the other great lovers of history. How had things seemed to them from the inside? Complicated, no doubt. Would she be part of history herself? The picture had got so big now, everything had enormous consequences. She had fought hard to retain control and she had lost. The feeling of the ship moving beneath exactly reflected how she felt, that it was out of her hands and someone else was guiding her destiny.

✦ ✦ ✦

On the return to London, Wallis found, waiting for her at Bryanston Court, a fat parcel of newspaper clippings from Aunt Bessie. They were not just American but from the foreign press too. Wallis's relationship with the king and the forthcoming divorce case were extensively covered in all of them. With a cold and churning horror she realized she was gossip subject number one for every newspaper reader in the United States, Europe and the Dominions.

She ran to her room and hurled herself under the bedcovers. Never had she longed for Ernest more, but he was in America himself now, with Mary. The faithful Lily appeared from time to time bearing trays of tea and bowls of nourishing soup, only to find her mistress still sobbing under the blankets. Only when, at her wit's end, she appeared with a large whisky could Wallis be tempted out. She knocked it back in one and felt something like resolve return. She looked at Lily with flaming eyes. "Bring me some notepaper, please."

The panicked, drastic note she now wrote to the king set out in balder terms still what she had already told him. Her life was being ruined, her reputation utterly destroyed. She loved him and always would but he must let her go now. It was over between them forever. She was going to return to America, find Ernest and beg him to take her back.

The next morning, the telephone rang. She lifted it with a shaking hand, hardening her heart against and yet longing for the tones of the hurt little boy. She heard, to her surprise, the icy voice of Tommy Lascelles.

"His Majesty wishes to know when you will be joining him at Balmoral."

"I don't want to go to Balmoral," she replied curtly. "He knows that already."

The king had suggested, on the return trip, that she join him at the family castle on Deeside. She had been doubtful to start with, but the news that the Yorks were to be there too turned doubt into absolute refusal. He had been so dismayed it had alarmed her and she had promised to think about it. But the press cuttings had only reinforced the need to say no.

"I see," said Lascelles distantly. "That may cause His Majesty a degree of difficulty."

"Well, I'm sorry about that," she said, politely unrepentant. "But it can't be helped."

There was a gentle cough from the other end. "His Majesty wished me to convey the fact that if you were unable to join him at Balmoral, he would slit his throat."

CHAPTER FORTY-SIX

"Deeside," the king remarked lightly, "has the lowest rainfall in Scotland."

"You don't say," returned Wallis. They were standing at the window of a Balmoral sitting room. The view outside was of unremitting rain. Coming at the building horizontally, it lashed at the glass like an animal. Wallis had never seen anything quite like it.

Nor had she seen anything quite like Balmoral. All gables and spires against a background of pines, it looked like a Grimm fairy tale plonked in a Scottish forest. A great gray tower with pepper pot turrets rose from a granite block festooned with domes.

The inside was spectacular in its hideousness. It was terribly dark, and yet despite the gloom no square inch was undecorated. Rooms ranged from fan-vaulted cathedral Gothic to gilded baroque with molded ceilings.

The decor was dominated by emphatic references to Scotland. Antlers sprouted from walls like branches of invisible trees. Wallpaper bristled with thistles. Tartan was everywhere, carpeted seas of it, sofas and chairs of it, enormous windows flanked with long curtains hanging from pelmets of the same. Even the lino was tartan.

Paintings of Queen Victoria, whose dream home this had apparently been, were everywhere. Her monogram decorated the fire buckets in the passage. Nothing in the whole place seemed to relate to the modern age at all.

Wallis turned from the window to find herself staring at a huge gold-framed painting in which a heroic sideburned figure was setting about an antlered creature with a knife.

"David, what on earth's going on here?"

He hurried to her side. "Prince Albert is gralloching the stag."

"Gralloching?"

"Gutting it."

The knife made her think of what he had threatened to do to himself. He had not mentioned it since she arrived; it was as if it hadn't happened. She felt both furious at his shamelessness and at the fact that she loved him more than ever. No one had ever needed her like this.

He beamed at her. "It's so wonderful to see you. I think that every time. I'm nearly forty but I haven't felt this way about anyone before."

She looked at him, half-thrilled, half-despairing. He started to look around at their surroundings critically.

"We need to pep the place up," he said. "American style."

She felt alarmed. The Fort had been work enough. She might be stuck here for years in the middle of nowhere, overseeing a complete overhaul.

He thought for a few seconds and then his face blazed with delight. "I've got it! I'll get hold of a projector. We could show a film. You could go down to the kitchens and show them how to make club sandwiches!"

She could imagine how that would go down. The servants at Balmoral seemed as grimly stuck in the past as the rest of the place. She doubted that they even had sliced bread. And as for olives and cocktail sticks to skewer the sandwiches together, forget it.

She smiled anyway. With any luck he would forget it. She felt exhausted. The journey up from London, earlier in the day, had seemed endlessly long. That Scotland was so enormous had been a surprise. She had been relieved to get to Edinburgh, but there was almost as long again to go.

Unexpectedly, he had been at the Aberdeen railway station to meet her, waiting in his sports car with his goggles on. He had imagined no one had recognized him, but it was obvious to her that people had and were being discreet.

"Good," he said. "Bertie and Elizabeth will be coming for dinner. It'll make a change for them."

Bertie and Elizabeth! Alarm clanged through her. Her heart plunged to the level of the tartan carpet. She had not realized they were here. The thought of them watching a film, eating club sandwiches, despising every second, blaming her, hating her. She felt faint.

She looked for somewhere to sit down. A small chair—covered in plaid, naturally—was positioned nearby. She was lowering herself down when the king's eyes bulged in horror.

"Wallis! *Stop!*"

She shot to her feet, nerves jangling painfully. "What's the matter?"

He was laughing. "You can't sit there! It's Queen Victoria's favorite chair. No one's ever allowed to sit there, *ever!*"

She was speechless. Queen Victoria's favorite chair? The woman had been dead for thirty-five years. She wanted to say, tartly, that the modernizing process was clearly some way off, when the door opened and, rather reinforcing her point, a tailcoated butler appeared with the afternoon newspaper on a silver salver.

She watched the king take it and read the headline. "What is it?" she asked as he raised his eyebrows.

"Oh, nothing."

"Show me."

Reluctantly, he passed the paper over. She read that he had been asked to open a new wing of Aberdeen hospital that day but had declined because of other commitments. Bertie and Elizabeth had opened it instead. The front page of the Aberdeen *Press and Journal* showed two photographs side by side, the Yorks before the hospital surrounded by an admiring crowd and the king in his goggles greeting her at the station. She, it seemed, was the other commitment.

Her mouth dropped open. It wasn't just the spectacularly bad judgment, but the absolute certainty at who would be held responsible. "David," she stammered when the ability to speak returned. "This is terrible. What must the Scottish people think?"

"I don't care what anyone thinks" was the predictable reply. "All that matters to me is you, Wallis."

She stood up and went to the window. The rain had eased and rich evening light now entered the long, gloomy room. Its intensity made the king's face more delicately pale, his eyes a deeper blue, his hair more powerfully gold. He was so beautiful, she thought, so innocent-looking. And yet. "If I matter to you, why did you do this?" She pointed at the paper. "They will blame me, you know that."

In reply, he felt in his pocket and produced a gold pocket watch. He flipped open the lid and showed her the engraving inside. "'To David on his birthday from GRI.'" He looked at her.

"Who's GRI?"

"George Rex Imperator. Quite embarrassingly affectionate and personal, isn't it?"

He was using his vulnerability as a weapon again. She knew this trick so well now. "Stop it!" she cried.

He took her hand, kissed it and said, wet-eyed, "You're the only person who has ever really loved me and wanted to care for me, Wallis. I love you so much."

She wrenched her hand away. "How can you love me?" she blazed at him. "You're suffocating me!" Then she rushed out of the room.

She struck out across the lawns, uncaring about her thin coat and that the water soaked into her shoes. She was sobbing, angry helpless sobs. Beyond the gardens, a rough track led into the hills between

copses of trees. She walked quickly up it; the way was stony and it was
as much as she could do not to stumble. She rounded a bend and was
surprised to see, ahead of her, two small figures in red. Nearing them,
she realized they were the little York girls. Were they lost? Her own
problems forgotten, she picked up speed, hurrying toward them.

"Lost?" Lilibet stared at her in amazement. Up close, she wore a
woolen jersey, kilt and ankle socks with stout brogues. Her sister was
identically clad. "How could we be lost here?"

"Well, it's not impossible." Wallis smiled ruefully. "I'm pretty lost
myself, I guess." And in more ways than one.

"Have you been crying?" asked Margaret, peering at her curiously.
"Your makeup's all smudged."

"It's the rain," said Wallis.

"But it's stopped raining now," the younger princess pointed out.
"Why are you looking at me like that, Lilibet?"

Lilibet stopped glaring warningly at her sister and regarded Wallis
with candid blue eyes. "You're that woman, aren't you?"

"What woman?"

"*That woman.* That's what Mummie and Papa call you."

Wallis blinked. "Oh."

"And Grandmama calls you an adventuress."

"So I've heard."

Lilibet was looking at her consideringly. "Does that mean you go
on adventures?"

"Well . . . I guess."

Margaret stirred beside her sister. "They don't like you," she said
in her piping childish voice. "But *we* do, don't we, Lilibet?"

The eldest princess nodded her chestnut curls decidedly. "Yes.
We do."

Tears sprang to Wallis's eyes at this unexpected tribute. She
blinked them away hard, and smiled. "What are you two girls doing
here anyway?"

"Waiting for the guns. They come back this way from a day on the hill."

"Oh, I see. This is stalking, right?" Wallis remembered Elizabeth's freezing inquisition in the garden at Royal Lodge. "How does it work, exactly?"

Lilibet looked delighted, as had been the intention. Wallis arranged her features into careful attentiveness as the elder princess started to explain, at a somewhat breathless high speed, how stag-hunting Balmoral-style required two ghillies and a stalker to lead the way, as well as a pony boy—a retired ghillie, usually.

"A retired what?"

"Oh, ghillie." Lilibet gave her monkey grin. "Well, a sort of guide, I suppose. For hunters." She rattled on with her explanation, obviously thrilled about the whole business and desperate to be a part of it. "Imagine!" she gasped to Wallis. "Having my own gun and wearing the special Balmoral tweed!"

"Imagine."

Something now appeared in the distance. Round the corner of the stony track came a pony moving slowly along under the weight of an enormous stag. "They're here!" Lilibet bounded excitedly off, with Margaret scrambling after.

"So exciting!" she yelled over her shoulder. "It looks like a royal!"

"A what?"

Margaret stopped and turned. "To qualify as a true Monarch of the Glen," she explained seriously, "the antlers need to have twelve points."

"Oh. I see."

"It is, it really is!" They caught up to find Lilibet jumping up and down. "Look! The trio at the highest point are quite large and deep enough to hold a glass of wine!"

Wallis looked at the huge dead animal, its flanks running with blood and its eyes rolling upward. She felt passionately sorry for it. She had to get away, she thought, before the same thing happened to her. But how?

✦✦✦

Dinner was death by a thousand cuts. The first was when, as Wallis greeted guests in the drawing room, the Duchess of York swept past, declaring, in her high, clear voice, "I have come to dine with the *king.*" Lascelles and Aird exchanged satisfied glances.

But at least the club sandwiches failed to make an appearance. The cook had looked so utterly disgusted at the suggestion that Wallis had half feared some deliberately botched ones, as sabotage. That the menu was salmon followed by grouse followed by raspberries felt like blessed deliverance.

"And all costing nothing because all grown on the estate," the king said proudly. Wallis examined her monogrammed plate, wondering if he really believed it actually cost nothing and wasn't a vast enterprise with hundreds of staff. But what the king believed was something she didn't want to think about. Not least because, once they returned to London, talk about marriage would start all over again. That he couldn't, for the moment, do anything about it was the sole advantage of this crazy place.

When the grouse had appeared, it had been carried on a silver tray by a butler in a plaid cloak. This was, it had been explained to her with stuttering difficulty by Bertie, because a servant predecessor had once stood in for Prince Albert when he was being painted as a shepherd by Landseer. She had been about to laugh hysterically when she suddenly realized he was serious.

The company listened politely as the king expounded on his favorite subject. "The committee examined the diets of over one thousand poor families and found that the lowest income group of four and a half million had diet 'inadequate in all respects.' *In all respects!*" the king repeated, pounding the venerable oak of the Balmoral dining table while guests in glittering diamonds raised silver soup spoons and looked dutifully concerned.

"Seebohm Rowntree found that forty-nine percent of all working-class children under the age of five suffered poverty," the king went on.

Ernest's voice came back to her. *Wallis, doesn't it strike you as a little weird that he always wants to discuss the poor while surrounded by the privileges of the very rich?*

Yes, Ernest. It does. But what can I do about it now? Oh dear, sensible, solid, sane Ernest.

She could see Elizabeth, across the table, staring pointedly at her Cartier diamond brooch. The duchess could not guess, Wallis thought, and would certainly never believe that she would give up all her jewelry in a heartbeat, all her imagined privileges and influence too, just to regain her former freedom, the husband she was on the verge of losing and the simplicity of the life she had once thought so dull.

CHAPTER FORTY-SEVEN

"Felix Toe? What sort of a name is that?"

"Felix*stowe*." The king smiled at her reassuringly. "It's on the east coast, Wallis."

Midge-plagued, rain-lashed Balmoral had been bad enough. She had only just got back to London and he was telling her she had to spend a fortnight by the sea in England in October. Her marriage to Ernest was to die in a courtroom in Suffolk, wherever that was, and, as the petitioner, she would be reading the last rites herself.

"But why there?"

"The London courts were full up," the king explained. "The only place they could hear your divorce was Ipswich."

"Ipps Witch?"

"Which is near Felixstowe, before you ask. Famous for being the birthplace of Thomas Wolsey."

"Who?"

"Henry the Eighth's fixer. Well, one of them."

She thought of Anne Boleyn. The net, closing in. Then she pushed the thought away. She was not quite helpless, not yet.

"What if I decide I don't want to go through with it?" she demanded. "What if I wanted to save my marriage?"

He took this calmly; he had so nearly got what he wanted, after all. "Well, Ernest has gone through with it. With Buttercup Kennedy. So there's not much of a marriage to save."

He took her hand swiftly. "And soon we'll be together. There'll be nothing to stop us anymore. You are everything to me, Wallis. I never knew I could be so happy."

The gratitude in his blue eyes sent a powerful wave of affection through her, even as she wanted to yell at him. It overwhelmed her that this man would do anything for her. This king, this emperor. It was adoration on a scale she had never experienced, that very few people ever got to experience. The urge to fight it was lessening all the time.

Felixstowe looked as appealing as any coastal town on the English east coast could expect to in October. It seemed to her heavy with metaphor. She walked along the beach, looking at the simple landscape and thinking how complicated her own life had become. The wind cut her ears and the briny air was sharp in her nostrils. She looked at the sea and thought it looked not like boundless escape, but like a great wall, gray or blue depending on the weather and extending in all directions. She looked at the sand and the worn, smooth stones and thought of the inexorable forces that had shaped them, forces they had had no option but to submit to.

Did she have to submit to it? When the king was away, she thought not. But when he came to visit, she thought the opposite.

"I realized I loved you when I felt actual physical pain when you left the room," he told her. "It's agony not to be with you."

He was like the tide coming in, sweeping over all before him. When they walked on the beach and he wrapped his coat about her against the gale, it was increasingly hard to imagine braving the winds alone. And yet, imagine it she did, even now.

He looked out to sea with a naval eye, assessing the conditions, wishing he had a boat. She too longed for a vessel, but only to take her

away. Where he pointed with delight at "white horses"—waves tossing like manes as they bounded in to shore—she saw long ridges of
water marching inexorably in. When he swooped triumphantly on a
piece of sea-worn glass, holding it up as if it were a treasure, she
thought of all the real jewels, those in his crown especially, that he
did not seem to value at all.

The hearing approached with the inevitability of the marching waves.
The day before, she walked through Felixstowe, feeling numb. It was
a wild day, and the wind screamed in the trees. Her hair lashed into
her eyes. A church rose on her left, ugly and Victorian. It was Catho-
lic, St. Felix, and she went in and sat down in one of the pews, looking at the crucifix on the plain white wall and the light through the
stained-glass windows. *God help me*, she thought. Dust specks were
dancing in the colored rays.

A priest appeared and asked if she wanted confession. It seemed
like a sign, so she followed him to a curtained booth. God had heard
her, and she prepared to talk to him.

The priest was murmuring through the curtain. "Show mercy
now on your servant . . . ?"

"Bessie." She couldn't risk that he would recognize her. There
would be reporters at the courtroom, that was for sure. She made her
accent as English as she could.

"Show mercy now on your servant Bessie and grant her deliverance pardoning all her sins whether voluntary or involuntary."

Voluntary or involuntary. Had she ever had any choice? Sometimes
it seemed that everything had happened by itself, almost as if it had
been predestined.

*You will have two more marriages in your life. You will become a
famous woman.*

"Reconcile her and unite her to Your Holy Church through Jesus
Christ our Lord to whom, with you, are due all dominion and majesty."

380 * Wendy Holden

Dominion and majesty. She knew something about that too.

"Now and ever and unto ages of ages, amen. So what is it that you wish to confess, my child?"

He sounded calm, understanding. She decided not to beat about the bush. "Well, Father. I'm in love with somebody who isn't my husband."

"You've been tempted to commit adultery?"

"Yes. And I'm afraid I yielded to the temptation, Father."

There was a silence. "I see," said the priest. "But now you want to go back to your husband."

Wallis took a deep breath. "Yes. I mean no."

"No? Which is it, my child?"

She curled her hands into fists, screwed up her eyes, felt the hot tears sluicing down her cheeks. "I don't know," she said, her voice choked. "I want you to tell me what to do, Father."

She expected him to say that it was her decision, between her and the promptings of her conscience, but instead he said, quite firmly, "I think you would regret abandoning your marriage."

A sudden anguish seized her. "But I have to!" she cried. "I love him so much, Father. He's like the air I breathe. He needs me so much. We're bound together."

"'If you love me,'" said the priest, "'keep my commandments.'"

"But what if I can't?" She was sobbing openly now. "Isn't there anything you can do?"

"Some sort of ritual, perhaps?"

"Yes!"

"I'm afraid not. But I can pray for you."

"Thank you, Father."

"And you can pray for yourself."

That night, sleepless and distressed, she paced the house's creaking wooden floors, praying for forgiveness for loving the king and also praying for Ernest to come and rescue her. She prayed for strength to endure what was coming, to help the king and to deserve his adoration. She wondered afterward if God had been able to make sense of any of it, contradictory and mixed up as her feelings were. After so long entirely alone, it was a shock to arrive at the courthouse to find it mobbed by journalists and to be escorted inside by the police. The judge did not conceal his hostility, and she felt sick with nerves as she answered the few questions that the barrister acting for her was obliged to put. But after uncontested proceedings lasting nineteen minutes, she was awarded a decree nisi with costs.

"I suppose I must," said the judge reluctantly, "in these unusual circumstances." Afterward, Wallis's barrister told her that the Bray hotel, considering itself superior to such things, had at first refused to allow its employee to present her evidence concerning Ernest and Buttercup Kennedy.

She laughed, it was so farcical. She wondered what Ernest had made of it.

There would, the barrister added, be an interval of six months before the divorce could be made absolute. She felt a gleam of hope. Anything could happen in six months. In that time, David might even find a suitable wife.

She returned to London to find she was to move from Bryanston Court. The king had had prepared for her a large and beautiful townhouse in Cumberland Terrace, Regent's Park.

"It's safer," he said.

She looked at him, puzzled. "But I felt safe where I was."

He looked so despondent that she tried to look pleased instead. "Thank you. It's very thoughtful of you to be so protective."

He looked back at her with besotted blue eyes. "Because you are everything to me, Wallis." Her heart turned over, as it always did.

Faithful Aunt Bessie had been persuaded to come over and move in too, to act as chaperone. Wallis threw herself into her aged aunt's arms and looked into the kindly, faded eyes.

"Don't say a word," Wallis said. "I know you told me so."

"Just one word," returned Bessie. "Does he *really* think he can marry you?"

"Yes. He really thinks he can."

"But it's impossible, surely."

"Let's hope so. I've got six months, anyway."

The king dined with them both on the first night. His irrepressible high spirits were, she guessed, because he had made her go through with the divorce in spite of her misgivings. She had now burned her boats and was his. Or very nearly.

The main course was snipe, shot on the Sandringham estate. He had been on a tour of the Durham coalfields and described the scene in some detail. The poverty had been appalling. There was a banner across the road saying WE NEED YOUR HELP.

"Something must be done," he said.

"So what will you do?" Aunt Bessie asked.

He grinned at her. "I'm trying my best." But Wallis knew that the energy that had once gone into improving the lives of the poor was now concentrated on trying to marry her. She felt ashamed to be such a distraction, and nostalgia for the impassioned campaigner he had been. Once this was all over, whatever happened, he must return to his causes.

The king was looking at her aunt's plate. "I say, Aunt Bessie, you're not leaving those heads, are you?"

Bessie gasped. "Eat the heads? I wouldn't dream of it, sir."

He grinned, reached across the table, severed the necks and impaled the heads on his fork to lift them to his plate. "But, Aunt, the brain is the best bit of the snipe!"

He gave Wallis a box after dinner, when Aunt Bessie had excused herself and gone to bed. It was a huge emerald ring.

"It came from an immense stone, as large as a bird's egg, which once belonged to the grand mogul," the king told her. "It had been divided up, as it was thought there was no one in the world extrava-

gant enough to buy the whole of it." He smiled his dazzling blue
smile. "But I would have bought the whole of it for you, my darling."
He showed her how he had engraved the date inside, and their initials, before slipping it on her finger. "This is to mark our engagement. WE are ours now!"

The jewel glowed like green fire on her finger. She felt thrilled by
its beauty, and also terrified at her situation.

"The oddest thing," he added as he was putting on his coat to
leave. "Baldwin came to see me. About the divorce."

"The prime minister?" she echoed, alarmed. "What did he want?"

"Well, he's a bit concerned about our marrying, to be frank with
you. But don't worry." He threw her a reassuring grin. "I'll be able to
fix everything."

Diana came to Cumberland Terrace with a bunch of pink roses.
"Gosh, how chic," she said, looking around the white-and-silver sitting room.

"Thank you. David had Syrie Maugham do it all." But having
once admired this style, Wallis now felt it clinical and contrived. It
was being worked on even before the stay in Felixstowe, it turned out.
The king had planned everything, as Ernest had said.

Diana waved her roses. "These are out of place. I brought them for
you from my rustic garden."

Wallis buried her nose in the petals. They had the delicious, fruity
scent of blooms that had fattened gradually under a country sun.
They were out of place, Diana was right, because they felt like the
only real thing in the room. "And how is Duff?"

Diana perched, in her tweed suit, on one of the spotless and spin-
dly white chairs.

"Busy with the king. His Majesty won't accept that your being
divorced is an impediment to marriage."

Wallis raised her head from the flowers. "He just refuses to face the facts. Baldwin's said he won't countenance him marrying a divorced woman."

"You sound quite blithe about it all."

Wallis wondered if she should tell her the truth. That she felt, if not blithe exactly, then certainly relieved. Given opposition like this it was surely impossible that the king should persist. They could go back to being lovers; perhaps she could even go back to Ernest. All might be well after all.

"But Duff's had a rather good idea. It might actually solve the whole problem." Diana leaned forward. "If the king waits until after he's crowned, he'll be so popular he could do what he likes, establishment or no establishment. His coronation will be the most glamorous spectacle in history bar none and he'll be right at the center of it. Afterward he could marry a monster from outer space if he wanted."

Wallis shot her a wry look. "Thanks, Diana."

"Don't mention it. So the idea is the king could be crowned and maybe attend a durbar in India or something, and after that he'd have the world at his feet. Don't you think it's actually quite brilliant?"

Wallis wondered what to say. Duff's idea was brilliant, but unnecessary. Stanley Baldwin had solved the problem already. She decided to be honest.

"Diana, I don't want this. I love David, and I don't think I could bear to give him up. But I don't want to be queen. I can't think of anything worse."

Diana looked surprised. Then she nodded. "I do see. But look at it this way. Following an inevitably gloriously successful coronation, the king might actually start to like being on the throne. He might actually start to look for someone who actually wants to be queen."

Wallis gazed at her in admiration. Diana was so clever. Her cool, pragmatic brain flew toward solutions, as straight as an arrow. Unlike her own crazed thoughts, which ran around in circles and lurched all over the place.

As she showed Diana out, hope soared within her. She could not remember the last time she had felt like that.

CHAPTER FORTY-EIGHT

T he king said no to Duff," Diana reported a few days later. "Absolutely refused to consider it, I'm afraid."

Wallis clutched the white-and-silver telephone. "Why did he refuse?"

"Well, the reason does him credit, actually. He feels it would be wrong to go through so solemn a religious ceremony as the coronation without letting his subjects know what it was his intention to do. He says he won't be crowned with a lie on his lips."

Wallis stared at the ceiling. She thought of all David had done to get to this point: ambushing Ernest and seducing his wife; forcing her into the Ipswich courtroom. Did he deserve to occupy the moral high ground? On the other hand, to be crowned and then find himself a wife while knowing, all the time, there was a mistress in the background he would never give up was wrong and cruel.

"What did Duff say?"

"He said he could not argue against such scruples, only respect them."

"So what now?"

"Beaverbrook and Churchill are trying the same line of argument. Winston's is quite hilarious, actually." Diana adopted Churchill's familiar growling tone and dramatic intonation. "Let His Majesty be anointed. Let him be given crown, scepter and orb and invested with the mystique of kingship. Let Mrs. Simpson make herself favorably known throughout the realm by modesty and good works."

She had a vision of herself touring hospitals, manning stalls at fetes. Doing what Elizabeth did.

Diana resumed her own light voice. "Don't you think that's funny?"

"Hilarious. Go on."

"Well, that's it. Modesty and good works. And then the marriage proposal could be raised again, and calmly."

"And how's that going down with David?"

Diana sighed. "To be honest, not with much success, it seems. He's sticking like glue to this determination not to be 'crowned with a lie on my lips.' Even if it means he won't be crowned at all."

Wallis reared up from the bed. "What? *What* did you just say?"

"Oh yes. The a-word has come up."

"A-word?"

"Abdication."

Wallis fell back down into the pillows. Nausea roared through her. The phone had dropped from her hand. She could hear, somewhere in the sheets, Diana's thin, disembodied voice.

"Wallis? Wallis? Don't panic! Duff has another plan. Or, rather, someone else does. Have you ever heard of Esmond Harmsworth?"

Going into the side entrance of Claridge's, Wallis's nerve broke and she dived into the ladies' changing room. She scuttled into one of the wood-lined cubicles, shut the polished door and sat down on the wooden seat.

Her hands were trembling, as they always were these days. Everything about her rattled and shook. She could not keep food down, so Esmond Harmsworth's lunch invitation was pointless on the one hand. Their meeting had had to be secret, timed for when the king was away. He was visiting the home fleet at Portland, a naval engagement of the sort he loved. He had been happily looking forward to it the night before, when she had seen him. But he always was happy these days, his mood in cruel contrast to her own. Having apparently resolved to give up his throne so he could marry her, his heart seemed as light as a bird's.

She could hear, outside, the attendant running a basin of warm water for her to wash her hands. She thought of the times she had been there with Thelma, and what Thelma had said.

Baby, have you any idea of what you're getting into?

Exactly what Thelma had known was something she reflected on often these days.

On the way out of the restroom, she caught a fleeting view of something skinny, black and haunted-looking in the mirror of one of the polished oak dressing tables. She looked like a vampire might, or an evil spirit. She wondered if Esmond Harmsworth, whose family owned the *Daily Mail*, was about to tell her that that was how the British people saw her. Perhaps he would say that the British press had decided to break the agreement they had made with the king. All was about to be revealed and she would become a national pariah. Her ever-convulsing insides convulsed again at the thought.

Pull yourself together, she told herself sternly as she crossed the elegant lobby and entered the airy restaurant with its arched silver screens. The air of quiet efficiency, the hum of a well-oiled machine, each part performing what it was trained to do, all contrasted with the turmoil within her.

Her host had chosen a table away from the main area of the restaurant, it seemed. The waiter led her through a screen of pillars to where he sat in a corner by a fireplace of honey-colored marble, against a velvet banquette. She felt a pang; it was where she had sat with Thelma that last time.

Esmond Harmsworth rose politely as she approached. He was thin and neat in a gray suit, with long light eyes and a slim mustache. He seemed friendly and had an air of mild determination. "I thought we would be more private here." He waved a hand at the empty tables surrounding them.

"But what if someone comes and sits next to us?" she asked.

"They won't," he said. "I've booked them all."

"Oh. I see." She felt a sudden terror of what he might be about to tell her.

"Do sit down," he urged her. "Let's get the ordering out of the way. The chicken pie is very good. And how about some oysters, as there's an R in the month?"

There was always an R in her month, she thought, slightly hysterically. Edward R, to be precise. She almost said so but held back. She must guard her words carefully. This was a newspaperman, after all.

Their chat was inconsequential at first. But Harmsworth seemed well-intentioned, direct and genuine. The oysters arrived, perfectly removed from their shells and put back again. She sipped at a glass of champagne, smiled, asked polite questions, answered them. All the time, her stomach rolled and tossed like a storm at sea.

The chicken pies arrived. They both watched politely as the waiters ceremonially removed the crusts, laid them aside and spooned the pie contents carefully on top. "I understand His Majesty wants to marry you," Esmond began once they had withdrawn.

She nodded.

"And there are, er, difficulties involved," Harmsworth went on.

She eyed him wryly. "You could say that."

"One of them being—and I'm sorry if this is not very flattering to you—that there is no question of you ever being queen."

Thank God. Aloud, she said, "No, of course not. And for the record, I don't need to be flattered. I like that you are straight with me."

He gave her a hesitant smile. "Good. I find that it saves time. So can I assume that you are one with the rest of us in desiring to keep the king on the throne?"

"Absolutely!"

"Quite so." Harmsworth sipped his wine. "Well, all that being the case, I wondered if any thought had been given to the idea of a morganatic marriage."

She knew the term vaguely. She had come across it in her history books. "Isn't that something romantic to do with the Hapsburgs?"

"Not romantic exactly. But to do with the Hapsburgs, certainly. The archduke Franz Ferdinand was shot at Sarajevo in the company of his morganatic wife."

She raised her napkin as if to conceal shock, but it was, again, an inappropriate urge to laugh. She was losing all her self-control.

"Admittedly that's not a particularly encouraging precedent. But for you and the king, a morganatic marriage could be the only compromise situation."

She listened carefully as he explained that a morganatic marriage could be contracted between two parties where one party, the king in this case, was of a higher social class than the other. In a morganatic marriage, the wife did not take her husband's title nor did the children of the marriage inherit it. So if she married the king, she would not be queen, nor any children be princes or princesses.

"It's a very interesting idea," she said when he had finished. Perhaps it might even work. The surging in her stomach had stopped, she realized. The hand holding her fork no longer shook. She felt a cautious optimism. She didn't want to be queen. Children had never been part of the plan. And this would allow them to get married.

He was looking at her mildly, but closely. "Perhaps you could suggest it to the king?"

"I'll certainly try."

"Some call them 'left-handed marriages,'" Esmond revealed as they finished their meal. Her appetite had returned too. "Because the left hand was sometimes given in the ceremony. They were actually fairly commonplace with royalty in the nineteenth century. Queen Mary's own father was the result of one."

Wallis almost choked on her champagne. "What? *Queen Mary?*"

Esmond nodded. "The House of Teck originated in a morganatic marriage."

"You are *joking*!"

"Not at all, and there are many others. King George the Third's sixth son, Prince Augustus, contracted a morganatic marriage with Lady Augusta 'Goosy' Murray. And after her death he contracted another with a Lady Cecilia Underwood, née Gore, next Buggin and finally Duchess of Inverness. Which was a step up in euphony as well as rank."

She eyed him merrily as she wolfed down her pie. "Esmond, you've certainly done your homework! You're an absolute expert in morganatic marriages."

He raised a pair of modest, sandy eyebrows. "I wanted to suggest for you the title of Duchess of Lancaster, which is an ancient and subsidiary title adhering to the sovereign, and so might be suitable."

She didn't say that she didn't care what she was called, if anything. Here, she was now certain, was the answer. Even the king could not find fault with it.

CHAPTER FORTY-NINE

The king did not, but the prime minister did.

"What did Baldwin say?" Wallis asked in alarm as the king collapsed in one of the white-and-silver armchairs at Cumberland Terrace, his handsome face creased with frustration.

"A lot of mumbo jumbo legalese, frankly. Morganatic marriage would mean changing the law, blah blah."

"In what way?" She was determined not to be fobbed off.

He sighed impatiently. "It's very boring, Wallis. But if you really want to know."

"I do."

He hurled his whisky about the inside of his tumbler. "Very well. He reminded me that the statutes require that any alteration in the law touching the succession of the throne or the royal style and titles needs the assent not just of Parliament but of the parliaments of the dominions since their tie to the mother country was through the Crown. Blah blah bloody blah," concluded the king, draining his whisky and staring fiercely into the fire.

Wallis sighed and looked at Aunt Bessie, knitting at the back of the room. She raised her eyes to the ceiling.

"He also said that if opinion was split, I should not try to force the issue by using my own popularity. As if I would!"

"But why not?" asked Bessie. "Your popularity is immense, and bound to be powerful. Why shouldn't you, if you feel yourself in the right?"

Standing at the fireplace, too agitated to sit, Wallis flashed her aunt a grateful glance. The pragmatic old lady had changed from disapproval and worry to a position of unflinching support. "What did you say to that?" Wallis asked the king.

He turned a proud blue gaze on her. "I said that marriage to you is an indispensable condition to my continued existence, whether as a king or a man. If I could marry you as king, well and good; I would be happy and in consequence a better king. But if on the other hand the government opposed the marriage, then I was prepared to go."

Wallis stared at him as the implications of this sank in. "You mean," she said slowly, "that you've put it to the vote?"

The king drew on his cigarette. "I suppose I have." A sort of thrumming horror was gathering in Wallis, increasing its cadence like a drumbeat. "You've given Parliament the power to decide your fate?"

"Basically, yes." He gave her a broad smile.

She shook her head disbelievingly. "You're always talking about the workingman, but you don't seem to know anything about democracy. Or history."

Surprise flashed in his blue eyes. "I'm not sure what you mean. My education wasn't as good as yours, evidently."

"Don't be sarcastic."

"I'm not. At naval college I once came forty-eighth in a geometry exam. Out of fifty-nine."

He could still make her laugh, even in this situation. "Stop it," she said.

"I mean that when an anointed king comes to blows with an elected Parliament, the king always loses."

There was a click of needles from the rear. "I believe," Aunt Bessie observed mildly, "that the last person to discover this was Charles the First."

Something in her calm tones put fresh strength into Wallis. She rushed to the king and took his hand. "David, they're never going to accept me. You've got to stop this! If you leave it with Baldwin, you're putting your head on the block!"

He shrugged. "A more comfortable place on the block, anyway."

Frustration rose within her. How could he be so calm, so fatalistic? "Take the proposal back from Baldwin and the Cabinet before they can act against you!" she cried.

He drew placidly on his cigarette. "Too late. It's already been committed to the political process."

"*What?*"

He met her horrified gaze calmly. "Oh yes, there's a special meeting of the cabinet called. The principal order of business is the morganatic proposal. Baldwin's agreed to ask the dominions as well. There are three choices, the first that I marry you as queen consort."

She had run to the mirror-fronted cocktail cabinet. The decanter stopper clanked violently in her shaking hand, echoing the action of her teeth.

"The second that I marry you morganatically, requiring this special legislation and whatnot."

Her body felt loose, as if it were boneless and might just collapse on the floor.

"And the third," he added simply, "that I abdicate."

Her eyes blurred and there was a rushing sound in her ears. She fell to the floor, her cheek against the white carpet.

Diana arrived at Cumberland Terrace looking flustered, as she rarely did. "Wallis? What's that written on the wall outside?"

HANDS OFF OUR KING.

"Oh yes," Wallis said wearily. "That's the politer end of what I've seen. I've had bricks through the window, even a bomb threat." She went to fetch the letter that had come that day, the latest of a series from "A Patriot," saying the writer was coming to London to kill her.

"This is terrible," said Diana, looking up from the note, her alabaster face a picture of beautiful amazement.

Cumberland Terrace, as it turned out, had not been particularly safe after all. Certainly not as secure as her old flat, safe within the confines of Bryanston Court, would have been. *Oh, Ernest!*

"But who knows?" Diana asked. "There's a press blackout."

"There is, but someone obviously knows something. Perhaps it's Lady Colefax. She bearded me a few days ago, after the state opening of Parliament."

"How wonderful he looked then," Diana reminisced dreamily. The image of the handsome young king, graceful and slender in his admiral's uniform, alone on his throne amid Parliament's ancient splendors, had dominated the news for days. "How proud he made us all feel."

"And I have the opposite effect, it seems," Wallis replied wryly. "Sibyl told me I was bringing the Crown into disrepute. And, of course, the whole of Mayfair is now suddenly discussing my torrid past in Shanghai. I'm the original scarlet woman, and to blame for everything. They're calling us Edward the Eighth and Mrs. Simpson and the Seven-Eighths. Quite good, I thought." She managed a brave but shaky smile.

"You seem remarkably composed," Diana remarked, standing at the window and looking out into the black November night.

"You're always saying that. But I'm a complete wreck inside. I have no idea what's going on anymore. David doesn't tell me. He used to ask for my advice but he doesn't now. He seems to be making all these decisions entirely by himself. He just appears in the evening and complains about it all. But by then it's too late."

Diana sighed. "I don't understand it. It's almost as if he wants to self-destruct and bring you down with him. As if he never wanted to be king at all, and this was all part of the plan."

Wallis, who had been standing by the fireplace, now sat down suddenly in the nearest armchair. A commotion was going on in her head. Cogs whirred, gears meshed. Lights came on.

"Oh," she said. "Oh my God." She pressed a hand to her mouth.

Of course. It was the only thing that made any sense. The only thing that could possibly explain all this madness. What had before seemed irrational and incomprehensible now showed itself as part of a pattern.

"What's the matter?" asked Diana.

Wallis tipped her head back against the chair. A wild laughter bubbled up within her. She was such a fool. It was so obvious.

The king's words in Windsor Great Park came back to her. *I can't be the right sort of king with the wrong sort of wife.* Was that the moment when he realized?

He had planned it all along. She had no doubt now. He had seen from their very first meeting that she was the perfect escape route. The only thing better than a divorced foreigner too old to have children was a double-divorced foreigner too old to have children. The British public, the church, the government, the king's own family would never accept it. It was impossible, and had been from the start.

But even then he was taking no chances. That was why he would not allow himself to be crowned first.

She had been entirely wrong about him. She had thought him damaged and dependent, but he had been clever and calculating. She could see how ruthlessly he had used her, how her reputation had been destroyed to serve his purpose. How he had placed her in the way of censure to attract criticism. The proclamation. The arrival at Aberdeen station.

"Awfully flattering though," Diana said, giving her a start. She had forgotten she was in the room. "To have a king love you so much he gives up his throne for you."

Wallis stared at the white carpet. Diana was wrong. It was not like that at all. The truth was not that the king had loved her so much he wanted to give up his crown. It was that he had never wanted to be king in the first place. His fatalism. His passivity. His refusal to use his huge popularity. His passionate overprotectiveness that might have hidden something else. It all made sense to her now. Perhaps she had been moved to Cumberland Terrace for other reasons. In a tiny, distant corner of her mind, one that she didn't quite dare look into, were the beginnings of the possibility that he might have even known who was behind the brick, the bomb, the letters.

When he came that night it was late. Aunt Bessie had gone to bed, shocked by all that Wallis had told her. She had advised her to leave, immediately. Go abroad. "It's no use," Wallis had told her. "He'll only follow me."

She sat in the chair by the window that had been repaired twice, looking out on the wall daubed with graffiti. She had not turned the lights on. It was like a stage set, and he would enter like a character in a play. She had her lines ready; she had been thinking about them all day. Despite everything, she felt oddly calm. Perhaps because, at this moment of realizing how powerless she was, there was a strength in finally knowing the truth.

When he arrived, letting himself in with his own key as usual, she did not move. He entered the dark room, and when he said nothing, she knew he knew.

"You deceived me," she said flatly.

He sighed. "Not exactly. Everything I told you was true. I love you like I love no other person. I need you."

"Because you don't want to be king."

He came silently over the carpet and sat down on a nearby sofa. "What can I say, Wallis? Who in their right mind would? It's pointless and lonely and perpetuates a social order that's completely irrelevant in the modern age."

"So why not be honest with me?"

"I thought I had been."

She thought of all he had said about hating it, being the wrong person. It was true that he hadn't concealed it. But neither had he really revealed it. "I took it all at face value. Why didn't you tell the truth?"

There was a silence. He lit a cigarette. The tip glowed; the smoke rose in the darkness. "I couldn't," he said faintly.

"I would have understood."

"You couldn't have."

"Why not, for Pete's sake?" She felt impatient.

"Because the only thing I love more than you, Wallis, is my country."

"Now you're confusing me."

He stood up, shoved his hands in his baggy trousers and went to the fireplace. The embers were dying. He took a poker and prodded them back into life. The light flickered on his face, which looked resigned and sad. "It wasn't selfishness that made me want to give up the throne. It was the certain knowledge that I was completely the wrong person. As I've told you before, I didn't want children. I hate stunting, the whole empty pageantry of it all. Bertie and Elizabeth would be a million times better."

"So you deceived me out of patriotism?"

He poked the fire. "If you want to put it that way."

"You bastard," she said.

"If only. Would have saved me a lot of trouble if I had been. But it's all worked out, don't you think?"

"Has it?"

He came over to her, took her hand. "You didn't want to be queen, did you?"

"Certainly not."

"And once this is all over we can just move back to the Fort and get on with our lives."

She thought about it. "That sounds good."

"You can see Ernest, as often as you like. He can come to stay with Buttercup."

"You mean Mary."

"Oh, yes."

She remembered, then, about the hotel not wanting to give evidence. She told him and he laughed. She thought how extraordinary he was, to pilot her so skillfully from blind fury to merry acceptance. He was a truly brilliant diplomat. Perhaps that could be his future.

He sat on her chair arm, dipped his head toward her. "I love you," he whispered into her neck.

"And I love you." She edged out of the chair onto the rug before the fire. He lay beside her and she pressed herself into his body as if she could press through him, or if she pressed hard enough they might merge and become one person. She wanted to crawl into his heart, curl up inside those mysterious chambers, see what they really contained. They began to move together and as always she felt desire and want and then afterward silence and stillness. She knew he would always be the place where she could come to rest.

Things began to move fast. As expected, the cabinet rejected the morganatic idea. The five dominions were also against the proposal. Canada, Australia, New Zealand, South Africa and Éire all said Edward VIII must abdicate if he wouldn't give up the idea of marriage.

"The Australian PM thinks I should go anyway, marriage or not, as the Crown has already suffered so grievously, as he puts it, from the connection with Mrs. Simpson," the king exclaimed.

"The cheek of the man," said Wallis.

"He says that he has no sympathy for divorced people and as a socialist he has no sympathy for the monarchy either! Bloody Australians!"

"He has a point that you can't be a socialist and a monarchist. That was one of your problems."

He smiled at her. "You're right. One of the things I'm looking forward to most is getting involved with working people. I'll be able to concentrate on it properly now."

He was certain that his brother would appoint him to some post where his popularity with the poor would benefit both them and the

Crown. It would be a sensible move on Bertie's part, Wallis thought. But then she remembered Elizabeth's cold stare.

It was in the same optimistic spirit that he went to see his mother. He came back full of rueful humor. "It took a while," he said. "You know my family. They never talk about important things. Shooting, the weather, a friend's marriage, the shocking behavior of the French. Anything except the subject gnawing their souls."

She smiled and waited.

"I rather had to force it in the end. I told Mama straight that I could not live alone as king and must marry you."

"What did she say?"

"She stared at me. I really think it was the very first time it dawned on her that I was going to abdicate. Then she said, 'Really! This might be Romania!'"

"What?"

He grinned. "King Carol the Second abdicated for love of his mistress, apparently. Mama then demanded to know why, when so many had sacrificed so much during the war, I could not make this lesser sacrifice."

"Did you tell her you were doing it out of patriotic duty?"

"I didn't bother, to be honest. I'm not sure she's capable of believing me with how she worships the monarchy. Papa was always her king first, her husband second." Here Wallis tried to imagine what this would mean in practice.

"Her final word was to wish me well for my forthcoming visit to the South Wales coalfields."

Wallis moved with Aunt Bessie back to the Fort. Here she resettled in the Queen's Room. Aunt Bessie was in the Blue Room, where she and Ernest had slept on their first visit so many years before. Remembering it, she felt a brief wave of wretchedness.

In the drawing room was a table with a great pile of unsigned state papers. "I may as well leave them for Bertie now," the king said.

He was back in London when another letter arrived. "It's from Hardinge," he said, opening it in the hall.

She raised an eyebrow. "Oh yes?" Hardinge, put there on purpose with Lascelles to antagonize and frustrate the king at every turn. "What does he say?"

Something the king had long wanted him to, obviously.

The king scratched his head. "He says that the silence of the British press about you is about to be broken, with potentially calamitous results."

She sighed. The savage headlines, packed with pent-up fury, were a hideous prospect. Shanghai, her marital history; it would all be there. And poor Ernest too. None of this was his fault. She felt, briefly, absolutely desolate.

"And the cabinet is meeting to discuss the serious situation that is developing." The king looked up, his brow furrowed. "Hardinge thinks that only one step can avoid a political crisis."

"Oh, does he?" She eyed him resignedly. "And what might that step be?"

"For you to go abroad without delay."

She thought for a few moments. "I have some American friends in Cannes," she suggested. "Herman and Katherine Rogers. I could go down there."

"Good idea," he said with a resolute look. "I'll look after things this end. It's all going to plan. God bless WE, my beloved sweetheart."

CHAPTER FIFTY

Lord Brownlow was chosen as her escort. He was an old friend of the king, a genial Midlands landowner whose nickname was "the Lincolnshire Handicap." It was not long before Wallis discovered why.

As the press embargo had now lifted and the story of their relationship had broken onto an astonished world, the gates of the Fort were mobbed with journalists. But no one saw the Rolls as, with lights dimmed, it raced to the far side of Windsor Great Park and away.

At Newhaven she passed some newspaper billboards. THE KING'S MARRIAGE, one read, in vast black letters. DUKE AND DUCHESS OF YORK RETURN FROM SCOTLAND was another, subsidiary headline. There was a picture of Elizabeth, looking dewily concerned.

The cat who got the cream, Wallis thought. The cat who got the queen.

But—so much the better. Whatever else Elizabeth might be, there was no doubt she was consort material. As for Bertie, there was even less doubt that he would be the steadiest, most conscientious and most traditional of kings.

On the Newhaven–Dieppe ferry, they became Mr. and Mrs. Harris. At Dieppe it all came apart. Brownlow had no sense of direction and frequently got lost. She had to help him read the map.

Meanwhile, the reports from England were all about abdication. Brownlow was appalled and upset. He insisted she call the king and try to persuade him from the course he had vowed to take because of her. Infected by his panic, she became convinced she must too. Now she was away from the king, it all seemed sheer madness. But the connections, as perhaps he had known they would be, were so bad they could hardly hear each other.

"Your husband's been in touch," Brownlow told her. He seemed to have more success in contacting London.

"Ernest?"

"He's offered to make a statement saying that the divorce was cooked up by him and the king."

Which it was, she thought, it absolutely was. "But why?"

"To get it overturned. So His Majesty doesn't feel obliged to marry you."

She was amazed. So even now, even at this stage, it might all be reversed. Ernest still cared enough to try. How lucky she had been, to have been loved by two such men.

"What does the king say?" She knew, of course. It was written all over Brownlow's disappointed face.

At Blois in Touraine the hotel was mobbed by local reporters and cameramen. They managed to escape after bribing a porter to smuggle them out of the staff entrance, but the press caught up again at Lyon after someone in the street shouted "*Voilà la dame!*" She escaped through one restaurant lavatory window, and through the kitchen of another.

She called the king repeatedly, over the ever-broken connection. He sounded tired but determined. He told her he had left London and withdrawn to the Fort, where reporters had besieged him to the extent he had to keep all the curtains drawn. Her heart ached for him. He was like a trapped animal. They both were.

"But it will be over soon," he reassured her. "Then we will be WE at last!"

Reaching Cannes in the early hours, four days after leaving London, Wallis swept through the gates of Lou Viei, home of the Rogerses, crouched in the car footwell with a rug over her head.

They were in the drawing room at Lou Viei—Wallis, Herman, Katherine and Brownlow—when the final act began. Wallis was lying on the sofa, hands over her face, when his voice floated out of the radio: "'Impossible to carry the heavy duty of responsibility and to discharge my duties as king as I would wish to do without the help and support of the woman I love.'" Finally it was over. She let out a deep, shuddering breath.

"'Who has tried up to the last to persuade me to take a different course.'"

"Did you hear that, Wallis?" Katherine was stroking her arm comfortingly. "He's just told the whole world that none of it was your fault. No one's going to blame you. It's all going to be fine."

Later, when Wallis had summoned the strength to move, she went to her room and looked out of the window. The Riviera night was cold and bright with stars. She stared into the darkness and thought of the nights at the Fort, with the great lit-up tower rising into the black sky. Soon they would be back there. She felt joyful at the prospect. He would be content there, pottering in the garden, doing whatever he could to assist the brother he always knew would be a much better king than him. They would get married there, surrounded by close friends, and grow old together in David's beloved England. It was all going to be fine.

Frogmore
Windsor
June 1972

The last part of the last ordeal. Two motorcades followed the hearse to Frogmore. Calm sunshine spread over a lawn screened by azaleas, rhododendrons and cypresses and in which, already, lay Prince George and Princess Marina.

His memorial stone, of cream Portland marble, was simplicity itself.

HRH THE PRINCE EDWARD

ALBERT CHRISTIAN GEORGE

ANDREW PATRICK DAVID

DUKE OF WINDSOR

BORN 23 JUNE 1894

DIED 28 MAY 1972

KING EDWARD VIII

20 JANUARY—11 DECEMBER 1936

She stood with bowed head as, in the shade of a plane tree, not far from the garden in which he had played as a child, David was lowered into the earth of the land he had loved but left so many years before. Finally, he had been allowed to come home. Windsor had come back to Windsor. She examined her own future resting place before making her farewells and leaving for the airport. Still in her black weeds and veil, she mounted the steps up to the airplane with a shaky determination. She did not turn or look back. That she would never come back here alive felt like a relief.

Grace waved a late edition of the London *Evening Standard* as the plane took off. Wallis learned that, even as the service in the chapel was drawing to a close, a Labour member called Willie Hamilton, a notorious Scottish monarch-basher, had made a speech about her in the House of Commons.

"Spare me," she murmured to Grace as they rose through the dirty gray clouds above Britain. "I really don't want to know."

"Wallis, it's not what you think. Just listen!" Grace looked down at the newspaper. "This is what he says. 'No woman could have behaved with more dignity and grace in the torrent of humiliation and indignity over thirty-six years.'"

Wallis had wearily closed her eyes; now they flew open in surprise. Beyond the cabin window the sky was a bright clean blue.

"He says he's planning a Commons motion condemning"—Grace glanced at the paper again—"'the hypocrisy and humbug of the current establishment, including the royal family, over the treatment meted out to the Windsors.'"

"Well, I'll be," said Wallis.

Grace gave a squeal of laughter.

"What's the matter?"

"He says he hopes that Prince Charles will marry a divorced hippie!"

Wallis cackled. "I don't think that's likely. The last thing that family needs is another divorced woman. Particularly an American."

Paris
June 1972

Back in Paris, the gates swung open. Ahead was the graceful golden house that had once been General de Gaulle's.

"David!" she called when she entered, as she always did. It echoed round the hall, fluttering the Garter banner that hung there before returning to echo in her heart.

How could she have forgotten? She would never hear his answering call again.

"I'm here! Darling, I'm here!"

Her health began to fail with the passing of years. She fell in the drawing room, then on the Riviera. Her bones were becoming like glass. She went out less and less. She hoped people would forget about her, but there were always interview requests. In the few she gave, she put a photograph of David on the table beside her.

The house became a fortress, the heavy gates always locked and guarded. David's suits still hung in his closet; his shirts remained in their drawers; his toilet articles still stood in his bathroom. His desk was ready for him, with stationery and pipe cleaners. She went to his room each night and wished him sweet dreams before retiring to her own. The dogs stayed on her bed. "It's flattering to know that there are still creatures who want to sleep with me," she quipped.

Charles got married. Uninvited to the ceremony, she watched on TV as he stood at the altar with not worldly Camilla Shand nor even a divorced hippie, but nineteen-year-old aristocrat Lady Diana Spencer. Would Camilla continue as his mistress?

she wondered. How would that work, in the modern age? Two consecutive Princes of Wales with two explosive relationships would look like carelessness.

Gradually, illness shrank her world until it was just her bedroom. It was crammed with flowers and photographs but the great empty space that had opened inside her remained unfilled. She knew she would die alone and felt impatient for it to happen. For so many years now there had been nothing whatsoever to live for.

She felt like the last member of a lost civilization. Her mind wandered further and further back. She existed mostly in her memory, increasingly unsure of the point where the past met the present. People wandered in and out: Thelma, Diana, Ernest. Music drifted through the room, the bands of long ago. She danced the Charleston in her dreams, or so she thought. But then the nurse came in and found her sprawled on the floor with a broken hip.

She ate less and less, apart from the iced vodka she sipped from a silver mug. She slept a lot. Pain kept her company. She would feel a sharp stabbing in the center of her chest, then the pain would spread down her arms and press from above on her skull. She would think the moment had come but then it would fade and she would be back in the white room, looking at the picture of David, eyes crinkled with mirth, a cigarette clamped between his teeth. *Don't worry*, the grin seemed to say. *It won't be long now.*

The day finally came and she felt something tilt within her. Her survival instinct took over; panic seized her and she called for the nurse. She came running in, a large girl whose short skirt reminded Wallis of what Cecil had once said on the subject: never had so little exposed so much that needed to be covered up.

Laughter rose in her throat, along with a feeling of suffocation. She had witnessed so much. The room began to spin and whirl and the pain spread in bands across her chest, arrowing down her arms. She felt something final and irrevocable take hold.

There was a brilliant light and she was outside, on a winter's day, beneath a bright cold sun. The chill pinched her nose and tweaked her ears. Her breath rose in a cloud into the air. She could see towers and a flag over the top of the trees and a frozen lake shining like a pale mirror. He was standing at the edge of it, amid the sparkling grass, blond and handsome, blue eyes creased with merriment. He wore a loud checked suit with exaggerated turn-ups and a quizzical look that made her heart turn over. There was a flash of silver cigarette case, the click of a lighter. He took a long drag, exhaled and smiled at her.

ACKNOWLEDGMENTS

Few people can say they spent lockdown with a legend. I was lucky to have Wallis Simpson as a companion. I have always been fascinated by her, and after I finished writing *The Royal Governess*, my novel about the inspirational young woman who taught the queen, I had no difficulty deciding that Wallis would be my next subject.

Like Marion Crawford, star of *The Royal Governess*, Wallis sent shock waves through the House of Windsor. But I had not realized before starting my research how alike the two stories were. They are both about women whose reputations were destroyed after their run-ins with the royal family. The more I read about Wallis, the more I started to question the traditional idea of her as a heartless gold digger who schemed to be Queen of England.

The Wallis who emerges from sources such as her amusing autobiography, *The Heart Has Its Reasons*; her private letters to Edward; and contemporary diarists such as Chips Channon and Diana Cooper is lively, funny, kind, unpretentious and, as the abdication crisis gathers momentum, increasingly appalled at the situation in which she finds herself. I realized there was enough evidence for a novel presenting her from an entirely new angle.

The Duchess was a thrilling novel to write, as I felt I was breaking fresh ground with my approach. And yet it felt strangely familiar. The points of comparison between the story of Wallis and that of a more recent American duchess are striking, while the idea that other truths may lie behind controversial royal figures has never been more current.

The books I read during my research were many and varied. They include *The Thirties: An Intimate History* by Juliet Gardiner, Harper-Press, 2011; *The Light of Common Day* by Lady Diana Cooper, Vintage, 2018; *Chips: The Diaries of Sir Henry Channon*, Phoenix, 1996; *Double Exposure* by Gloria Vanderbilt and Thelma Lady Furness, Andesite Press, 1959; *Coco: The Life and Loves of Gabrielle Chanel* by Frances Kennett, Victor Gollanz, 1989; *Counting One's Blessings: The Selected Letters of Queen Elizabeth the Queen Mother*, edited by William Shaw-cross, Macmillan, 2009; *Wallis and Edward, Letters 1931–1937: The Intimate Correspondence of the Duke and Duchess of Windsor*, edited by Michael Bloch, Summit Books, 1986; *King's Counsellor: The Diaries of Sir Alan Lascelles*, edited by Duff Hart-Davis, Phoenix, 2006; *A King's Story: The Memoirs of the Duke of Windsor*, Prion, 1998; *The Heart Has Its Reasons: The Memoirs of the Duchess of Windsor*, Michael Joseph, 1956; *Wallis in Love* by Andrew Morton, Michael O'Mara Books, 2018; *The Duchess of Windsor* by Michael Bloch, Weidenfeld & Nicolson, 1996; *That Woman* by Anne Sebba, Weidenfeld & Nicolson, 2011; *The Windsor Story* by J. Bryan III and Charles J. V. Murphy, Dell Publishing, 1979; *Edward VIII* by Frances Donaldson, Omega, 1976; *King Edward VIII* by Philip Zeigler, Collins, 1990; and *The Duchess of Windsor* by Diana Mosley, Sidgwick & Jackson, 1980.

The Duchess would not have seen the light of day without the brilliant people it is my privilege to thank here. My agent Deborah Schneider at Gelfman Schneider, and at Berkley, Kerry Donovan, Claire Zion, Jeanne-Marie Hudson, Craig Burke, Bridget O'Toole and Danielle Keir. In the UK, Jon Elek, James Horobin, Nico Poil-blanc, Rosa Scheirenberg, Annabel Robinson, Rob Cox and Alexandra Allden at Welbeck. My agents Jonathan Lloyd and Lucy Morris at Curtis Brown in London.

Having now written two novels about "difficult women" in the House of Windsor, I think I might have hit on a theme! I am currently working on a third, *The Princess*, about the early life of Diana, Princess of Wales.

THE
DUCHESS

WENDY HOLDEN

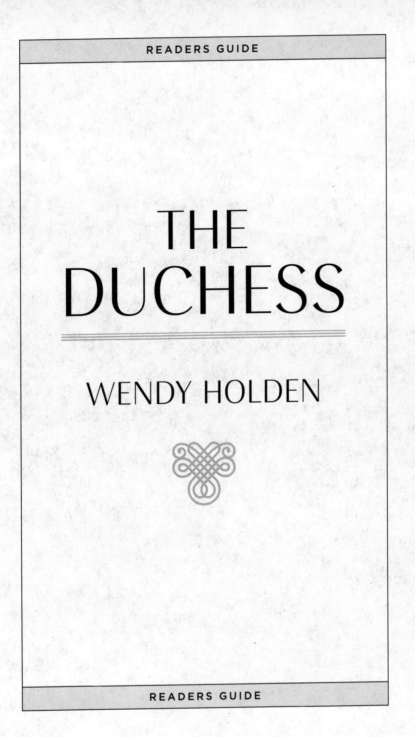

DISCUSSION QUESTIONS

1. To what extent has reading *The Duchess* altered your perception of Wallis Simpson?

2. Has reading *The Duchess* altered your view of Edward VIII? In what ways?

3. In what ways has history treated Wallis and Edward fairly or unfairly?

4. What does the novel reveal about the English class system and the relations between rich and poor?

5. Would Wallis's story be different if it were happening today?

6. What do you think of the character of Ernest, and Wallis's relationship with him?

7. Thelma and Freda, royal mistresses: What did you make of their characters?

8. What would you have loved and hated about high-society social life during Wallis's time?

9. How would you characterize Wallis's relationship with her mother?

10. How would you characterize Edward's relations with his family, and with the Crown in general?

11. Could an American ever successfully join the British royal family? Why or why not?

12. How important are the settings in the story in conjuring up the spirit of the times?

13. To what extent was the abdication a bad thing? Might it have been avoided?

14. What does Wallis tell us about social mobility—or social climbing?

15. Do you think Edward VIII was just using Wallis to avoid being king? Could he have done anything differently?

16. In Wallis's shoes, what would you have done?

17. To what extent was Wallis a feminist?

Wendy Holden is a number one bestselling British novelist. She has authored eleven *Sunday Times* top ten bestsellers and has sold millions of copies worldwide.

CONNECT ONLINE

WendyHolden.net

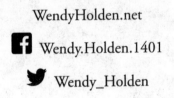

Wendy.Holden.1401

Wendy_Holden

Ready to find
your next great read?

Let us help.

Visit prh.com/nextread